D0466931

ll

Mt. Desert Island

*SOMES
SOUND*

Pretty
Marsh

*BLUE HILL
BAY*

Northeast
Harbor

Southwest
Harbor

Swans
Island

PENOBSCOT BAY

AND ITS APPROACHES

ONE FELL SLOOP

VIKING
Mystery
Suspense

NOVELS BY SUSAN KENNEY

Garden of Malice
In Another Country
Graves in Academe
Sailing

ONE FELL SLOOP

SUSAN KENNEY

VIKING

VIKING
Published by the Penguin Group
Viking Penguin, a division of Penguin Books USA Inc.,
375 Hudson Street, New York, New York 10014, U.S.A.
Penguin Books Ltd, 27 Wrights Lane,
London W8 5TZ, England
Penguin Books Australia Ltd, Ringwood,
Victoria, Australia
Penguin Books Canada Ltd, 2801 John Street,
Markham, Ontario, Canada L3R 1B4
Penguin Books (N.Z.) Ltd, 182–190 Wairau Road,
Auckland 10, New Zealand

Penguin Books Ltd, Registered Offices:
Harmondsworth, Middlesex, England

First published in 1990 by Viking Penguin,
a division of Penguin Books USA Inc.

10 9 8 7 6 5 4 3 2 1

Copyright © Susan Kenney, 1990
Map copyright © Viking Penguin, a division of Penguin Books USA Inc., 1990
All rights reserved

Library of Congress Cataloging in Publication Data
Kenney, Susan.
One fell sloop / Susan Kenney.
p.   cm.
ISBN 0-670-83537-4
I. Title.
PS3561.E44505   1990
813'.54—dc20   90-50050

Printed in the United States of America
Set in Times Roman
Designed by Bernard Schleifer
Endpaper map by Virginia Norey

For Pat, my sister:
Who made the coffee
And read the doughnut

And
with special thanks
to the members of
the Tuesday afternoon
Literary and Detection Society
Amherst College, Spring 1989:
Quentin T. Ewert
Nathan L. Frank
Eric A. Harris
Lauren K. Heggestad
Jeanne M. Lambrew
Andrew N. Thomases
Sarah G. Wade
Heather R. Wall
Julia R. Whaley
Professors Richard J. Cody and Geoffrey R. Woglom

AUTHOR'S NOTE

Although most of the place names used in this book can be readily located on any map of Maine or chart of Penobscot Bay, the reader will search in vain for the endangered islands of Rebel and Restitution. These as well as the characters and events depicted are the products solely of my imagination and have no counterpart on the coast of Maine or elsewhere in the real world. Happily not fictitious, however, are those organizations named and characterized herein as passionately devoted to the cause of protecting the world's wildlife in its natural habitat, the Nature Conservancy, the National Wildlife Federation, the Wilderness Society, Greenpeace, and the Sierra Club, who with their constant vigilance and imperishable resolve continue to monitor and publicize that most important of all issues—the fate of the earth.

The creation of a fictional world is a complex process, involving the gathering of information from many sources. Here are some of them.

For answering bizarre and unrelated questions in their own particular areas of expertise without once asking, "Now, what could you possibly need to know that for?," for reading and rereading rough drafts, and for patience lo, these many years, these friends have been at it long enough to qualify as the usual suspects: Ed Barrett; Lou Day; Ed, James, and Anne Kenney; Maxine Groffsky; Gene Long; Jessica Munns; Patricia Onion; Barbara Sweney; Heidi, John, and Erika von Bergen; Sid and Ellie Wertimer and family. These are new to the lineup: John Ames, Alida Milliken Camp (Mrs. Frederic E.), Robert Nilson, Skip Pendleton, Alex Turner, and the residents of Bayside, Maine; and my editor at Viking, Mindy Werner, whose middle name has to be Job.

For information on the process of identifying, gathering, and preserving plant life, Professor David Firmage and the library reference staff of Colby College; for support in this as well as in the writing and production of my previous books, all of my colleagues, the administration and staff at Colby College.

For background, interior layouts, and general history of wind-jammers and other remarkable sailing vessels: the members of the Maine Windjammer Association, who annually hold an open house in Camden, Rockland, and Rockport, Maine, where members of the public can reconnoiter the schooners and ask questions to their hearts' content, in particular Captains Orville and Ellen Barnes of the schooner *Stephen Taber*, and Captains Bill and Julie Alexander of the schooner *Timberwind*; *Windjammers of the Maine Coast*, by Harry W. Smith; *Nautical Quarterly*; and the National Maritime Historical Society, whose complimentary copy of *Sea History*, with its article on canalboat schooners, arrived at my house one day, just in time to provide a further twist to the plot.

And last but not least, for background on the international exchange program for students and officers in the fields of criminal justice and forensics and for providing Alan with a place to hang his hat: Neil Richards, of the Police Staff College, Bramshill, Hampshire, England; Nancy Jacobs, Barbara Price, and John Collins, of the John Jay College of Criminal Justice, New York City; and Peter Strawbridge, of New Scotland Yard, London.

My thanks.

CONTENTS

O N E   The Body on the Beach   1

T W O   Messing About in Boats   81

T H R E E   Jolly Roger   167

F O U R   The Fell Sloop   235

ONE

THE BODY ON THE BEACH

1

It had seemed like a good idea at the time, Roz Howard thought as she rolled over and carefully rearranged herself in the somewhat confined vee-berth of her Aunt Jessie True's old wooden sailboat. Of course, the berth was not nearly so crowded now as it had been when she and Alan Stewart were both sleeping in it, but at that point she hadn't really noticed. Alan had moved into the main cabin late last night, after the disagreement that had begun before they even left the dock at Northeast Harbor had blossomed into a full-scale row. Now they were hardly speaking.

She sighed heavily; it looked as though they were more or less stuck with the situation, at least until they got back on dry land. And then what?

Through the bulkhead she could hear faint rustling noises. The door to the main cabin, however, remained shut. With a pang she remembered other mornings, waking early, face to face. . . .

"Ouch!" he said, wincing and rubbing the back of his head vigorously. It was the second time he had reared up without thinking and cracked his head on the low cabin clearance. Roz

shifted slightly to give him more room. "We could lie the other way, with our feet in the narrow end," she suggested. "Or move into the main cabin and sleep in the two settee berths." He looked down at her in mock horror, his damaged head cocked to one side, tousled mahogany-colored hair brushing against the roof of the cabin top, heavy shoulders and long body filling the small space, leaned closer and murmured in her ear: "Fair Rosamund, you must be joking." . . .

Roz sat up carefully, taking care not to crack her own head (though nowhere near Alan's size, she was still no pygmy), and peered through one of the portholes. The heavy fog they had been sailing in last night had almost completely lifted; a few flimsy rags of vapor swirled up from the surface of the water, shone briefly incandescent in the glare of the early-morning sun, then vanished into thin air. There was no hope of going back to sleep, but after last night she was reluctant to confront Alan, especially this early. Anyway, the sounds from the other cabin had subsided for the moment. She stretched out on her back with her arms behind her head and watched the oblong patch of light grow brighter, trying to collect her thoughts.

It had all begun with a square blue envelope, addressed to her at the college in the familiar upright Spencerian hand, grown even more spidery in the last few years since Roz had heard from her: "My dear Rosamund . . ." Aunt Jessie had arrived for her usual summer in Maine in mid-May, but hadn't discovered Roz's presence at Canterbury College in nearby Southwark until she had worked her way through several months' worth of back newspapers and read all the publicity about the sensational series of murders at the college the previous winter. She wasn't an aunt, really, actually a first cousin once removed on Roz's mother's side, but Roz had been fond of her as a child, regularly visiting the cottage in Maine with her parents, sailing around Penobscot Bay with Aunt Jessie and Uncle Lou in their one-of-a-kind 1936 vintage Herreshoff sloop. But Roz's parents had been dead for several years now, killed in an automobile accident, and she and Aunt Jessie had lost touch after the funeral.

First there had been all the emotional turmoil over the bitter end of her long affair with Tony, the tension over her upcoming contract renewal at Vassar. Her reappointment as an associate professor hanging in the balance, she'd taken herself off to England to do the edition of the Lady Viola papers, and gotten embroiled in that awful mess at Montfort Abbey. But she'd also met and gotten to know Alan there, and after they'd disentangled themselves from that debacle, they had gone to Scotland together, spending several idyllic months in and about the rustic little cottage near his family's ancestral manor at Pittenweem, on the eastern coast, near St. Andrews. They had hunted rare plant species along the sheeptracks of Glen Clova, swung from the sheer rock faces of Ben Lawers, and investigated other botanical meccas for a catalogue of endangered native, casual, escape, and volunteer wildflowers Alan was illustrating for the Royal Botanical Society of Edinburgh. When that had begun to wear a little thin (and the weather had grown a bit thick), they had embarked on an extended tour of the Highlands, Alan delivering fascinatingly detailed lectures on (in alphabetical order) archaeology, architecture, art, classical literature, horticulture, painting, paleobotany (his specialty), rock-climbing, and Scottish history, as well as a running line of casual chat from his vast store of miscellaneous information on—it seemed—virtually every other subject that happened to come up. All this in addition to various other interesting pastimes involving considerably less talk. But when was life with Alan ever *not* interesting?

She groaned softly, then rolled over, burying her face in the damp pillow. The sounds from the front cabin were once again audible, more systematic. Alan must be getting up. Would he make the first move toward reconciliation? She waited tensely for a tap on the door. None came, just various faint creakings and rustlings.

The boat rocked slightly. She wondered what he was doing

now. Probably packing to leave as soon as they got back to port, which could be as early as this afternoon if they sailed straight for Aunt Jessie's. Well, if he was, she had only herself to thank. Speak in haste, repent at leisure. But how could it have come to this so quickly?

The noises stopped. Relaxing slightly, she thought back to what she could now discern, with the dubious luxury of hindsight, as the beginning of the end.

Dropping like a stone into their heady pool of bliss had come the news that the powers-that-be at Vassar had decided that her services would in all likelihood no longer be required after next year. But, in an odd stroke of timing, almost simultaneously she had been invited—make that begged—to fill a most unexpectedly and inconveniently (it was almost mid-semester) vacated post at a small liberal arts college of excellent reputation in the heart of Maine. It would be temporary, of course, a one-year replacement, but it was still a job, a chance to get back on track, professionally speaking.

There had already been talk of her staying on with Alan—even, on several occasions when they were both in a weakened state, of marriage. This had worried her somewhat; she was still skittish (recalling the thick wool blinders through which she had gazed lovingly at Tony for so long) about long-term commitment, the threat of passionate admiration combined with strong physical attraction overcoming any hope of self-determination, let alone independence. Though she could not bring herself to tell Alan this (how could he possibly understand; he was both independently wealthy—well, comfortable anyway—*and* self-employed, as an amateur but no less expert and well-respected plant taxonomist, as well as a much-in-demand free-lance artist), she had felt this as a blow not only to her professional pride but to her sole means of livelihood. Alan had been wonderfully understanding about not pressuring her to make a decision, not pressuring her at all, in fact, but she had still felt suspended, professional and personal life left hanging, herself impaired, mostly by the nagging doubt ("the fault, dear Brutus, is not in our stars, / But in ourselves, that we are underlings . . .") that she simply wasn't good enough to hack it in the groves of academe. So, what to do?

During her long walks through the fields of gorse and heather (alone, please, she told him; she had to concentrate), she reasoned that it would be better for her to resign from Vassar right now than to try to wait them out or stay on another year as an all-too-visibly lame duck. That still left the burning question of her blighted career versus life with Alan. " 'Versus'? Why 'versus'?" she could still hear him saying in a puzzled tone. "What's to be against? Whoever said you need choose one and not the other? Why can't you—we—have both?"

Ay, there was the rub. With his casually self-confident (and, she had to admit, generally justified) air of universal expertise, how could he begin to understand, let alone credit, her need to pursue a sterner ideal of academic professionalism, to be in a position to choose instead of being so unceremoniously unchosen; most of all, her determination not to leave unfinished something in which she had invested so much time and energy. Which is precisely why she wasn't about to discuss it with him until she had made up her own mind.

She strained her ears once more for sounds from the other cabin; all was silent except for the rhythmic lapping of small waves against the hull. Had Alan gone back to sleep? She pictured him in slumber, the spare sleeping bag barely covering his chest, an arm flung back over his head, long, fine artist's fingers curling slightly, the other shoulder cocked in an unconscious shrug. Or was he lying there thinking, just as she was, about the sudden collapse of their relationship?

She had finally torn herself away, sniffling into his faintly resinous tweeds at the Edinburgh airport, still wondering if she was doing the right thing. But they would keep in touch by phone, letter, and the occasional transatlantic visit, while they recollected in tranquillity the presently all-too-lyric possibilities of their future together. Her teaching job would end in late spring, there was the prospect of another summer together; she was certain they would work things out.

Then, as if to complicate matters, in the spring the English Department at Canterbury had offered her a full-time position that was not only tenure-track, but in her fields of medieval and women's studies. It had all seemed too good to be true after the string of professional and personal disasters she had experienced lately—not the least of which, come to speak of it, had been her renewed relationship with her now closest living relative, Aunt Jessie True herself.

After a great deal of thought (and some rather unsatisfactory long-distance phone calls) she had decided to take the job at Canterbury, at least for the foreseeable future. Since the swotting up of a full load of new courses meant a considerable amount of preparation on her part, it was decided that Alan would come over here for a month or so during the summer. But what was she going to do (at least during the day) with his rather large and energetic presence in the cramped one-bedroom faculty apartment she'd been allocated until further notice? How much rock-climbing, bog-stomping, and plant-sketching could she expect him to do on his own? She didn't know the first thing about Maine botanical lore, and not much more about its history; she didn't have a car, and all her new friends at the college had left on various summer junkets elsewhere. And aside from the odd art flick at the Depot Movie House, let's face it, in terms of cultural events, downtown Southwark (pronounced *Suth-wuck*) left something to be desired.

Ah, but wonder of wonders, here was the blue envelope, its contents announcing Aunt Jessie's presence in her summer cottage in the charmingly picturesque seaside haven (formerly a Methodist tenting ground) known as Bayside. Visions of the sloping village green with its row of lacy Victorian gingerbread cottages lined up like the folded-back corners of Great-grandma's tatted handkerchiefs danced in her head, an artist's dream. Well, Roz certainly knew a good thing when she saw it. She fired a note right back. Would Aunt Jessie like to meet her "friend" from Scotland, and could they spend some time together on the coast with her this summer? And what had become of that wonderful old boat they used to sail?

The upshot was that Roz and friend were more than welcome, and not only that, they could even do her old Aunt Jessie a huge favor. Because of her arthritis, Aunt Jessie hadn't done much sailing in the last several seasons, but she had recently had both hips replaced, and now she and "the girls"—her crew of contemporaries, all of them at least seventy-five if they were a day—were eager to get back at it. So the famous old twenty-seven-foot wooden sloop had spent the winter being refurbished at Farnham-Butler's Boatyard in Northeast Harbor, and was now ready to go. But the doctor had told her to go easy at first, and so would Roz and this friend of hers (assuming he had *some* experience sailing boats; she knew Roz was perfectly capable but two heads were always better than one, for safety's sake, and so on) be willing to bring the boat down from Mount Desert? They could even keep it for a week or two as recompense, take it on a more extended cruise if they liked.

Roz's heart leaped up. Better and better. This was just the ticket: a chance to repay Alan in kind for that lovely summer in Scotland, something special she could do to show *him* a good time for a change. She'd sailed most of her life, mostly on small boats on the lake where she grew up, but also summer after summer well into her teens on the bay with Aunt Jessie and Uncle Lou. She knew the boat, she knew the area. It had seemed like *such* a good idea, and when she called Alan to propose the plan he was more than enthusiastic: "Good Lord, fair Rosamund, a twenty-seven-foot one-off Herreshoff centerboard sloop, vintage era and yard-maintained? Say no more," he chortled. "I've had a bit of experience messing around in boats; I daresay the two of us can sail her with no trouble. How soon can we get on board?"

So they had opted, with Aunt Jessie's blessing, for a two-week cruise around Penobscot Bay. And off they'd gone on that Saturday morning, driven by Aunt Jessie herself in her

1948 wood-paneled Ford Estate Wagon, to Northeast Harbor on Mount Desert Island, a trip that took a little over two hours by car but was some seventy sea miles and a good three days by sailboat.

The boat had already been recommissioned and was waiting for them. Aunt Jessie had seen to everything, including the latest edition of the *Maine Coast Cruising Guide,* tide tables, a dozen yards of rolled-up nautical charts, and enough food, gear, and assorted yacht-type clothing to get them wherever they wanted to go. "Enjoy yourselves, my dears, go anywhere you like, do a little gunkholing, sail her hard, she'll stand right up and love you for it," Aunt Jessie had told them ("she," in context, presumably meaning the boat, not Roz herself, since Aunt Jessie had been addressing both of them, though Roz was not at all sure Alan had taken it that way, from the shockingly salacious look he had given her behind Aunt Jessie's back). Then, since parking was at a premium in Northeast (as well as everywhere else within a mile of the Maine coast in July), she had waved goodbye and roared away. And so they were off.

Alan had chuckled appreciatively when he saw the name on the transom. "I say, fair Rosamund, whoever named this boat was too clever by half." When she looked blank, Alan obligingly (if somewhat unnecessarily; after all, as a medievalist she was no slouch herself at languages, including Latin) had translated: "*Verorum*—'Of the Trues.' Well, not quite literally, but near enough. One of the benefits of a classical education," he added, jostling her with a jolly elbow, "instant free translations of your odd—in the sense of occasional, but also in the sense of eccentric—boat names."

Well, she'd known that, of course; she had just never given it much thought. Uncle Lou had named the boat way back when; she didn't know about the too-clever part, but he'd been fond of puns, classical or otherwise. Anyway (she thought with a mild but unexpected surge of annoyance), as far as she was concerned, a boat was a boat, name or no name; you sailed in it, you didn't address it—or her—by name.

But Alan did. "Now then, *Verorum,* old girl, let's see what you can do!" Without further ado he'd jumped right on board, turned around a few times taking it all in, and before she could even say "Ahoy there," assumed the role of captain, barking orders right and left. "Here, you take the helm while I run the sails up. Just keep her pointed right into the wind."

So there she was, hanging on to the tiller for dear life, obediently heading the bow into waves as high and white-crested as snowbanks, while the wind gusted, the sails slapped and banged, the boom knocked violently back and forth right over their heads, huge threatening clouds scudded across the sky, and the cold, iodine-colored, seaweed-infested ocean slopped up over the deck, pelting her face with salty droplets. Meanwhile there was Alan swarming busily all over the boat, hanking on sails and running back lines, stowing this gear and grinding that winch, whistling merrily the whole time. And as if that weren't enough to give her pause regarding this whole enterprise, he hadn't even bothered to use the antiquated but perfectly adequate gas engine, had just cast off the docking lines and given the bow a mighty shove, then vaulted neatly over the lifelines into the cockpit. Then, as the sails filled with a *whomp!*, he had snatched the helm from her without so much as a by-your-leave and steered them straight out the harbor into open water. "Say no more," huh? "Bit of experience," eh? Oh, right.

Roz sat there fuming. Something was wrong with this picture. Somehow her vision of this adventure had involved only the sunny hours—fair winds, calm seas, clear skies—and herself in charge, not huddled over the tiller meekly following orders, or, worse yet, doing nothing. A naïve notion, she supposed, but the really aggravating thing was that even though this was supposed to be her bailiwick, her party, her special area of expertise, the truth was, in this, too, as in every other activity she could think of, he was completely knowledgeable and most competent, infuriatingly competent, most competent indeed.

And that was just the beginning.

2

Well, where to? Alan had consulted the charts, tracing his finger over possible routes: Bass Harbor, Seal Cove, Pretty Marsh, Blue Hill Bay. Deer Isle, Eggemoggin Reach, Cape Rosier, Castine. Perhaps a spot of island-hopping in the East Bay. They were in no hurry to cover the distance; after all, they had two weeks, did they not?

So they had not gone far that Saturday, after an initial comprehensive shakedown cruise (during which Alan did virtually all the "shaking down") around the Cranberry Islands, spending the night on a guest mooring below one of the great shingled "cottages" just around the next headland in Somes Sound.

For a while, that night and most of the next day, it had seemed to her as though everything were going to be all right after all, in spite of the inauspicious beginning. She had almost forgotten how charming (if that was the word for, among other things, the gift he had of making everything seem so effortless, yet somehow special) Alan could be on a daily, even an hourly, basis, the cheerful line of chatter, the wit, the casual but welcome expressions of affection, verbal and otherwise, the long, fond, speculative looks in her direction, as though he couldn't quite believe he was really here, with her, at last. Once or twice she had caught him looking at her with a serious, bemused, almost anxious expression on his face that made it seem as though there were something important on his mind he wanted to say to her, but one way or another the business of sailing seemed always to intervene.

But that was all right; there would be time enough for serious discussions about their future later. She was more than willing to let him choose the right moment, particularly since (she suspected darkly) such a discussion might present some difficulties. So during those first two days (and nights—one had certainly to take into account the nights) in the cozy quarters of the well-appointed if elegantly narrow and slightly super-annuated boat, just the two of them, an extended cruise of two weeks had still seemed like a perfectly wonderful idea.

Then things *really* began to fall apart.

First there was the incident of the mooring ball. They had put into Stonington on Deer Isle at the end of the second day's sail, and she was minding her own business, leaning over the lifelines, about to fish up the mooring line, when suddenly Alan was at her side, snatching the boat hook out of her hands and snagging the mooring ball as it sheered past, shouldering her handily out of the way even though she had everything under control. Of course, the mooring line had been as big around as her wrist and weighed a ton, but she was perfectly capable of hauling it in on her own. He had apologized afterward, but for Roz this was only one more example, writ however small, of what she was beginning to feel more and more as not so much caring but actual oppressiveness, an obsessive need to assert control. Perhaps it simply went with being on board a boat, a natural reaction to a potentially threatening situation. After all, somebody had to give the orders or everyone might drown; hence the concept of Captain. Why, even mild-mannered, soft-spoken Uncle Lou had turned into an order-barking tyrant of sorts on occasion, never mind fragile little Aunt Jessie hollering like a stevedore.

But still. The fact was, like Lucifer (who had a point) she

felt herself impaired—or not so much impaired as impinged upon, hovered over, smothered.

For the moment she had said nothing (after all, he'd just gotten here), but in her heart she knew this could hardly bode well for their future together, let alone the next two weeks. It wasn't the first time he'd shown up ready to take charge and keep her safe at all costs, rushing to her side during those awful days at Montfort, or flying over at the drop of a hat when he thought she was in danger (which she had been), in the series of murders at Canterbury College. But however self-deprecatory and apologetic he might be (His words in the airport, that day she'd left Scotland to come to Maine: *"If ever there was a maiden—metaphorically speaking, of course—who could manage her own rescues, it's you, fair Rosamund . . . while I, in the best tradition of the White Knight, do little more than tumble off my horse at your feet . . . after the fact, of course"*), he couldn't seem to help himself, and while this sense of being watched, worried about, and hovered over had been tolerable, even comforting, on an occasional or long-distance basis, it was now beginning to weigh heavily on her. And this sudden, intense, and unrelieved proximity in the confined quarters of an elegant but extremely narrow boat after six months' separation wasn't helping matters any.

Even so, that was probably no excuse for the flaming row that had erupted last night and seemed to have put an end once and for all to the question of their future together. Just thinking of it now made her cheeks hot; she squirmed uncomfortably inside the sleeping bag, tangling her feet in the process. "Flaming row" was not entirely accurate; *she* had gone up in smoke; he had simply gone ashen. And, finally, ominously silent.

Not that she could blame him, after the way she had carried on. Bleakly she wondered if she would ever find out what those significant glances were all about, what it was he had been meaning to tell her. Squeezing her eyes shut, she put her arms back over her head and stretched full-length, trying to dispel the sense that she had provoked him beyond the limits even of *his* remarkably good nature, and lost him truly.

There was a thump from the main cabin, then another; again the boat rocked slightly. More thumps, systematic, purposeful. Alan must be awake. Not only awake, but up and around. She waited tensely for the sound of footsteps coming in her direction, a tap, a soft, tentative murmuring of her name.

What she heard instead was the sound of the companionway hatch sliding open, the rasp of a dropboard being removed. Alan's morning ritual; business as usual. She sighed. Life would go on as before, end of the affair or not. But there was nothing that said she couldn't peek, was there? Disentangling herself from the double sleeping bag, she quickly swung her legs over the side of the vee-berth and surreptitiously opened the door separating the two compartments.

He was standing with his back to her at the bottom of the companionway, stooping slightly (even though there was no danger of knocking his head here; it must be force of habit), one foot on the first step, while he lifted out the rest of the dropboards that closed off the companionway. Though he'd spent most of his time on board shirtless (while she shivered), after two days of austere sunshine at best, his back was still only lightly tanned, its satiny, faintly bronzed texture ending in a demarcation of slightly paler flesh just below his waist. She noted once again how much less bulky-looking he was stripped, quite fine of limb really. Even so, his tall, broad figure dwarfed the main cabin, out of scale, an eagle hunched in a henhouse. Watching him unobserved, she felt a moment of sharp longing for the baggy corduroys and rough, rumpled, turpentine-impregnated tweeds, followed by an even sharper longing to have things back the way they were just three days ago. If only she could take back what she'd said. Well, most of it, anyway.

She blinked as the bright sunlight streaming through the open hatch was blotted out by his suddenly fast-moving, triangular silhouette dashing headlong up the steps and out the hatch. A hearty shout, a slight pause, then the sound of a huge splash as he hit the water flying.

Roz took a sweatshirt and pair of pants from a peg in the hanging locker, slipped them on, and went through into the main cabin. She stood a moment looking down at the still-rumpled settee berth he'd occupied last night, considering what to do next.

These other mornings she had been content to sit on the deck, warming herself in the sun, while he splashed back and forth in his powerful and violent crawl (necessary, she was certain, to keep his limbs from freezing solid in the frigid water). After fifteen minutes or so he would paddle back to the boat, climb up the detachable swim ladder, take the towel she held out to him, and rub himself briskly all over, red as a boiled lobster and covered in goose bumps. Then they would adjourn below for what Alan referred to as "a bit of a warm-up," emerging (eventually) to make the coffee and fix a hearty breakfast.

Come on, Roz, she chided herself, no sense moping around. Even though things had changed fairly drastically since yesterday, it didn't necessarily mean they had to ignore each other completely, did it? They could still be friends, couldn't they? Besides, there was always the possibility he might catch a cramp and drown if she weren't watching.

And if he didn't drown first, he'd freeze to death getting out. In his rush to get airborne and over the side, he'd forgotten to take his towel; there it lay, thrown down casually on the other bunk. Tucking it under her arm, she climbed up the companionway and out into the bright sunshine to see what she could see.

He was already some distance out, churning briskly away from the boat, arms flailing, feet sending up little geysers of spray. As she followed his progress, she idly ran through her own version of the man-overboard drill she'd amused herself by concocting on the off-chance he ever did need rescuing—faint though that possibility might be. She would row out in the dinghy, and fish him in, then lash him alongside like the big marlin in *The Old Man and the Sea,* until she could get him back to the ladder. Ah, but then how would she get him back on board in his crippled or unconscious state? Hook him to one of the halyards and reel him in like the aforementioned fish? Get serious, Roz, hook what? He was out there without a stitch on. She'd have to do it the way Aunt Jessie had shown her all those years ago: drop the mainsail overboard like a hammock, scoop him up, and winch him in.

Not that she could seriously imagine any such occasion, or, for that matter, his requiring rescue in any form. She didn't really need to watch his every move; at this point it was sheer self-indulgence. Rolling the towel up and tucking it behind her head, she stretched out along the cockpit seat in the early-morning sun and closed her eyes.

It was those hours of white-knuckled sailing in the fog that had finally done it. After a full day of hiking Deer Isle, including a nerve-racking rock climb to an almost inaccessible but eminently sketchable granite quarry, they had taken their time getting up and going the next morning, and had not left Stonington until Monday noon.

They had just entered the East Bay and were wending their leisurely way across on a beam reach toward their ultimate destination on North Haven, looking forward to drinks and dinner at a well-recommended restaurant as a nice change from the rather limited fare on board. Alan was down below sorting through the sail inventory, considering whether or not it would be worth it to change headsails to give them "more of a lift," while Roz had the rather dull job of minding the tiller. Yawning with boredom, she looked back over her shoulder . . . and saw to her great dismay a thick bank of fog inexorably rolling in from the north like some great impenetrable cliff of chalk. In a panic she had called down to alert Alan, and was astounded when he popped up, grinning from ear to ear, chortling merrily. "A jolly old pea-souper fog! Haven't seen one this good since the Clean Air Act came in! Shades of ye auld banks and braes of bonnie Doon! What ripping good fun!"

Well, maybe *he* thought it was ripping good fun to be surrounded by white stuff as heavy and smothering as sopping wet cotton batting (except, she found to her relief, thick as it appeared, you *could* still breathe it in), unable to see your hand in front of your face, let alone any other boats, rocks, caves, lakes, fens, bogs, dens, and (to complete the quote from Milton), shades of death, but it wasn't exactly her idea of a good time. In fact, she was getting more and more frightened by the second.

Her main worry was that they would either run into or be run into by something large, hard, and fatal, if not to them, then to poor Aunt Jessie's pride and joy, the good ship *Verorum*, entrusted to her care. Thus she was at first grateful for Alan's calm imperturbability as they inched their way toward what the charts indicated was the nearest safe anchorage, between two islands alliteratively named Rebel and Restitution, a mile or so off Cape Rosier. He had remained completely unruffled the entire time, sitting below at the navigation station with his chart and dividers and stopwatch, shouting orders ("Ten degrees five seconds north-northeast for three minutes, ready, set, go!"), while she sat damply in the cockpit in Aunt Jessie's ancient oilskins, one hand glued to the tiller, while the other blew the raucous, eardrum-shattering foghorn-in-a-can at regular and, as far as she was concerned, much too infrequent intervals; if it were up to her she'd keep the damn thing going constantly, even if she went deaf in the process. There she huddled, eyes glued to the deck compass, surrounded by fog as opaque and sticky as cotton candy, its pinkish tinge emanating presumably from the west the only indication she had of the sun going down at close to 9:00 p.m. The moon was no help either; just two days past new, its light was too feeble to penetrate the murk. And, as if that weren't enough, last but not least, rain had started coming down in buckets. There she sat, soaked and shivering, listening to Alan's disembodied voice (she couldn't *see* him, of course; she had to bend forward and wave the white stuff out of the way even to make out the compass), calmly giving orders as though nothing were amiss— and why not? *He* was warm and dry.

Not that he hadn't offered to trade places. He had come up, composed as you please, and offered to take the helm while she took over the navigating. Drenched and miserable as she was, she had shaken her head.

"But why ever not?" he inquired, giving her a puzzled look. "Because I don't know how to navigate," she answered through clenched teeth. "But I thought you said you knew how to sail," he said. "I do," she snapped. "I just never sail in fog. Or in the dark." Furious, she turned away. "Sorry, I didn't mean that the way it sounded," he said. She didn't answer. He stood there for a moment, then without another word went back down below and resumed his evenly measured calling out of one direction after another: "Bear ten degrees to port, now hold it at one-thirty due east. . . ."

And so it went. The rain had stopped after a while, but the fog persisted. Through a combination of Alan's navigation, dead reckoning, and what Roz preferred at the time to think of as sheer luck but was in fact, she grudgingly had to admit, sheer skill, after ghosting for several hours through the fog under sail (the engine was too noisy for them to hear each other, let alone anyone else who might be around), ears pricked for horn and gong and bell, going from navigational aid to navigational aid like a floating connect-the-dots puzzle, they had fetched up right on the mark, a bell-buoy at the entrance to the channel between the two islands. Ding-dong, said the bell. "Dead on!" cried Alan triumphantly, sticking his head up through the hatch and waving the stopwatch under her nose. "That's the number ten bell-buoy! Eleven on the dot and here we are!"

Ding-dong and here they were indeed—wherever that was. All very well and good, but after hours of bracing herself in between obligatory spurts of the foghorn to avoid the innumerable imminent collisions suggested by the varying shadows and degrees of density of the fog before her, teeth either clenched or chattering, stomach churning, eyes burning, ears ringing, Roz was a trembling wreck, too undone to be relieved. All she wanted to do was crawl into her half of the sleeping bag, shut her eyes, and get warm.

But first they had to find one of the moorings the *Cruising Guide* had so cavalierly promised were available for visitors. The fog had been so thick they couldn't see their own bow, let alone the surface of the water, so after several minutes of futile circling, during which Roz gritted her teeth and bit her lips against the almost irresistible urge to start screaming hysterically, they had decided to run the anchor drill.

Or rather Alan had, seeing the state she was in, quietly and efficiently bringing them to a halt in waters the depth sounder identified as between twenty-five and thirty feet deep. This was quite adequate scope for a boat the *Verorum*'s size, he had reassured her as he perused the chart with the flashlight, even at dead low tide, which would not be until more than six hours hence in any case, as high tide was occurring more or less this very moment, or, to be precise, five minutes to midnight on this Monday in mid-July. They had battened down the hatches and begun preparations for a light supper, with drinks first to celebrate their attainment of safe harbor.

And then it happened.

Exhausted almost to the point of tears, she was curled up on one of the settee berths in a semi-comatose state, barely sipping at her wine, when Alan had raised his glass and drained it, then looked over at her and said in an unforgivably hearty tone: "Well, then, fair Rosamund, there's something I've been wanting to tell you. I've been thinking about this affair of ours, and I must say, I for one have had quite enough of this transatlantic back-and-forth business, seeing each other only every six months or so, rationed weekly phone calls, letters crossing in the mail, neither of us ever really knowing quite what the other one is up to, all the worry . . ." He cleared his throat, eyes fixed on her face. "And these intense reunions—rather nice, actually—but still, there's always the difficulty of picking up where we left off, only to have to wrench away again. So, fair Rosamund, to make a long story short, I decided to take matters into my own hands. I've gone ahead and arranged—"

Her look of stunned incredulity stopped him in mid-breath. She sat there speechless, staring at him in disbelief. Then something inside her just let go, like a watch-spring wound too taut. She sat forward so that they were practically nose-to-nose, eyelashes nearly meshing. "Oh, really," she said in an ominously level tone. "*I* see. In your infinite wisdom, *you've* taken matters into *your* own hands and ar-*ranged* everything." She cocked her head and put a studious finger to her chin, making owl-eyes at him. "So what's it to be this time? Come live with me and be my love in my little cottage in the glen and string up hollyhocks? We'll go roamin' in the gloamin' in the heather on the hill?" She paused for effect, drilling her finger into her chin, and frowning in a caricature of deep thought. "Noooo, that's too easy; we've already tried playing house in the Highlands—"

He leaned back away from her slightly, regarding her with an intensely startled look. "Roz, I—"

"—No, wait a minute, don't tell me! You've decided to take that professorship they offered you in paleo- . . . paleo- . . . paleolobotomy! . . . at St. Andrews after all, the one with the apartment thrown in, all the mod cons, even a nice sop for the little woman as visiting lecturer—"

"Paleobotany," he corrected with some dignity.

"Whatever!" she yelled, trying to keep herself from shouting in his face and not succeeding; it was, after all, a very narrow boat. She jumped up, waving her arms, and glared down at him. His face was flushed, his expression one of surprise mixed with a tinge of what she took to be guilt. Ha! She was right! "That's it, isn't it! Caught in the act! Without even bothering to consult me, you've made this happy little arrangement with one of your old-boy buddies, and now you expect me to just fall in behind, pack in my job, pack up my bags, and follow after!"

"Roz, I—"

"And just what am *I* supposed to do with *my* job in *my* chosen profession? Resign? I've signed a contract for at least a year, maybe three, or six, or forever. It's what I do, Alan! I teach literature! And not on an honorary do-us-a-favor visiting-wife or paramour basis, either!" She paused to catch her breath. "Not only that, you may be interested to know, I'm even getting to *like* it there!"

"Rosamund, my very fair Rosamund," he said in an almost beseeching tone. "Please listen—"

"Stop telling me what to do, damn it!" She turned away and began to storm around the cabin, insofar as it was possible to storm in a space not much larger than a luggage compartment.

"Roz, wait. I just assumed—"

"Well, you can just assume again, buster! Ever since I met you, you've been doing the assuming, the arranging, the coming and going, the deciding, the ordering around! Roz do this, Roz hold that. Then when I finally try to arrange something for us on my own for once"—she waved her arms around the boat's interior, slopping a fair amount of the very best late vintage *blanc de blanc* onto the cabin sole in the process—"you *still* take over. Goddammit, it's *always* you!"

Lifting her wineglass, she took an inadvisably large gulp and choked, but recovered before Alan could get a word in. He was sitting there, staring at her, completely thunderstruck. "So just let me get this straight," she sputtered. "In the guise of pledging me once again your undying love and loyalty and care, you are now presenting me with another *fait accompli*—or perhaps I should say '*eald-gewyrht*'; that's Anglo-Saxon for 'service or reward rendered for earlier deeds' in case you were wondering—benefits of a nonclassical education! Well, thank you, Sir Alan. What more could any little woman want!" she finished in a withering tone. She did a little curtsy, batting her eyelashes demurely, taking perverse pleasure in the totally bewildered expression on his much-too-clever, faunlike face. Right now he looked like Pan with a toothache.

"What *do* you want?" he said quietly.

"Oh, give me a break," she groaned, "not that old snore— straight out of Sir Gawain and the Loathly Lady! 'What does every woman want?' " she mimicked, rolling her eyes and bobbing her head from side to side in a pantomime of puzzlement. Then she leaned forward, fixed him with a look, and prodded his chest with a sharp forefinger. "Well, for one thing, you can stop calling me 'fair Rosamund' all the time! I'm not some flaxen-haired floozie, some diaphanous nightie–draped damsel in distress you have to swoop down on, tuck under your arm, and protect from evil all the time, you know!"

His face flushed crimson. "What am I to call you, then? 'Old sock'?"

"Just plain 'Roz' will be fine! And while we're on the subject, you're driving me nuts with this White Knight business! I'm perfectly capable of taking care of myself, and doing things on my own. So will you please, please, *please* stop trying to rescue me all the time!"

She could still remember his stricken expression as, finally out of breath, she had turned and stomped up the companionway, her progress slightly impeded by the dropboards she had to dismantle one by one, a feat she accomplished in relatively short order, however, considering she had not bothered to put down her wineglass first.

Emerging on deck was like coming up into the bottom of a well full of lint. But she was used to it. Slamming down the dropboards one by one behind her (and, to her great satisfaction, emphatically walling in Alan's stunned visage in the process), she had groped her way into the cockpit and sat down. The mist, thick as it was, was very cooling on her burning cheeks, but clammy in its dewy condensation on the seat and everywhere she touched; even her wineglass was sweating beady little rivulets onto her fingers. The dampness had quickly begun to soak through her clothing, but she'd sat there awhile anyway, trying to calm down.

Everything was so quiet, sounds muffled by the thickness of the fog, only the gentle creakings of the boat, the regular cowbell clanking of the rigging that echoed faintly as the old wooden hull rocked gently in its cocoon of angel-hair, the waves mere ripples now, weighed down by the heaviness of the atmosphere. Creak, groan, ding-dong, lap, lap, slosh, slosh, and various other vague, non-human rustling noises caused one way or another by beast, bird, fish, or boat.

She was beginning to shiver. It was late, time to call it a night and go to bed. Dumping the rest of her wine over the side (it had gone flat anyway), she stood up, undid the dropboards one more time, and went back down below, to find that Alan had moved his things into the main cabin and was perfectly happy to leave her alone for as long as she liked. In fact, he seemed more than willing to give her all the time and space she needed to make up her mind about what she wanted to do, or so he had indicated by his careful avoidance of virtually any contact, particularly physical, with her whatsoever.

For her part, Roz was already beginning to regret her knee-jerk recalcitrance, her hardness of heart, her pride. She had been hasty, had overreacted, behaved badly, said things she hadn't meant to. Obviously she had hurt him. She had also effectively put an end to any further discussions about their future, at least for the moment. What *had* he been going to tell her? Suppose it wasn't what she had assumed? How was she going to find out?

Up until now, she could have just asked. But their quarrel had changed everything, and she couldn't bring herself to raise the issue this soon. Maybe in a day or so, after things cooled off, *if* he hadn't already decided to pack up and leave. But, meanwhile, how were they going to get on together? Closeted by herself in the tiny, pie-shaped bunk, she wondered sadly if there was any way, without appearing abject, that she could restore their relationship to at least a semblance of its former easy give-and-take. At least they could be friends, couldn't they?

But lying there alone in the dark, when she had tried to formulate a way to tell him how she really felt, the words just went round and round the same old track. How could she make him understand her sense when she was with him—and often even when she wasn't—of being hovered over, watched and guarded under the guise of being taken care of and kept safe, her own sense of self overborne and trampled as he rode incessantly to the rescue in thought, word, and deed, whether she required it—let alone *wanted* it—or not?

Maybe she was being unjust, but she couldn't help feeling that if she allowed matters to progress in this fashion she would cease to be her own person altogether. She could just imagine what it would be like, being Alan's wife in England, far from home (but what was home, her parents dead, no close relatives to speak of except for Aunt Jessie), no job, dependent, coddled, Alan always on the alert, ready to gallop to her side the minute she ventured out on her own. That was why, if she were to go with him, even marry him (not such a horrible idea in the abstract—or was it in the concrete that it wasn't so horrible?), she had to know that she had some aspect of her life—her professional career—that was hers alone. Once she felt she had achieved that, they could begin to address the question of their future together. But even now she could imagine the bitter irony of his all-but-certain response: "And when will *that* be, Roz? If ever?"

So that was how she had left it; she had kept to her closet and said nothing. Maybe tomorrow, if the weather cleared, they might have a last picnic together on one of the islands, and after that, who knows? And so they had bedded down for the night, or what was left of it, in their separate quarters, Roz in due course sleeping the sleep of the not-very-just, albatrosses and ancient mariners aside, alone, alone, all, all alone, alone on a wide, wide sea.

$$3$$

Well, not so wide, she observed now that the sun was up over the treeline, the fog completely gone, the air crystal-clear as far as the eye could see. The water was flat and shiny as a mirror, as though the fog had cleaned and polished it. She shielded her eyes and looked around at the small cove they had come into last night.

Hmmm. Not so all, all alone either; there was another boat riding at anchor closer to shore. Maybe a little too close? But she supposed it was all right; the tide must have turned already, judging from its progress up the little beach toward the high-water mark, and she suspected the crew knew what they were doing; probably they were more familiar with the anchorage.

The real question was, Had they been close enough to the *Verorum* to overhear last night's altercation? She hadn't heard anything that would make her think there was anyone else in such close proximity, but then whoever it was obviously hadn't been screaming and yelling and throwing pots, either. And had Alan noticed its presence, or missed it entirely in his headlong leap overboard?

Both boats were in what appeared to be little more than a

recess in the fairly narrow channel between the two islands, a cove formed by a small crescent of sand and shingle beach, with a spit of land spiked with tall evergreens curving around to one side, with a high bank covered with scrub on the other. Glancing down at the chart, she saw that there was in fact another cove on the other side of the spit of land; maybe that's why they hadn't been able to find the moorings. Then she realized that the other boat, perhaps a dozen feet longer than the *Verorum*, its shiny dark-green hull and honey-colored brightwork sweeping low and sleek to the water, single tall aluminum mast swaying in the slight ground swell, was attached to what appeared to be a partly submerged log, except that submerged logs were seldom painted white with Day-Glo orange stripes.

She hoped Alan's raucous commotion as he came up under and flushed several smug seagulls wasn't disturbing the occupants at this early hour. But no, they must already be up and presumably exploring; she could see a white dinghy pulled up on the beach just above the high-water mark, and what looked to be a bundle of clothes or the makings of a picnic not far beyond it.

A slight movement caught her eye. She turned to look, and was startled to see what she had taken to be a further stand of evergreens in the process of detaching itself and moving outward from behind the spit of land. She watched as the shadowy peaked evergreens resolved themselves into the pointed topsails of a large sailing vessel. It must be one of the many windjammers that plied the Maine coast every summer, bearing several dozen passengers from all over the country. There was probably a whole swarm of them behind that headland; Roz thought she could make out at least one more tall mast, or was it just more pointed firs, their dark silhouettes momentarily resembling shadowed sails?

She sighed. So much for her fantasy of a romantic reconciliation between the two of them on a remote, deserted island. Not only are we not all, all alone, she thought, this is practically Grand Central Terminal.

As it turned out, however, only one windjammer had

emerged from behind the fringe of evergreens. Black of hull with weathered sails that looked tattletale gray in the oblique morning light, fully twice as long as the *Verorum,* the boat was now bearing toward them from the far end of the channel at a surprisingly good clip, considering the almost total lack of wind. She had read that few of them had engines, but that they could make progress even in the lightest of airs because of their enormous sail area, wide beam, and relatively slight hull resistance. Maybe this one did have an on-board engine; she didn't see any yawlboat pushing it along. If so, it was an awfully quiet one, no muffled throb or hum that she could hear. But then Alan was still making a terrific racket, churning back toward the *Verorum* in a strong racing crawl, head buried in the water, full speed ahead.

She looked back speculatively at the windjammer. From this distance she could make out only a couple of people on deck, one at the wheel, another leaning over the stern occupied with some task involving the transom. But it was early yet, not even seven; the rest of the passengers and crew were probably still below chowing down one of those hearty windjammer breakfasts she'd read about in numerous articles in *Down East* magazine detailing the delights of cruising aboard such vessels. Either that or they were all sleeping in; after all, it was still practically the crack of dawn, and she'd heard there was a fair amount of happy (and, to their credit, generally nonalcoholic) late-night carousing on these trips. But obviously someone had to be up and about to see they caught the first tide, or else a boat that size would surely run aground trying to get through the relatively narrow channel.

Roz watched the windjammer's rapid progress toward them. One of the figures on deck, sex uncertain, was now staring through binoculars apparently aimed at her. As she watched, the glasses swept quickly in an arc over to where Alan's bare flanks twinkled through the water like pale dolphins. The figure—female, Roz guessed from the mop of dark, curly hair, though that was no longer any guarantee—lowered the glasses momentarily, leaned over, and shouted something to the gray-haired person at the stern, who hurriedly tossed a large tarpaulin down onto the stern rail and scurried down the forward hatch.

Roz smiled. She could guess what was going to happen next. Briefly she contemplated letting Alan (who had so far seemed to take their privacy for granted, or else, like many Europeans, simply didn't care) charge right up the ladder as usual, blowing and puffing and naked as the day he was born, completely oblivious to the fact that he was being observed by a cheering throng of happy vacationers, not to mention the possibly female crew member with the binoculars, all lined up along the windjammer's rail, catcalling and whistling and waving handkerchiefs.

But that would be a dirty trick, and she had no real desire to cause him any embarrassment. After all, even though their relationship might be on the rocks, there was no reason they couldn't still be civil to each other, was there?

"Alan!" she called, trying to attract his attention. He flailed on, almost to the stern of the *Verorum,* which had swung around so that it was directly facing the rapidly approaching windjammer. She reached over and pulled up the ladder.

"Hi, Roz! Where the devil's the ladder got to?" Alan gasped, treading water and groping about blindly, mahogany hair even darker wet, plastered down so slickly over his eyes and forehead that he momentarily resembled a seal. He pushed a few strands out of his eyes to look up at her as he treaded water; the rest, recalcitrantly wavy, had already begun to spring up in stubborn little tufts. "Is this your idea of a joke?" he gasped.

"I'll put it back down if you want, but you might look over there first," she said equably, pointing behind him in the direction of the passing boat. "I wasn't sure how modest you were about appearing in front of an audience."

Alan cast a quick glance back over his shoulder. "Damn and blast! Where did that ruddy great ark come from?" he exclaimed as he vigorously frog-kicked himself around the far side of the *Verorum*'s hull. Trying not to laugh, Roz wrestled the ladder over the side to where he could grab the bottom rung.

"Hurry it up, please!" he protested. "I'm bloody freezing!" Because of the curve of the hull, the ladder swung outward slightly, just barely reaching down to the surface of the water. With some difficulty Alan climbed up so that just his eyes and eyebrows showed above the rail. He glared at her, teeth chattering like dice in a cup. "I don't suppose there's such a thing as a towel anywhere about?"

Trying to keep a straight face, Roz thrust the towel toward him, only to have it snatched rudely away as Alan's head disappeared again. She heard him cursing quietly to himself as the ladder brackets wriggled violently against the rail. She hoped they would still hold at that awkward angle; she might end up running the man-overboard drill after all. But shortly Alan's head, followed by the rest of him, reemerged. He stepped over the rail and into the cockpit with as much dignity as possible, considering he was wearing only a skimpy bath towel wrapped ever-so-decorously around his waist.

Meanwhile the windjammer was passing by about fifty feet away, but when Roz looked over again there was no longer anyone on deck to enjoy the spectacle; the boat appeared for the moment to be sailing along on its own. The only thing hanging over the rail was the large tarpaulin, which seemed to have fallen down over the transom so all that was visible of the lettering on the stern were the last two letters—RD—of the name, and only -*land* of the port of call.

Alan wiped the hair out of his eyes and turned a baleful glance in the windjammer's direction. "What do you mean, an audience?" he demanded, turning back to her with an indignant look on his face. "There's not a bloody soul in sight!" He took a threatening step toward her.

"There was a moment ago, Alan, I swear it!" she said, holding up her hands and backing toward the companionway. "Maybe it's a whole boatload of nuns, and the ones on deck went below to tell the others to hide their eyes. Ow! No! You're cold and wet!" she howled as Alan grabbed her, picked her up bodily, and started for the rail. She felt a shock, not so much at the coldness, but at the sudden, welcome contact of his flesh with hers. Maybe things were going to be all right after all. Without thinking, she playfully kicked her legs and beat her hands against his bare chest, shrieking in mock outrage, "Put me down, you big bully!"

And immediately regretted it as he stopped dead, gazed at her for a moment, then gently lowered her to the deck. "Ah yes, there is that, isn't there?" he said quietly, the hurt once again visible in his eyes. "Sorry, I forgot myself for a moment. I assure you it won't happen again."

With that, clutching the towel tightly around him, he disappeared down below.

4

"Hmmm," said Alan as they rowed the dinghy *Mendax* ("Look at that: 'true' or 'false,' a matched set," Roz had translated earlier, thus forestalling any further demonstrations of the benefits of his classical education) toward the long curve of sandy beach at the head of the cove on the nearer of the two islands. "Who was the rebel, I wonder? And who got restitution for what?"

It was midmorning now, and after a leisurely breakfast of fruit, Muesli, and several cups of hot coffee, they had agreed in a mildly roundabout fashion, neither mentioning their argument, that they were in no real hurry to head across the bay to Aunt Jessie's. After all, the weather was fine, their final destination was less than half a day's sail, and here were not one but two interesting-looking, reputedly deserted islands close by. Even if their romance had come a cropper, as Alan might say (but, ever the courtly gentleman, did not), they were grown-ups; they could get along quite nicely for the rest of the brief time they were going to be together, before they docked and Alan went on his way, presumably back home to Scotland forever.

So they had decided to start their exploring on the smaller of the two islands, which, according to the chart, was somewhat mysteriously called Restitution. The other went by the even stranger name of Rebel Island. It was Roz's observation, after poring over the charts and coastal guide at some length, that most Maine islands seemed to be named in one of four ways: for a prominent physical feature, as in Flat Island; for something they resembled either by sight or on the chart, as in Saddle or Horseshoe; after birds or animals they had once been (and in some cases still were) inhabited by, as in Deer Isle or Fox Islands; and, less commonly, after the families who owned or had settled them originally: Torrey, Pickering, Holbrook.

Neither Rebel nor Restitution fit any of these categories, as far as Roz could tell, though Rebel Island could just as well have been called Sheepshead. That's what it looked like, with its wedge-shaped outcropping of rock at one end, the rest covered by pale deciduous trees as thick as wool. Probably there was already an island called Sheepshead nearby; too confusing for ancient mariners, no doubt, or modern ones, for that matter. Restitution, on the other hand, slightly sinister-looking with its flat shape and dark, dense, tall pine woods coming almost to the edge of the sandy beach, could just as well have been named Mysterious Island.

"It says here," she read from the guide on her knees, "that Rebel, the larger of the two islands, was settled in the early nineteenth century by the Fell family of Ireland, who raised sheep and operated a flax-importing business that grew into a flourishing textile empire—"

"Read 'smuggling,' " interpolated Alan.

"Mmnn. Nothing here about rebels, though. 'In later years the family had a falling-out. . . .' " Roz glanced up quickly, wondering if Alan would take any reference to their own falling-out, but he appeared oblivious.

"Ouch," he said with a pained expression. "Who wrote that? No, don't tell me. One of your relatives, right?"

"They don't have a corner on bad puns," Roz protested.

"What other kind is there?" he replied mildly.

Her frown went unnoticed. After a moment, Roz went on. " 'The holdings, including substantial family estates on the mainland, were divided between two brothers, Roger and Brian, the older acquiring sole title to Rebel Island, the younger receiving'—hold your sides—'Restitution.' " They both groaned. " 'The islands remain divided between the heirs of the two branches to this day.' Hey, listen to this. 'There have long been rumors about buried treasure on Rebel Island. The name is thought to date back to prerevolutionary times, when Loyalists, or Tories, maintained a garrison at Castine.' Ah, here we are, about the name. 'Legend has it that a group of revolutionary soldiers, or *rebels* as they were known to the Loyalist citizens of Castine, used this island as a staging area for an attack on the garrison, but the invasion never materialized, and historians think the story is probably apocryphal. There are,' " she read, " 'also rumors of a huge treasure trove left behind, either buried or in a sunken vessel, or possibly in an elaborate treasure pit on the order of Oak Island. But even after considerable exploration in the nineteenth century and more recent scientific excavations, no evidence of such a treasure has been unearthed to date. The so-called treasure pit is thought in reality to be a mine shaft abandoned when the bottom flooded, and the remains of the large sunken vessel off the western head are most probably those of an eighteenth-century fishing smack.' " Roz looked up from the page. "Smack? Is that a kind of boat? I thought it was another word for dope."

"Cutter or ketch, anywhere from forty to seventy-five feet or so, originally used in commercial fishery," Alan said matter-of-factly as he feathered the oars preparatory to a new stroke. He rowed so strongly that every time he pulled on the oars the dinghy shot at least ten feet through the glassy water; at this rate they'd be on the beach in no time. "Usually not this far offshore, though. More likely it was a British customs vessel; many of them were pressed into service as revenuers to prevent contraband, which lends further credence to the buried-treasure story. Not to mention the smuggling."

Here we go again, Roz thought with a little prick of her earlier irritation. Wasn't there *any* subject this man could not comment on at length and in great detail? Classical languages, rare plants, paleobotany (or whatever), sailing and navigation, and now (it appeared) British maritime history and nautical nomenclature as well. What other unsuspected areas was he an expert in? More to the point, where had he gotten *this* specialized information? She knew Britain was a seafaring nation, but this was ridiculous.

"And where did you get all that?" she asked.

"What? The nautical lore?" He shrugged. "Oh, there and about. Mostly browsing the Greenwich Maritime Museum at weekends, I suppose."

I might have guessed, Roz thought. Of course he would have picked it up the way he seemed to most things, in true *Homo universalis* fashion: by osmosis. Granted, there were the various degrees from Oxford and London (both earned and honorary), but the fact of the matter was, Alan was a prime example of that almost exclusively British breed, the gentleman amateur who (not without a certain amount of unconscious arrogance) is ready to take all knowledge as his province—however maddeningly miscellaneous, willfully eccentric, and seemingly unrelated—just for the fun (if not the sheer pedantry) of it, a species endangered in these ever more specialized, technocratic, goal-oriented United States, but whose existence continues to flourish throughout the United Kingdom, as can be demonstrated on a day-to-day basis by perusing the weekly program guide of the BBC. But what can you expect from a country whose most popular superhero is the decidedly low-tech Dr. Who, careering about the universe in a tatty old police call box, mowing down evil-doers right and left, armed with nothing more than a seventeen-foot muffler (hand-knit), a sonic screwdriver (Phillips head *and* regular), and his own ingenuity (unlimited). In fact, now that she thought of it, he did rather remind her of Alan, baggy tweeds and all.

With his gift for ferreting out and retaining esoteric information, he probably *had* picked up all the nautical lore browsing around the Greenwich Maritime Museum on weekends. What it all came down to was that, at least on the surface of things, he appeared to know something about everything and was perfectly prepared not only to say so but to act accordingly. And that was the real reason, she realized, for her reluctance to commit herself—her sense of his endless, mind-boggling competence. How could you constantly be around a person like that without always feeling at a disadvantage? Or as Milton put it in his definitively sexist fashion: "He for God only, she for God in him." That was it, purely and simply; like Lucifer, like Eve, she felt herself impaired. But why should she penalize Alan for that? The only thing he'd done, after all, was love her enough to want to protect her, marry her if she'd have him, and take her away with him. Well, she'd fixed that. Now all he wanted to do was take himself back home without her, as soon as possible.

She studied his profile, his face now turned away from her, looking intently over his shoulder as he gauged the dinghy's progress toward the little crescent of beach. He turned back, caught her watching, smiled briefly, and bent to the rowing again, effortlessly, with grace.

Feeling her cheeks redden, she bent her head back to the guide and read on. " 'All excavations and explorations on Rebel Island were halted some years ago by order of Roger C. Fell,' blah, blah, and blah. . . ." She turned the page. "Ah, here's the part about Restitution. 'Unlike its close neighbor, Rebel Island, still in the hands of the Fell family, Restitution Island has never been inhabited. The island is currently owned by Mr. Peter Onterdonck'—Whoops! What happened to the Fells? Oh, wait a minute—'an ardent conservationist who inherited it from his mother, a descendant of Fell the younger, at which time all explorations on both islands were stopped by agreement of all the heirs.' Whoop-de-do, now hear this: 'Whatever the truth of the rumors, the real treasure of Restitution Island is not a matter of legend; it lies in the great natural bog that covers most of the island's five-hundred-acre interior, home to a number of species of endangered plants and wildlife that occur only rarely, if at all, elsewhere. Similar habitats are thought to be present, though to a much lesser extent, on Rebel Island as well, though this has never been scientifically verified. Both islands have in recent years been the focus of efforts by the Nature Conservancy, which seeks to acquire them both as a preserve, to eliminate the possibility of commercial development'—oh, horrors!—'particularly of the larger island. But by the terms of the original division, neither of the two islands can be sold or otherwise developed without the permission of the owner of the other. Although the terms of the covenants have been contested a number of times, at this writing' "—she flipped to the front of the book—"third edition, revised and updated a year ago, 'the issue is unresolved, and both islands remain in a relatively unspoiled state. While hiking and picnicking are permitted, visitors to the island are asked to refrain from building fires, camping overnight . . .' et cetera. Well, there you are," she said to Alan, who was leaning on upraised oars, letting the dinghy glide slowly toward the beach while he studied the green-hulled boat. "Anchored right next to a lovely bog, chock-full of who knows what unclassified, even as yet possibly undiscovered flora and fauna, right up your old field botanist's alley. Did you bring your glassine envelopes—or as we call them in this country, Baggies—your magnifying glass and tweezers?"

"Never leave home without them," Alan replied absently. "A pretty sight, that sailboat over there," he said, nodding in the direction of the other boat. "Hinckley, see the cove stripe? Newer model, fiberglass and aluminium, but still a regular poppet of a boat. Forty feet or so, wouldn't you say? Probably a Southwester. A miracle she didn't ground at low tide, must be one of those keel-centerboard models. Either that or whoever's sailing her must know this area like the back of his—or her—hand. Hmm, another odd name for a boat, in Latin as well," he mused. Roz glanced without much interest at the green-hulled boat, apparently named *Nonamote* (was that Latin? Not in her book), then went back to sizing up the picnic possibilities of the little beach. "No tender tied up to her anywhere," Alan observed, still studying the other boat. "The crew must be off somewhere."

"That's probably theirs pulled up over there, don't you think?" she replied, pointing out the dinghy behind him on the beach. "It's been there since first thing this morning; I saw it while you were swimming. Maybe they went exploring, in which case we'll probably meet them. The island isn't that big." She glanced quickly at Alan to see if he showed any signs of disappointment that they weren't going to have the island all to themselves, but he was absorbed in looking over his shoulder for a place to land as he bent to one last stroke. In a matter of seconds the bow of the *Mendax* was plowing a V-shaped trough in the wet sand at one end of the gently sloping beach.

"If you will just take charge of the picnic hamper and stay put for a moment while I haul the boat up," Alan said, hopping out of the dinghy, feet bare and tan duck trousers rolled up to his knees. "What with these whacking great tides you've got in Maine, our friends from the Hinckley must have had themselves quite a trek up the beach with that tender if they came in early this morning." He glanced at his watch. "Just gone nine, so it's barely half-tide now; must be a good fifty yards to the high-water mark at low tide, and all uphill. We, on the other hand, have cleverly arranged it so that all we have to do is pull our craft up a few reasonable yards, have our picnic, explore a bit until the next high tide, then just give it a shove and we're off."

He paused briefly to look around the little cove. "I wonder where they've got to? I hope they don't mind if we join them, inadvertently, as it were. Perhaps they'll be getting ready to go off soon, now the tide's nearly in, and we can have the place to ourselves," he added.

Roz looked up hopefully, but his face was inscrutable as he splashed through the few inches of water, dragging the dinghy with her still in it up far enough that she could step out without getting her feet wet. As if I'd melt, she thought with some amusement. Always the gentleman, even barefoot in rolled trousers with his shirttail hanging out. She noticed that he had left his sketch pad behind on the *Verorum*; could it be that he had other things in mind besides sketching plants that might possibly require having both hands free?

She reached behind her and picked up the wicker hamper from the fancy London store Fortnum and Mason. She had admired just such a hamper in passing by a store window the last night they'd spent together in Edinburgh before she flew home to take the job at Canterbury, but it had been so outrageously expensive she hadn't dared to dream of owning one, resigning herself instead to the usual pedestrian array of paper plates and napkins, Dixie cups and Tupperware in a brown cardboard box.

Then Alan had stepped off the plane bearing the deluxe model, with willowware china and silver table settings for two, wineglasses, linen napkins, tablecloth, the rest of the hamper stuffed with pâté de fois gras, capers, cheese, English biscuits, water crackers, and other such delectable edibles that she could feel her stomach start to rumble now just thinking about them. Though the delicacies had long since been devoured and the basket now held the Maine version of a plowman's lunch, it was the thought that counted (his other gift she was not so sure about—a giant-sized box of Elasto-plast adhesive sticking plasters in assorted shapes and sizes to replace the ones she'd used up last winter during the series of assaults and murders at the college, the enclosed card bearing a pointed reference to "that underdeveloped sense of danger of yours"). But enough of that. He had seen her yearning for the pretty picnic hamper, and presto, here it was.

She walked up the damp sand of the gently sloping beach toward the high-water mark, thinking she would put the basket down on that small outcropping of rock almost like a table, and then help Alan carry the dinghy up far enough that they could explore the island—and whatever else might come up—without having to worry about the *Mendax*'s going out with the next tide and leaving them stranded. As she neared the other dinghy she glanced past it at what she had taken for a pile of clothes.

And stopped dead in her tracks, staring. It was not a pile of clothes after all. Or rather it was, but there was someone in them.

5

At first she thought he was simply asleep, napping on the beach in the sun, but as she moved closer, ready to apologize if necessary for disturbing him, she realized there was something odd, the quality of stillness perhaps that brought a sudden chill to the air and made her shiver. She carefully laid the hamper down and wrapped her arms around herself, but did not move any closer.

The man was lying on the sand several yards up from the dinghy, some distance above the high-water mark but not quite to the place where the sand turned to pebble and beach grass before it met the fringe of great evergreen trees that eventually merged into the dense, dark woods beyond. He was sprawled face down, head turned to one side, with one arm outstretched and bent slightly at the elbow, as though he were trying either to attract someone's attention or get somewhere—the woods perhaps?—and had simply fallen over in his tracks.

Those tracks, sharply incised in sand that was still firm from last night's downpour, led straight up the beach from the dinghy, which had been pulled several feet above the highest line of seaweed, driftwood, and other flotsam that marked the farthest incursion of the tide. Otherwise the surrounding sand lay undisturbed, except for Roz's own tracks coming from the lower part of the beach where she and Alan had landed.

She watched the figure closely for a moment from where she was standing some ten feet away, eyes riveted on his back, but could not detect any rise and fall of breathing. Oh, no, she thought, here's death, right here, right now, in this beautiful place. She turned and was about to scream to Alan, who was hauling their dinghy up beyond the high-water mark, but something stopped her. It was so quiet here, so still, she didn't want to disturb the peace. Or wake the dead? Leaving the picnic hamper where it was, she started back down the beach.

Alan had already noticed there was something wrong—that weird sixth sense he seemed to have about these matters—and was running up the beach toward her, awkwardly trying to shuffle into his boat shoes as he went. But then he seemed to catch himself, stopped short, stuffed his hands in his pockets, and strolled nonchalantly the rest of the way up to meet her. "Trouble?" he asked casually. All Roz could do was gulp and nod.

Together they hurried over to the body. Alan knelt in the sand by the man's head, while Roz watched from a few feet away.

"He's dead, all right," Alan said, as he replaced the man's stiffly upraised arm back in its indentation exactly as it had lain. Roz noticed a line of very faint, curved scratch marks in the sand running from near his shoulder to just past the top of his head as though he had clawed faintly at the sand in his last moments. "At a guess," Alan continued, "I'd say he's been dead for some hours, since the rain stopped anyway, from the look of his tracks. Rigor's quite well advanced, even considering that he may have been lying in the sun all morning. Heat hastens the process, as I'm sure you know," he added almost as an afterthought.

And how do *you* know that? she wondered distractedly; an expert in forensic pathology too? But that was unjust; more likely it was the same way she did, from reading detective stories. But never mind that now. "He's been here since seven this morning, anyway. I saw him while you were swimming. I thought it was a pile of clothes." She put a hand over her mouth. It was all she could do not to simply cut and run, crying and gibbering down the beach like a hysterical idiot. She bent closer and forced herself to look down at the body.

He had been a good-looking, even handsome man, tall and well set-up, about Alan's size. He looked to be about forty, his blondish hair just starting to gray at the temples, a few deep laugh lines around his eyes and mouth. He was wearing a white shirt open at the neck, worn khaki pants rolled up like Alan's, and well-broken-in boat moccasins that had evidently come off as he stumbled, and were now splayed pathetically pigeon-toed by his feet. His skin was weathered as though he had spent much of his time in the sun, the deep tan still visible as a faint shadow over the waxen paleness of his complexion. She swallowed hard and made a conscious effort to unclench her fingers. "What do you suppose happened to him to make him drop dead in his tracks like that?" she asked quietly.

"Heart attack, most likely," Alan replied, sitting back on his heels, hands dangling between his knees. "Or stroke. He looks like he might have been trying to go for help, doesn't he? Though where he thought he'd find it on an uninhabited island I can't imagine."

"Maybe he didn't know it was uninhabited."

"Hmmm. But if he didn't know the island, would he risk bringing that boat of his so close to shore in the dead of night, never mind the fog? Assuming that is his boat, but I hardly think he'd row all the way out here from the mainland in a dinghy, and besides, look there, it's got the boat's name spelt backward on it in small letters—'*et oma non.*' Of course '*oma*'s' Greek, not Latin, but that's beside the point. Though I say, Roz," he went on in an oddly digressive tone, "must everyone in Maine have boats named with classical allusions or puns or both? Whatever's wrong with plain old 'Lively Jane'? 'Sea Smoke'? Or 'Winter's Dream'?"

Roz looked at him curiously. He was staring out over the

water as though frozen in place—except that his lips were twitching. He looked up, saw her watching, and clamped them shut, his eyes darting back and forth over the sand. For all his calm demeanor, Roz suddenly realized, he was just as unnerved as she was. Well, why wouldn't he be, suddenly coming upon a dead body in the middle of a deserted beach in the middle of the morning in the middle of July in the middle of nowhere? She was feeling pretty rattled, not to say downright sick, herself.

Alan cleared his throat and turned his attention back to the body. "It's clear he was alone at the time," he said, gesturing at the single line of footprints leading from the dinghy to where the man had fallen, "so there can't be any question of foul play. . . ." He leaned closer to the body, studying it.

Roz choked back a wave of nausea as he slid a hand under the man's face. "Still, he seems awfully young and fit to just drop over like that. Of course, that doesn't mean—here, what's this?" Alan was carefully lifting the man's head, his expression suddenly one of rapt concentration. To her horror, Roz watched the head and shoulders come up off the sand all at once, upraised arm and profile locked at an angle of salute, stiff as a pharaoh. She looked away, feeling even sicker, as Alan probed delicately through the longish, sand-encrusted hair. "Over the right temple the skullbone's gone all squishy, some sort of depressed fracture. No blood to speak of, but that doesn't signify." Carefully he laid the body back down and looked up at her with a puzzled expression on his face. "That's odd. It appears he's gone and got himself coshed."

"Coshed? You mean hit on the head?" Roz looked at the man on the beach, the footprints, then back at Alan. "But . . . but how?"

"Exactly," Alan said, standing up and dusting his hands off on his pants. "Here's a chap lying dead with his skull bashed in, all alone in the middle of a sandy beach on a deserted island, not another soul in sight . . . and just the one set of tracks." He peered around once more at the single line of footprints leading from the dinghy to where the body lay. "It's all well above high water, so there's no question of the tide's washing them out. Now there's a charming puzzle, wouldn't you say?"

"But surely he must have done it to himself somehow?"

"I daresay. The question is, how? Not to mention where and when. Not here, obviously, no rocks in sight, nothing to fall on but nice soft sand. And the tracks appear to be quite remarkably straight and firm except for the last few; he doesn't seem to have staggered much until right at the end. Apparently he stopped, dug in a bit, then fell right out of his shoes, just like that. Odd," he said thoughtfully. "Most odd."

"Couldn't it be a delayed reaction, swelling of the brain or something, some sort of cerebral hemorrhage . . ."

"Mmmm, there's a thought. You're pottering about at something or other when *bam!* stars all over the map; you come to after a bit, not even knowing what hit you, go about your business—granted, a tad groggy—while unbeknownst your brain is busily swelling up inside your head, and then in due course, while getting up to have a pee or walk the dog, you simply fall over dead." He regarded her gravely. "Is that what you had in mind?"

"It'll do." Roz gulped, feeling slightly queasy again. "Isn't that why they wake people up every two hours after a head injury, just in case?" Alan was watching her now with a worried look on his face; she suddenly found herself wishing he would just step forward, put his arms around her, and tell her it was going to be all right.

But he didn't. "Right you are," he said briskly, turning his attention back to the body. "Of course, tracks aside, that still begs the question of how and when and where he got himself bashed."

"Maybe he got clipped by his own boom, or something like that," she said. "Then later, when he felt himself getting sick or dizzy—or whatever—he knew he had to get help, so he rowed into shore—"

". . . Too disoriented by then to know where he was or exactly what he was doing, pulled the dinghy a few yards up the beach, staggered a few steps . . . and fell down dead. That must be it." Alan contemplated the body a moment longer, then took a deep breath. "But never mind that now. Let's just see if we can find out who the poor sod was." He knelt back down and began to go through the man's pockets, carefully so as not to disturb the body any more than he had to.

Roz suppressed a shudder; she couldn't imagine even touching it—him. "Back left pants pocket: handkerchief, unused, no wallet," Alan was saying. "Loose change and two paper clips in the right hip, nothing but lint in the left." Lifting the body slightly, he slid his hand underneath the man's chest. "Hullo, what's this?" He pulled a crumpled plastic envelope containing a few remnants of what appeared to be some sort of plant material out from under the body. "This from the pocket of his shirt, still quite damp and muddy, not to say a bit slimy into the bargain." He wiped his hand on the sand with an expression of distaste, then held up the envelope for her to see. "What do you think of this? Either it's a few precious flakes of cannabis, which dampness does not improve, or our friend's been out collecting specimens of some sort, and not too surprising, that, considering what you read off to me earlier about this place. If so, this particular item's gone largely missing. Not marked at all, either, more's the pity, but whatever it was must grow nicely in a swamp." He unfolded the little envelope, studied what was left of its contents for a moment, sniffed it, and put a small particle on his tongue. "Hmm, not pot at any rate," he said thoughtfully. "Must be some other kind of dead weed." He spat the flake out. Lifting the body up slightly once more, he carefully replaced the envelope where he had found it, and laid the body down. Then he stood up very straight, thrusting his hands deep into his pockets. "Well, then. Are we not neglecting the most pressing matter at hand?"

Roz stared at him dumbfounded. What could that be, other than the body? And how could he be so calm? Then she noticed his fingers working inside the thin cloth of his pants pocket.

Stepping backward from the body in the tracks he'd already made, Alan gave the whole area a wide berth as he came to stand beside her. "Which is, as they say in your country, to call the cops. One of us will have to row out to his boat, see if anyone else is on board, which I strongly doubt, see if we can find out who he is—was—and radio the authorities. The other should stay here with the body, in case . . ." His voice trailed off as he looked down at the sand.

In case what? Roz thought wildly. The corpse woke up? A gang of murderers came running out of the woods waving huge boomerang clubs? Her scalp prickled. She didn't particularly like the idea of going out to the boat, but she certainly didn't want to be the one left alone on the beach with a dead body. "I'll go," she said quickly.

"Fine," Alan said absently, apparently distracted by something he saw in the sand. He was staring down at his own footsteps, looking perplexed.

"Alan?"

"Mmm? Oh, right." Abruptly he jerked his hands out of his pockets. "Let's get you on your way. Just step round here, will you?" he said as he motioned her down the beach away from the body and the tracks.

Together they hurried back to the *Mendax*, and pushed it down to the water's edge, Alan holding it steady while Roz jumped in. "Look for things amiss," he said, giving the dinghy a hard shove that sent it several yards out into the water.

Wait a minute, she thought as she moved into the center seat and picked up the oars. Look for things amiss? What did Alan mean by that? What things? Blood and hair and other signs on board the boat of what might have caused the head injury? Or did he have something else more sinister in mind? Unwashed extra glasses with lipstick on them, half-burnt cigarettes from exotic places, fingerprints on doorknobs (did boats even have doorknobs?) as in some Humphrey Bogart movie? But that would suggest that there had been—worse yet, still was—someone else on board! She stopped rowing. Did he really think that was a possibility? Of course he did. She could just hear him saying now—Alan, not Humphrey Bogart—"Ah, fair Rosamund, we must consider all the possibilities." Except that he hadn't called her "fair Rosamund" since last night. And furthermore, he'd sent her out to search the boat all by herself.

That alone, along with his well-known penchant for overprotectiveness, pretty much dismissed *that* idea, didn't it? . . . Besides, there was just the one set of footprints. Right?

As she pivoted the dinghy around and began to row out toward the green-hulled boat, she saw him walking slowly back along the beach toward the body, head bent, hands clasped behind his back, completely absorbed in something he had seen in the sand. All he needed was a calabash, a deerstalker's cap, and a mackintosh to complete the picture of the ultimate detective hot on the scent. She knew for a fact he already had the magnifying glass.

6

It wasn't far to the other boat, the water still relatively smooth, with only a slight chop beginning to show in the channel between the two islands, and Roz was alongside in a few moments. She maneuvered the dinghy around to the stern, where there was some sort of ladder arrangement affixed next to the name: NON-AMOTE, *Southwest Harbor*. The stern counter was of the traditional swept-back style, high off the water, and the ladder did not go all the way down, but when Roz reached up and grasped the bottom rung, the whole thing extended downward smoothly like a miniature fire escape. So far, so good.

Tying the dinghy to the end of the ladder, she stood up, staring along the full length of the long, sleek green hull. Was it really possible for one person to sail a boat this size? Wasn't it all too *likely* that there was someone else on board, perhaps as yet completely oblivious to what had transpired on the beach? Or, worse, completely aware?

She looked back toward the beach; Alan was now crawling around on his hands and knees with his nose practically *in* the sand, completely engrossed in scrutinizing whatever it was he had seen on the beach. Obviously he didn't for a moment think there could be anyone lurking on board, or he'd be standing there watching her like a hawk, wringing his hands. At the moment, he couldn't be less concerned. Well, so what? She was perfectly capable of taking care of herself.

All right, then, what was the etiquette in a situation like this, just in case? Shout "Ahoy there!" "Permission to board?" She finally settled on a loud "Hello!" from the dinghy, then a louder "Hello there! Coming aboard!" from midway up the ladder.

No answer. She paused at the top, peering between the polished steel rails of the stern pulpit, and yelled one more time: "Hi! Anybody home?"

Silence. She stepped over the lifelines and down into the cockpit.

The deck stretched in a long sweep before her, covered with a bewildering array of winches, pulleys, cleats, and a veritable cat's cradle of lines running every which way, ending in neatly coiled piles at various intervals along the deck. Roz stared in amazement, feeling slightly reassured. With all this gear, one person could easily sail a boat this size alone.

But that didn't mean there *wasn't* someone else on board. She—or he—would have to be sleeping, or . . . or what? Come on now, Rozzie, she chided herself, don't let your imagination run away with you. You're a big girl now. Look for things amiss, but not that amiss. She pricked up her ears, listening carefully for any sounds of life, but all she heard was the lapping of small waves against the hull, the gentle cowbell clank of the rigging against the mast as the boat bobbed slightly in the swell.

As she moved past the wheel toward the companionway, she heard an ominous swishing noise. Ducking just in time, she felt rather than saw the boom swing violently across the cockpit and crash with a loud *bang!* out the other side.

Heart walloping, trying to catch her breath as she watched the boom sway in a diminishing arc over the cockpit, she thought: Now that's odd. Shouldn't that be lashed down?

Ah, here was the problem; the mainsheet had come uncleated, and the lines between the pulleys and the traveler were pulled loose and tangled in a knot. Not only that, the mainsail was not furled but piled loosely on the boom and bound up, as though rather hurriedly, with sail ties. A little puff of wind had caught one of the folds hanging down and sent the boom flying over. Not so shipshape after all. She grabbed the lines just under the block, then hauled slowly on the sheet until it pulled free of the snarl. Just then the wind gusted again, ballooning out the loose sail, and the huge boom reared in her hands like a spooked horse. Dangerous. A loose boom could be a lethal object. As perhaps it had been.

With some difficulty—it had almost enough force to lift her off her feet—she yanked the boom back down and popped the line into the jam cleat. She was about to furl the sail and fasten it down when it occurred to her that she should leave everything the way she found it, just in case. There was no danger really, the boom resting tight and immobile easily a foot and a half over her head, well over seven feet above the cockpit floor. It was a good six inches in diameter, capable of putting one hell of a dent in someone's head, all right—but only if that person happened to be in the wrong place at the wrong time, and not paying attention.

And that would take some doing. He'd have to be Kareem Abdul-Jabbar to be standing around with his head up there in the first place. The only other way would be to stand upright on the cockpit seat—or kneel on the cabin top—which would be totally unnecessary to accomplish any sailing maneuver she could think of. Pretty damned stupid, in fact, not to say downright suicidal, never mind totally unyachtsmanlike. Somehow she didn't think the person who sailed this boat, presumably the man on the beach, had been in that category.

Nevertheless, cautiously climbing up on the seat while taking care to keep her head well out of the way, she examined both sides of the end of the boom. No evidence of blood or hair that she could see. That didn't rule out microscopic traces, but that was a job for the experts.

As long as she was up here, she might as well have a look at the rest of it; she turned her attention to the foredeck. Unlike the main, the jib was furled up tightly on the forestay, thanks to roller reefing. This boat seemed to have all the other latest improvements, so why not a self-furling main? Or maybe it was, and he had decided not to furl it for some reason. Careless of him, especially given the shipshape and Bristol-fashion appearance of the rest of the boat. Maybe it was nonfunctional at the moment; things were always going wrong even in the best maintained of vessels. Another example of Murphy's law, no doubt: the more complicated an arrangement is, the more things can and will go wrong. Take herself and Alan, for instance. But never mind that now.

She moved all the way forward, stepping over various piles of neatly stowed gear, to where a good-sized anchor, chain and all, hung in place at the bow, obviously not needed since the boat was tied up to one of the moorings. The anchor, with its large double-pronged fluke, would certainly be adequate to bash a person's head in right and proper if such person happened to slip and fall on it just so. The fact is, she thought to herself, boats are a floating stockpile of things to bump into and injure yourself on—stanchions, pulpits, blocks, pulleys, winches, knobs—and she had the bruises herself to prove it. She bent down and peered closely at the anchor, but there was no blood or hair on either prong, or on the shaft, the bow pulpit, or anything else that she could see.

That completed the deck inventory. What next? Find out the man's identity, and contact the authorities as soon as possible.

And that meant going down below. Where there might or might not be someone lurking.

She marched back to the cockpit, stood squinting into the darkness of the open companionway, held her breath and listened for a moment. Silence. But surely any person on board would have heard her tramping up and down and come to by now—any live person, that is. Good thinking, Roz.

Taking a deep breath, she stepped cautiously through the hatch and—somewhat awkwardly facing forward, but she wasn't about to *back* down—negotiated the steep wooden steps into the main cabin.

As her eyes accustomed themselves to the dimness inside,

station, her eye was caught by a two-tiered bookshelf in back of the right-hand settee berth; there might be a bookplate or something there. *Wind in the Willows*—ah, messing about in boats indeed—*Between Wind and Water*; *Wind, Sand and Stars*; Joseph Conrad's *Tales of Land and Sea*; *Riddle of the Sands*; *Adrift.* A fairly predictable assortment of yacht literature. Chapman's *Piloting,* this year's tide tables, an edition, bound in green and apparently brand-new, of Bowditch's *American Practical Navigator.* Several volumes of *Nautical Quarterly* in hardcover. A recent issue of *Sea History.* No *Cruising Guide,* however; as Alan had surmised, the owner must have known this area like the back of his hand. The hand that now lay stiff and cold in its frozen upraised greeting . . . Stop it, Roz.

She took down several books at random and flipped open the covers. No names or bookplates in any of them. The second shelf was a little change of pace from the nautical compendium: *Field Guide to Rare and Exotic Plants of the Northeast, Life in a Bog, Peat Barrens of the Western World, Extinct and Endangered Plants and Wildlife of the Atlantic Coastal Zone.*

Hmm, she was beginning to have her suspicions about the identity of the owner of this boat. But what was this? A small, unlabeled volume that looked like a diary of some kind. Ah, she thought, now we're really on to something!

She pulled it from the shelf and leafed through it. Each page had a number, and a series of notations scribbled hastily in pencil, so that she could hardly make out what it said. But whatever it was, at least part of it was in Latin, followed variously by *R, Red-, Reb-, Rest*-something—obviously abbreviations of the names of the islands—and what looked to be a geographical location and directions. Obviously a log or a notebook of some sort. Hmmm, she thought; I wonder.

As she riffled the rest of the pages, a loose piece of paper fluttered onto the cabin sole. She picked it up: more sets of coordinates, and then an odd series of letters and numbers, almost like the combination to a safe. She turned the paper over. On the other side was a crudely scaled drawing of what appeared to be a cylinder, with various demarcations along its length, wavy lines, cross-hatchings, and several of what appeared to be legs or tubes running off at angles to the main cylinder. More letters and numbers. Could it be some sort of code?

She wondered what Alan would make of this. Should she take it back to show him, along with the log? No, better leave things just as they were, in the unlikely event there had been foul play—for which possibility, frankly, she hadn't seen a shred of evidence. Personally she was putting her money on the loose boom; the rain last night could have washed off any visible traces of human contact. But that was a problem for the authorities.

Who, she reminded herself, should be contacted right now. She replaced the notebook and paper on the shelf just as she had found it, and headed for the navigation station.

The documentation papers and radio license she found tucked neatly in a drawer underneath the navigation table confirmed her suspicions. The captain and owner of the documented vessel *Nonamote* was indeed Peter Onterdonck, who was also, according to the *Cruising Guide* she had been reading from what now seemed like aeons ago, owner of the island known as Restitution, on which he now lay dead. A wallet containing a driver's license with his photograph on it laid to rest any further doubts she might have. Roz sighed. He had been quite a good-looking man, even from that mug-shot angle, and only forty-one years old.

She turned her attention to the complicated-looking VHF on a shelf above the navigation table and studied it briefly, long enough to determine that in spite of all its dials and buttons and digital readouts it worked in approximately the same fashion as Aunt Jessie's beat-up two-button Radio Shack model. Tuning the channel indicator to 16, she picked up the transceiver, held the button in, and called, "Mayday, Mayday, Mayday! This is the—" she hesitated, finally settling on "*Nonamote,*" to rhyme with "boat."

She waited; nothing happened. Would anyone answer? Well, of course not—her thumb was still on the button. She needn't have worried; as soon as she let go, there was the crackle of a response.

"*Nonamote,* this is Marine Patrol, call sign Maine two zero niner three five. Received your Mayday. Please give your call sign and position and we will proceed to your aid. What seems to be the problem? Over."

She stared at the transceiver as though it were a live toad. Call sign? Damn! The voice had caught her off guard; she should have known better. Where the hell was the call sign? She flipped through the papers in front of her for any set of letters and numbers remotely resembling a call sign, to no avail.

"Excuse me," she said desperately, "but is all this really necessary? There's been some sort of an accident. There's a man dead here."

"All right, *Nonamote,* just take it easy. What are your co-ordinates? Over," the voice repeated through a veil of static.

Coordinates! Roz smote her head. Now they wanted latitude and longitude! How the hell was she supposed to know those off the top of her head? "Listen," she said evenly. "All I can tell you is that I am in a boat with a green hull—a Hinckley about forty feet—in the channel between Rebel and Restitution Islands in East Penobscot Bay, and there's a dead body lying on the beach at Restitution Island. I don't know the coordinates," she explained as best she could to the disembodied voice, trying to suppress the impulse to scream loudly and bash the transceiver against the wall, "but it's somewhere near Cape Rosier." That should be enough, let them figure out how to get here, and fast. She released the button, forgetting to say "Over." She quickly pressed it in again. "Sorry! Over!"

"Hey, that's good enough, *Nonamote*; we'll send someone to assist you. Proceeding to your position from Stonington, ten degrees north-northeast, at twenty knots, estimated time of arrival twelve hundred hours plus thirty." Then in plain English: "That's half an hour from now, ma'am. Try not to worry, help is on the way. Over and out."

Roz hung up the transceiver. Just like that. Help was on the way, for which she was grateful, even if the voice on the radio had sounded fairly condescending. Speaking of which, she paused to consider, why hadn't the dead man—Peter Onterdonck! What an idiot! After all that, she hadn't even told the officer who the dead man was!—used the radio to call for help? After all, it was right here, and anybody, even a semiconscious person—or a semicoherent one, as she had just demonstrated—could raise somebody in a pinch.

But she couldn't stop to ponder that now. She had looked for things amiss, found out the man's identity, and reported the accident. Mission accomplished; it was time to go. She hurried back up the steps and into the cockpit. She could just make out Alan's tall figure, still bent over, still studying something on the beach.

And there was the body, no longer resembling a pile of clothes. She closed her eyes for a moment, trying to distance herself from it; saw it as though from a great height, like a figure at the bottom of a gorge, one arm outflung, head slightly turned, removed, abstract, pristine. It was only the idea of death that bothered her, really, wasn't it? Not the body itself. Right?

Wrong. It was the body of a man named Peter Onterdonck, who had lived and breathed and read books and sailed his boat, who had cared about the life around him, and it bothered her a lot. Climbing down into the dinghy, she rowed slowly and thoughtfully back to the island.

By now, past noon (twelve hundred plus ten, to be exact), the tide was approaching the high-water mark. Pulling up onto the beach, she caught sight of her precious Fortnum and Mason's hamper lying forlornly in the sand where she had left it, now perilously close to the water's edge. Abandoning the dinghy, she went up and rescued it, noticing that the tide had obliterated all their tracks farther down the beach, though not the ones still clearly visible in the damp sand above the line of sea wrack. She placed the hamper under a large tree just beyond where the beach ended and walked back down to where Alan was standing.

"All is changed utterly," he said, turning to her, his face grave. "I'm afraid our chap's been murdered."

7

"Just look here," Alan said as she stared at him, openmouthed. He pointed down at the set of tracks that led from the dinghy to where the body lay.

Obediently Roz looked down. The prints were clearly impressed in the damp sand; they looked like the same old footprints to her. All around, the sand was clear and undisturbed, except for the V-shaped trough made by the dinghy where it had been pulled up above the high-water mark, a faint lengthwise indentation where the painter had been dragged, and the tracks they themselves had made earlier.

Alan reached into his pants pocket and pulled out what Roz recognized as his prize purchase from their 2:00 a.m. foray into L. L. Bean on the way from the Portland airport (Alan had declared after his visit to Maine last January that there would be no more trips in the tiny commuter plane that served Southwark and points north. "My latest idea of hell on earth," he'd told her upon alighting, "is to be yo-yoed for an hour in a prop-driven aircraft I can barely sit upright in that doesn't even have a loo, should the need arise, which, luckily, it didn't"). This particular item was a gadget-infested pocketknife the likes of which Roz had never seen. At least an inch thick, it contained, in addition to its lone knife blade, a stapler, a miniature saw blade, a screwdriver, scissors, a hole punch, a magnifying lens, tweezers, a toothpick, and a metric rule—"Everything you'd ever need to survive in the wild except an outboard motor," the salesperson had cheerfully explained, happily demonstrating the full range of possibilities. "Even a chain saw." "Chain saw? Surely you jest," Alan had remarked dubiously, at which point the young man unwound a long, flexible, tooth-edged steel cord. "Good Lord!" Alan had responded in awe. "It looks just like a garrote! I must have it!" Right now he was fiddling with the metric rule; she was glad to see he'd found at least one way to put the instrument to use.

"You weigh roughly nine stone, yes?"

"If that's a hundred and twenty-five pounds," Roz answered, looking at him curiously.

"And I weigh fourteen stone. Or, calculating rapidly, one ninety-six, slightly more than half again as much. Now if you will just step aside . . ."

Roz did so, and watched while Alan bent down and slid the metric rule into one of her footprints, marking the rule with his thumb. She wondered if the magnifying lens would be next. "Twelve millimeters at the heel." He stood up and stepped back, then bent over and repeated the procedure in his own footprint. "Eighteen millimeters. Precisely half again the depth of yours, the slight difference accounted for, at a guess, by the weight–to–surface area ratio."

Roz nodded, wondering what he was getting at.

"Now, considering our unfortunate victim here, wouldn't you say he was approximately my size and weight?"

"Hmmm, well, he is lying down," Roz said. "But, as a matter of fact, I'd say he's just your size, give or take a half-inch. Six-one and a half, one ninety-five on the nose. Gray eyes. Born under the sign of Aquarius."

"What, so exact?" he said, looking at her in surprise.

"I saw his driver's license," she admitted.

"Ah. Then you can confirm my conclusion, based on the evidence at hand, taken together with certain information from the *Cruising Guide*, that this is in fact the body of Mr. Peter Onterdonck, late the owner of this island," Alan said as he bent over one of the dead man's footprints and inserted his measuring device. "Twelve millimeters deep at the heel and not a penn'orth more." He stood straight, carefully folded up his device, replaced it in his pocket, and regarded her impassively.

Roz looked down at the footprints and back at Alan. "But . . . but those *must* be his footprints. I mean, they're his shoes, aren't they?"

"Ah, yes, my dear, ah—Roz. These are indeed the prints of his shoes. What I am saying is that his feet couldn't have been in them."

Roz looked again. One line of footprints leading to the body, none leading back, the footprints not the body's but those of someone else wearing his shoes. Foul play indeed. Murder meant to look like an accident, the old backward-footprint ploy, as old as Hercules. So that's why he hadn't used the radio. Her head buzzed, and she felt slightly faint. Finding a nameless body on a beach had been one thing. Looking down at him now, knowing who he was and suspecting that he had been murdered, was quite another. The buzzing grew louder; the treetops overhead seemed to converge, began to whirl. She shut her eyes.

"Steady on, Roz love, are you all right?" She felt his arm go around her and quickly pull her to him, turning her so that she could no longer see the body. She sank heavily against him. His arm tightened around her.

She took a deep breath and opened her eyes, pushed away slightly, and smiled up at him. "Thanks," she said, "I'm fine now." He dropped his arm precipitately and stepped back away from her. She gazed at him for a moment, then went on as before. "So what you're telling me is that whoever killed him carried the body over here wearing his shoes, dumped him down, and then walked backward in the same footprints?"

"Not exactly. Here, just hop on my back a second; no, do it," he said in answer to her look of stunned bewilderment. "No one's watching."

"How do you know?" she demanded. But that wasn't the real reason she was hesitant; none of this was her idea of the ideal way to reestablish close physical contact, falling against him in a near faint, then turning around and climbing up his back like a monkey on a stick. She hadn't done anything like this since fifth grade. Well, maybe tenth. But he didn't seem to think anything of it, as he motioned to her impatiently. "Come on, then," he prodded, turning his back and bending over slightly.

Feeling profoundly self-conscious, she scrambled up onto Alan's back. He took several steps with her clinging like a knapsack to his shoulders and hips, then let her down gently without comment and once again brought out the measuring device. "Twenty-eight millimeters, thirty minus two, not quite as deep as yours and mine together."

"Why isn't it yours plus mine?"

"Effect of compaction, at a guess. I'm no physicist, but even so, the exact difference hardly matters, does it? The point is, he couldn't have walked up here by himself and left those tracks, nor could anyone remotely human-sized have walked over here carrying him. No, someone a good bit lighter than Onterdonck made those tracks, emphatically without the addition of his body weight on board. So—how did the body get there?"

Roz thought for a moment. No other tracks, no telephone poles, no lines, just a bare expanse of beach. "Skyhook?" she replied in a feeble attempt at humor, glancing around at the beach, the sand, the trees—anywhere but at the man's body. Suddenly it was all too much; tears stung her eyes. She moved away from Alan and went down the beach toward the water. Such a beautiful day, so bright and clear, she thought as she looked across the channel toward Rebel Island. The island lay green and peaceful, the late-morning light glancing off the tall white steeple of the little church . . .

Wait a minute. What church? There was no church on Rebel

Island. As she stared with a strange sense of displacement at the tall white peak, she saw that it, not the island, was moving, gliding slowly behind the farthest headland of the island, taller than the evergreens, taller than . . . Roz blinked, and blinked again. The white peak resolved into a triangle, the triangle into a sail. A sail as tall as a church steeple? It couldn't be.

But it was, she saw shortly, as the sail billowed around the headland and an enormous sailboat came into view, with a single mast so tall it seemed to dwarf the landscape, tall firs and taller pine trees, headland, islands, rocky bluffs, and all. It was the biggest single-masted sailboat Roz had ever seen, the hull more than twice the length of the green boat, a hundred feet at a guess, the mast towering over it at least that high, more like a pylon than a mast.

In a matter of seconds the huge boat was swooping up the channel toward them at what seemed to be the speed of light. She couldn't see any crew on board! The boat was sailing itself and it was going to ram right into the island! A giant ghost ship run amok with no captain, not even an apparition of one, on deck to steer!

Wait! There *was* someone, a lone, dwarfed figure standing in what must be the cockpit—but where was the wheel? All the figure seemed to be doing was madly waving its arms! For help, obviously! The boat was out of control! But what was she supposed to do? Oh, no! Here it comes!

She was about to turn and run for cover when the boat suddenly veered and, with a noise like thunder, massive foresail shuddering, came about. It glided a few more feet toward the island, then, with the rumble of an engine reversing, came to an abrupt halt (much to Roz's relief) some hundred yards away, standing off in the middle of the channel. There was a whir and a whine of winches, and two mammoth plow anchors shaped like giant fishhooks plopped off the deck and into the water, apparently untouched by human hands. As Roz watched with her mouth open, the massive jib instantly disappeared into the forestay, like the flicker of a snake's tongue. If that was the jib, the main must be the size of a football field. But where was it? She didn't see any signs of a sail on the boom (which was the size of a giant fallen redwood), just a little triangle the size of a hankie with a rope attached sticking out of the mast near the bottom.

The lone figure now visible on deck, in shorts and a shirt and long hair tied back in a ponytail, was standing in what must be the cockpit—though it was higher up on the deck and closer to the center of the boat than any cockpit she had ever seen, and in fact resembled a parapet. The person appeared to be playing some sort of keyboard instrument, hands hovering over and occasionally touching down here, and here, and there. But what was being orchestrated?

Why, the landing, what else? As Roz watched, the huge boat briefly backed up to set the anchors. A hand fluttered and swooped, and the engine noise stopped abruptly. All was suddenly quiet once more. Silently the giant hull swung around until it came to rest in the deeper water some fifty yards beyond the *Verorum*.

"Alan!" Roz called, her eyes still riveted on the new arrival. "Do you see this?" Stupid question, how could he miss it? The boat was so enormous it dwarfed everything around it. Roz felt like a pygmy perched on a hummock surrounded by toothpicks.

Alan was standing where she had left him, and he, too, was staring out at the monster sloop with a bemused expression on his face. "Amazing. Haven't seen a maxisloop that big since the America's Cup. Looks like a J-Boat knockoff. Do you suppose that's her skipper running in here hell-for-leather in the inflatable?"

In no time at all, the rubber dinghy with its disreputable-looking passenger swooped up onto the beach. "Ahoy there!" came a distinctly male voice. "Are you the party in distress?"

"Are you the Marine Patrol?" Roz asked in disbelief. She rather doubted it. Not only did he have a ponytail, but a full, somewhat scraggly beard and a rolled bandanna tied around his brow, restraining whatever stray wisps of shoulder-length hair had escaped the ponytail. But who else would have answered her Mayday transmission?

"Hell, no," came the reply. "I was on my way upriver to Bucksport, cruising by the other side of Rebel there with the distress channel open, and I heard your call, so I decided to buzz around."

From the looks of his attire—worn T-shirt with a skull and crossbones prominently displayed, ragged cutoffs, and no shoes—Roz guessed he must be a deckhand. She wondered where the captain and the rest of the crew were. Meanwhile the man yanked his dinghy up onto the beach, then walked over to Roz and Alan, his hand outstretched in greeting. "Roger Fell's the name. That's my boat, the *Jolly Roger*. What's up?"

8

Could this be the very same Roger C. Fell, mentioned in the *Cruising Guide*? But he didn't seem quite old enough; that must have been this man's father. He was a slim, wiry man in his early forties, Roz judged by the crinkly lines around his eyes, the few streaks of gray in his sun-washed hair. He looked like a fugitive from the sixties, his bedraggled, even ratty appearance considerably at odds with the clean, high-tech elegance of his boat. But maybe that was the whole idea. Yet there was something rather attractive about him, in a vaguely piratical way. Not to mention the fact that with a boat of that size and technological elegance he must be a multimillionaire.

After Roz and Alan had introduced themselves, the three of them walked across the sand toward the body. As they approached it, Alan directed Fell to steer clear of the footprints.

Fell looked at him curiously, then said, "Oh, sure, no problem." He hopped up on the grassy verge and peered at the body stretched on the beach, then did an intense double take. "Hey, what the hell! I'll be damned. That's my cousin Peter!" He hopped back a few steps, shaking his head. "Jeezum, I thought that looked like the *Non-Amo-Te* out there," he said, pronouncing the boat name in four syllables, to rhyme with "tray." Alan looked up sharply at the mention of the boat name, his attention suddenly riveted on Fell. "Jeezum-crow-binius," Fell said. "Are you sure he's dead?" He began to pace back and forth along the verge in an agitated fashion, eyes fixed on the body.

"The family feud still on, eh what?" Alan said quietly.

Fell stopped short, turned slowly to face Alan. "Now how the hell did you know that? Wait a minute! You some sort of detective?"

Alan smiled faintly and shook his head. "Your family history according to the *Cruising Guide,* and the name of your cousin's boat. *'Non amo te, Sabidi, nec possum dicere quare . . .'* "

Roz could not believe her ears. What was Alan thinking of? This was hardly the time for Latin epigrams!

Roger Fell was staring at him as though he had taken leave of his senses. "Yeah, um, well . . . he was fond of possums, and he sure liked to dicker . . ." he said in a bewildered tone. Obviously Alan had him at a disadvantage. Somehow Roz didn't think Mr. Fell was one to take very kindly to that fact.

Nor, obviously, did Alan. "Er . . . sorry," he said quickly, glancing over at Roz, who just shrugged; too late now. "It's an epigram from Martial," Alan explained. "I thought surely you must know; my mistake."

"So?" Roger Fell said in an unmistakably hostile voice. "Know what?"

Alan cleared his throat and continued. "Yes, well. In the latter part of the seventeenth century, one John Fell, Dean at Christ Church, Oxford, caught a feckless young rogue named Tom Brown at some mischief and demanded he construe a Latin epigram on the spot or be sent down. Nothing if not quick on his feet, Brown ripped right into the one from which I just quoted the first line, and translated it thus: 'I do not love thee, Doctor Fell, the reason why I cannot tell, but this alone I know full well, I do not love thee, Doctor Fell.' Since he'd only done exactly as he was told, Fell had to let him off. No relation, I expect," Alan added in an obvious attempt to change the subject. "Your Fells are Irish, aren't they?"

"Were," Fell answered. "And I suppose you're British or something, huh?" he inquired, apparently more interested in Alan's not-quite British accent then his feat of erudition.

"Or something," Alan replied.

"Yeah? Well, fine, welcome to the U. S. of A.," said Fell; Alan relaxed visibly. "So anyway," Fell continued, "you hit it right on the nose, pal. His dad and mine couldn't stand each other. Politics, mainly; his old man didn't approve of anyone who'd support those, and I quote, 'fanatical outlaw Republicans.' My old man told him to mind his own goddamned business." He shook his head. "No love lost between ol' Pete and me either, far as that goes. Always sticking his nose in where he wasn't wanted, him and his wacky environmentalist ideas. Degrees up the ying-yang, Harvard Ph.D. and all—and look where it got him. Didn't know when to quit, the stupid son of a bitch."

" '*Nil nisi bonum . . .*' " Alan said gently.

"Oh, Christ, not more Latin," Fell said in an exasperated voice. Wiping his face with a loose end of his headband, he glowered at Alan. "So what the hell does *that* mean?"

" 'Never speak ill of the dead,' " Roz translated quickly, hoping to head off what promised to be a noteworthy show of wrath on Fell's part.

"Oh. Oh, right." Fell fixed his less-than-friendly glance on her. "Quite the lady Latin scholar yourself, aren't you?"

Roz glared right back at him. Hmph. "Lady scholar" was it? So Fell was not just an aging pseudo-hippie, but a sexist male as well. Yet there was something attractive about him, though what it was she could not tell. Certainly not his manners; his restless energy, perhaps, and the fact that he obviously didn't take any nonsense, Latin or otherwise, from anybody. There was nothing reserved or cautious about Roger Fell. But wasn't he behaving rather oddly about his cousin's death? Just the least bit callous, feud or no feud? Or was it all part of his macho-buccaneer image, the bluff exterior hiding a heart of mush?

Fell had turned his attention back to the body. "Well, looks as though he's dead, all right," he said after a moment. "Too bad. Harumph. Not that it's any skin off my nose. We didn't even speak, hardly. Oh, well, it'll make things a whole lot easier for me, and that's a fact. It's an ill wind and all that." He paused, sniffing the air speculatively. "Speaking of wind, maybe we should move him into the shade. The fuzz may not get here for a while."

As Roz stood there wondering if Fell could possibly demonstrate any more ways to be completely offensive, he suddenly leaped down onto the sand and started for the body.

Alan stepped forward quickly and put an arm out to hold him back. "I don't think that would be a good idea," he warned. "There's a good possibility that there's been foul play. The fact is, his skull's been bashed in."

Fell stopped in his tracks. "Been bashed in," he repeated slowly. "I take it you mean not accidentally on his own hook, but by someone else on purpose, as in, like—murder?" He thumped his hands onto his bony hips, and deliberately perused the scene again. He cocked his head, looking derisively from one of them to the other. "Oh, right," he said in a tone of utter contempt. "Hey, are you guys nuts? What are you trying to pull here, anyway? I may not be able to reel off Latin epitaphs or whatever-you-call-'em, but I'm not stupid, and I can read footprints as well as anybody." He gestured impatiently toward the body. "These big ones by the head are yours, aren't they?" Alan nodded. "And those smaller ones over there are obviously the lady's here. That leaves just those, from his dinghy to . . . here," he said, marching over to point down at Onterdonck's feet. "So you tell me how he got his head beat in by somebody *while* he was walking all by himself on a deserted beach surrounded by sand, *with only his own footprints to show for it.*"

"To be sure," said Alan. "It's your regular locked-room mystery."

Fell stopped short, obviously thinking that one over. "Oh, *I* get it," he sneered. "My cousin's standing all alone out here in the middle of the sand with his thumb up his ass, and a giant orangutan swings out of those trees and drops a coconut on his head—whoops! That can't be it! No coconut!" Fell executed a little dance step, twirled around, and stopped, hands splayed out in an exaggerated shrug, as if to say: ta-da! "No, wait, I've got it!" he chortled. "Superman flies through the air and thumps him a good one upside the ear just to say hi, and breaks his skull, right? By mistake, of course."

Fell stepped back and folded his arms over his ragged T-shirt. His glare would have withered a persimmon. "Hey, get real, you guys. So what if I don't have a Ph.D. from Harvard, Yale, Oxfam, or whatever! I'm not dumb! You're looking at an A.B. from Bowdoin and a Wharton M.B.A. here, and I could have bought and sold Pete Onterdonck ten times over if he'd've let me. So *read my lips.* Apes aren't native to Maine, and neither is Superman. You're looking at an *accident,* pure and simple. Any idiot can see that." Roger Fell paused to catch his breath, then, to their combined astonishment, added, "He's just lucky he didn't try any funny business on *my* island, or it might *well* have been murder." With that, he turned and stomped off down the beach, still shaking his head.

They both stared after him. Roz wondered what Alan was thinking. Could it be Roger Fell was protesting too much? "Read my lips" indeed.

"I daresay," Alan murmured, as though echoing her thoughts. "Dancing on the grave isn't even in it, is it?"

Just then their attention was distracted by the high-pitched whine of what sounded like dueling chain saws moving closer at a high rate of speed. They looked up just in time to see a dull, khaki-colored, medium-sized powerboat, with a windscreen, a weather-beaten canvas canopy, and a radar dish like a big cake tin on a stick affixed to its cabin top, roar around the edge of the island. It headed straight for them at top speed, its wake cutting a sharp, translucent swath that momentarily rocked all three sailboats one after the other, setting them nodding at each other like Chinese wise men. Roz took an involuntary step backward. *They* really *are* going to ram right into the island, she thought.

And so they did, in a matter of speaking, cutting the engine at the last moment and gliding nose first up onto the beach, coming to rest with their engine still in the water. Two khaki-clad figures with mirrored sunglasses leaned out from under the awning, buttons and badges flashing. The Marine Patrol had arrived.

9
_____

The officers, who introduced themselves as Sergeant Stiles and Officer Rancourt, were quite efficient and courteous, questioning each of them in turn, carefully noting down the responses in an ordinary secretary's spiral notebook. Roz supposed they didn't have much call for a full murder investigation kit in these parts—they were probably more used to dealing with midnight poachers and boats with inadequate personal flotation devices. But they seemed to do just fine, even if their dialogue did sound a bit like something they'd heard on television. Thus of Roz: "Yes, ma'am, and when did you first become aware of someone lying on the beach? And when you saw the body, did you approach or otherwise touch or disturb the remains?" Of Alan: "Yes, sir, now, when Ms. Howard here informed you about the body, you went over, and could you tell me exactly what you observed?" Of Roger Fell, with whom they already seemed to be acquainted: "And exactly when did you arrive on the scene, Mr. Fell?" They also seemed to know already that the body was that of Peter Onterdonck, Rancourt remarking in an aside to Stiles: "See, I tol' ya it had to be *Non-Amo-Te* [pronounced to rhyme with *tray*], not some other slab called *Non-amote* [to rhyme with *boat*]."

"Well, guess we're going to have to call in the M.E. for an unattended," Stiles said when he'd finished taking notes. There was a brief discussion about exactly what county jurisdiction the islands were in, Hancock or Waldo, since the border more or less bisected (invisibly, of course) this part of Penobscot Bay. Roger Fell settled the argument by informing them that the islands were split between the two, Restitution lying just inside the boundary of Waldo, while Rebel went with Hancock, because of its closer proximity to the mainland, a little over a mile from Cape Rosier at dead low tide. "Belfast it be, then," said Rancourt. "I'll call 'er in."

"Make it snappy, will you, Archie?" Fell said. "Let's get this show on the road. I've got a zoning board meeting over to Ellsworth tonight at seven."

"Over to"? Roz noted—funny way for an A.B. from Bowdoin to talk, unless they'd left off teaching grammatically correct English some time back. Then she remembered; native Mainers, however well educated, tended to lapse into a lingo all their own, including such gems as "over to home" and "from away," which they employed at will, particularly when talking to other natives. So he and Stiles and Rancourt were old buddies—on a first-name basis, anyway. Maybe they'd even grown up together, here on the bay and thereabouts.

Rancourt went back to the patrol boat to radio the mainland, while Stiles remained on the grassy verge talking to the three of them. "Not that it's necessarily one of your suspicious deaths, y'know," he said, "but in this business you gotta go through all the motions."

Somewhat absently nodding his agreement, Roger Fell turned and walked off by himself. Roz looked at Alan incredulously. A man lying dead on an isolated beach with his head bashed in, and it wasn't suspicious? Who were these guys kidding? But all Alan did was to raise his eyebrows at her with a barely discernible shrug.

Oh well, she was sure the medical examiner and the state attorney's office would sort it all out one way or another. There would be an autopsy, an inquest, an investigation. Their presence—hers and Alan's—would surely be required as witnesses. Roz thought this over for a moment. That meant Alan would have to stay around indefinitely; they both would. She wondered if he'd figured that out yet. Or if he cared.

If he had, he wasn't showing any signs of it, at least not to her. He had collared Stiles and was deep in conversation with him. She heard him ask when and how the medical examiner and all his paraphernalia would arrive, by yet another boat, or possibly a helicopter? "Seaplane," she heard Stiles answer. A seaplane, hmm? Roz thought, momentarily distracted from her contemplation of the possible hitch in Alan's plans for a speedy departure. That would mean three sailboats, three dinghies, a motorboat, and an aircraft, not to mention five live human beings and one dead one, all on one small, supposedly uninhabited island in the bay. Even counting the other island as part of a pair, this was an awful lot of activity for such ordinarily remote and isolated small acreage. She wondered what the assorted local flora and fauna thought of having their peace disturbed in this way. Probably not a great deal. After all, they had persisted here for centuries, while human beings (and their Latin) just came and went, on their way to becoming, like A. E. Housman's Roman and his trouble, "ashes under Uricon." Some little uproar, a flurry of noise and activity, and then all would be peace again. This in turn made her recall once again that strange comment Roger Fell had blurted out earlier. What "things" would Onterdonck's death make easier for him? And why had he been so concerned with Onterdonck's possible presence—make that "funny business"—on *his* island?

Alan, meanwhile, had his shoes off and was showing Stiles the soles; they were British boat shoes, and had a distinctive pattern cut in a spiral that was clearly distinguishable from the tracks made by anyone else. He and Stiles then walked off down the beach, examining the tracks all the way back to all three dinghies, occasionally bending down together while Alan pointed something out to Stiles.

They came back to where she was standing, Stiles nodding and pursing his lips. "Thank you, sir, you've been a great help. Ma'am." With a polite nod in Roz's direction, he turned and walked down the beach until he caught up with Roger Fell. In spite of Fell's disreputable appearance, it was clear that he commanded the respect of both the officers. Stiles addressed him in an almost deferential way, and after a moment the two of them moved down the beach out of earshot.

"What were you and Stiles talking about?" Roz asked Alan as they moved down the beach away from the body, which had, to Roz's relief, been covered with a blue plastic tarpaulin, awaiting the arrival of the medical examiner. Alan was gazing after Stiles and Roger Fell, frowning slightly, apparently lost in thought.

"Hmm? Oh, sorry. I was trying to convince him of the jiggery-pokery with the footprints, but I'm not sure he believed me. All he did was look rather skeptical, ask me what line of work I was in, and when I said I was an artist at the moment, but that I'd had some experience in certain aspects of the forensic sciences, he looked straight at me and said, 'Is that so?' which I did not take to be a question. Then he made a sound like a cross between a throat-clear and a grunt"—here Alan approximated the sound of "Ayuh"—"and said he'd let the medical examiner know, 'for whatevah that's wuth. They got their own procedures to foller,' " he continued in a quite credible imitation of a heavy Maine accent, " 'them folks down ta 'Guster, though most of it sure beats me, and that's a fact.' " As he was talking, Roz noticed him reaching into his pants pocket. "The fact is, I don't think he believed a word I told him." The world's fattest jacknife appeared in his hand, metric rule extended once again, as he unobtrusively stooped down to probe the indentation of a bare foot.

"Well, you've done your part, haven't you?" she said curtly. "You pointed out the discrepancy; let them work out how it was done. They're the ones in charge now, and so it's their problem, isn't it? We've done all we can here, haven't we? Can't we just go?"

Giving her an odd look, Alan stood up and repocketed the knife. He was silent for a moment. "Ah, yes, we'd best just be done with it, hadn't we? Well, let's just hope the authorities can work it out. Then we can all be on our merry ways."

Roz nodded. Of course, she thought sadly, on our oh-so-separate ways; he was, after all, anxious to be gone. She looked away down the beach toward the officers. They were still talking with Roger Fell, who was clearly getting impatient. He, too, wanted to be gone. Just then Stiles turned toward the two of them and beckoned them to come over.

"Just a few more questions, folks," he said apologetically as they joined the little group. "Did you observe anyone else in the area either last night or this morning, other than Mr. Fell here?" Fell glowered.

"There was a heavy fog last night," Roz said. "We couldn't see anything, not even the *Non-Amo-Te*. . . . But wait, there *was* a windjammer of some sort that went out early this morning, twin masts, seventy feet or so, weathered canvas sails, dark-green or black hull."

Stiles looked at Rancourt, eyebrows raised. "Well, that only describes about half the skinboats—'scuse me, schooners—in the fleet," he said dubiously. You didn't happen to get the name, did you?"

"No," Roz answered. "There was a tarpaulin or something hanging down over the back. All I saw was a few letters—capital RD—and the end of one word—*land*—underneath. It was fairly early, around seven a.m. They had been moored around the other side for the night, I assume. But the body was already there—"

"That's strange," Roger Fell said. They all turned to look at him. "Both these islands are supposed to be off-limits to the schooner fleet."

"Maybe they was just passing through?" offered Rancourt.

"At seven o'clock in the morning?" Fell replied sarcastically.

"Hey, wait a minute! Now that I think of it, there's a Canadian vessel been doing test borings on Rebel for some environmental impact study, name of *Sea's Garden*. Could be that was her. Was she a topsail schooner?"

Roz looked at him blankly. What the hell was a topsail schooner? She turned to Alan, who simply shook his head, indicating it wasn't.

"Well, don't worry about it," said Stiles. "We'll get everything checked out. There's only about twenty windjammers hereabouts, one or two more down Portland way. But it's most likely one of the local fleet. I doubt it they would've seen anything even if they *were* here last night, all sittin' down below singin' songs and tellin' stories the way they do." He turned to Alan. "Now, sir, could you give me an idea of your itinerary for the next few days?"

"We don't have one, actually," Alan said with a quick glance at Roz. "We are—were—on holiday."

"I see. Well, we'll have to ask you not to leave the area for the time being, until we get this business cleared up." He handed Alan a card with a number on it. Alan glanced down at it, seemed to be studying it, his face without expression. Stiles said, "If you'd just call this number wherever you put in for the night so as we can keep track of you, in case we have any more questions . . ." He turned to Fell and handed him one, too.

"What the hell is this, Stiles?" Fell snarled, waving the card away. He drew himself up belligerently, almost losing his shorts in the process.

"Come on now, Mr. Fell. It's just a formality. We may need you for an inquest, if there is one. We're just trying to cover all the possibilities here."

"But I wasn't anywhere near here last night! I didn't come into the East Bay until midmorning, on my way to Ellsworth via Bucksport, just like I told you."

"With all due respect, Mr. Fell," Stiles began, obviously trying his best to avoid a confrontation, "we have only your word for that. With that humongous sailing machine of yours, you could be over to Blue Hill and back again ten times every hour of the day *or* night."

"Am I a suspect, then?" Fell demanded in an outraged voice.

"Nobody suspects anybody of anything at this point. We're just asking you to keep yourself available in case something comes up."

"This is ridiculous! What if I refuse?"

"We'll just send the Coast Guard after you," Stiles said cheerfully. "You're kinda hard to lose."

Fell was clearly not amused. He snatched the card out of Stiles's hand and stalked off to his dinghy. In a matter of seconds he had pushed it into the water, fired up the motor, and roared off. Roz, Alan, and the two officers watched wordlessly as he scrambled up what looked like a three-story fire ladder onto the *Jolly Roger*. In another moment his hands were hovering wildly over the instrument panel. With his look of furious concentration he reminded Roz so much of the Phantom of the Opera madly orchestrating some grand overture that she expected to hear organ music boom out over the water.

But the only sound was a low thrum followed by a splashing noise as the anchors churned up out of the water. Then the huge hull gracefully executed a 180-degree turn, sluicing around in a wide arc before heading straight down the channel between the islands. A mainsail the size of a football field cut crosswise came sliding out of the mast along the boom with the smoothness of a stage curtain; the boom itself began to swing out mightily downwind to port, then halted abruptly, as with a soft hum and a whir the mammoth sail appeared to trim itself.

As they watched in stupefaction, another sail the size of a three-ring circus tent fluttered up out of the deck. "My God, will you look at that?" Alan crowed happily. "It's the biggest ruddy spinnaker I've ever seen!"

With a great *tha-womp!* the mammoth spinnaker filled with wind, floating in front of the sailboat like a giant hot-air balloon. They barely had time to note the black skull and crossbones emblazoned across the belly before the *Jolly Roger* shot off like a spaceship in warp drive and disappeared downwind.

"How do you like them apples?" said Rancourt. "It's all hydraulic. No wheel or nothing; he does it all by pushing buttons. Ain't it some amazing?"

"Mr. Fell's quite a character," said Stiles. "Nice guy—well, most of the time, anyway—even if he is as rich as stink."

At that moment there was a roar out of the sky, and as they all looked up, a small airplane with what appeared to be two canoes where its wheels should be swooped down out of the sky, circled once, then plowed to a landing at the mouth of the cove.

"Jeezum, it's about time they got here," said Stiles.

"Speaking of characters," Alan muttered under his breath into Roz's ear, "what would you say our friend Mr. Fell weighs?"

"About one-fifty," she muttered back. "Just a guess, of course. I didn't see his driver's license."

"Hmmm," said Alan. "That fits." He jiggled the contents of his pants pocket briefly, then withdrew his hand and stared straight ahead. As they watched the plane taxi in toward the beach, Roz heard him muttering softly to himself, "I do not love thee, Roger Fell . . ."

TWO

MESSING ABOUT IN BOATS

10

"Well, that's damned peculiar," Alan said as he marched down onto the floating dock belonging to the Dark Harbor Boat Yard. He was carrying a newspaper. Roz looked up from where she was reading in a corner of the cockpit.

"What's peculiar?" she asked. Alan didn't answer; he had stopped dead in his tracks and was now standing on the dock, totally engrossed in reading the paper, apparently in its entirety, flipping pages—all six of them—over furiously. It was two days since their adventure on the beach, and they had tied up at the dock to get some supplies after spending a quiet night on a guest mooring in Gilkey Harbor.

By the time the medical examiner and the other officials had indicated their services would no longer be needed at the scene of the crime it was well past five o'clock in the evening. The wind had come up from the southwest, so Roz and Alan had decided to sail around Cape Rosier and up into Castine, even though this was in the opposite direction from North Haven and points south, where they had been headed originally. But Roz had declared during the monumental case of the shakes she had suddenly developed after getting back on board the

Verorum that although she was sure Pulpit Harbor was very nice, it was also very isolated, and at that moment she would really prefer to go where there were more likely to be lots of lights and people. Alan had agreed readily.

Roz had secretly hoped that after their disturbing experience on Restitution Island some sort of reconciliation might be in order. But after they had treated themselves to a dinner in an excellent French restaurant up the road from the town landing (where there were not only bright lights and people but a Maine Maritime Academy training vessel the size of a battleship, chock-full of frolicking young persons), upon returning to the *Verorum* replete with food and drink, Alan had simply bid her good night once more in a polite and formal manner and bedded himself down in the main cabin. Lying alone once again in the forecastle, Roz had tossed herself to sleep, thinking over and over, Now who's the pigheaded one?

Alan had faithfully made the call both days, but there had been no word as yet on the disposition of the case. The next morning they had continued on their way, insofar as it did not take them too far afield—or rather a-sea—from their possible summons as witnesses, no farther than a day's run from Belfast, just in case. So they had ventured only so far as the southernmost tip of Vinalhaven, Alan gazing longingly out to sea in the direction of a shadowy, far-off Monhegan Island with its famed artists' colony, shades of Henri, Bellows, Kent, Tam, Jamie Wyeth, et al. But eleven nautical miles was considerably more than a day's sail from Belfast.

So back they came to Gilkey Harbor ("I shall just have to settle for the summer digs of a lone, lorn Charles Dana Gibson," Alan had grumbled), formed by the juncture of Islesboro, Seven Hundred Acre (Gibson's home), and Job islands, smack in the middle of the bay. Roz was beginning to feel as though she were on board one of those ghost ships doomed to sail the seas from Cape Verde to Cape Horn forever searching for—what? Safe passage? "Don't worry, love," she wistfully recalled Alan saying on an earlier occasion, and in another context, "you're safe with me."

This current passage with him was certainly safe enough; *too* safe. At this point, Roz was willing to settle for "this nettle, Danger," if it meant the end of the awkward rift between them, this stiff formality of his space, her space, and never the twain shall meet except by accident, bumping elbows or unwittingly colliding near the head.

Not that things weren't congenial enough on the surface. In fact they had settled quite amicably into what Roz regretfully recognized as a foreshadowing of their soon-to-be-separate lives, Alan doing ten things at once, coiling and whipping lines, tinkering with the engine, hiking around their various stopping places, looking for interesting plants, noting this and sketching that, while Roz sat in the shade and doggedly read selections ranging from Beowulf to Virginia Woolf for her courses in the fall. Who said that two people couldn't get along perfectly well without great sex—or any sex, for that matter—though in truth Roz couldn't say she'd recommend it. But what difference did it make now, anyway? Obviously the only reason he was staying around now was that he had to. As soon as the case was wrapped up, he'd be on his way, and she would never find out what it was he'd had to tell her. He certainly wasn't about to divulge it now. And she wasn't about to ask.

They had awakened this morning, in their separate quarters, to another day of bright sun and calm seas. For a little change of pace they had decided to make their next landfall a picturesque but guaranteed-to-be-uninhabited (and therefore phoneless) island in midbay with the chance of an old farm ruin or two in addition to the various plant specimens Alan had been sketching (obviously for lack of anything better to do with his hands, she thought grumpily), so Alan had gone right after breakfast to make the obligatory call to Stiles's office.

She watched him now as he hastily swatted the paper back together, swung one leg over the lifelines, and stepped down into the cockpit, lean and tan in his short-sleeved shirt, several days' growth of beard glinting red in the sunlight (he had stopped shaving when they had stopped sleeping together), that old familiar look of perplexed concentration on his almost faunlike face. Once more she felt a pang of longing; if only things could go back to the way they were. But, as he had said earlier, also in another context, all was changed utterly.

Suppressing a sigh, she repeated her question: "What's so peculiar? Wasn't there any answer?"

He came and stood over her, close enough for her to feel the warmth emanating from his body, but still carefully avoiding any direct physical contact. She wondered how long they were going to go on like this. Right to the very end, she supposed, as he waved her goodbye at the airport with a nod and a salute.

"Oh, there was an answer right enough," he said, slapping the paper against his thigh. " 'No need to call in on this one anymore, sir,' " he went on, imitating the reedy, long-distance voice of a female dispatcher. " 'The officer in charge has indicated your services will not be needed.' When I asked why not, all she would tell me was, 'Sorry, sir, I have no further information,' and that was that. Then I went up to the little grocery and bought a newspaper. Here's the full rundown. You might like to read it yourself. It won't take long."

He thrust the paper at her and went below. She could hear him thumping around, stowing gear and turning on the batteries. What was he up to now? She tried peering down into the cabin, but it was too dark to see what he was doing, and he was making too much noise at the moment for her to get his attention and ask.

She turned to the paper in her hand. The full rundown consisted of two paragraphs on an inside page.

SCION OF PROMINENT LOCAL FAMILY FOUND DEAD

The death of Peter Onterdonck, Ph. D., age 41, son of the late Maria Fell and Valerian Onterdonck of East Blue Hill, found dead last Tuesday on Restitution Island, has been ruled accidental, due to a head injury sustained while sailing alone in his sloop, the *Non-Amo-Te*. Educated at Hotchkiss, Amherst College, and Harvard University, Mr. Onterdonck was a well-known amateur naturalist, a board member of the Jocelyn Society as well as the Sierra Club and the Nature Conservancy. He was also active in politics on the local and state levels, as well as a member of the Republican National Committee. He leaves a cousin, Roger Fell, of East Blue Hill. . . .

Roz put the paper down and turned to see Alan's head and shoulders framed in the open hatch. He was leaning on his elbows, waiting for her reaction. "So what do you make of that? And I don't means the odds on the general public recognizing the word 'scion.' "

Roz considered. "Looks like they took the easy way out."

Alan slammed a hand down on the companionway so hard she jumped. "Right-o! The old Occam's razor approach. Sweeping a good bit of the shavings under the carpet in the process, one might add. The question is why? And how so quickly? There's barely been time for a postmortem, I should think, let alone a formal inquest. Or isn't there such a thing as a coroner's jury in Maine? Surely an unattended death under suspicious circumstances . . ." He regarded her with skeptical eyebrows.

"I really don't know," Roz replied. "Maybe the medical examiner decides. It's possible they do things a bit more casually here—"

" 'Casually' be damned! What about the evidence? We were witnesses, or near enough. Not to mention the bogus footprints!"

"They must have figured it wasn't suspicious after all. Maybe they found something that convinced them it was an accident . . ."

"It couldn't have been—you know that and I know that, Roz! The fact that the footprints were faked should have been enough to give them probable cause whatever else they found! Come on, then, it was such an obvious setup!"

"Obvious or not, apparently they just didn't—" She stopped in midsentence. She had been going to say, "they just didn't believe you," but at this moment, Alan was clearly a man whose pride had been hurt, whose opinion had been flouted, whose competence had been called into question—no, worse—ignored. She didn't need to add further insult to injury. "—think it was worth pursuing," she finished lamely.

"Well, they can think again," Alan said as he vaulted up over the hatchway, reached across her, and started the engine. The old gas four-cylinder coughed, shuddered, then began to thump out a loud but steady rhythm.

"Where are we going?" she asked as he whipped the tie-downs off the tiller and handed them to her, then jumped up onto the deck and started stripping the sail cover off the main.

"We're off to Belfast, fair Rosamund—sorry—Roz," he announced as he ran the main up and cleated it. The sail hung limp, the boom twitching listlessly with the motion of the boat. "Obviously someone has brought pressure to bear to get this case neatly and quietly disposed of. No muss, no fuss, no murder." He hopped onto the dock and began casting off the docking lines and tossing her the fenders. "I'm just a wee bit curious to find out who—not that I can't make a guess. Aren't you?" He didn't wait for an answer. "But even more than that, I shan't be able to rest until I know how that footprint dodge—ye olde riddle of the sands—was managed! What we have here is not your mere garden-variety murder-in-the-vicarage-brand whodunit, but a rollicking good *how*dunit!" He stopped and drew a breath, favoring her with a heartier-than-usual version of his familiar spade-shaped grin. "How can one resist? Just give us a hand with the tiller there, will you?"

With a strong push he sent the bow surging away from the dock, then leaped onto the boat at the last moment, catching the stern rail and pulling himself aboard, apparently not noticing the hand she had extended. He rushed forward, leaving her at the helm. Roz bent down and put the engine into gear, then laid the tiller over and trimmed the main as he bent to hank on the jib.

The next moment they were barreling their way at top speed out of the narrow harbor. She watched him as he balanced himself with his legs firmly planted on the cabin top, cranked the jib halyard down hard and made it fast, arm muscles bulging with the effort. That accomplished, without even a glance in her direction he bent to tidy up and coil the lines that were squirming every which way over the deck like newly hatched snakes.

She looked up just in time to see the long dark hull and twin masts of a medium-sized windjammer coming down the far side of the point, and turned around quickly to see if it was by any chance the one that she had seen leaving Restitution the other morning—though what made her think she could tell one schooner from the next at this distance she had no idea. She was too late, anyway; the near headland of Seven Hundred Acre Island with its fringe of tall fir trees and odd little brick-gabled folly had already come between them and blotted it out of view.

11

The wind was still from the northwest, light and variable, so after an undistinguished and time-consuming series of tacks in an attempt to beat their way to Turtle Head, they ended up motoring most of the way up East Penobscot Bay, the noise of the antiquated engine making conversation impossible, for which Roz decided she was grateful, since she was feeling slightly confused about matters between the two of them, not to mention Alan's outraged response to the latest developments—or rather the lack thereof—in the so-called case.

Having coiled up and neatened all the lines, Alan hopped down into the cockpit and offered to take the tiller from her. She took her book, a new one she was thinking of using in her women's studies course, called *Women's Ways of Knowing,* and went down below, ostensibly to read, but actually to try to sort a few things out on her own. But she did not get very far, and presently she put down her book, went back out on deck, and sat down across from Alan. Smiling amiably at her, he reached over and turned off the engine. Silence settled around them like a benediction. Alan adjusted the tiller; the sails puffed out gently as the boat began to glide across the wind. "Hadn't we better talk things over while we've got the chance," he said finally, gazing out toward the horizon.

Roz froze. Could this finally be it? She looked up at him expectantly, her heart pounding a lively beat.

"Right, then; as to the case before us . . ." (I should have known better, Roz thought bitterly; of course he'd meant the case.) "I thought we might engage in a spot of what Edgar Allan Poe calls 'ratiocination,' " he went on. "I believe the usual questions are 'who, what, where, when, and how.' "

"Aren't you thinking of a newspaper story?" she replied curtly.

"Right you are. My mistake," he replied cheerfully. "You pick, then."

She sighed under her breath. Oh well, it was a long way to Belfast; the important thing was, as long as he was so obsessed with the case, he wouldn't be leaving, right? And somewhere in here there still might be time to sort things out between them.

Meanwhile, there was always the old adage: If you can't beat 'em, join 'em. She'd read her share of mystery stories, including the works of Edgar Allan Poe *and* Arthur Conan Doyle, and she was no stranger to real-life murder investigations. "I suppose it's as good a place to start as any," she said, trying not to sound too cross. " 'Who' is easy enough. We know who the victim was, so I guess the next question is 'what?' In other words, did a murder actually occur?"

"A definite 'yes' to that one. We know that from the phony footprints. Whoever took it upon himself to send our Mr. Onterdonck to Fiddler's Green took great pains to make the death look like an accident. Covering of tracks—sorry, but quite literal in this case—equals presence of guilt."

Roz let the pun—such as it was—go. But Fiddler's Green? "Where's Fiddler's Green?" she asked.

"Oh, sorry. It's the sailor's version of heaven. Not a real 'where.' "

"I see. Well, then, we also know where—"

"Ah, but do we?" Alan interrupted. "We know where the

body was found, but not necessarily where the death occurred."

"The newspaper said: 'while sailing alone in his sloop, the *Non-Amo-Te.*' "

"A likely story, as you well know, but one may presume that the authorities found some evidence to support this idea, even though *you* didn't see any—not too surprising," he added charitably, "since it may have been only minute traces of blood and hair on the boom and you're not in the habit of carrying a microscopic lens around on holiday with you" (but *you* are, she thought) "and then went about matching traces of metal from the boom and so forth in the wound during the medical examination, and that's what tore it for the powers-that-be, even though that sort of thing could easily have been planted after the fact and our man could just as well have been taken off with a spanner in a used-car lot. They would surmise that he was clipped by the boom while anchoring, in the way these things can happen; he'd sailed for years but just got careless, all it takes is a little squall of wind before you've managed to quite furl the sail, or perhaps it was the fog; he didn't quite know where he was in regard to the rigging. At any rate, the blow caused an epidural hematoma, swelling of the brain in the temporal-parietal lobe, compression of the brain stem—in other words, delayed but certain death, and Bob's your uncle. Case closed," he finished gloomily. "Except that someone else set the whole thing up."

"Shades of Mr. Noakes in *Busman's Honeymoon,*" Roz remarked, thinking of the delayed-death part. She wasn't about to argue with his medical terminology, much less inquire where he got it. "Do you really think that's how it was done?"

"Well, not the loose-rigging part; as I recall, in that case it was some sort of flying aspidistra, but that's the general idea, yes."

"It was a cactus," Roz said. "And every bit as preposterous now as it was then. Or so the local authorities must have thought, since they never even considered it in the first place." Not that she wasn't a great admirer of Dorothy L. Sayers's last mystery novel, but for reasons other than its plausibility.

"Come, come now, I'll have no aspersions cast against the masterful Miss Sayers and her unmatched resourcefulness in the matter of the hitherto undreamt-of means; those poor law-enforcement coves simply don't know what they're missing, do they?" he said. "Let's just take it as read—or, rather, ruled," he went on, moving his speculative glance past her out over the water to some distant point beyond. "Sometime after the initial insult, our unfortunate Mr. Onterdonck felt himself losing consciousness and tried to go for help. Of course he was completely disoriented by then, but he nevertheless got into the dinghy, rowed to the beach, got out and started across to wherever he fancied he was going, waving an arm in distress, and fell over dead. Hmmmm. Makes perfect sense, except for the faked-up footprints, of course. It was Herbert Spencer, wasn't it, who said that tragedy is a theory killed by a fact? Or as my illustrious Scottish ancestors would have it: 'One mustn't burke a fact to support a thesis.' "

Alan paused to make a minor correction in their course. He stood up, uncleated the main, pushed the boom over to the other side, yanked it down tight to stop the sail from fluttering, and re-cleated it, all in one fluid motion, while guiding the tiller with his knee. Then he plopped down on the seat right next to her. Well, why not? The boat was on the other tack now, wasn't it? It probably didn't mean a thing.

"So what you're saying," she said after a moment, "is that some person or persons unknown, faced with the necessity for the disposal of the body, carefully arranged the footprint ploy to foster that assumption—that it had to be an accident."

"Right-o. That's where the similarities end, however. While the aforementioned fatal event in the Sayers novel was also no accident, the delayed-death part of it *was* completely unforeseen—the victim getting up and walking away, only to go tumbling down the cellar stairs, where he wasn't found for days, which threw our gentle sleuths—not to mention our villain, who had taken great pains to concoct an invincible alibi for precisely the wrong time—into a muck sweat for three hundred pages, thereby neglecting the matters at hand more appropriate to the title of the book." He reached forward, gave the port winch a turn, then fixed his attention once again on a point off in the distance, one long-fingered hand resting on the seat between them.

Roz tried to ignore the vibrations that seemed to be emanating from the small margin of space between her thigh and his hand. "So what's next?" she asked.

Still staring off into space, Alan silently ticked off questions on the seat between them, his fingers drumming perilously close to her. "We're up to 'when,' " he said presently. "Judging by the rigor, I'd say he'd been dead about ten hours, twelve at the most, when we found him. That was rising nine in the morning, so calculating rapidly . . . Ha!" Suddenly he raised both hands and slapped his own thighs. "That means it could well have been going on even as we arrived on the scene the night before. By Jove!" he chuckled. "There's a jolly thought! Whoever did it must have been having fits when we came barging in!"

Roz blinked at him. She was not sure that "jolly" was the adjective she would have used to describe the idea of Onterdonck's body being disposed of while they were, say, running their anchor drill. Or carrying on their quarrel.

Alan went right on. ". . . Whoever that whoever is, which is the next question: 'whodunit?' Followed directly by the even more fascinating question of 'howdunit': that is, how the body got where we found it, not so much how it got dead," he added, "though I'm quite sure the two are all part and parcel of the same skulduggery." He lifted his hands and this time folded them neatly behind his head, looking perfectly relaxed and unconcerned as he leaned back, controlling the tiller with his foot.

"But Alan," Roz said, "we didn't hear or see anything. . . ."

"Not in that fog we didn't, but then we were hardly paying attention then, were we? We had enough on our plates, looking about for the nonexistent moorings, then the emergency anchor drill, never mind the usual creaking and groaning, dinging and clanking, sloshing and lapping of your typical old wooden boat."

And the yelling and screaming and pot-banging of your typical old knock-down-drag-out quarrel, he might have added. But he didn't. Ever the gentleman.

"There's something very isolating and muffling about a good old-fashioned fog," he was saying now. "Take summers in the Highlands, when the mist drops in so thick you can't even guess where your own feet have got to, let alone your neighbor's. I think that's where the Celtic notion of fairy magic comes from— all those people vanishing away only to turn up years later. *Brigadoon* and so forth; the rest of the world just disappears and you have to stand stock-still lest you walk straight into a bog or run afoul of a cowpat. At any rate, after that we were preoccupied, you'll recall, what with one thing and another, dinner to get and . . ." His voice trailed off. He fell silent again, apparently at a loss for words. And what? Roz thought. As if she didn't know.

After a few moments he seemed to come to, glanced at her, his face inscrutable. "Yes, well. I think we can agree that what with . . . er . . . one thing and another we never took in the fact there was another boat close by, nor for that matter that thumping great schooner that came tearing by next morning. If your windjammers are anything like the holiday-for-hire boats we have at home, the passengers and crew must have been having a fair rumpus on their own, so I wouldn't expect they'd have heard anything. No, however the deed was accomplished, and by whom, it must have been quietly and under cover of fog and darkness. You didn't hear anything odd when you went up on deck, did you?"

That's right, she had almost forgotten. In the aftermath of their quarrel—which Alan had so circumspectly referred to as the 'er . . . one thing and another'—she had rushed up on deck and stayed there for a good fifteen minutes. If anybody had heard anything, she would have been the one.

She turned her attention to remembering what noises she had heard under cover of fog and darkness that night in the cove at Restitution Island. Lap, lap, creak, creak, dong, dong. She hadn't even been able to tell there was another boat—the *Non-*

Amo-Te—or even an island nearby, let alone something so obviously surreptitious happening on the beach.

They both sat quietly for some minutes, thinking their own thoughts as the boat glided along, seemingly under its own direction.

After an interlude of racking her brains to no avail for any kind of missed detail that might shed some light on what had transpired, Roz began to wonder whether Alan was justified in his insistence that Onterdonck had been murdered. After all, there was nothing in the evidence, even allowing that the footprints were faked, that said it had to have been murder, was there? Perhaps it *had* been an accident, a blow dealt during the heat of an argument, say—but over what?—and whoever was responsible had panicked and done his—or her, let's be fair—best to cover the whole thing up. A chance meeting, a fight, an accident of some kind; that's probably what the authorities believed, a finding of involuntary manslaughter at most, so why bother? After all, their prime—their only—suspect, Roger Fell, even if he was filthy rich, was still a Maine native born and bred; in Joseph Conrad's terms, "one of us," just as Onterdonck had been. She had the feeling that a kind of Yankee frontier justice still operated in parts of rural Maine; take care of your own, avoid outside interference. Or, in a vernacular restatement of Alan's favorite tool of logic: keep it simple, stupid. Of course they would take Roger Fell's word over hers and Alan's. Taking a deep breath, she turned to face him, and recounted her reasoning.

"Aha, another shave of the old Occam's razor come home to roost, if you'll pardon the mixed metaphor. But hold on for a bit; let me get this straight. If all the locals are 'us,' then who are we? Or rather those of you who live here, since it's obvious as soon as I say two words that I'm not native to this country."

"That's easy. If you weren't born here—that is, in Maine, even in a particular locality, Belfast, say—and preferably your parents and grandparents before you," Roz explained, "then you're 'from away.' You're an outsider. You're one of 'them.' "

"Ah, I see. And 'we' take care of 'our' own, brooking no

interference. All very well and good, although if true, not exceptionally flattering to the local constabulary." Alan paused for a moment, considering. "But if what you say is true, why would Fell—I mean, the murderer, let's not be hasty—even bother with a cover-up? Why not leave the body wherever it came to grief, and simply turn up with head hanging, hand over heart, saying, 'So sorry, sir, I didn't mean to.' The old Cock-Robin defense."

Damn, she thought testily, leave it to him to find the flaw in her reasoning. Not too surprising, though, come to think of it, considering a Scottish logician (one of his "illustrious ancestors"?) had practically invented the discipline in the first place. She sat there in silence, watching him make minute adjustments to the tiller with his toe. His arms were stretched out behind him (and her) along the coaming in an attitude of relaxed contemplation. Which was more than she could say for her attitude. She wished he would just reach over and pull her in close. Enough of this "ratiocination" nonsense!

"No . . . reasoning from what we know so far," he continued, "the aforementioned cover-up—however it was accomplished—could hardly have been something cooked up on the spur of the moment, which further knocks the idea of accidental homicide or manslaughter in the heat of the moment into a cocked hat. Hmmm." He heaved a sigh, then sat forward, removed his foot from the tiller, brought his arms up and over and rested them on his knees, leaving the tiller to wobble along on its own for the moment.

"Well," he said finally. "We appear to be getting no 'forrarder'; we still haven't the foggiest notion how the dastardly deed was accomplished. It's too late now, obviously, to convince anyone else the footprints were tampered with, let alone how, but if we could get an idea of how the body could have got there *not* under its own power, then perhaps we could convince the powers-that-be—'we' being 'them' aside—to reopen the case. Or, I should say, open it in the first place.

"However, we seem to be stymied on that aspect—skyhooks, orangutans, and Superman aside, of course. We surely would have heard a helicopter coming over, they make such a shocking racket even the fog wouldn't have absorbed it. That rules out every means I can think of offhand by which one might plant a body *sine* footprints to match in the middle of a deserted beach. So how *did* the body get there?" He flicked a finger at the tiller, which was swaying gently between his knees, then continued in a resigned voice, "I'm afraid we're well and truly stumped, Roz. Barring a divine revelation—or, even less likely, a confession—there's virtually no possibility at this point of determining the 'how.' We'll just have to think of something else." He leaned back and stretched; Roz watched his chest and stomach muscles tensing under the thin shirt. The tiller bobbed in her direction. "Nicely balanced, isn't she?" he said in an offhand tone. "Your turn."

She grabbed the tiller, adjusted the boat's course, and stared straight ahead. "If it's all so damned impossible," she said irritably, "maybe there wasn't a cover-up after all. Maybe you're mistaken about the footprints."

"Actually I only meant your turn at the list of possibilities," he said mildly, looking rather pointedly at her clenched hand, the knuckles as white as a row of molars. But that's all right, you can steer if you like. It does help to pass the time, as does the conversation."

"Oh," she said, and twitched her fingers loose, feeling reproached. She had the sense she had behaved badly again, jumping down his throat like that. But really, couldn't he think of a better way to pass the time?

"Right, then," he said somewhat cautiously. "Perhaps we'd best leave the manifest impossibility of 'how' aside for the moment. So it's your go."

"All right," Roz said, in what she hoped was a conciliatory tone. "How about motive, means, and opportunity?"

"New list! Jolly good!" He rubbed his hands together in a parody of anticipation; to her relief, Roz felt the tense atmosphere dissipating somewhat. "All right, then. We've scratched means, at least for the time being, so let's try opportunity. You don't mind going both ends toward the middle, do you? So.

We need to ascertain who was in the vicinity at the time Peter Onterdonck was knocked dead and his body transported by means as yet unknown onto the beach to make it look as though it could only be an accident when he was alone, by himself, solo and unattended."

"Well, that's easy enough. As far as we know there were only three boats in the area during that time other than Onterdonck's. Ours—"

"Stop right there. We can immediately rule out ourselves. Detectives aren't allowed to be the perpetrators of the crimes they are solving. It's one of Father Ronald Knox's rules of detective fiction."

"Oh, I see. That's a relief, to know we didn't do it," Roz said with a straight face. "Then there's the windjammer we saw taking off while you were swimming."

"Hmm, I'd forgotten about them. Not terribly likely, though, do you think, what with a whole boatload of passengers, as witnesses; it's hardly the sort of thing you'd do accompanied by a cheering throng, fog or no fog. Besides, as far as we know, they were just passing through; *persona non grata* as far as those islands go, according to Fell. No; I think we can rule them out as well. Carry on, then."

Roz could see where this was leading. "That leaves Roger Fell, who was seen skulking about the other side of Rebel Island early that morning. That certainly puts him in the vicinity. Even though he denied it when Stiles brought it up."

"Hmmm," said Alan. "Curiouser and curiouser."

"Also obviouser and obviouser," Roz replied. "Too obvious, in fact, don't you think? If he did it, why would he blurt out all those incriminating things about how much he disliked Onterdonck in front of witnesses?"

"Witnesses who were never called," said Alan. "And even though he did deny it," he went on, "it would hardly signify. With that huge rig of his, as Stiles said, he could have been in and out of there like a thief in the night any number of times, with no one the wiser. What's the odd whir and a clunk or two when you've got your own boat noises going on all the time?

No, if I may ring a change on Harriet Vane's exceptionally clear-headed but somewhat limited formulation, when there is only one person who could have done it, however obvious, then you have your murderer.''

"Wasn't it Lord Peter? And doesn't it go like this: 'If a thing could have been done only one way, and if only one person could have done it that way, then you've got your criminal, motive or no motive'?"

"You're quite right, of course, now that I think of it. The solution by way of the unexpected means; I forgot that part. Which puts us back even more, since we haven't the foggiest notion as to that one way, never mind the motive, leaving us rather pathetically still with only a smashing good idea about the 'who.' " He sighed. "But tempting as it is, though, we mustn't jump to conclusions. If Fell is in fact the murderer, it would be disingenuous, to say the least, for him to stick around and then turn up like that, so soon after the fact, wouldn't it? *Unless* he was morally certain no one could possibly drop to the footprint dodge—that bloody 'how,' again—and just wanted to gloat over our stupidity! Sheer arrogance, in a word.'' Alan sat forward, snapping his fingers. "Ha! The shoe fits, footprints or no footprints! The man's clearly a born criminal. He absolutely does carry on like some sort of robber baron, don't you think?''

"More like a pirate," Roz said, "but more to the point, now who's jumping to conclusions? And if that's true, you must have given him a nasty shock when you started voicing your suspicions. But he never turned a hair.''

"No," Alan said, sitting back again. "That's the odd thing. The perfect stonewall. Of course he must have been betting no one would take me seriously—what with my being 'from away,' and a long way away at that, your bona fide untrustworthy foreigner, not to mention your impractical artist-type fella— which in fact turned out to be the case.'' Alan sighed heavily. "Leaving out once again the ineluctable problem of means, I'm sorry to say that with what we have to go on at the moment, we couldn't prove in a thousand years he did it just by virtue of proximity, any more than we could prove—Knox's rules aside—we *didn't* do it.''

"So it's a dead end," Roz said, sympathizing with his disappointment. She needn't have bothered, though, as his face instantly resumed its expression of chipper fixation.

"Not to worry. We've one more detective conundrum left to apply; you know the one I mean—*Cui bono.*''

More Latin. But never mind, this had to be the end of it. He'd said one more, hadn't he? " 'To whom the good?' " she translated, "Or, in plain English, 'Who benefits?' Who would profit from the killing? Or, as per my list, Motive with a capital *M*. The old question of 'why,' which brings us back to none other than our dear friend Roger Fell, and whatever things he thought would be made easier for him if Onterdonck no longer stood in his way, in terms of the covenants, say. At the very least it would mean the end of the feud. And according to the death notice," she added for good measure, "he's also next of kin.''

"And thus stood to cop the lot, no matter what, speaking of obviouser and obviouser. But in all fairness to the writ-all-too-large Mr. Fell, would you care to consider other *cui*s? Or should I say *bono*s? Actually it's *quibus bonis,* come to think of it, but I shouldn't like to be pedantic. At any rate, we must leave no stone unturned.''

All right, Roz thought. I'll give you a turn, in case you've forgotten. "Sex. *Cherchez la femme.*''

"Hardly," he said without missing a beat. "If any *femme* toted his body up the beach and planted it there, even with little tripping-toes, she would have had to be a tenth the size of Tinkerbell and twice as magic to make imprints anywhere near the depth of the ones we found. Ditto any *homme*, for that matter. No, she—or he—would have had to have help, which more or less rules out sex for its own sake as the motive, unless it was a team effort." Alan shook his head. "It simply doesn't add up. No, I think we shall have to dismiss squalid passion as a motive for virtually any part of this, if that's all right with you.''

Roz nodded. What else could she do but agree? She hoped he hadn't noticed her telltale blush.

"Right then," said Alan. "My turn. Drugs. Onterdonck caught someone dropping off stacks and stacks of illegal substances from far-off Colombia and Ecuador, and had to be bumped off."

Roz snorted. "With three thousand miles of coastline available, most of it right along U.S. Route One, why risk unloading a major shipment on an island with no access except by boat? You'd just have to load up again. Besides, that's boring. It's *always* drugs when anyone gets murdered in Maine. Either that or hunting season. Come on, Alan, get serious."

"Seriously, then, what about money? You know what the Pardoner said. '*Radix malorum*' and all that."

Roz did know what the Pardoner said, and then some; she wasn't a professor of medieval literature for nothing. "—'*est cupiditas*—Love of money is the root of all evil.' But money from where? Surely not from selling phony indulgences. And why would Fell care about the money anyway? You heard what the officer said: he's rich as stink, but not immorally so."

"At least not that we know of. All right, then, just for the sake of argument, let's leave Fell's name out of it for the moment. That's the prologue. Think of the tale."

Roz thought a moment. The tale—three greedy men and a pile of gold. "Buried treasure?" she said dubiously. And shouldn't she be the one giving the Chaucer lecture?

"Why not?" said Alan. "It has to be something to do with the island. Suppose Onterdonck had found some sort of map or clue to where the treasure was—in whatever form it was, you'll recall from the guide that it was multiple choice: pirate treasure pits, sunken ships, and so forth—and that showed how to get to it."

"I thought all that was supposed to be on Rebel. So then what was he doing on Restitution Island?"

"Aha, that's the irony of it. Perhaps he'd discovered the location of the booty on his island, gleefully announced the fact to ah . . . whomever, but *à la* your dog-in-the-manger, wasn't about to share, just rub said person—or persons—unknown's face in it."

"Isn't that still just greed? I mean, it's all love of money, whether it comes in bucks or bullion."

"Come, my dear, buried treasure does have a certain fascination that your ordinary filthy lucre lacks. But you're right. I think we're getting onto pretty shaky ground here. Better known as rampant speculation. We seem to be reasoning far ahead of the evidence. A capital mistake, as Sherlock Holmes would have it."

"I'll say."

"Well, in aid of remedying that, there is one other rubric regarding the nature of evidence that we might find useful." He leaned forward, peering under the limp foresail.

"Which is?" Roz said wearily. She was beginning to feel as though she'd been rubricked within an inch of her life.

"All evidence fits basically into three categories, if you will: the evidence of one's own senses, hearsay, and analogy. In other words, one, what you yourself see, hear, smell, feel, or taste; two, what you read or someone else tells you; and three, what you can figure out by putting yourself in someone else's place and reasoning from your observation of the general principles of human behavior. Of course evidence of one's own senses is the best kind; the other two can get a bit dicey if you're not careful about overinterpretation."

"Oh, really?" Roz said. "And where does all this come from?"

"I made it up," Alan replied, still squinting past the genoa at something ahead of them. "I find it quite useful for keeping things sorted out in any kind of investigation." He gave the tiller a tweak and sat back, apparently satisfied with their progress. "Which is precisely why we're on our way to Belfast, my dear Watson, in case you hadn't guessed. To gather more information, by whatever means at our disposal, and continue our investigation. After all, if not us, who, and if not now, when? And if I am not mistaken and that's the nun I think it is—'nun' as in aid to navigation, not religious vocation," he said, pointing out a hooded red shape bobbing some yards ahead, "we are coming hard upon the entrance to Belfast Harbor even as we speak."

12

It was just past three when they passed the triangular pile of stone called the Monument at the entrance to Belfast Harbor. Ten minutes later they were tying up at one of the floats in the little boatyard sandwiched between a sardine factory and a railroad yard. Roz was furling the main when she heard the whine of an outboard motor, and turned to see an obviously homemade skiff shaped like a flatiron skimming toward them at breakneck speed, its operator balanced more or less upright in the center, steering the engine with what appeared to be a broken broomstick. "Look, he's probably going to tell us to move," Roz called to Alan, but as the boat came closer to the *Verorum* it veered to one side, cutting a deep arc in the water, and swooped on by, shedding paint chips off its weathered hull as it went.

But not before Roz caught a glimpse of the skipper, a slight, wiry man of indeterminate age with narrow shoulders and legs bowed like a wishbone, a fringe of beard around his jaw that matched the longish wisps the color of old rope blowing out from under the navy seaman's beret on his head, and an unlit corncob pipe clamped in his mouth. He was dressed in a sailor's middy blouse and wide-bottomed work trousers. "Why, it's Old Stormalong!" she exclaimed as she looked after him in amazement.

"It's who?" said Alan from belowdecks, where he was tending to some mystery of the bilge.

"That man who just went by us in the little skiff! He's the spitting image of Old Stormalong!"

Alan popped his head out the front hatch. "And who, may I ask, is Old Stormalong?"

"He's a legendary sea captain in American folklore, a sort of maritime version of the tall tale—you know, Paul Bunyan and Babe the Blue Ox, Pecos Bill? I used to read about him in a set of children's books we had, called *My Bookhouse*. There were lots of funny pictures, and that man tearing around in the boat looks just like him!"

"American folklore?" Alan said in a puzzled voice. "I thought your fields were medieval and women's studies, mostly the latter, judging from your current reading list."

"All knowledge is my province," said Roz.

"I see," said Alan. "Well, then, may I call your attention to the fact that your mythical Old Stormalong is currently dancing attendance on a familiar-looking green-hulled boat?" He pointed past her toward the middle of the harbor. "If I'm not mistaken, that is none other than *Non-Amo-Te* out there on that mooring. What do you suppose she's doing lying up here?"

"Maybe they needed it for the inquest?"

"I thought we agreed there couldn't have been an inquest, not a formal one at any rate. A postmortem at best, no findings, case closed, thank you very much."

Briefly Roz considered the presence of the *Non-Amo-Te*. "They must have found something on board to establish that it was an accident," she said. "After all, Alan, they couldn't just dismiss the whole thing, even in Maine. They probably had it towed here. Or maybe it's impounded, pending further investigation. Just because they don't need us anymore doesn't mean—"

"Of course it does," Alan interrupted. "We're the only ones

who can testify to the fakery of the footprints. You saw what the place looked like after Stiles and his cronies got finished. It might as well have been a ruddy pig's wallow." Flexing his shoulders, Alan hoisted himself without apparent effort up through the open hatch and swung his legs out onto the deck with all the ease of a gymnast. He sat down on the cabin top and gazed speculatively over the water at the *Non-Amo-Te*. "Hmm. I don't suppose we could possibly get aboard her, do you?"

"No, not really," Roz said. "I'm sure it's locked up tight, waiting for the next of kin to come along and claim it. And where I come from, we don't approve of breaking and entering."

"Of course not," Alan said, turning his gaze—still speculative—back to her. "Silly thought." He sat awhile longer, apparently lost in thought. "All right, then," he said presently, heaving himself up with a sigh. "Let's paddle on in, fix it up with your Old Stormalong about a mooring, and take in the sights of beautiful downtown Belfast. Perhaps we could even have tea or, as they say in your country, a late lunch."

Meanwhile, the aforementioned spitting image of Old Stormalong had accomplished whatever task he had set out to do in the harbor, and was on his way back to the wharf. Roz and Alan reached the floating dock at just about the same time he did, and for a moment the two boats bobbed around each other like boxers before Alan made the *Mendax* fast. He then stretched out his hand to help Roz out of the dinghy, somewhat unnecessarily since she was as capable as anyone of balancing on one leg while tossing up and down in one moving object while stepping upward onto another.

She took it anyway. It was the first time they had touched voluntarily since that day on the beach, and Roz was startled by the little shock it gave her, the electricity of the contact between their flesh. But Alan apparently didn't notice; as soon as she had both feet on the boards, he dropped his hand, turned to Old Stormalong, and extended it to him, introducing himself and Roz.

Old Stormalong looked them up and down, pulled the pipe out of his mouth, and squinted, rolling from one bandy leg to the other with the motion of the floating dock. He looked so salty in his tattered pullover and wide-legged pants flapping at the ankles that when he opened his mouth Roz fully expected him to break into a sea chantey.

What he actually said was "How do," as he extended a callused, thick-fingered hand. "Thaxter Waite's the name. Was wonderin' who that was in Jessie True's boat. Heard she was still laid up. Thought maybe she would've sold her, what with her hip and all. You must be that perfessor cousin a' hers from away."

By the time Roz had sorted out whose hip was whose and who was selling (or not, as it happened) whom, not to mention how he knew, if not who she was by name, then where she was from (or rather not from, that is, Maine), and how she was related to Aunt Jessie, she was already well into a lengthy explanation of who she and Alan were and where they had been on their cruise in Aunt Jessie's boat. Thaxter Waite nodded, encouraging her account with a series of "uh-huhs," pronounced in several different ways ("*uh*-huh," "uh-*huh*," "uh-*huh!*") indicating variously agreement, curiosity, and surprise. Alan had casually walked off down the dock, apparently looking at one of the boats tied up there, a long, low, sleek mahogany powerboat in the process of restoration. He was eyeing the boat with great interest, but she could tell from the set of his head and shoulders that he was all ears.

She paused in her account after the part about finding the body on the beach, thinking that Thaxter Waite might offer something about what had happened since, but all he said was "Uh-huh? You don't say so. Bad business, real bad business. Got his boat out there now, waiting for one of the Hinckley boys to come pick 'er up. Guess she'll be sold now; don't expect Roger'll want 'er; he's much too high-tech. Personally I don't think he likes to sail one bit, just likes punchin' buttons. Pity, she's a sweetheart of a boat. Uh-huh." He rocked back on both heels just as a swell sloshed under the floating dock, so that

Roz had to restrain herself from grabbing his shirtfront to keep him from going over backward. But he just rolled with it, continuing to chew his unlit pipe unperturbed. He rocked back upright, turning at the same moment to say to Alan, who was just coming back toward them, "Like her? That's my Beals Island lobster boat, ain't she a beauty? 'Sharpshooter,' they calls 'em, torpedo-style, like them old bootlegger boats." Waite gazed proudly at the sleek mahogany hull. "Goes like a rocket, she does. Picked her up for a song, port side was stove in. Rest of her's just fine, though. I'm fixin' to restore her right up proper when I get the time." Alan nodded appreciatively.

Waite turned to Roz and said, "There's a man knows a good thing when he sees it. Uh-huh! Well, got to get back to work. You can take that mooring out there, fella it belongs to hasn't got his boat in yet, and won't for at least a coupla more days." Chortling inexplicably, he added, "Or so he says, anyways. Meanwhile, I'm using it for visitors. You got things to do uptown? I'll put her on for ya soon's I can get to it. Save ya another trip out 'n' back in the dinghy."

And that was all. With a brisk nod, he rolled up the gangway on what appeared to be permanent sea legs. A moment later they heard the raucous splutter of a clearly unmuffled engine and looked up to see Waite wheeling around in an ancient front-end loader minus its tires, a block of granite chained to the rear.

"Didn't get much out of him, did you?" Alan said. "Nice try, though. Shall we be off? I'd like to investigate the possibility of a shower and a shave."

13

After availing themselves of the surprisingly good municipal bath facilities just up from the town dock, Roz and Alan walked up the rather steep main street lined with old brick storefronts.

"Aren't they wonderful?" Alan commented. "Look at those granite lintels and Flemish gables. All largely original and unspoiled, from the looks of it."

"Also largely unoccupied," Roz observed, gazing from one FOR LEASE sign and window swirled with whitewash to the next.

"Apparently Belfast is a town whose time has not yet come," Alan continued in a conversational tone as he strolled along the sidewalk.

"Or already gone," Roz replied somewhat curtly. She wasn't feeling quite up to a lecture on colonial municipal architecture. Couldn't they just get on with things?

"Pity they ran out of bricks for these sidewalks," Alan went on imperturbably, scuffing his foot along the curb at the intersection of the two main streets. "Those old-fashioned gig lamps are nice, though. Oh well, never mind. Back to our riddle of the sands; the question of motive. Given Onterdonck's feelings about the islands, not to mention the family feud, I think it would have been a bit of an oversight on his part to leave everything to Fell, don't you? Wouldn't he have made sure the property was protected?"

"We can find out easily enough," Roz replied, shading her eyes and peering around her. "If I remember correctly, there's a newspaper office—actually two of them—in the next block up the street. I'm sure they've got the story on file. What about you?"

"I think I'll just browse," Alan replied. "There's some sort of art gallery back there that looks interesting. Perhaps I can pick up something by way of local gossip. Art dealers have a way of picking up odd bits of information, what with people coming in and wandering about totally oblivious to anyone else's presence, chatting on about this and that as though one were simply fried eggs up against the wall. I'll meet you at that café around the corner in an hour, and we'll compare notes. Right then? Cheerio!"

With a jaunty wave he thrust his hands in the pockets of his stand-by-themselves rock-climbing shorts and marched off down the street. Roz watched him for a moment, admiring the broad line of his shoulders and the muscles of his back in the light summer shirt, the slimness of his hips even in the bulky shorts, the long, sturdy legs. He had shaved for the first time since their fight. She wondered if that meant anything. "Ah, my dear," she pictured him saying as they settled down for the night on board the *Verorum,* "all this ratiocination may be very well and good, but are we not neglecting the matter at hand?"

But this was mere wishful thinking on her part; as far as Alan was concerned, the matter at hand was obviously "the case." She paused a moment to consider the situation: as long as the case remained unsolved, it, not she, would continue to be the main focus of his attention. But if he—or they—did solve it, or even put into motion the means to a solution, there would be no further reason for him to stay on. A cleft stick if there ever was one.

She considered yet another possibility: that they would get absolutely nowhere in their quest for further evidence. Suppose

Roger Fell *had* inherited everything and the authorities had ignored this obvious motive, never mind Alan's evidence indicating that Onterdonck had been murdered in the first place? If this was in fact what had happened, then she didn't think there was anything more they could do. They would have to let the whole thing go—and Alan would go with it. End of case, end of romance. She sighed heavily. It all looked pretty hopeless at this point. Oh well, in the interest of truth, she might as well try to find out what she could. As Alan had pointed out earlier, it helped to pass the time. She turned and went up the street toward the first newspaper office.

She spent the better part of the hour going over back issues and questioning several busy but helpful occupants of the cubbyhole offices. Thus when she met up with Alan again at Darby's Restaurant, an ersatz Irish pub with an old paneled bar, booths, and several tables, she was full of information. As, apparently, was he.

"What-ho, Roz!" he chirped as they sat down in one of the more isolated booths. Roz could tell from his chipper tone and happy grin that he was quite pleased with himself. She wondered what he'd found out to make him so jolly.

"Okay, you first," she ordered.

"As it happens, I was in luck. The art gallery is run by an inordinately tall man with a large head, huge jaw, and legs right up to his chin, thus giving him a startling resemblance to the figure of the Nutcracker in Tchaikovsky's ballet. At any rate, he talked a veritable blue streak the whole time I was there, an unending stream of fact, rumor, gossip, and speculation about Fells, Onterdoncks, the islands, the bay, the harbor, the town of Belfast, as well as the world of art here in Maine and beyond, while I ostensibly pawed through his surprisingly impressive collection of etchings, lithographs, collographs, and such. As a result, you are now sharing a table with the proud owner not only of an amazing amount of miscellaneous information, but also of a not-so-well-known and therefore reasonably priced print by your distinguished as well as semi-local contemporary artist Alex Katz, which I have arranged to have framed and sent back home to Pittenweem. Not only that, the owner has asked to see some of my sketches."

"Hmm," said Roz. Just then the waitress came, and they put off comparing notes until they had chosen from a menu unexpectedly featuring homemade Mexican dishes (in Belfast, Maine, former Broiler Capital of the World?) and were busily engaged in downing glasses of ice-cold beer from the tap. The waitress brought their food in short order (the restaurant was not terribly busy at this hour), and they tucked in with a vengeance.

"So what *did* you find out?" Roz asked when they had finished eating and ordered their second beers.

"Hmm, well. The owner of the art gallery—Ian James is his name—and Onterdonck were extremely close friends, according to him. He's a former New York art dealer, and, mind you, there's nothing the least bit taciturn about him. It was rather like standing in front of a fire hose. Terrible shock, Onterdonck being found dead like that, tragic accident, terrible loss to the family and to the town, not to mention the world of conservation, and so on. The upshot is, however, that there was a sort of a mini-inquest, they did indeed find traces of blood and hair on the boom, and concluded just as we thought: the loose boom caught him a nasty whack, causing a depressed fracture, swelling of the brain, delayed trauma reaction; hence the verdict of accidental death. Case closed. Your turn."

That's it, Roz thought in surprise, the sum total of his information? It hardly seemed like a lot to her, no more than what they already knew, or had guessed! But never mind that now; she couldn't wait to launch into her own recitation. "There wasn't much more than we already knew about Onterdonck's death—basically what you found out from the art dealer, and the will hasn't been probated yet, so there's nothing on that score—so I started looking up stories about Roger Fell, and listen to this, Alan." She leaned forward. "According to various newspaper reports, Fell is a major real-estate entrepreneur, responsible for developing big tracts of land here and all the way up along the coast, or what native Mainers call 'down east.'

It seems that right after the death of his father last winter—
that was the Roger C. Fell mentioned in the *Cruising Guide,*
by the way, who had a long-standing commitment to keep Rebel
Island just as it was—our Roger Fell put forward a plan to
make the island into a marina and an exclusive condo development, possibly a theme park centering on the idea of buried
treasure. He planned to rename the island—get this—Treasure,
and manage it himself. Remember the Ben Gunn getup? He
must be practicing for the role."

"Oh, the horror!" Alan gasped, his eyebrows shooting up
like twin circumflexes. "The fascination of the abomination!
How perfectly dreadful!" He thought a moment. "But Roz!
How would people get on and off? A ferry trip's hardly worth
it, and it's not as though you could run a bridge out there. It's
a mile or more offshore."

"Right, not even the Verrazzano Narrows Bridge is that long.
Fell did, however, go to the trouble of investigating the possibility of a causeway between the island and the mainland at
Cape Rosier, from land he already owns. It would be the longest
causeway on the East Coast, and thus another possible tourist
attraction. Most of the locals thought it was a swell idea. He
wooed the town fathers, county officials, and so on. It would
mean lots of new jobs in a fairly depressed area, so naturally
they were all for it."

"Wouldn't it muck up the tides?" Alan said, his eyebrows
still in his hair.

"Apparently not. The Maine Department of Environmental
Protection, or DEP, did an impact study and came down in
favor of it. Ditto the Army Corps of Engineers. As the editor
of the newspaper remarked, and I quote, 'Asking the Corps of
Engineers to evaluate a project like that is like asking a monkey
to evaluate a banana.' The EPA is yet to be heard from, but
that's a federal agency, and folks around here don't think much
of them. As one local they interviewed (and who chose to
remain anonymous, for obvious reasons) put it: 'There's allus
ways of getting around them nosy feds.' So virtually all the
official channels had been gone through, and it looked like a

sure thing as far as the authorities were concerned." Roz leaned forward even more, eager to expound her full theory. "Here's what I think must have happened. Fell tried to get Onterdonck to agree, either sell Restitution to him outright—"

"For what, a parking lot?" Alan interjected, his eyebrows disappearing into his crown. He began tracing what appeared to be a line of bumper-to-bumper cars in the condensation on the tabletop.

"—or enter into a partnership. And you can just imagine what Onterdonck the naturalist had to say about the whole enterprise. Of course he must have vetoed it on the spot. And according to the covenants, he had the power to stop it. Fell couldn't develop his island or sell so much as a square inch of it without Onterdonck's permission." She paused and sat back, almost at the end of her story now, watching Alan's face closely for his reaction. Would he rejoice that the pieces were all coming together just as they had speculated? "Alan, I think this is what we've been looking for. That's what Fell must have been referring to when he said Onterdonck's death would make things easier for him. With Onterdonck out of the way, as next of kin he would inherit, and it's full speed ahead. There's your *cui bono,* your prime motive, your 'who,' 'what,' 'where,' 'when,' and 'why.' If anybody did it, he did!" She plopped her hands down on the table for emphasis. "So that's it!" She looked across at Alan. To her surprise, he didn't seem particularly elated by this confirmation of his theory; he was still idly doodling on the tabletop. "Isn't it?"

"Well, not exactly. According to the loquacious Mr. James, Fell *is* next of kin, but *not* Onterdonck's heir—"

Roz stared at him in dismay. Could this be true? There went the prime motive! She watched the whole edifice of her argument crumble. What was it Alan had said earlier, "Tragedy is a theory killed by a fact"? Not to mention the fact that he had picked up more in a pleasant half hour spent in casual hobnobbing and chitchat while browsing through various kinds of interesting wall art with his left pinkie than she had in close to an hour's worth of interviewing half a dozen reporters and pawing through musty clippings with both hands. She had a nasty suspicion that he and the putatively prognathous Mr. James were two of a kind in the miscellaneous information-gathering sweepstakes.

"—just as we suspected might be the case," Alan went on (generously including her in the category of detective master-minds, knowing full well that he alone had suspected it). "On-terdonck had the foresight to make a will some years back—as soon as he inherited, in fact—leaving Restitution Island to the Nature Conservancy, about which he wasted no time serving notice to the various Fells *pater* and *filius*, and anyone else who was interested." Alan shrugged. "Of course, this is all by way of hearsay, but it seems pertinent."

"Well, so much for the 'makes it easier' motive," Roz said, staring glumly at her plate. "You can bet the Conservancy will give him a good run for his money. With those protective cov-enants to work with and that powerful lobby of theirs, they'll have him back in court in ten minutes. Fell would have been better off trying to negotiate with Onterdonck; the Conservancy is nothing if not persistent. He'll probably end up turning Rebel Island over to them just to get himself off their mailing list, never mind his back. So much for Fell's grand plan." With a wry chuckle, she looked up at Alan, wondering how *he* felt about seeing their whole case come apart before his very eyes.

"Again, not exactly," said Alan. "There's more. About a month ago the state supreme court finally overturned the pro-tective covenants. According to James, Onterdonck was fit to be tied, even though he'd been expecting something of the sort for months. So the fact of the matter is that Onterdonck, as mere owner of the adjacent island, no longer had any power over what Fell could or couldn't do with Rebel Island. Unfor-tunately, neither will the good old Nature Conservancy, though I expect, as you say, they'll give it a right go. No, I'm afraid it appears to be full speed ahead for our Mr. Fell, with or without Onterdonck. Groundbreaking is scheduled for mid-August. Thus our theory about a motive for Fell's involvement regarding

Onterdonck and his covenants, is totally and irrevocably up the spout."

"Wait a minute, Alan, let me get this straight. So what you're saying, courtesy your Mr. James, is that Fell wouldn't have benefited one way or the other from Onterdonck's death, unless he had no idea about the will, which, given the information from James, he clearly did."

Alan nodded. "So it would appear. And we are right back to square one, as my favorite literary character, the White Knight, was wont to say."

"Oh, really?" she remarked, looking at him curiously. "I don't remember that from *Through the Looking Glass.*"

"Or was it the Mad Hatter? No, that was 'You can't fall off the floor,' or words to that effect. Not that it matters, really." Alan paused and took a good long swig, draining the mug in front of him. He waved to the waitress for another. Roz watched him as he sat there quietly contemplating his beer. The odd thing was, though he was clearly not elated by these latest developments, he did not seem particularly downcast, either. But maybe his joy was in the doing—the journey, not the arrival, that matters. Or maybe he was happy it was over, looking forward to his getaway.

"So where do we go from here?" she inquired after several seconds had passed. "If anywhere?"

"Ummm, well. I've been thinking," Alan replied. "I'm still not quite ready to give up on our Mr. Fell. If square one is the body on the beach and Fell's reaction to it, given all the benefits—the *quis* as it were—that have been eliminated, I still wonder how 'things' could be made easier for him. And *what* things?" He gazed thoughtfully at her. "What are some of the other possibilities? It has to involve the islands somehow; that remains the only real connection and source of animosity between the two men. Given the present circumstances, what difficulty could possibly yet have stood in Fell's way that Onterdonck's death would remove from the picture?"

Alan was looking at her oddly, almost expectantly. Hmm.

Did he somehow already know something, or was he making it up as he went along?

"Think about everything we observed that day," he said now, still gazing at her. "Your garden-variety motive will do for a start."

Garden variety? Garden as in what—the only one she knew about in this context was at Montfort Abbey. What could that possibly have to do with it?

They sat silent for a while longer, arms propped on the table. The waitress was beginning to hover. Roz, ostensibly looking out the plate-glass window, knew that Alan was still watching her. She had the aggravating sense that he knew the answer perfectly well. If there was ever anyone who looked as if he had something up his sleeve, it was he.

The waitress came and collected their plates, with a slightly bewildered-sounding "Was everything all right?" at the sight of Roz's leftover green salad. "Would you like that in a doggy bag?" Roz nodded absently, and shortly the waitress returned with the salad greens carefully sealed in a plastic bag.

Roz looked at the bag and then at Alan. "The plastic envelope we found on Onterdonck's body," she said.

"Exactly," Alan replied, thumping his hands down on the tabletop. "Given a choice, for what obvious reason might an ardent amateur naturalist be fossicking about on an uninhabited and environmentally threatened island? We had already reached the conclusion that Onterdonck had been out collecting plant specimens. But to what purpose?"

When Roz looked blank, Alan paused, then leaned forward eagerly. "You've spent time in Maine, you must be familiar with the famous *Pedicularis furbishiensis* case some years ago."

Roz shook her head, staring at him in astonishment. What in blue blazes was a *Pedicularis furbishiensis*? In the context of the conversation so far, it must be some sort of rare species, most likely vegetable in spite of the sound-alike etymology that suggested a tiny eight-legged pest. After all he wasn't a world-renowned obsessive-compulsive plant nut for nothing, although she wouldn't put it past him to know a thing or two about bugs as well.

"There was a proposed hydroelectric project that involved building a dam at a place called Dickey-Lincoln, on your northern border, which would have flooded a good part of the Saint John River valley and parts of the Allagash. The sportsmen and the environmentalists got themselves into an uproar, because it was one of the last habitats of an endangered plant species, the aforementioned *Pedicularis furbishiensis*—that's Furbish's lousewort," he added helpfully. "Flooding the area would have destroyed two thirds of the extant plant populations, so to make a long story short, the environmentalist groups took it all the way to Congress. They didn't exactly stop the project, but they held up the process so long that it became financially unfeasible, and the whole thing was scrapped. Claps and cheers all round and Dickey-Lincoln down the drain."

Roz smiled at the thought of the great big power plant scuttled by an itty-bitty green one. Plants and more plants, plant power, in fact—no pun intended—that's what he had meant by "garden variety" motive. "I get it," she said slowly. "Failing the protective covenants, you think Onterdonck was doing his damnedest to find another way to scuttle the cargo port."

Alan nodded and leaned closer, resting his elbows on the table. "What else could Onterdonck possibly have done to foil Fell's plan at this point in the project—the midnight hour, as it were?"

"He'd been looking for some sort of extinct or endangered plant species that had no other habitat but Rebel Island, which would certainly make the EPA sit up and take notice, as in the lousewort case. And you think he'd found it." Roz thought this over briefly. "But wait a minute, Alan. He was on the wrong island. What good would it do to find something on Restitution?"

"Ah-ha, he was *found* on the wrong island, all the better to fool us with, my dear. But you know my methods, Watson. Reasoning by analogy, we begin to fathom, if not the riddle of how the body got there, then a faint glimmer of a feasible why. Put yourself in Fell's place. Just suppose that our friend Onterdonck had been snooping about on Rebel for the express purpose outlined previously, and not only that, had actually come up with the goods, witness the glassine envelope. Then he met up with Fell, probably on board the *Non-Amo-Te,* and told him in no uncertain terms how he was going to stop the project once and for all and see to it that both Rebel and Restitution islands remained forever wild. Not the wisest move to make on his part, but then I doubt that most people ever imagine that someone is going to rear up and strike them dead just like that, reason or no.

"So, at any rate, Onterdonck naïvely taunts Fell with the news that he's found something rare, strange, and endangered that will put Fell's multimillion-dollar project on the rocks. A furious Fell knocks him senseless. Then, when he realizes Onterdonck is injured unto death, puts him ashore on Restitution Island to steer attention away from Rebel, making certain (or so he thinks) that it will look like an accident—by means we have not yet established, but if we've proved Fell's motive it hardly matters; motive plus opportunity will serve quite well in lieu of the solution by means of only the one way. Or, more simply put, when you know how then you know who. And there we have it." He sat back, laced his hands behind his head, and regarded her impassively. "All the evidence—senses, hearsay, and analogy—present and accounted for?"

Maybe too much present, Roz thought, spying a flaw in his reasoning. "Wait a minute, Alan," she said. "If Fell knew enough to get rid of the plant specimen, why in the world would he leave the plastic bag right there on the body for anyone to find?"

"Ah, good point." Alan pondered this a moment. "I said Onterdonck was naïve and unwise, but I don't think he was stupid. He must have taken the specimen out of the bag himself beforehand and put it somewhere for safekeeping. Put yourself in his place. Wouldn't you?"

Reasoning from analogy; put herself in Onterdonck's place.

Brr, no thanks. Yet Roz had to admit it all made sense. She nodded.

"So there we have the motive as well as opportunity, the chain of reasoning complete, at least in the abstract." Alan paused, looking pensive.

"Well," Roz said after a moment, "it sounds as though you've got the whole thing in the bag . . . no pun intended," she added quickly in response to his stern glance.

"Unfortunately not," he said. "When I said this was all in the abstract, I was speaking quite literally, and that's where I fear it must remain, since without the specimen, or at the very least the glassine envelope—what was it you called it, a Baggie?—we have no concrete proof. Even without the plant itself, if we'd had that bag I might still have been able to do something with the bits left given the run of a decent laboratory for a day or so, but it's clearly too much to hope for that the envelope in question is still extant, much less that we could get our hands on it at this juncture. Who'd pay any attention to a silly old plastic bag with traces of some old weed in it, as long as it wasn't hash or some other illegal substance? Since the case is officially closed—or, rather, never opened—it's probably gone with the rest of Onterdonck's unregarded trifles, straight into a dustbin somewhere. So much for the hard evidence to prove our supposition. Without the plant specimen, the whole thing remains mere speculation, and Mr. Fell's cargo port–*cum*–Buried Treasure Adventure Park is in the clear. And without any further evidence to reopen the investigation, we shall never know how the body got where we found it. So that's the end of that." Shoulders slumping, Alan heaved a dejected sigh, the first real sign he had shown of discouragement. "I'm afraid this means we're well and truly stumped, Watson," he said in a depressed tone. "We can't even make this into a problem for which the solution is the sole reward, as our old friend Sherlock Holmes would have it, let alone make the world safe for louseworts." He sat forward, chin on hands, as glum as Roz had ever seen him since this all began.

It certainly looked—and sounded—like the end of the line.

Contemplating his usually cheerful countenance, his heretofore resilient, forever resourceful disposition, qualities that she treasured but had recently taken too much for granted, Roz felt a wave of urgent sympathy. I can't just leave things like this, she thought. Maybe their relationship was past help, but what about the so-called case?

She sat there toying with the plastic bag full of salad greens, thinking not so much about how nice it would be to pin the murder on Roger Fell as how nice it would be to scuttle his plans for the ruination of those lovely islands, for if Rebel went, there would be no saving Restitution. Maybe its wildlife could tolerate the odd sail- and motorboat, a seaplane or two, a gang of sometime detectives, but she hardly thought it could survive a wholesale commercial enterprise. Far from being a Greenpeace-style environmentalist guerrilla, she was hardly even a run-of-the mill nature activist, but she'd done her share of lobbying and picketing here and there against nuclear waste dumping and power plants, and she had faithfully sent in her annual contributions to the Wilderness Society, the Nature Conservancy, and the Sierra Club, even if she seldom had time to do more than skim their publications. She was sure they would have had plenty to say about Fell's little plan, once they got wind of it. But could they actually do anything to stop it? Or was this really up to her and Alan? She thought of the two islands, lying quiet and peaceful and undisturbed all these generations, with so much to offer as they were. It was a big enough crime to despoil all that, without committing murder into the bargain.

She knew Alan was watching her, but she did not look up, not wanting to confront the look of disappointment in his face. After a moment he placed several bills and some change next to the check, obviously getting ready to leave. Meanwhile, all this talk of preserving plants had made her think back to her high-school biology class, waxed paper, and her mother's ruined iron.

"Alan, how exactly does a naturalist go about collecting plants these days? I mean, do you just dig them up and put them in plastic bags? Don't you have to dry them or press them to preserve them somehow? And what about identification?"

Alan glanced at her curiously, then stared past her out the window. "In the field," he began in a formal tone, as though he were lecturing to a class, "you would carefully dig up a specimen—if it can be spared—of the whole plant and put it in a plastic bag. Then you would give it a collection number and record the number and information about identification and type of habitat, along with some kind of directions to where it was found, in a field notebook. Once back at your field camp or wherever you were working from, you would place the specimen into a plant press. Then when you'd got back to your permanent base, you would mount the pressed, dried specimen on acid-free paper, label it, and store it in a herbarium case—"

"Alan, wait a minute," Roz interrupted. "What exactly does a plant press look like?"

He gave her a puzzled look. "Two end pieces made of wood slats cross-hatched like a lattice, about this big"—here he made an oblong shape a foot or so long with his hands—"and this wide, with bits of cardboard with blotting paper and newspapers folded in between. You sandwich each of the specimens—as many as you want—in between the folded newspaper, then the blotting paper, then cardboard, and cinch the whole thing together with two straps. It can be any thickness, depending on—"

Roz stood up so fast she nearly knocked the remaining contents of the table over into Alan's lap. Without thinking she grabbed his arm, yanked him to his feet, and hurried out the door.

"Alan, listen," she said when they had gone a little way down the street. "There was one of those things on Onterdonck's boat—I thought it was some sort of portfolio or artsy-craftsy briefcase!" She turned to face him, almost babbling in her excitement. "The rare plant specimen could very well be in there! Wouldn't that be the logical place to put it for safekeeping? If we could get hold of that plant press and find the specimen, it would give us positive proof of a motive for Fell to get rid of Onterdonck! New evidence! We could take it to the police and get them to rethink their conclusions about Onterdonck's death. I mean with that strong a motive plus his proximity to the area at the time of death . . ." She stopped to catch her breath—and realized she was still hanging on to his arm for dear life. Suddenly self-conscious, she let go. "And even if we don't get anywhere with them," she went on in a more reasoned tone, "if we were to bring all this to the attention of the EPA as well as the nature groups, we might be able to scuttle the theme park ourselves, and save the islands, not to mention the East Bay. Alan, think what the lousewort lobby could do with this!"

Alan had stopped still and was looking down at her with an expression of wonderment. "Fair Rosamund! All in one fell swoop! Sorry, it just slipped out," he said, shrugging apologetically. She couldn't tell whether it was for the pun or the "fair Rosamund" or both, but it didn't really matter. She was relieved to see his natural good humor reasserting itself once again. She stood on the edge of the sidewalk, smiling up at his handsome, clean-shaven face. She caught her breath as he reached out and pulled her to him—just as a pickup truck came roaring around the corner, the dangerously projecting Western mirror sweeping the air just where her head had been. "Sorry, there I go a-rescuing again," he said, bowing formally as he released her. "A mere reflex. I'm sure you would have ducked in time. More to the point," he went on coolly (as she stood there with her cheeks aflame), "does this mean you've changed your mind about having another go at searching *Non-Amo-Te*?"

"Well, yes, in the abstract," Roz said as matter-of-factly as she could, her excitement subsiding along with the blush, along with the tingle in her flesh from the brief, hard contact of his arms. "But it doesn't change my mind about the boat's being locked up, which appears to me to be a fairly insurmountable obstacle. Unless you think we could just go up to Thaxter Waite and ask for the key." They had resumed walking, and now were just crossing over the railroad tracks at the entrance to the boatyard.

"I rather doubt that will be necessary."

Roz looked at him suspiciously, wondering if here was yet another area in which he was unexpectedly competent: breaking and entering. She wasn't at all sure she wanted to go *that* far, even if there was a moral issue—and more—at stake. Two issues, really, the murder of a man and the proposed despoliation of the islands.

Alan must have read her thoughts, for after a brief pause he looked down at her dispassionately. "Or would you just prefer to let the whole thing go? We could just get back on board and take the boat on down to your Auntie Jess's in no time; it can't be more than a half hour's sail from here. We can just have done with it; I'll pack my things and be on my way. Just say the word." He stood looking down at her, face inscrutable, hands stuffed into the pockets of his sailing shorts as if he weren't quite sure what to do with them.

Here it was again, the unresolved issue between them, with its unspoken necessity on her part to make a decision. But here, too, was a mystery right at hand, a perfect way of avoiding the inevitable and getting Alan to stay on, at least for a while longer. All she had to do was say the word, one way or another.

"All right," she said. "I'll give it a try."

"Ah, good show!" Alan said, grinning down at her. He thrust his hands deeper into his pockets and hunched his wide shoulders up in an attitude almost of anticipation. "I knew you were game."

14

When they got back down to the floating dock they found that Thaxter Waite had not only moved the *Verorum* from where they had left it, but had moored it in close proximity to the *Non-Amo-Te*. "Birds of a feather," Alan said in response to her expression of disbelief at this stroke of luck. "Boats of like size moored together. Either that or it was meant, as in 'fated to be.' Why don't you search out some dark clothing for your foray while I reconnoiter?"

With that he left her on the *Verorum* and set out for a row around the harbor, while Roz rummaged through her duffel bags for the darkest outfit she could find. Occasionally the sound of his voice drifted back to her as he went about conversing casually with the inhabitants of the other boats wherever he came upon them—with virtually no trace of his Oxford-*cum*-Scots accent, she noticed. He seemed to be mimicking the downeast intonation perfectly; for all they could tell, probably he was just another fellow Mainer out for a row, checking out the latest arrivals. She wondered if he would learn anything of use in his rambles. Anyway, she was sure he was enjoying himself. Leaving him to it, she went down below to hunt up some dark clothes.

When she emerged sometime later she looked for him among the boats, but he was no longer in sight. Nor could she hear his cheerful rumble floating back to her over the water. Hmm, where had he gone, and what was he up to now? Some plan of his own he wasn't telling her about? Surely he hadn't taken it upon himself after all to search the *Non-Amo-Te*? He'd better not; that was supposed to be her job, she thought crossly, searching for a glimpse of him among the various bobbing hulls.

What he had been up to, it turned out, was shopping. He returned just as dark was falling with a loaf of crusty French bread, some cheese and wine, a salmon pâté, and assorted other delicacies from the local co-op natural food store. They fixed themselves a light supper, then sat on deck waiting for the moon to go down, watching the lights of the harbor go out as several dinghy-loads of day sailors rowed in to shore from their boats, chatting and laughing, and those who were staying on began one by one to extinguish theirs.

Finally Alan declared the harbor dark and deserted enough. He descended below and to Roz's surprise emerged on deck a few minutes later dressed in a navy sweater, watch cap, and dungarees.

"Hey, wait a minute!" she protested. "I thought I was going to do the searching. I'm the one who knows where everything is, remember?"

"Ah, to be sure, my dear Watson. But as you may recall, there is the difficulty of the lock. Also," he went on imperturbably as he hauled the dinghy alongside, "you might consider this point as well: a strange dinghy—in fact any dinghy at all— tied up to yon *Non-Amo-Te* would certainly be deemed suspicious, while a warmly dressed person seen messing about in a boat in the harbor late at night would be taken for nothing more than a harmless insomniac out for a bit of a row in the dark."

She had to admit he did have a point. "All right. You can row me over there and pick the lock. Then I'll go down below and find the plant press. There's also a notebook just like the one you described, with reference numbers and names and directions."

"Right-o. Just stay down out of sight until I bring the dinghy round the back where no one can see you getting in." Alan dropped over the side and into the *Mendax,* while Roz slid around the far side of the cabin and ducked down out of sight.

At first she heard nothing except the lap of water percolating randomly against the *Verorum*'s hull. Then there was the slight thump of the dinghy as he maneuvered it around to the side away from shore. A faint whistle almost like a snore floated up, her signal to lower herself down into the dinghy. Feeling like a character in a John Buchan novel, she scrambled down into the dinghy herself.

They set out for the *Non-Amo-Te,* keeping the hull of the *Verorum* as much as possible between them and the rest of the harbor. Alan rowed silently, timing the dip of the oars to blend in with the desultory slopping of water against the hulls of many boats rocking gently in the ground swell, the rhythmic clank of rigging against masts. Soon they were coming around the other side of the *Non-Amo-Te.* Roz was relieved to see it was the farthest out in line, with no other boats beyond to overlook them. "Up you go, then," Alan whispered, motioning her to climb on board. She clambered up, had just flattened herself out and was creeping along the deck on her elbows when she realized what appeared to be an oversight on their part.

"Alan," she whispered. "You should have come up first! I don't know how to pick the lock."

"Nor do I," he whispered back in a maddeningly offhand tone. "But not to worry. I said earlier I didn't think that would be necessary; to that end, in my explorations this evening I observed that the lock in question is a combination. If my experience of boatyards is anything to go by, good faith and expediency operate here as elsewhere. In other words, the lock has almost certainly been left on the combination. Just give the shank a smart shove in and then pull the whole thing back toward you and I'll give you odds it unlocks on the spot."

Unlocks on the spot, huh? So much for the necessity of his coming along to see to the difficulty of the lock! He could just as easily have told her all this back in the *Verorum*! So why had he insisted on coming with her? But she already knew the answer. For all his efforts not to hover (stopping short at letting her be run over by a truck, of course), when push came to shove, he *still* couldn't quite bring himself to let her go it alone! He just *had* to be here, in case she got herself in trouble or, worse yet, missed something important.

Oh, well, they were both here now, they might as well get on with it. She reached up and grasped the lock as he had directed, and sure enough, it came open in her hands with a barely audible click. She waved the lock in the air to show Alan, who nodded and gave her a thumbs-up sign, then pushed off silently and began to row away, looking perfectly innocent and unconcerned. Hmm. Locks aside, she had to admit he had a point about the dinghy. She had misjudged him, jumped to hasty conclusions once again. He had intended all along to let her go in alone.

Well, get to it, then. Quickly Roz dismantled the dropboards, stepped over the sill and down several steps of the companion-way, then carefully replaced the boards from inside, sliding the hatch closed when she was finished, so that from the outside the hatchway would appear undisturbed to even the most careful observer.

Neck prickling in the inky blackness, she backed down the rest of the steps until she could feel her feet scuff on the cabin sole. Cautiously she turned around so that she was facing the interior of the cabin.

It was odd, eerie even, being back inside the boat, especially all closed in like this. This must be what being inside a chamber at Pompeii would feel like, she thought, everything left just as it was, only the fact of death falling over everything like ash, altering all your perceptions. She shivered violently in the pitch dark.

Okay, Roz, get cracking. Pulling out the tiny penlight Alan had given her (yet one more purchase from L. L. Bean), she switched it on and swept the little circle of light around the navigation station, galley, bunks, bookshelves, as far forward as the bulkhead door into the forecastle.

And stared in disbelief.

Everything was gone. Everything that could be moved, that is. The main cabin had been completely stripped, charts, utensils, personal effects, books. Only the built-in cabin accoutrements, the instruments, the radio remained. And yes, the Tiny Tot, now swept clean of ash. How could this be? The cupboard was completely, utterly bare.

Edging past the table, she shone the light into the hanging lockers; nothing. No liquor, no foul-weather gear. And, needless to say, no plant press. She didn't really need to check the forecabin, but she did, running the narrow beam all along the peaked interior, looking in one empty drawer after another. The head, too, was bare, polished clean. The whole boat was now characterless, bland, resembled nothing so much as a vacant hotel room.

The question was, who had removed everything? Surely not the Nature Conservancy; the wheels of any bureaucracy, even the most benevolent, grind at only one speed, exceeding slow, so it was a safe bet they hadn't even sent anyone to look the boat over yet, let alone implement a wholesale removal of Onterdonck's things. And what would they want with a bunch of personal effects anyway? Not to mention the fact that the will couldn't possibly have been probated yet.

So who had taken everything away, and why?

She plopped down on one of the settee berths. All right, then, suppose the police *had* been suspicious and had gone around collecting evidence after all? But there were no other signs of a search, no fingerprint powder daubed here and there, no tracks of big or little muddy feet, no mess, no fuss of the kind one might expect from an official going-over. Everything was just too neat. The interior was so spick-and-span tidy it looked as though a professional cleaning outfit had been through with Q-tips. Even if the police had removed Onter-donck's personal effects, why bother to clean and polish?

Maybe the boat had been put up for sale already? But there hadn't been that much time; the *Non-Amo-Te* had only been here since Tuesday. No, whoever had done this must have made pretty quick work of the whole matter, just swept up everything as though with a huge vacuum cleaner and taken it away, lock, stock, and barrel, evidence and all, swabbing the whole place out with a vengeance afterward.

She stared at the empty bookcase across from her. There went their plan to prove the once and future crimes of Roger Fell. The notebook was gone as well, along with every other sign that Peter Onterdonck had ever inhabited this boat. But what in the world had made her—and Alan, too—think that Roger Fell would leave incriminating evidence on board the boat a second longer than he had to, next of kin or no next of kin? He'd anticipated the whole scenario and managed, by hook or by crook, to cop the whole lot after all.

So. It seemed her mission was over as soon as it had begun; no plant press, *ergo* no specimen, no notebook, therefore no case. There would be no stopping Roger Fell now. Soon Rebel and Restitution would be the downeast version of Disney World, or worse. And Alan would be on his way home to Scotland. Alone. Unless they could somehow manage a reconciliation first.

She was still glumly considering the implications of this wholesale disappearance of the evidence when she heard a tapping on the hull; Alan returning to check her progress. She was supposed to shine the light briefly through the porthole when she had found the plant press; he was probably wondering what was holding things up. She knocked softly three times, indicating that she'd heard him. With one last look around the bare interior, she put out the light and groped her way out of the cabin of the *Non-Amo-Te*. Quickly she replaced the dropboards and clicked the lock shut behind her, giving it a good twist just for spite.

As soon as she was seated in the dinghy she told Alan the

whole story of what she had found, or rather, not. They rowed back to the *Verorum* in silence, tied up the dinghy, and descended into the main cabin.

But if she imagined Alan's shower and shave that afternoon meant anything, she was sadly disappointed. After a brief, inconclusive discussion about what, if anything, to do next, Alan simply nodded and said, "Tomorrow, then," and gave her his usual polite but distant salute, a clear indication he meant to sleep yet once more in the main cabin. She was left to retire to her lonely vee-berth, where she lay awake far into the night, finally falling into a restless slumber just before daybreak.

15

When Roz awoke it was midmorning, and the sounds of the boatyard and harbor were noisily apparent. So was the smell of the coffee Alan was brewing on the propane stove. She pulled on a sweatshirt and a pair of jeans and went into the main cabin.

Alan looked up. "Good morning, Roz. Did you have a good night?" he said cheerily. Roz looked sharply at him, but could detect no signs of irony, other than the fact that he himself looked well rested, from which she grumpily concluded that he must have considerably vaster stores of what Keats had called "negative capability" than she did. He handed her a cup of coffee and a bowl of cereal, then suggested they have breakfast on deck.

They lingered over their second cups of coffee, thinking their own thoughts. Finally Alan put his cup down. "All right, then, let's begin at the beginning. The first question is, who would have had reason to remove the specimens between Tuesday morning, when you saw them on board, and last night? Let's assume for the sake of argument that the authorities did not. They would have no reason to, there being, at least in the newspaper report of Onterdonck's death, no mention of foul play; the case appears, from their point of view, to have been closed before it was ever opened. Then there is the legal heir apparent, your redoubtable Nature Conservancy. But I suspect that unless they had already been supplied with some clue about what was on board, which seems unlikely, they would have little interest in lugging off Onterdonck's personal *lares* and *penates*. If they had been supplied previously with said clue, which could only have been by Onterdonck himself, I can't imagine them keeping it to themselves for even a second— Onterdonck either, for that matter, which argues perforce that he must have only recently come upon his find—that very day, in all likelihood—when he met with his unfortunate end. But alas, there has not been even a whisper of any possible discovery, any indication of Fell's show not being able to go on, which I gather, from the sentiments expressed to you at the newspaper office in that marvelous red-brick miniature Victorian gothic château at the top of the block, would be very big news indeed. So, these two aside, who else would have had both motive and opportunity?"

Roz sighed, trying to pull herself out of her depressed mood. "Only Roger Fell had the motive, if we're right about the contents of the plant press and what Onterdonck was intending to do with it."

"Opportunity?"

Surely they weren't going to have to go through the whole detective catechism again, sifting the evidence through micromesh, leaving no tern unstoned? She fervently hoped not. "Not so certain," she said wearily. "He stormed right off the island after the body was found, so it must have been after the boat was brought back here. He's had at least two nights to do it in, *if*, she added for good measure, he did it in the dark—as in illegally."

"Good point. Let's imagine him, then, gaining access as we did, under cover of darkness. From your description, wholesale removal of Onterdonck's belongings would have necessitated a regular caravan of dinghies. About as inconspicuous as a trail of ants making away with the toast crumb by crumb over the breakfast table. And even if he just decided to dump the lot overboard on the spot, it would still be a rather touchy job, wouldn't you say? Imagine the number of kersplashes it would entail. Certainly you'd run the risk of someone taking notice and catching on. What ho! Alarums and excursions, man overboard, drag the harbor—"

Alan jumped up and began to pace up and down the narrow space between the cockpit seats. The *Verorum* rocked slightly in response to his movement. Roz looked around, hoping no one was watching. "—and lo! there's the booty sitting ever so suspiciously in a nice little collection right under the boat. 'And what might this be in aid of, my fine sir,' murmur the aghast authorities, 'sending said contents of said boat straight to Davy Jones?' " Alan stopped in midgesture and, with a "so-much-for-that-idea" glance at Roz, subsided back onto the cockpit seat across from her. "Incriminating, to say the least. No, I don't think he would have dared to do it surreptitiously. He must have managed it somehow so that it would appear strictly on the up-and-up."

"We could ask Old Stormy," Roz suggested. "Fell must have gotten around him somehow."

"Hmm. But how? Let's think. Fell *is* Onterdonck's nearest relative—feud or no feud—and blood is thicker than water. I can see Fell just turning up, saying he wanted something to remember his old coz by, and marching right on board as though butter wouldn't melt in his mouth. After all, there was no reason to believe, as far as Waite knew, anyway, that any crime had been committed, no doors taped shut, no police lines—"

"Not to mention the fact that Fell's one of 'us'—"

"—Unlike the Nature Conservancy for a start, so Waite just tipped him the wink and told him to take whatever he fancied, no questions asked. Brilliant." Alan nodded vigorously. "Here's a similar scenario that doesn't even require the complicity of your good Stormalong: A grief-stricken Fell calls up the Nature Conservancy and asks"—here Alan put his fist to his ear and imitated a telephone exchange in nasal Yankee tones—"if he could please (sniff, sniff) have his dear departed (sniff) cousin's personal belongings (sniff, choke) for old times' sake, hate to have them go out of the family, et cetera and so forth, don't you know? How could they say no? What else would they do with the goods? They'd probably be grateful to him for cleaning everything up and leaving the boat empty so they could put it up for sale. 'Oh, *would* you mind?' 'Oh, no, of course not, no trouble really. I'd be ever so happy to take all that old stuff off your hands and clean the boat up for you.' "

"So he goes aboard, takes away the evidence—along with everything else—that indicates his motive for murder, giving Rebel Island a clean bill for the EPA in the process, and proceeds to destroy the specimens at his earliest convenience," Roz concluded.

"You don't suppose it's possible, do you," Alan mused, "that having acquired the whole kit and caboodle safe in his own hands, he mightn't just leave the evidence lying about on board the *Jolly Roger* for a bit, where the casual visitor might just come across them? No? I thought not. One more forlorn hope blasted. I'm afraid it's all been sent long since to a watery grave." Alan fell silent, knitting his long fingers into some sort of complex geometric arrangement.

Roz sat quietly, going back over the logic of it all, using the argument from analogy: putting herself in Fell's place. "I just thought of something, Alan," she said after a minute or two. "If Fell actually killed Onterdonck on board the *Non-Amo-Te* that night, why didn't he just drop the plant press and all the stuff that went with it overboard in the cove right there and then? Why leave it all behind and then have to come back later?"

Alan's hands sprang apart; he sat forward. "Ouch, there's a difficulty. Hmmm. First of all, we don't know that he did kill Onterdonck on board; the evidence of hair and blood could have been planted later. But I suppose the simplest explanation is that he didn't know what he was looking for until afterward, when the glassine collecting envelope turned up on the body. It must have been then that he realized Onterdonck had had everything right there with him on board all along. I don't imagine Fell's spent a great deal of time in the botany lab pressing plants, so he'd have no more idea what that funny-looking wood and waxpaper arrangement was than you did. And anyway, didn't you say it was stashed out of sight in the hanging locker?"

"But Alan, doesn't that scuttle the whole idea of motive? If Onterdonck hadn't threatened him then and there with the endangered plant specimen . . ."

Alan jumped up again and thrust his hands in his pockets, restlessly pacing. "Not really. Let's go through the scene again. He and Onterdonck meet on board the *Non-Amo-Te,* and Onterdonck taunts him with the news that he's found something that will put a real spoke in Fell's wheel—the Rebel Island equivalent of Kate Furbish's famous lousewort—but doesn't let on he has the very same threatened *flora* right there on the premises, hidden in plain sight amongst like items *à la* your 'Purloined Letter,' as it were. Picking it up where we left off over lunch—in the heat of the moment, Fell kills Onterdonck, bashing him with whatever comes to hand, the fire extinguisher, say." Roz ducked as Alan made a quick backhanded swipe with one large arm in the air over her head. "Then he has to cover up the killing, so he sets to work making it look like an accident by planting the body on the beach, somehow managing to cover his tracks into the bargain, and off he goes. But then next day, when he realizes we've been all over the body and turned up the plastic bag for our pains, he twigs it that the specimen had to be on board after all . . ."

Alan suspended his dramatic re-creation of the crime for a moment, whirling to face her. "No, that's too *ad hoc,* and anyone who could engineer that body-on-the-beach ploy in the dark and fog is anything but that." Off he went again, stomping back and forth like a bear in a cage in the confines of the cockpit. "Fell's no dimwit; of course it would occur to him that the plant specimen might be there and he'd jolly well better search the boat as his first order of business as soon as he'd put paid to our Mr. Onterdonck. So the question is, why didn't he? Let's think again. Suppose he did know the specimen was there, but it took him a lot more time and energy than he thought to set up the footprint dodge—however he did that, but never mind—I swear I won't be sidetracked by that again—so there he is, having worked the footprint fiddle somehow, on his way back to Onterdonck's boat to get rid of the incriminating plant material, when we arrive, anchor cheek-by-jowl with the *Non-Amo-Te,* and begin clattering about and carousing and generally making our presence known, so that he can't risk it, and has to silently fold his tents and steal away, hoping he can sneak back the next morning when we're up and gone, and extract the evidence."

"Which he did, or tried to," Roz added, "except he couldn't because we were still there. I'll bet he was lurking on the other side of the island the whole time, just hoping we would shove off early in the morning. Which we emphatically did not." Roz sat silent for a moment, recalling her early-morning impressions of the island. "Alan, here's another possibility. Let's suppose that however he managed to fake the footprints, he had to get in the water to do it. That means he would have had to get wet, right? Not just damp as though from the rain, but really wet, like dripping."

"A fair assumption."

"But when I boarded the *Non-Amo-Te* it was completely dry. So he couldn't have gone right back and down below or he would have left damp tracks that would have shown someone else had been on board."

"And that's why he didn't go back right away to get the specimens! He couldn't risk leaving a trail."

"Right. He rowed his and Onterdonck's dinghy in with the body, left it and the body there—"

"The means by which we cannot tell—"

"—then got into his dinghy and zoomed out to his own boat to put on dry clothes, leaving the evidence to be collected later. But when he went to go back and search for it, there *we* were."

"The engine on that rubber launch of his makes an awful racket; there'd be no mistaking it, especially in the middle of the night. No, of course he couldn't risk it. By Jove, I think you've got it! Excellent deduction, my dear Watson! Not only that, it has the virtue of great simplicity. But why," he began to ruminate, "would he have had to get in the water? . . ."

Suddenly irritated by what she took to be the note of condescension in his voice, not to mention his insistence on endlessly analyzing what seemed to her to be an increasingly abstract problem—who gave a damn about every little detail of how, as long as they could incriminate Fell, and anyway, couldn't they just get on with it?—Roz stood up impatiently. "This is stupid, Alan. We just keep going around and around, and I for one think all this speculation is getting us nowhere. All we're doing is whipping away at an attenuated analogy based on hearsay. Whatever happened to your evidence of the senses?"

"Ooch." Alan winced. "Flogged with my own stick."

"Let's go back to the simplest explanation," Roz went right on, "that Roger Fell didn't know the specimens were there on board in the first place. Maybe he still doesn't! Maybe he had nothing to do with it at all! Or maybe he was just curious!" Pausing for breath, she went on more calmly. "What we want is bare facts, and so far we've gathered precious few of them. Obviously the first thing we have to find out is whether Roger Fell actually *did* clear out Onterdonck's boat. Which is what I'm going to do right now."

"Ah, the old Occam's razor technique," said Alan in an admiring tone. "Well done, my dear Watson. Perhaps you'd best wear the Sherlock mantle—or I should say inverness—from now on."

"Don't be condescending," Roz said curtly. "And I'll thank you to cut the Holmes and Watson crap as well. Just call me Roz from now on, okay?"

With that, she climbed into the dinghy and set out for shore to question Thaxter Waite.

16

But if Thaxter Waite had any useful information about Roger Fell and the missing contents of the *Non-Amo-Te,* he was not about to divulge it. Roz had some trouble getting him to stay still long enough to ask him anything in the first place, and once she got him started, found he was a past master at deflecting even the most direct of questions. Asked whether Roger Fell had been in the boatyard anytime this week, his only comment was "Roger Fell? Couldn't tell ya."

Couldn't or wouldn't? Roz wondered suspiciously, chasing along behind Waite as he bustled around the yard, his rolling gait making her feel as though the ground itself were undulating.

"And if he was," he went on after coming to a brief standstill beside a powerboat of some sort with a gaping hole in the hull, "you can bet your bottom dollar he wouldn't be comin' in here with that monster sloop of his." Here Waite stuck his head, pipe and all, inside the opening. Smoke poured out around his neck and shoulders. Sniffing apprehensively, Roz backed up several steps, wondering about the possibilities of an explosion. Weren't there all kinds of toxic fumes and noxious chemicals constantly in use in boatyards?

"No, sirree," came Waite's voice, echoing hollowly from the interior of the boat. "Pulls too much water, that one; purt'near fifteen feet if she draws an inch. Ain't that kind of water heah. He'd have to tie up to the town dock, and even then he'd only get away with it risin' high tide. Naw, he'd have to anchor way to hell and gone, and that's too in-con-*veen*-yunt," Waite drawled with an unmistakable note of irony. "Not that he's got much use for Belfast anyways." Waite's head emerged; he reached up and began peeling off parts of the hull as though it were the shell of a cracked hard-boiled egg. "Not fashionable enough for him, I guess. He usually lies up in Camden when he's not tearin' around the bay scarifying lobster pots. One week he dredged up three dozen on that dratted winged keel of his, and took a purse seiner net all the way to Owls Head. Not too popular with any of the locals, far as that goes." Waite shook his head, but Roz couldn't tell whether it was at the wrecked boat hull or the depredations of Roger Fell. "Not for lack of trying, though," he went on after a moment's consideration, the object of which was again uncertain. Oh well, thought Roz, at least I've got him going. "You hear about the boat-naming contest?" Waite suddenly offered. "Thousand-dollar prize. Decided to rename the *Jolly Roger* somepin' else, using 'Fell' this time, redo the whole shebang, can you believe it? Guess he got some sick a' runnin' around like some danged pirate, so now he's trying to change his image around here, git folks to come around to him. It'll never work, though; they'll just take the money and run. Then there's that new boat a' his a-buildin' over to the yard down Brunswick way. Mebbe he's fixin' to make *that* one the buccaneer boat. Uh-*huh*."

After getting a detailed but largely irrelevant earful about the design, specifications, and expense of Fell's soon-to-be-built bigger and better giant yawl ("Guess he figures one mast ain't enough, so he'll try one and a bit—'spect he'll work himself up through ketch-rig to a ten-masted schooner the size of the *Queen Mary* 'fore he's done with it"), Roz gave up on the topic of whether Roger Fell had been seen anywhere near the boat-yard in the past week, let alone aboard the *Non-Amo-Te*. But

Thaxter Waite had reminded her of something else she had nearly forgotten.

"Have you seen or heard of a black ship anywhere around here, medium-sized, with a name ending in -RD, from either Rockland or Portland?" she asked. She couldn't think of any other ports of call ending in -land.

Waite was hauling on a huge length of rusty, mud-encrusted chain that disappeared into the water between what appeared to be two railroad tracks. "Black ship, uh?" he responded without looking up. "Sorry. Ain't no square-rigger—black, green, or purple with pink polka dots, medium-sized or otherwise—around these parts that I know about."

Square-rigger? What had given him that idea? "Actually, I meant one of the ones with two masts that take passengers," Roz explained patiently. "A schooner of some kind, maybe?"

Thaxter Waite looked up and regarded her briefly, then went back to hauling chain, oblivious to the shower of rust and slime now spattering over him. "Why didn't you say so? There's all kinds a' schooners, but ain't none of 'em a ship." Then he proceeded to give her a thoroughly academic (and largely gratuitous, as far as she was concerned) lesson in the differentiation of types of sail rig, from barkentine to ship of the line: "Two or more masts with only the mizzen rigged fore and aft is a bark. . . ." Standing there at a safe distance from the seemingly endless, as well as increasingly foul-looking (and -smelling) chain, helplessly listening to a description of the sail plan of a "ship, strictly speaking," Roz wished perversely that she could set Alan on him; they were obviously two of a kind. Come to think of it, unless it was her imagination, Waite even sounded different as he stood there delivering his disquisition on sail rigs. It wasn't until he was well into his monologue that she realized he seemed to have temporarily lost his good-old-boy Maine accent.

The upshot, which Roz nearly missed, as it coincided with Thaxter Waite's throwing the massive hank of chain with a sound of thunder into a nearby wheelbarrow that staggered drunkenly under the weight, was that he hadn't seen or heard of any schooner, bark, barkentine, ship, or other large sailing vessel of that kind or description in Belfast, nor was it likely that there would be. "Not exactly the hub of the universe" was his comment. In other words, well off the beaten track, so to speak, particularly for the tourist-oriented windjammer trade.

"Let's face it," he said finally, turning to her with a trace of irascibility as well as the familiar Maine drawl back in his voice, "this here harbor ain't that picturesque to begin with, though it's better now they've tore down that big ugly chicken-feed tower left over from the days when Belfast was the Broiler Capital a' the World. But who wants to come in and tie up next to a smelly old sardine factory? By gorry, on discharge day the gulls alone are enough to drive you right outta here; you need a durned umbrella just to walk down the dock, never mind the stench! No, ma'am, this is a workin' harbor; we deal in lobster traps, not tourist traps. And even if it weren't for that, there still ain't enough shoppin', just what uster be called the Grasshopper Shop, and a coupla wicked good bookstores, but there's bigger ones in Camden, never mind all them boutiques and such strung all the way down Route One to Kennebunkport." Here he shook his head, muttering. "Frankly, I hope it never comes, but it will. Be druve right up the coast to Nova Scotia 'fore we know it."

With that remark, stated in a tone of finality, Thaxter Waite ducked his head in a quick nod, then stood stock-still and waited for her to speak, a clear indication to Roz that the interview was over as far as he was concerned. Obviously he had better things to do than chew the fat with her. At this point, after noting his unusually literate use of the subjunctive, Roz gave up any further hope of fathoming the mystery of the missing personal effects, never mind Waite's on-again, off-again Maine accent and grammar, and asked to settle up for the night's mooring.

"Five'll be plenty; after all, Jessie True's an old customer, hate to see her get all het up. Thankee, come again," Waite said with a smile, pocketing the bill Roz gave him. Then he added, much to her surprise, "Come to think of it, I suppose that boat you were askin' after could be around for the Great Schooner Race. Lot of 'em come in for that. But that's all down t'other end of Islesboro by Camden and Rockland, not way up here.'' With that he nodded politely and rolled off toward the boat shed where he kept his noisy homemade tractor-forklift, in due course reemerging saddled up on said contraption, which he proceeded to wheel about the yard with either reckless abandon or amazing dexterity (or both), rearranging huge boat cradles. Roz began skirting her way past the small shack that housed the boatyard office and ship's chandlery.

"Looks like a' ant with a load a' matchsticks, don't he?" remarked a voice behind her.

Recovering from her lurch into the wall of the shack, Roz turned around several times, trying to locate the owner of the disembodied voice. She hadn't noticed anyone other than Thaxter Waite anywhere in the boatyard since she'd been here. There was one boat still in dry dock, or whatever you called it when they were out of the water propped up on stilts or jacks, a fairly big full-keel boat with most of its bottom paint sanded off in blotches. She peered around one side and then the other, and still didn't see anyone.

"Up here," said the voice in a Maine accent so strong it made Thaxter Waite's sound mild in comparison, the "here" more like "hee-yaw." Shading her eyes, she looked up and saw a round, cheerful face peering down at her over the high wood cockpit coaming. "Mind reachin' me that pipe too-wull ova-theyuh byah feet? Be much obliged, save me anutha trip down th' laddah."

Roz picked up the large wrench the voice apparently was referring to and mounted the ladder leaning up against the hull, shortly coming face-to-face with a cherubic-looking man of indeterminate age whose shy expression, sunburned cheeks, and large brown eyes heavily fringed with lashes blinking in the sun reminded Roz of Bashful in *Snow White and the Seven Dwarfs*.

She handed the wrench over. "Thankee," he said, and extended his other hand, still somewhat grease-stained and streaked with rust even though he had just wiped it vigorously on his shirt. "Name's Clyde Math-yew. That's *M-e-r-i-t-h-e-w.* Math-yew."

"Roz Howard," she replied, shaking his hand warmly from her perch on the ladder. She looked across the cockpit past Mr. Merithew / Matthew at what she could see of the harbor. From this inconspicuous vantage point a person could see not only everything that was going on in the boatyard but every boat moored out in the harbor as far down as the town dock. "Nice boat," she commented casually. She didn't want to start right in firing questions and frighten Mr. Merithew back into his den or his bilge or wherever he'd been while she was trying to get some answers out of Thaxter Waite. She wondered if he'd overheard.

"You can come up over on deck and set a spell if you want. I'm still a-workin' on her. Should get her launched in a coupla days though, if I can just get this dratted sea cock loosened up. Froze up on me end a' last season. Wife won't sail unless we got a workin' head, and there ain't no fixin' her once she's in the water. So here I set, tinkerin'. Oh, well, bettah late than nevah." He rummaged briefly in a tool tray, then climbed back down the companionway. Roz heard a clanking noise, some muttering, then Mr. Merithew reappeared in the companion-way, mopping his forehead. "Phew, think I finally got 'er. Now all I have to do is pack her good, and we're in business." Presumably he was referring to the sea cock (female in gender, odd as that seemed), and not his wife. He smiled shyly at Roz. "You ain't from around here, is ya? Saw you and your . . . husband, is it?—"

"No, just a friend," Roz replied somewhat awkwardly, thinking that Clyde Merithew didn't miss much from his bird's-eye view overlooking the boatyard.

"—friend come in on Jessie True's boat, though. Now there's a nice rig; can't beat them old Herreshoffs. Matter of fact, that's my mooring you're on out theyuh."

"Oh, really? Ah, that's nice." Not sure what else to say, Roz beamed broadly at Mr. Math . . . Merith . . . make that Clyde, then sat down on one of the few clear spots in the cockpit. She could see Alan leaning against the cabin of the *Verorum*, a sketch pad in his lap, looking off into the distance and drawing something in an unhurried fashion, apparently minding his own business. Watching him now from this slight distance, she felt a pang of regret that she had been so snappish earlier. He had done nothing—well, almost nothing—to deserve her display of bad temper. But enough self-recrimination for now; back to the matter at hand—finding out what, if anything, Clyde knew about the removal of Onterdonck's belongings. Beyond him, the *Non-Amo-Te* swung lazily around the mooring. "That's a pretty boat, too," she said, pointing at the *Non-Amo-Te*.

"Ayuh," said Clyde. "A real beauty. Pete Onterdonck's boat, but he went and brained hisself good on it t'other day and done got killed. Jeezum, ya nevah know." Clyde shook his head, looking back at her. "S'pose you heard?"

"Yes, I did. It was in the papers. What a sad story," Roz replied.

"Ayuh, turrible, turrible. His only kin, that's Roger Fell, now *he's* not one to appreciate a boat like that, not with him likin' all that gadgetry and fancy stuff. Doesn't matter, though, word is Onterdonck left everything to the Wildlife Conservancy or some such. Haw!" Clyde crowed unexpectedly. "Serves old Roger right, far as that goes!" Seeing the unalloyed joy on Clyde's face, Roz remembered Thaxter Waite's comment about Roger Fell's lack of popularity among the locals.

" 'Spect they'll be putting the boat up for sale now," Clyde added, examining what looked like a partially melted-down Slinky he was holding in one hand. "That's prob'ly why they had 'em come get all the gear and sich. S'pose that nature outfit couldn't make any use of Pete's stuff. Wicked decent of 'em, if ya ask me, for all he cared—there was awful bad blood between those two families, ya know, and all ovah them two littly islands over Cape Rosier way."

Wait a minute! Roz kept on nodding politely, her ears twitching like Thumper's, desperately trying to sort out Clyde's use of pronouns. "He" who? " 'Em" what? "Gear and sich"? Was he saying what she thought he was?

"Ayuh," Clyde continued, purposefully tinking his wrench on the Slinky, which began to disassemble in his lap. "Ol' Roger couldn't even be bothered to do it hisself; sent a coupla his yard apes up here with a bunch a' packing boxes. Course, he's been out a' town all week on business I hear, down Boston way. Prob'ly in a vault somewheres countin' his money. Hoo-eee!" Clyde guffawed. "Anyway, as I was sayin', yestiddy noon this was, they come ter gid it; had to catch the tide, a' course— jeezum, she's some piece a' work, that *Jolly Roger*—plunked them big plow anchors down t'other side a' the town dock, and came toolin' over here in the twenty-foot lifeboat they usually keep hung up on davits for rescuing people what jump over-board during them big drunken parties a' his'n. Saw 'em myself, took back a dozen or so boxes all sealed up with tape nice and neat and stowed 'em aboard just like that. Betcha Fell don't even know what's in 'em, and don't care, neither. He never did have no use for Pete, nor Pete for him. Probably send the whole lot straight to Goodwill without even openin' 'em, far as that goes. Course poor ol' Pete's likely rolling in his grave already at the thought of *Non-Amo-Te* shove up hyar in Thax's yard 'stead of at the Hinckley boys' over to Southwest. Those two couldn't agree on anything—they uster go at it hammer and tongs, and that's a fact. Some kind of rivalry there, all right— oh, you leavin'?"

Roz had risen so fast the boat was rocking slightly in its cradle. "Ah, yes. Sorry to rush off like this, but I think I see my ah . . . crew waving, must be time . . . to go!" she blurted, as visions of the sealed boxes, contents unexamined by the absent Roger Fell himself and therefore possibly with all the goods still intact, danced like sugarplums in her head. New evidence after all! She had to get back to Alan and the *Verorum*, let him know there was still a chance if they acted quickly. "So nice to have met you, Mr. Mer—Matthew," she said, pumping his hand vigorously as she edged toward the ladder. "You've been a great help."

Leaving Clyde Merithew with a puzzled expression on his face, Roz scrambled down the ladder and sprinted for the dinghy. She lost little time rowing back to the *Verorum,* where she found that Alan had not only done the breakfast dishes but also made everything shipshape. He had put away his sketch pad and was sitting by the mast whipping lines with waxed cord from a ditty bag he had picked up at a marine supply store in Searsport. He looked up interrogatively as she pulled alongside.

"Ahoy there!" said Roz. "Let's go!"

"May I ask where?" he inquired as he tied the dinghy to and extended a hand—automatically, to be sure, but she took it anyway—to help her on board.

"Camden," she said breathlessly. "We've got to catch up to the *Jolly Roger.* Fell did remove the goods, but it's possible he hasn't done anything with them yet! He had everything taken off by a couple of flunkies just before we got here, so there's still a chance! This may be just another wild-goose chase, but it's worth a try. Come on! I'll tell you all about it on the way."

"You mean you actually got something useful out of the monumentally unforthcoming Thaxter Waite?"

"Not from him, exactly," Roz said as she ran forward and began to untie the mooring line. "Unless you count the part about a three-masted, fore-and-aft-rigged mizzen barkentine. . . ."

"No such thing," Alan said matter-of-factly as he reached over to start the engine. "That's a bark."

"Grrr," said Roz. There was no time for further comment as they got under way.

17

Spurred on by Roz's sense of urgency, they cranked the protesting engine up to top speed and motored out to just beyond the triangular stone monument marking the entrance to Belfast Harbor. The wind was already blowing briskly straight across the bay from the west; with any luck they could set the sails for a beam reach and be in Camden in an hour or two. Roz took the tiller while Alan raised the mainsail and then shook out the genoa and trimmed it with a few quick grinds of the winch, the muscles of his shoulders and forearms straining, so that Roz, watching him unobserved, was reminded once again that sailing is not for the small and weak of mind or body. As the sails filled and snapped taut, she shut off the engine, amazed as always by the sudden silence and sense of peace, the only sound now the occasional vibration of the luff against the shrouds, the creak of the old hull, the lazy squeak of the rudder post as she held the tack.

Alan came back into the cockpit and sat down next to her. "Now then, why the thrash?"

"Okay," Roz began excitedly. "Here's what I found out, not from Waite, but from this guy named Clyde Matthew—that's spelled *M-e-r-i-t-h-e-w,* in case you wondered—who's been in the yard all week working on his boat. All of Onterdonck's stuff was taken off the *Non-Amo-Te* yesterday afternoon in *sealed* boxes and put on the *Jolly Roger* by a couple of Roger Fell's 'yard apes'—I take it that means 'employees.' According to Clyde, Fell's been gone all week on business, 'down Boston way.' "

Alan nodded, listening attentively.

"So here's what I think happened: Fell, thinking he's cleared it on the murder, gives his men orders to clean out Onterdonck's boat before he leaves for Boston. So they just pile everything in boxes any which way and take it all back to the *Jolly Roger* to await his return. This was just yesterday, so there's a good chance the boxes are still on board, contents unexamined *and* intact. If we can just get our hands on those boxes before he gets back . . ."

"I hate to cast a pall on your enthusiasm," Alan interrupted, "but how do you know Fell's flunkies didn't have orders to pack up *all* Onterdonck's personal clobber, socks and drawers and drink and such, and, once out of the harbor, quietly deep-six the lot?"

"Why should they?" Roz protested. "I mean, I really can't conceive that they'd be in on it with him in the first place, and even if he weren't curious, he'd hardly give them orders to pack it all up, carefully seal it, and then proceed to heave it all overboard, would he? Wouldn't that seem awfully suspicious, not to mention wasteful—even to 'yard apes'?"

"Hmm, yes, you've got a point there. He'd hardly want to risk that." Alan sat forward and gave the starboard winch a twist. "So your idea is that they had orders to take the boxes back straightaway to the *Jolly Roger,* where they would remain untouched, awaiting Fell's return. After all, he wouldn't be in any hurry to go through them once he'd got them safe. . . . Hmm, it's just possible. I suppose it's possible as well that there's something else other than the plant press among those belongings he wants or needs to find before ditching everything."

"But listen, Alan, if we can just get to them before he does—"

"Good Lord, Roz!" Alan exclaimed. "How do you propose we do that? I mean, it's not as though you could row over in the dark of night, clamber aboard, and pop the lock the way we did on *Non-Amo-Te*—"

"Well, it's worth thinking about, isn't it?" Roz countered. "Anyway, aren't you the one who's always saying we must consider all the possibilities?"

"Ah, to be sure, 'Expect nothing, be ready for anything,'" he said, giving her a glimpse of that jaunty triangular grin that had always reminded her of an Elizabethan comedy mask.

"Did you make that one up, too?"

"Not quite. It's Zen, more or less; just a little something I picked up in the Orient. But while we're on the subject of who's thinking what, I had rather thought I'd keep myself entertained by trying to sort out the question of 'how.' For lack of any further evidence, I had quite resigned myself to dealing with the problem in the abstract over time, a little deduction here, a spot of ratiocination there, settling for the solution of the puzzle as the sole reward—whoops, sorry, I forgot Sherlock Holmes has been interdicted," he said. Shifting his glance from her to the rapidly passing shoreline, he continued. "However, I must admit this latest discovery of yours puts rather a new face on things. . . ." He fell silent, staring off into the distance, leaving Roz to wonder what was going through his mind. As far as she was concerned, it was time to give the subject a rest. After all, they wouldn't be in Camden for at least another hour.

"Look," she said, pointing to a sprawling red house with cream gingerbread trim and several turrets, on a bluff overlooking the rocky shore. "There's Aunt Jessie's cottage."

Alan turned obediently to look. "Oh, Roz, I say! There's a bonny sight! Hold on, where's my sketchbook?" he said, rising precipitately. "I must draw that green sward with all those cunning little houses lined up like bits of lace fancywork."

Just then the boat heeled sharply, its speed increasing markedly. "On the other hand, we seem to be passing by at a rather good clip," he added, grabbing onto the nearest handrail. "How's the weather helm?"

"Fine," Roz said, keeping her eyes on the telltales. "No problem; everything's under control. Why don't you just go ahead and sketch if you like. I'll tell you about Fell's boat-renaming contest."

"Bad luck to rename a boat barring a change of owner," Alan remarked absently, his hands busy scribbling in an outline of the little rickrack and and lace-tatting village. "He'll be sorry."

"Maybe we should enter," Roz suggested. "How about 'Fell Odyssey'?"

" 'Fell About'? No, I have it: 'Fel-ony'!"

" 'Most Happy Fell-a!' " countered Roz. " 'Fell's Naph-tha!' " And so it continued until Roz terminated the contest with "Fell-atio."

This kept them well occupied and in relatively good spirits until they were passing the place where the West Bay narrows between the mainland and Islesboro some two miles to the east. Here the wind grew a little skittish, changing direction around the three islands ranged along the shore of Islesboro, and Roz had to harden up several times as they came abreast of Seal and Ram Islands, and passed the outcropping of ledge called Flat Island where harbor seals congregated in the sun, plastered over the rocks as fat and glistening as garden slugs. For a time a pair of dolphins accompanied them, revolving in their twin arcs a short distance from the boat, before gliding off to parts unknown. Although Roz felt perfectly at ease handling the tiller, at one point the boat heeled over so sharply that it was all she could do to keep from letting go, and though she might at this juncture have been quite willing, even relieved, to relinquish the helm to Alan, to his credit he said nothing, did not even turn a hair, just kept on sketching in a desultory way, apparently preoccupied with his own thoughts.

Shortly past the narrows the wind settled down, and Roz swung the boat into a easy broad reach down the western shore of Islesboro. As they sailed past Gilkey Harbor, Warren, and then Job Island, she told Alan the rest of what little she had managed to glean from Thaxter Waite and how he had deflected her questions, including the one about the mysterious black ship.

"I don't suppose he means to be perverse," Alan murmured, blowing charcoal crumbs off the drawing he was working on. "He was probably raised in that old tradition of 'Loose lips sink ships.' After all, he's got a business to run that depends on goodwill and reliability, and, your Auntie Jess aside, you too are 'from away,' are you not?"

"Not exactly. I was born in Maine, you know. Right up the road. We were visiting Aunt Jessie, and I was early. But of course he doesn't know that."

Alan stared at her in amazement. "*I* didn't know that," he said finally. "But then there's a lot we don't know about each other, isn't there?"

Roz did not reply. She sat silent, hardly daring to look at him. Was he finally going to break down and tell her what it was he'd been keeping to himself ever since their quarrel?

"But never mind that now," he said briskly. "Go on with Thaxter Waite and the black ship."

Roz hid her disappointment as best she could. "Well, I did find out something vaguely useful: wherever our black ship— excuse me, schooner—went off to, it wasn't Belfast."

"Well, that's a blessing," said Alan, as though nothing had passed between them. "I fear at this point the identity of said mystery schooner is largely academic, though if there's a big fleet that sails out of Camden, perhaps one of the captains will be able to give us a clue to -RD from -*land*. I don't suppose we can completely rule out the possibility that said passengers of said windjammer might have seen or heard something and simply not realized the significance. Though tracking them down at this late date seems a further exercise in the forlorn-hope department. Which springs eternal."

Mine, too, Roz thought; when am I going to learn? "Personally," she said in an attempt at humor, "I'm convinced it was a ghost ship, an hallucination brought on by a surfeit of cheese and good wine—"

"Or bad plums," Alan returned promptly, "as the phantom Spanish sailor admonished Captain Slocum before he hopped back on the *Pinta* and sailed off with the rest of Columbus's crew." He grinned at her and she grinned back, as much as anything relieved at the sheer silliness of it all.

They fell silent once again, gazing at the shoreline in the near distance. The atmosphere was hazy, with a ghostly inversion layer reflecting the line of horizon, so that it was difficult to see where the water left off and the sky began.

"I say, Roz." Alan's voice came as though from a great distance.

Taking her eyes off their course for a moment, Roz turned to him. His eyes were on her once more, serious, intent, searching her face.

"About ah . . . things . . . I mean, us . . ." he began tentatively. Then, to her dismay, he broke off with a sharp exclamation. "Good Lord!" he said, shielding his eyes and squinting at something over her left shoulder. "I say, Roz, what the devil *is* this? A *Flying Dutchman* convention?" He was pointing at something off the port bow. "I mean the opera, of course, not the Olympic class," he explained unnecessarily, humming a few bars from Wagner's overture.

Damn, Roz thought, of all the times to be interrupted by an operatic allusion. She turned and looked where he was pointing. Sure enough, not a hundred yards away, ranging across their path from behind the southern tip of Islesboro, wavering like a heat mirage in the haze and apparently suspended in midair, were what appeared to be many huge peaked icebergs gliding along in a ghostly fashion. As Roz watched, fascinated, these apparitions resolved themselves into at least twenty complicated tentlike configurations of sails, now seen in fact to be churning across the bay toward them at a rapid rate, accompanied by the deafening sound of many great birds flapping in unison.

"Seriously, Roz!" Alan was having to shout now over the din of the approaching boats. "Ghost ships aside, what *is* this really, some sort of windjammer jamboree?"

"It must be the Great Schooner Race!" Roz yelled back. "Thaxter Waite did mention something about it, but I didn't realize it was today!" Now that she thought of it, she had a vague recollection that it was usually the second Friday in July.

One by one the tall ships, white hulls with rose and tanbark sails, green hulls with white sails, black ones with weathered canvas the color of parchment, came up on them and passed by, moving with deceptive speed through the water, peeling back the surface in a running wake that hissed against their long, sleek sides. Hordes of yellow-slickered figures lined the rails, hung on the huge winches, manned the wheels, or simply tried to keep their balance on deck, laughing and shouting and calling out to one another over the noise of the thundering sails.

Roz heard a louder hissing, splashing sound behind her, and turned to see a huge, dark shape bearing down on them with every sail flying, its dark hull foaming fiercely through the water, coming on so fast that hull, sails, passengers, and all were nothing but a blur.

"Alan, look out!" She barely had time to shriek before the huge sails blotted out the sun. She covered her eyes and quickly put the tiller over, hoping they could tack out of the way in time. The huge windjammer sluiced by, its wake washing up and drenching the cockpit. A near miss.

"Bloody lunatics!" Alan howled in outrage, shaking his fist after them. "Did you see that? They nearly ran us down! Roz, quick! Get her name!"

Roz opened her eyes, but it was too late; the boat had already rounded the mark, a bell-buoy near the largest of three small islands in the bay, and was sailing away broadside to them, pulling into the middle of the pack. One by one the rest tacked around in a more sedate fashion, their triangular scooting silhouettes turning to narrow quills as they proceeded down the bay.

Alan turned to Roz in a positive fury, water streaming down his face. "Damned idiots!" he muttered, wringing out his shirt. "The crew have no business letting a bunch of amateurs handle a boat like that in these conditions. But they'll be sorry. We'll jolly well report them to the Coast Guard for not giving way and sailing to endanger. We'll have their license before we're done."

"I didn't get the name," Roz said, watching the long line of schooners sway one after another down the bay like a string of shark's teeth.

Alan stared at her in disbelief, water still streaming down his face as the *Verorum* bobbed gently in the confused, still-washing wake of the massed schooners. "You didn't?"

"No, but we're in luck."

Alan looked at her dubiously. "May I ask how nearly getting swamped by a large, apparently nameless ketch-rigged sailing vessel run amok qualifies as luck?"

"That's every schooner in the fleet out there, and more besides. If I remember correctly, they finish up at the Rockland breakwater, then all head back to Camden for a big boat parade."

"Oh, that explains it," Alan said acidly as he wrung out the bottom of his shirt.

"No, Alan, you don't understand. It's a challenge race. All the big boats in the whole area take part in this race, not just the schooners. You can't refuse if you want to keep on the good side of the locals: it's just not done. That means the *Jolly Roger*'s bound to be here. Maybe even our so-called black ship, too! After the boat parade, there's a big bonfire and party on the beach, even a beer tent. Everybody goes—skippers, crew, passengers, the whole bunch. *Everybody*," she repeated, trying to impress on Alan the significance of this wholesale exodus. Or had he forgotten their real purpose in being here? "Don't you suppose," she prodded, "while they're all over there carousing, a person might have a chance to do a little poking around?"

" 'A person,' eh? 'Poking around,' is it then?" He planted his hands on his hips, frowning at her. "And what, may I ask, happened to that nice scruple of yours about violating other people's property? I note, however, that your underdeveloped sense of danger is still intact."

"Oh, come on, Alan, it's perfect!" she said in exasperation.

He did not look convinced.

18

"Given this schooner soiree of yours, don't you suppose the harbor is likely to be full up?" Alan said as they rounded the neck of land at the mouth of Camden Harbor and motored their way between a rather large, rocky island and an impressive array of red nuns, green cans, and orange day beacons.

Roz had gone forward to break down the foresail, leaving Alan at the helm for the tricky business of threading the gauntlet into Camden Harbor. He was steering with one hand and with the other endeavoring to turn the pages of the *Cruising Guide* he had balanced on his knee. "It says here," he said now, "that as a place to spend a quiet night Camden is a 'dead loss.' Rather odd choice of words, wouldn't you say, not to mention its curious relevance, puns aside, to the case in point?"

"It's not *my* schooner soiree, it's the Chamber of Commerce's," Roz replied as she finished bagging the jib and tying it down around the forestay. "And who said anything about spending a quiet night?" She glanced over her shoulder at him to see if he had made anything of her inadvertently suggestive choice of words. Apparently not; there he sat, head bent, poring over the pages of the *Guide*. What were you going to tell me?

she wanted to say to him. What is it we don't know about each other? But his mind was clearly elsewhere.

"There follow," he said now, "some extremely detailed directions on how to find a mooring, on the order of 'failing this and failing that, please go on to Plans C, D, E, and F.' At which point we shall find ourselves parked back out in mid-bay, which is, I needn't point out, a very long row to get to where, in your estimation at any rate, the action is," he concluded, looking up at her with an expression of mild reproach.

"Don't worry," Roz said, turning her attention to the release of the main halyard. "It's early yet. The schooner parade isn't even in sight. They've got to come all the way up from the Rockland breakwater. There'll be room."

"Ever the optimist, I see," Alan replied. "I hope you're right; according to this there's a crackerjack bookstore in town. One could conceivably browse that. There's a book I want to find. How about you? Got enough to read?"

She looked at him for signs of irony, but his attention had been distracted by the necessity of avoiding a large catboat barging its squat way out to sea. Cursing under his breath, he reached down and turned on the engine, then stood up to steer while hauling in the mainsail with his other hand.

As it turned out, Roz was too optimistic. As they chugged their way into the inner harbor, it was clear the place was already chock-a-block with floating vessels of every kind and description: sailboats, motor cruisers, lobster and fishing boats, skiffs, rowboats, shells, wherries, runabouts, even a pair of windsurfers dipping and looping precariously around the floats and various boats rafted together in twos, threes, and fours on either side of the narrow channel and all along both sides of the narrow harbor. "One wouldn't even have to wet a slipper to get to the other side," Alan remarked as they slowed to a crawl and scanned the floating docks for enough space to land the *Verorum*.

"How they're ever going to get all those schooners in here I can't imagine," Roz said. "What this place needs is a traffic cop."

"None other than," Alan said, nodding toward a harried-looking figure in a battered but official-looking launch with what appeared to be police cruiser lights on top. He was wearing a white yachtsman's cap with a large shiny badge attached, and as they watched he began gesticulating with one arm and shouting through a bullhorn to some windsurfers, who collapsed with their finlike sails into the water, laughing, and began to paddle toward shore.

"I say, Roz, it doesn't look terribly promising."

"Look, there's a big empty space over there," she said, pointing to a well-kept wharf above a series of floating docks several hundred yards long that took up nearly the whole east side of the harbor, all the way up to what appeared to be a fancy condominium complex on the point. With its turrets and bays, fancy woodwork and wide eaves ranked in terraces up the hill, it looked like a gray-shingled version of Angkor Wat. Several good-sized sailboats were docked in slips at either end of the wharf, but the rest was bare. "It looks like they have plenty of room. Let's head over."

"Right-o," Alan replied agreeably, and carefully began maneuvering the *Verorum* between a pocket schooner attached to a large white mooring ball and its near neighbor, a lobster boat bobbing practically in mid-channel. "Hmm. Spiffy ramps and pilings, all on the straight and level, boards look to be quite new, barely weathered, not a barnacle in sight. And, I might add, some very expensive-looking yachts tied up at either end. Looks a bit pricey. We may have to skip dinner," he added solemnly.

As Alan brought the *Verorum* alongside the floating dock, Roz hopped off with the docking lines and was just wrapping one around a cleat to pull the boat in when a young man in a blue coverall ran down the gangway, waving at them, followed at some distance by an elderly man in a khaki shirt and trousers. Embroidered over the pocket and on the back were the words *Seafarer's Marine*. "I'm sorry," the young man said officiously, "but you can't dock here. This is reserved for another boat."

"All of it?" Alan remarked with a look of disbelief. "My

dear lad, there must be nearly two hundred feet here. Surely you can spare ten yards or so.''

The young man shook his head, clearly impressed by Alan's manner, if not his reasoning. "Sorry, sir—"

"That's okay, Jack," the older man interrupted. "I'll handle this." He had come down onto the dock and was standing with his hands on his hips, looking the *Verorum* up and down, grinning his head off. Ha, another old Herreshoff nut, Roz thought. Maybe we'll get some dock space after all.

"Well, now, will ya look who's here?" he crowed. "If it ain't *Verorum,* as I live and breathe. Heard she was back on the briny! Lookin' good, old girl, lookin' good."

As Roz stared at him, wondering at his tone of familiarity, he squatted down and patted the *Verorum*'s bright mahogany toe-rail, admired the bronze winch-mounts, and ran his fingers up and down the nearest stay. "Hmmm, brand-new standin' riggin', brightwork taken right down to the bare wood . . . They sure do good work over to Northeast, I'll say that for 'em. Ayahwp." He stood up, hands folded over his belt, eyes crinkled into slits, nodding like a porcelain mandarin doll. "Slack off that docking line there, Jack. This here's Miz Jessie True's boat, and we can always find a spot for an old cuss like her." He turned to Roz. "Where's Jessie at?" he said, ducking down and peering through the nearest porthole. "Jessie True, you old rascal," he called, "you in there?" He stood up again with a mildly disappointed look. "Where's she got to? Never knew the *Verorum* to sail without her." An expression of horror crossed his face. "Don't tell me she's up and sold 'er?"

Roz quickly introduced herself and Alan, hoping the lack of Aunt Jessie actually on board in person would not cause him to rescind his offer of dock space. She went on to explain the circumstances of their cruise—an edited version, that is.

"Hip replacement, huh? In't she a caution! Can't wait to see her and those gals of hers tearin' up the waves again." He shook his head, chuckling. "Okay now, let's get you folks squared away before the schooner fleet gets here—you happened to hit the big race day, you know it? But we'll take care a' ya.

Just bring her down around there," he directed, gesturing toward an empty slip at the far end of the dock toward the condominium-infested point. "Better make it toot sweet, too. My dock boy wasn't just whistlin' 'Dixie' about that space being spoken for; it's reserved for the *Jolly Roger,* belongs to a guy name of Roger Fell. Biggest goddamned sloop you ever saw, hundred-twenty feet on the waterline if she's an inch, mast like a jeesly conning tower." As Roz and Alan exchanged a glance, he nattered right on. "Don't know where they're at right now, but the crew radioed awhile back that they'd be in tonight, so I expect we'll be seeing 'em sooner or later. There you are, this oughter do ya. Any problems, anything you need, you just lemme know." And with that, before either of them could say "thank you," he was off down the wharf.

With the aid of Jack the dock boy, they had just settled the *Verorum* into her slip when the first of the schooners appeared in the outer harbor. Under full sail, topgallants and streamers, flags and ensigns flying, one-, two-, and three-masted, with white hulls and black hulls, tan and green and red hulls, spanking white and weathered cream sails, tanbark and rose-colored, they passed through the narrow channel between the outer islands. Moving now in close formation, they reminded Roz of a line of stately cathedrals seen from a distance, ghostly towers and steeples and flying buttresses that seemed as you moved toward them rather to be moving themselves across the landscape, immense, deliberate, possessed of some lofty secret knowledge. They reminded her of nothing so much as the sight of Ely, that magnificent cathedral seen from afar standing so gloriously high and serene above the flat English fens. Ely: also the town where she and Alan had spent their first night together. She wondered if Alan were having similar thoughts. She looked over at him. He was gazing around at all the boats. She sighed. Probably not.

Meanwhile, one by one the tall ships were rounding the point of the rocky island and came up into the wind, huge sails fluttering and rumbling like thunderheads, and suddenly it was impossible to make out each boat individually as they milled about, some dropping sail, running out anchors amid shouts and screams and sounds of great hilarity. Spectators lined the docks and shores of the harbor, many with binoculars and cameras at the ready. Several of the boats, their sails now down and being furled by gangs of passengers, continued into the inner harbor either under their own power or nudged along by smaller boats like pilot fish, finding their way into berths reserved for them as members of the Camden windjammer fleet: *Roseway* and *Adventure, Mattie* and *Mercantile, Mary Day, Angelique,* and *Stephen Taber,* as well as a number of other, smaller boats whose names Roz could not make out. Many more schooners slowly bobbed at anchor in the cove back in between the island and the further headland.

"Quite a show," Alan said at her shoulder. "Gives a whole new meaning to one's concept of the Spanish Armada, does it not? Look at them all gathered there, like so many birds of paradise." She turned her head to look up at him, but he had already moved off down the deck and was gazing speculatively, not at her, but at the massed windjammers. "Hmm," he said. "I'd rather like to have a go at finding those lunatics in the overcanvassed ketch-rig that nearly ran us down out there. There can't be too many of those about; most of what we have here appear to be mostly your run-of-the-mill schooners, barring a Friendship sloop or two."

"I thought they were all schooners," she said.

"Not a bit of it. All may be referred to as windjammers, according to local usage, but the term *schooner* can only be used to describe your large sailing vessel with two or more masts, fore-and-aft-rigged, the fore or mizzenmast—that's the one in front—the same height or shorter than the mainmast. Didn't Thaxter Waite cover that in his lecture?"

"Maybe he did," said Roz. "After a while I stopped listening. So what does that make the black ship, then?"

"Our old friend the mysterious -RD from -*land*? You had a better look at her than I did; I was rather preoccupied, if you'll recall," he said. "I only saw her from the rear as she was pulling away—hard to tell exactly what's what in sail plans when you're looking up the back of a boat tearing by under full sail, clinging to a ladder mother-naked and bloody freezing into the bargain.''

"You saw enough of her—it—to let Roger Fell know it wasn't a topsail schooner," she said accusingly.

"Yes, but that's perfectly obvious, a whacking great square topsail set on the foremast; you can hardly miss it," he said. "It certainly wasn't one of those."

"Well, it had two masts, all right," Roz replied. She tried to recall the configuration of sails, but all she could see in her mind's eye were two high, peaked sails like dark evergreens. Foresail and topgallant? But which mast was higher? "I'm pretty sure the rear mast was taller, or maybe they were the same height—oh, I don't know, Alan! All I'm really sure of is the long, dark hull and shabby-looking sails, and those letters on the stern."

"Transom," Alan corrected absently. "Well, we'll just take it as read that she was a schooner, not that it really matters a great deal. We do have the letters to go on as well. I suppose we might as well have look for her while we're trying to locate that renegade ketch. If, as you say, it's likely every large vessel in the reasonable vicinity is either here or on the way, we should make quick work of our reconnoiter. On second thought," he remarked as he scanned the harbor, "dark hulls do appear to outnumber light by roughly two to one, tatty canvas sails abound, and names are not uniformly visible, at least from my particular angle of vision. And damned few ketches as well, from the looks of it. Still, I expect we'd might as well be at it." He bent down, untied the dinghy and swung it around, hopped down into it, and began fitting the oars. He glanced up to where she was still standing by the mast. "I say, you are coming with me, aren't you?"

"I'm feeling a bit tired; I think I'll just stay here," she said. "You go ahead, though." She slid down into a sitting position on the cabin top, her back propped against the mast, and gazed out to sea.

Alan rowed a few strokes around the hull and sat in the dinghy facing her. He seemed about to say something, then obviously thought the better of it. "Goodbye for now," he said, then bent to the stroke, dug the oars in hard; the little dinghy spurted through the water.

She watched him row away, face now turned away from her in profile, looking over his shoulder as he stroked his way evenly around one boat after the other in the crowded harbor, his figure growing smaller and smaller as he rowed toward the schooners, until he resembled nothing so much as some strange water bug as it scooted into the thicket of boats moored behind the rocky point, and disappeared.

Then she turned her attention to the other direction, where she could just barely make out a large billowing shape striped in multiple hues of red, gold, and green bobbing along the horizon out beyond the farthest channel marker, looking about as much at home as some great, exotic bird of paradise. As she watched, the balloon resolved into a giant balloon-shaped sail, and behind it, the absence of skull and crossbones notwith-standing, unmistakable, the tall mast and long, sleek shape of none other than the *Jolly Roger,* coming home to roost.

THREE

JOLLY ROGER

19

She supposed it was possible for a boat to have not one but
two spinnakers the size of football fields; she was vaguely aware
that certain sailboats belonging to serious, not to say completely
obsessed, sailors—those "on the circuit," for example—had
whole wardrobes of sails that took up more cabin space on
board than passengers and crew. Or perhaps this gaudy red-,
green-, and gold-striped number served a slightly different function of which she, not being the world's foremost expert on
sail-rigs, was unaware.

At any rate, it ought to be amusing to watch, from her ringside
seat on the *Verorum,* the maneuvers necessary to bring this
enormous vessel through the crowded harbor and alongside the
dock at Seafarer's, where space the length of two football fields
had been reserved. Getting a camel through the eye of a needle
was nothing to this; the boat looked more like a small aircraft
carrier than a yacht. She wondered whether Alan had noticed
its—whoops, make that "her"—arrival from wherever he was
now; "she" was a little hard to miss, the great mast towering
over all the other boats in the harbor so that she—or they—
looked oddly out of scale, as though she were the one life-sized

boat surrounded by a bunch of toys, a fat white mother goose surrounded by a fleet of tiny goslings. And the heck with this "she" business; as far as she, Roz, was concerned, boats always had been and could go right on being referred to, at least by her, as "it."

The great hull slowed perceptibly as soon as the *Jolly Roger* had passed the first channel marker, almost as though someone had slammed on the brakes. The multicolored sail suddenly shivered, then narrowed down to a pulsing funnel shape like a tornado, and was instantly sucked down into some sort of hole in the foredeck. Behind it the mainsail began to shrink vertically in a rapid fashion, and shortly disappeared into the mast with a hissing noise. From her vantage point, Roz could see a whole troop—half a dozen, anyway—of figures clad in black overalls with white piping, swarming over the deck attending to this or that part of the landing drill. She couldn't see anyone in the cockpit steering—if that is what you called it, as opposed to aiming—the way Roger Fell had been that day they saw him at Restitution Island, but she presumed someone must be running the boat from somewhere, as it by no means seemed to be operating at random.

With truly admirable grace and efficiency the *Jolly Roger* threaded its way through the maze of boats as if by magic, turning here and gliding there, the thrum of its engines a barely audible vibration in the air, presently sliding by Roz and the *Verorum* and coming to a standstill precisely one yard away from the floating dock, an instant after a row of cocoon-shaped rubber fenders the size of trash barrels had exploded out of the hull at various strategic locations to cushion—unnecessarily— the landing. Ha, thought Roz from where she sat in the shadow of the huge yacht, craning her neck upward the full three stories of the superstructure, this is not a boat, it's a floating precipice.

The hum of the engines stopped abruptly, and all was quiet. Just as Roz was beginning to wonder how people got on and off—she was thinking in terms of an elevator of some sort and had begun to scrutinize the lower part of the hull for an appropriate opening—one of the black-overalled young men appeared at the rail approximately amidships and flung open what turned out to be a gate of some sort, which in turn initiated the operation of an apparatus consisting of accordion-pleated metal plates that proceeded to arch outward some twenty feet, unfolding as it went, until it gently settled into place with a clank on the upper tier of the wharf.

Jack the dock boy came running up and bent to the application of several clamps or screws that apparently served to affix the ramp to the wharf, nodding to one of the overall-clad young men, who shouted, "Thanks," turned, and disappeared through a door of the cabin on the main deck. Meanwhile another young man at the stern and one at the bow had thrown down coils of rope the size of fire hoses to two others waiting on the dock, who wrapped them around wooden cleats the size of fire hydrants. So much for docking lines, thought Roz.

She went down below and got out the binoculars, and, taking up what she hoped was a fairly inconspicuous position in the companionway of the *Verorum,* continued to watch the activity on the *Jolly Roger.* So far she had seen no sign of Roger Fell himself, but that wasn't too surprising, since he was supposed to be "down Boston way." She counted five crew members— all compact, muscular-looking young people with sunburned faces and sun-streaked hair, a matched set in overalls with skull and crossbones cleverly appliquéd on each back and the name *Jolly Roger,* along with "Tom," "Dick," "Harry" (actually the name on his back was "Steve W.," and he was the only one with dark hair; the rest had hair in various shades of red-gold, with accompanying freckles), "Pete," and "Sheila" (and why not, there was nothing that said a deckhand couldn't be female, was there?) embroidered over the front pockets—going about numerous making-fast and shipshaping activities.

But who was in charge? She'd been a witness to Roger Fell's remarkable solo virtuoso performance in the cove between the two islands, but this was obviously a whole new operetta with a different set of players. Who had brought the boat in so expertly? And where was he—or she; there wasn't anything that said the skipper couldn't be a woman, either—hiding? The balconylike cockpit in the center of the uppermost deck that Roz, for lack of a better term, still thought of as the *Phantom of the Opera* set, had remained conspicuously empty throughout.

As if in answer to her question, a rather gnomish-looking, weatherbeaten, but clearly authoritative older man wearing an unadorned khaki-colored uniform of pants and shirt that accentuated his barrel chest, a matching hat with a captain's badge affixed to the center above the visor, and "Capt. Sidney" something-or-other embroidered on his pocket strutted out a door on the second deck—really more of a mezzanine between the open cockpit and the main deck—and stood for a moment looking around the boat, glancing in turn at the gangway, the docking lines, the mast, the various coils of rope and gear. In due course he nodded, went back inside, and emerged onto the main deck a few minutes later with a large duffel bag. He paused at the gangway to speak to one of the hands, who was busy coiling lines into shapes resembling beehives. Struggling to read his lips, Roz made out only "Mr. Fell . . . back Tuesday . . . in charge." Lowering the binoculars, she watched Captain Sidney duck-walk across the gangplank onto the wharf and away up the driveway toward a waiting taxicab. Shore leave. Either that or he was going to do his laundry. Somehow she didn't think the *Jolly Roger* lacked such facilities; she wouldn't be surprised if there were an entire laundromat tucked away in there.

Hmmm, thought Roz. A crew of six, including a professional captain. These must be the hired hands, kept at the ready to run the boat when Fell wasn't on board to do it himself, probably to help out on more extended cruises as well. She lowered the binoculars and sat herself down on the top step of the *Verorum*'s companionway, continuing to observe the proceedings on board the giant yacht.

The boat's arrival had already attracted considerable attention, and Roz noticed that there were several young women now lined up along the wharf near where the gangplank had been attached, whose presence in turn appeared to have attracted the attention of the crew member to whom Captain Sidney had spoken about being in charge as he was leaving. As Roz watched, one of the young women, tall, blond, quite fetchingly clad in shorts and a halter top, engaged him in animated conversation across the gangway, smiling and giggling. After several minutes of this, the young man, smiling and nodding, beckoned the girl and her friends to come aboard. Squealing with excitement, they advanced over the gangway one by one, stepping gingerly on the panels, and were graciously handed onto the deck by the young man. They stood around him, craning their necks and oohing and aahing, pointing at various fittings around and about the main deck, the young man responding with short explanations, accompanied by much flashing of very white, very straight teeth. Shortly he motioned to them to follow him through one of the doors into the superstructure, and they all disappeared inside what appeared to be the main cabin. They must be about to get the grand tour.

Roz sat in the companionway of the *Verorum* for a few more moments, thinking. Then she went below to check her wardrobe.

When she emerged some ten minutes later, mascaraed and rouged within an inch of her life, the young women were just trooping out onto the uppermost level of the yacht. Three male crew members were now in attendance, and the little group milled around the top deck for a brief period—the young women clearly not as interested in the technicalities of sailing a ship this size as they had been with the fascinations of its interior. Then the group, chatting and laughing amiably, descended a steep, almost ladderlike stairway to the main deck, and proceeded past two lifeboats hung on davits to a glass-enclosed rear deckhouse that appeared to be some sort of lounge. Rock music boomed, but not before Roz heard the clink of ice cubes, the setting up of glasses, the popping of beer tops.

Scanning the harbor for any sign of a returning dinghy, Roz

adjusted the neckline of her low-cut, nearly backless sundress. Sorry, Alan, but there are times when one just has to seize the moment. But really, with all those people on board, and Roger Fell clearly not, there could hardly be any danger. Flapping her heavily mascaraed eyelashes experimentally, she stepped off the *Verorum* onto the floating dock, put her slingback high-heeled sandals on, and sashayed along the wharf as far as the metal gangplank that led to the *Jolly Roger*.

It took her several minutes to attract the attention of one of the two remaining crew members not involved in the jollities taking place in the glass-enclosed lounge, but that was all right; it gave her time to rehearse her story. She had decided to stick as close to the truth as possible regarding time and place, with one or two important exceptions, so when the serious-looking black-overalled young man with "Steve W." inscribed over his breast pocket came over to the opening in the rail and inquired politely, "May I help you, miss?" she was ready.

"Hello, my name is Roz Howard, and that's my boat over there," she responded in a firm voice with just a hint of a Maine drawl, gesturing back at the *Verorum,* which was looking very small in the shadow of the hulking *Jolly Roger* but also very classic in its lack of ostentation, an appearance not entirely lost on the young man, who glanced appreciatively at it and then back at her, also appreciatively. "I . . . ah . . . was with Mr. Fell on the *Jolly Roger* last weekend. . . ." She paused, smiled sheepishly, letting Steve W. work out the possible implications of that statement, then breezed on in a tone of mixed relief and embarrassment. "I'm so glad to have caught up with him again, because after I left I found I'd left my bag on board, and I was just fit to be tied—you know, my driver's license, passport, Gold Card, the whole works."

Steve W. nodded with polite interest, standing almost at attention by the gate. Roz leaned closer, burbling on, "I just couldn't believe my eyes when I saw you coming in, such luck, I was really desperate, thinking about making all those damned phone calls"—here it occurred to her to supply a convincing detail or two to imply a certain, one might say, intimacy—"of course I didn't recognize you right away without that outrageous skull-and-crossbones spinnaker of Roger's—"

"Yes, ma'am," said Steve helpfully. "Mr. Fell's trying out a new one. He's changing the name. So we had to get all new sail insignia, refit the—"

"Oh, what a pity! I thought *Jolly Roger* was so appropriate for dear old Roger—he's such a dashing buccaneer himself! What a pirate!" Roz gushed as she placed a foot on the metal bridge, hoping to forestall a technical discussion that might take too much time and possibly blow her cover. And then there was the time factor. She wanted to get on and off before Alan came back and started wondering where she'd gone, or, worse yet (since, let's face it, that would be fairly obvious), came looking for her. She moved cautiously toward the middle of the gangplank, trying not to catch her heel. Squeals and giggles mixed with bits of dialogue floated over from the glass-enclosed deckhouse.

"All that Italian marble, travertine, alabaster, different-colored stone in each bathroom, and gold taps. . . . I never dreamed . . ." "That's 'head,' Diane, on boats they're called heads. . . ." "Even when they have Jacuzzis?" came a puzzled female voice. "And the three kitchens . . . ," chimed in another. "That's 'galleys.' " "Yeah, but one's really only a wet bar. . . ." "Okay, whatever, but you know what *really* got me was the organ in the saloon or whatever you call it—I mean, I thought the two grand pianos in the upstairs lounge were pretty wild. . . ."

"Listen, ah . . . Steve," Roz said, sidling confidentially toward the young man, "I know Roger—ah, Mr. Fell—isn't available at the moment, but I'm leaving first thing in the morning, and I wondered if you could just let me look for my bag. . . ."

"Oh, no problem," Steve said amiably, standing aside to let her pass. "You know where you left it?"

"Um, I have a pretty good idea," Roz said, fluttering her eyelashes and mustering the best unmaidenly blush she could under the circumstances.

"Yeah, okay, well, I guess you must know your way around,"

Steve said, apparently without irony. "Why don't you just go ahead down below and find your bag while I report in? Just holler if you need any help."

"Thank you so much, Steve." She watched him start to climb the stairs to the mezzanine, then turned and went through the nearest doorway into the main cabin of the *Jolly Roger,* just as though she knew exactly where she was going—and nearly fell headlong down an elegant but extremely steep and narrow flight of stairs.

20

Quickly recovering herself, she grasped the brass railings on either side of the tunnellike stairwell and tiptoed down.

The stair opened into a large space, obviously the living room—make that "main saloon." It took a few seconds for her eyes to become accustomed to the dark interior, and when they did, she could hardly believe what she was seeing. If the *Non-Amo-Te* had been the nautical equivalent of a swank Park Avenue apartment, *this* was something else entirely. It was as though she were standing in a scaled-down version of one of the grandiose receiving rooms at Hampton Court or Versailles. Fell—or his decorator—must have bought out the interior of some Jacobean manor and installed it all—the whole nine yards and more—right here. This isn't a real sailboat, she sneered to herself, it's Roger Fell's designer playpen. What we have here is a seagoing stately home. It all fit—in more ways than one: Roger the Raider strikes again. The National Trust should get a load of this; piracy isn't the half of it. She tiptoed into the center of the room and peered around her.

Dark, richly patinaed linenfold mahogany paneling lined the walls and ceiling, lit softly by brass chandeliers with tiny flame-shaped bulbs. The fireplace, of rose-colored marble in a swirled pattern resembling clouds at sunset, was surmounted by a mantelpiece carved in the ornate style of knobs and arches, fluted pilasters and cornices, a large murky oil painting of indeterminate but obviously violent subject over it. The deep rose color of the marble was repeated in the velvet-covered settee and matching chairs arranged around the fireplace, and luxuriant, ruby-toned Oriental rugs covered the hardwood floor. Opposite the fireplace was another ornate wooden paneled fixture that Roz, moving forward in a daze, recognized as an intricately caparisoned pump organ of ancient and clearly religious provenance. On either side were a pair of framed and backlit stained-glass windows—Fell must have hit a church or two while he was at it.

Looking around purposefully (after all, she was supposed to be searching for something, wasn't she? Suppose there were hidden cameras?) while she backed toward the far side of the room, she was momentarily confused by a kaleidoscopic picture of herself reflected in the mirror backs of several gallery display cases let into the paneled walls, softly lit and full of all kinds of delicate-looking bric-a-brac—if that was the term for such obviously precious objects of silver, gold, and gemstone arranged along the shelves, including a series of scroll-shaped conch shells burnished to a pearly sheen, lined up in graduated sizes from one the size of a thimble up to one as big as a megaphone. But what do they do when the boat heels? Roz wondered. Or isn't it allowed to? She gave the largest conch shell a little push. It didn't move. Neither did any of the other items, all firmly fixed in place. So that's how it's done, Roz thought. Everything glued, nailed, or screwed down. A place for everything and everything in its place.

Everything, that is, except the boxes.

Making a show of lifting up a tapestry-covered throw cushion, she ostentatiously shook her head and looked perplexed, then plumped it up carefully and put it back. Okay, so they're not in here. Where to next?

There appeared to be only one way out, other than back up

on deck. Roz marched through the paneled opening into the passageway beyond. A door to her left opened on what was obviously the "powder room," with its gold-streaked, translucent alabaster walls and matching marble vanity, blond porcelain fixtures, and, sure enough, gold taps and faucet. Even the flush handle was gold. Sleeping Beauty's bathroom. She couldn't imagine anyone actually using it except a fairy-tale princess, and everyone knows they never have to.

The short passage opened out onto what must be the dining room: chinoiserie fabric wallpaper above pale wood wainscoting; sconces with candles lit; another fireplace in gray speckled stone flanked by two cupboards full of fine china and glassware; a long, stately table surrounded by eight Louis XIV chairs in cream enamel gilt; champagne-colored, tapestry-embroidered seats; a silver-gilt epergne in the center; two silver-gilt peacocks set at either end. Nice, but what happened to this stuff in heavy weather? Did Tom, Dick, Pete, Steve, and Sheila rush down and replace everything with plastic cups and paper plates at the first sign of a swell? Hardly likely. But surely all this couldn't be glued down too, could it, all just for show? But that wasn't what she was here for, to check out Roger Fell's housekeeping arrangements. Time to move on.

As she passed, Roz gave a gentle nudge to one of the peacocks; to her surprise the bird skittered easily across the polished surface. She leaned forward against the edge to put it back . . . and recoiled as the whole table seemed to give way under her. Stepping back, she watched it sway gently back and forth, contents and all. Of course, that explained it. It was hung on gimbals, capable of staying level even when the boat heeled. She walked over to the nearest cabinet and gave it a good shove. It gyrated briefly in several directions, then swiveled to a stop without rattling a single glass. Maybe this wasn't such a pantywaist boat after all; it was well set up for heavy weather, even ninety-degree rolls. Of course, all the passengers would be standing on their beam-ends, but the table and glassware would be just fine.

Having ascertained through her seemingly random, slightly

distracted explorations that there were no boxes stuffed anywhere in here, Roz continued through the door at the end of
the room and found herself in a narrow, rather more utilitarian
passageway lined with several sliding doors. This looked more
like a storage area. She opened the first door; a gleaming
kitchen assaulted her eye with stainless steel, fluorescent lighting, white porcelain restaurant-sized appliances, huge steaming
tables, an industrial-model dishwasher, a walk-in refrigerator-
freezer, and cupboards galore. But no boxes. This was followed
by a series of pantry-sized rooms, the last announcing with its
low hum of machinery and complicated array of pipes, dials
and valves its function as the utility-generator–engine room. It
took Roz a moment to realize that what she took for a huge
ovoid stainless-steel boiler running up through the ceiling was
actually the bottom of the mast. No boxes here, either. Roz
was beginning to feel as though she were getting rather far
afield—or awash.

Just past the engine room, a metal ladder led upward through
a well-like opening. Cautiously Roz climbed up, listened briefly,
then poked her head above the rim of the well into what appeared to be an auxiliary control room for NASA: buttons and
dials and screens and digital readouts, half a dozen radiotele-
phones and wirelesses, walls covered with charts. And there,
in front of a lavish padded-leather swivel seat, was a wheel
affixed to a large pedestal compass, and next to it a lever conspicuously marked "Autopilot." Ha! So that was it. This must
be where the action was, as far as running the ship went, when
Fell himself wasn't doing it from the *Phantom of the Opera*
cockpit upstairs.

Craning her neck in the other direction, she saw through a
set of sliding glass doors a modern-looking lounge area with a
long, polished brass-and-mahogany bar, leather-covered set-
tees—and, sure enough, two white baby-grand pianos standing
face-to-face. Loud laughter sounded close by; Roz ducked down
quickly and scurried away from the stairwell. She waited a few
moments, then opened the last door. A large cabin with an
arrangement of bunks and hammocks, built-in drawers, all very

plain, must be the quarters for the crew. It looked as though she had come to the end of the line as far as this level went. But she hadn't seen any guest staterooms, let alone the master suite; she must have missed them somewhere along the way. She would have to retrace her steps, and that meant traipsing all the way back aft. But she had to locate the boxes before Steve W. realized how long she had been down here. She wished she'd thought to bring along a purse to bolster her story. But it was too late now. And where were the boxes? Maybe Fell had simply deep-sixed them after all.

Hurriedly making her way back to the saloon, she found what she had missed on her headlong entry down the flight of stairs. Adjacent to the companionway, almost hidden in the paneling, was a door that opened into another passageway. Opening it, she found herself in some sort of square foyer with more doors—six of them to be exact, counting the one at the far end. All except the one facing her were ajar, the interiors visible. Pausing to listen once again, all she heard was the hiss and gurgle of the built-in tropical-fish tank at her elbow. Opposite was another head, done in black and chrome, including two urinals, the Prince Charming counterpart of the Sleeping Beauty powder room.

She peered quickly into one after another of the guest staterooms, for that is what these obviously were, each done in a different period style, from Early American with its antique four-poster and candlewick spread to Art Nouveau, from Watteau to Warhol, Augustus John to Jasper Johns artwork on the walls—all with private baths, complete with whirlpool tubs and showers. Feeling like Goldilocks in the house of the Three Bears, she could barely restrain herself from wallowing in the bedclothes and sitting on all the chairs, and had to remind herself sternly that she was on someone's boat, and not just any boat at that. This was the lair of some other kind of bear. And she had business here.

That left the closed door. So far she had had the free and uninterrupted run of the place. Was she pushing her luck? One last fairy tale came to mind—"Bluebeard." She glanced at her watch; though it seemed forever, she had been down below only twenty minutes or so. And this was, after all, only a boat; even if it was 120 feet on the waterline, there had to be an end to it somewhere. How much more boat could there be? The boxes—if they still existed—must be in Roger Fell's private quarters, and this door must lead to them. She stood with her hand on the knob, rehearsing what to say if there should happen to be anyone on the other side. Oh, dear, I got a little lost and went the wrong way, but really, my bag has got to be in here somewhere. Hoping she wasn't about to precipitate herself into someplace really inappropriate to this fabrication, such as another boiler room or the crewmen's john, she pulled open the door.

Well. If she thought she had finally come to the end of the line in this direction, she was sadly mistaken. Yet more doors, suggesting still more boat. But it looked as though she had finally achieved Roger Fell's sanctum sanctorum—or at least its outskirts. This seemed to be a game room or den, its paneling somehow inlaid in such a way as to resemble tiger stripes, a pool table, gaming boards, and several video-game consoles bolted to the floor. In the far corner, beyond a wall of bookshelves filled with leather-bound books-by-the-yard, was a semicircular wood-paneled bar with elephant-tusk railings, a full complement of crystal barware on a gimbaled shelf behind it.

Hmm, she thought, averting her glance from the stuffed elk head over the bar, heads on stakes as well. In fact, everything in the room seemed to have a certain reference to violence, dark places of the earth, the theme of the hunt. She stared with an odd sense of *déjà vu* at a large, gloomy picture of a terrified horse being mauled by a leopard on the back wall by yet another door, this one slightly ajar. Shades of Stubbs, she thought, why does that ring a bell?

Suddenly she knew what all this reminded her of, not just this room, but the whole place. Dark places of the earth indeed. Brrr. Not a grand hotel, not a royal palace, not your average stately home, but something much more personal and familiar to her: Montfort Abbey, garden of malice, so-called stately home of the late Lady Viola Montfort-Snow and repository of her so-called papers, as well as her son Giles and assorted other lunatics, Alan being the one fortunate exception. She stood still for a moment, fighting the urge to forget the whole thing and simply cut and run.

Instead she strode across the room and pushed aside what she devoutly hoped was the last door into the last room—and stood in the doorway, staring openmouthed at the *Jolly Roger*'s *pièce de résistance,* the master suite.

Even in her wildest dreams, Roz could not remember reading, hearing about, or even imagining—let alone actually *standing* in—a bedroom done entirely in black leather. The walls, the built-in chairs, the headboard were covered in what seemed like acres of glove-soft, smooth black material, the bedcovers and pillows of the huge round bed as well, all emanating that pleasantly pungent, distinctly organic odor Roz associated with brand-new luxury-car interiors, clearly indicating to her that she was not staring transfixed at a roomful of expanded vinyl. She wondered if the bedsheets were leather, too.

The black expanse was not entirely unrelieved, however. The bed itself was lit from underneath so that it appeared to be floating on a soft pale cloud of luminescence. Over the bed—she might have guessed—hung an entire Holstein cowhide whose black-and-white pattern bore a striking resemblance to a grinning skull and crossbones. Poor cow. Here and there were accents of chrome in the track lighting and drawer handles, all reflected in the shiny black japanned-enamel built-in chests and dressers, as well as in the mirrors along one wall and on the ceiling over the bed. On the black wall-to-wall carpeting in front of the (naturally) black marble fireplace lay a polar-bear rug, its wide-open eyes staring, ivory teeth bared in a grin. Beyond an archway, its sliding mirrored door half open, Roz glimpsed a black-marble Jacuzzi sunk into the floor; the rest of the master bath was done in chrome, black marble, with mirrors all around.

Well, fan my brow, thought Roz, I wonder where he keeps the whips and chains? Roger Fell's decorator was going to have his or her hands full when it came to doing *this* over in a new theme. She started to chuckle in spite of herself, then found herself snorting and choking with mirth, finally falling helpless with laughter into a chrome-and-leather armchair that promptly tilted backward into a supine position under her, and sent her into fresh paroxysms of glee. Catching her breath, she sat up, wiped her eyes, and looked more calmly around her at the full extent of the room.

And there, sure enough, piled in a corner on the other side of the bed were several rows of large cardboard boxes. She was up out of the chair and across the room before she realized with a sharp pang of disappointment mixed with alarm that not only were the boxes no longer sealed, but someone had obviously already gone through them.

Oh, hell. She was too late.

But wait a minute. She was here, and she might as well make sure that all was in fact well and truly lost. Bending over the first box, she plunged her arms into it, and felt only the softness of clothing. The second, books; the third . . . wait! Here, among the various articles of foul-weather gear . . . muttering softly to herself in a frenzy of renewed hope, she rummaged further, grasped and pulled. And here . . .

" '*And he-rrrre* . . . ,' cried the Baby Bear, '. . . *she is!*' " warbled a falsetto voice behind her.

Roz whirled, eyes wide, hands clutched around the plant press.

Roger Fell was leaning in the doorway, regarding her with an oddly vulpine expression on his face, especially for a bear.

21

"What are you doing here?" Roz gasped, swinging the plant press around behind her back in a frantic attempt to conceal it. She stared at the figure framed in the doorway. He was dressed in a white sharkskin suit with a black shirt and pastel-striped tie, and his hair and beard had been neatly trimmed and combed so that instead of looking like a pirate, he looked merely satanic.

"Shouldn't I be asking you that?" said Roger Fell. "After all, this *is* my bedroom. But, that being the case, maybe I don't need to." Slowly but deliberately he began to move toward her, taking off his jacket in one fluid motion and tossing it aside, then loosening his tie and pulling it off with a sinuous hiss that ended in an abrupt snap.

Roz backed up until she felt the row of boxes pressing against her calves. She let the plant press drop into the nearest one as quietly as possible. "I . . . I thought you were away on business until Tuesday," she said by way of conversation.

Roger Fell shook his head and began unbuttoning his shirt. "It's my captain who isn't coming back until Tuesday. I flew back into Owls Head this afternoon so I could meet the boat here. As you can see, I haven't even had time to get undressed.

These are my business clothes." He pulled the shirt out of his pants and threw it on the bed, kicked off his shoes, then reached down to unbuckle his belt.

Roz began to move sideways along the row of boxes, thinking that if she could get a better angle between herself and Fell and the bed, she might sprint for the door as soon as he dropped his pants, before he had a chance to step out of them.

"Steve told me you had come aboard to 'look for your bag,' " Fell said as he unzipped his fly. Roz stood poised, ready to run. "I told him it was all right. I wanted to see what you were up to." He raised one leg, standing storklike the way all men do at this point in undressing, and began to pull off the first leg of his trousers. Roz took off for the door.

Fell snaked out a hand as she went past, grabbed her arm, and snapped her around as easily as a child at the tail end of crack-the-whip. She went sprawling flat on her back onto the leather-covered bed, Roger Fell on top of her.

"I'll scream," she said through gritted teeth.

"Good luck," said Roger Fell. He rolled off her, sat up, and began untangling himself from his pantlegs. He finished pulling them off and dropped them onto the floor, revealing white silk boxer shorts with a tiny black skull embroidered where the designer mark would usually be. So, she thought distractedly, he'll have to get all new underwear, too. "Nobody's here. They've all gone ashore to join in the windjammer jamboree. I told them I'd look after things," he said, chuckling softly. "So unless your boyfriend decides to come looking for you, it's just you and me, kid." He leaned back on his elbows, turning to Roz and giving her a lascivious look. Alan, she thought desperately, where are you? She closed her eyes, wondering if she should fight or just give in. After all, hadn't the man already murdered once and gotten away with it?

"So let's get down to business." The bed shook briefly; there was a soft grunt, then a rustling of clothing. Roz braced herself. "Okay," said Roger Fell, his voice sounding farther away. "Forget this 'bag' business. Tell me what you were *really* looking for. *And* why."

Roz opened her eyes. Roger Fell had gotten up off the bed and was in the process of pulling a striped Rugby shirt over his head. As she watched in amazement mixed with profound (if temporary) relief, he pulled a pair of white duck trousers out of a closet and stepped into them. "Don't look so surprised," he said. "I'm not a rapist; I can tell when someone's not in the mood. On the other hand, you're not a bad-looking chick, and if you should change your mind . . ." He gave her an interrogative look, then shook his head. "No? Okay, then. Maybe later. Just let me know." He reached into the nearest box and hauled up the plant press. "So what's the deal? And, I might add, what the hell *is* this funny-looking thing, anyway?"

Roz got up from the bed with as much dignity as she could muster, considering that her backless sundress had rearranged itself to be more or less frontless as well. Giving the waistline a quick jerk to bring it back around to where it belonged, she briefly contemplated making a fast break for the door and getting herself the hell out of here while she still could.

But something stopped her. Not only was Roger Fell not behaving in the way she would expect him to (or any other suspected murderer, for that matter) on finding a strange woman gotten up like a floozy rummaging through boxes that might very well contain evidence to incriminate him, he was behaving in a way that indicated he had absolutely no idea what she was looking for. Even more incredible, he appeared to have absolutely no idea what *it* was when he saw it; the plant press might as well have been an old fruit crate as far as he was concerned. She stood there staring at him, completely baffled, trying to think of something appropriate to say in the circumstances—whatever *they* were.

Roger Fell returned her gaze for a moment, as though waiting for an answer. Then he shrugged, tucked his arm around the plant press, and headed toward her. Roz braced herself once more, but Fell passed right by with barely a glance in her direction. "I'm going to have a drink," he said over his shoulder as he went out the door. "How about you?"

22

Roz stood there in the middle of the black-leather bedroom staring at the empty doorway. All around her the black lacquer, the chrome, the marble, the skull-and-crossbones wall hanging, the jumbled boxes replicated themselves crazily in the mirrors, like a fractured Cubist painting by Braque. Something nudged her foot; she recoiled sharply, then looked down—a jawful of bear teeth yawned derisively next to her bare toe. Her shoes must have fallen off when Roger Fell flung her on the bed. Quickly she put them back on, smoothed her dress, straightened her hair, and followed Roger Fell into his private lounge— or, perhaps more appropriately, given the wild-animal decor, his "den."

The den appeared to be empty, but from behind a half-open sliding door that had been concealed in the paneling she heard the sharp crack of an ice tray, the sound of ice cascading into a bucket. The plant press had been carelessly set down on the edge of one of the leather lounges; she gave it a little tug and sat down next to it. Through the open door she glimpsed an array of cupboards done in a lightish wood, two stainless-steel sinks, a microwave oven, a range top, a walk-in refrigerator.

Galley number two, or was it the wet bar? she wondered distractedly. And what difference did it make, anyway? The real question was how she was going to get out of here, gracefully or otherwise, and whether there was any possibility, outlandish as it might seem, that she might manage to take the plant press with her. But then everything was seeming pretty outlandish at the moment, particularly Roger Fell, whose behavior hardly seemed to fit in with the elaborate hypothesis about his guilt and motivation for the murder of Peter Onterdonck she and Alan had been so busy developing these last few days. But suppose Fell knew he was caught red-handed, and this was all an elaborate bluff on his part. Could it be that—in what Alan had identified as his all-consuming arrogance—he didn't think for a minute anybody else could possibly know what he'd been up to, let alone prove it? Or perhaps he simply didn't know any such evidence existed, or thought it existed in an entirely different form? Alan was right on one point: Roger Fell had obviously not spent any of his time in a botany lab making waxed paper, newsprint, and weed sandwiches.

The real point was, here was the evidence she and Alan had been looking for in the form of the intact plant press, literally right at hand! She should just grab the thing and make a run for it while Roger Fell was so improbably occupied with playing *mein* host in his wet bar amid his magic ice-cube maker, cheese tray, and microwave hors d'oeuvre cooker. They could always figure the rest out later. She moved to the edge of her seat, plant press in hand, poised for flight.

Too late. Roger Fell emerged from behind the door with an etched-crystal-and-silver ice bucket. He marched over to the brass-and-elephant-tusk-railed bar, deposited the ice bucket to one side, and plunked two frosted old-fashioned glasses the size of small wastebaskets down next to it. Tiny etched skulls grinned at her from the glassware. Enough is enough, she thought wearily.

"What's your poison?" he inquired, giving her an ever-sogracious smile with just the suggestion of a sardonic cast. "I've got just about everything," he said, ducking down behind the bar.

Roz contemplated putting the plant press under her skirt, in the hope he might have forgotten about it. She could hold it between her legs, have a drink or two, and then casually get up to leave. . . .

"So what'll it be?" Fell prodded, popping back up from behind the bar like a jungle jack-in-the-box.

A drink, a drink? What should she have to drink? Nothing too alcoholic; she had to keep her wits about her. She had to make this look good, play for time, so she could figure out what to do. Alan should be coming back to the *Verorum* any minute now, would find her gone, come looking. . . . No, she couldn't count on that. She'd told him to stop rescuing her all the time, hadn't she? And he was certainly taking her at her word.

"Ah . . . a white wine and seltzer?" she said tentatively and then mentally kicked herself; what she really should have asked for was some exotic party drink that took a while to mix and required bizarre ingredients—a banana daiquiri or a gin sling or something—then, while he was occupied with his blender or his cocktail Cuisinart, she could take off.

"Aw, come on, be a sport," said Roger Fell. "How about a mart?"

Mart? Roz's mind went blank. Mart? What's a mart? Idiot, a martini, of course: what Alan always called a gin and It— straight gin with a dash of vermouth. She suddenly got a picture of her father, mixing drinks on the veranda back home in Marcellus, New York: cracked ice, a silver cocktail shaker, elaborate ceremony, drinks consumed slowly, with great gusto, everyone so polite and mellow. Well, if the staid society matrons of Marcellus could drink them . . . "That will be fine," she said to Roger Fell.

She watched as Fell brought out what appeared to be a powder horn made from the tusk of some large animal, but which she gathered—as he began to pour into it half the contents of a large green bottle with a red seal prominently stamped into it and a red ribbon tied around its neck—was actually some sort of cocktail shaker stoppered with a screw-on cap at the narrow end and a flat, hinged silver lid covering the top. Fell then added ice cubes and began to shake the horn-shaped flagon vigorously. Okay, the green bottle was obviously the gin, so where was the It?

With some dismay she realized that Fell's idea of a martini was straight hundred-proof gin on ice, and he was serving it up right now by the jugful. He reached underneath the bar and brought up a wooden stand carved for the express purpose of holding the shaker upright, set the horn in it, then came around from behind the bar holding two glasses full of gin and ice.

"Cheers," he said amiably as he handed her a still-frosty glass. He sank down in the leather lounge chair across from her, lifted his own drink in a courtly salute, then took a hefty swig.

Roz waved her glass at him and took a good swig herself, followed by a vain attempt to suppress the shudder that came with it. Whew. The gin was so cold she could hardly feel it going down, and it had practically no taste at all. It was like gulping frozen air.

"Okay, Miss Howard, let's get down to business," Fell said. "As they say in the old country, what gives?"

"Oh, please call me Roz," she said brightly, stalling for time. "And may I call you Roger?"

Fell's eyelids closed in a gesture of assent, only to fly open almost instantly, so that he was still regarding her intently.

Fighting the urge to seriously fidget, Roz took a good slug of her drink, crossed her legs, and looked around the room, then back at Fell. "Well," she said. "I guess I've got some explaining to do." She cleared her throat, recrossed her legs, and took another swig.

"Um-hmm," said Roger Fell. He stood up, retrieved the martini horn from the bar, refilled her glass, then sat back down again.

"The fact is . . ." Roz paused and took another gulp of her drink. What was the fact? Come on, Roz, get with it. "Well, to begin at the beginning," she began, "I'm sure you remember the first time we met, the day your cousin Peter Onterdonck was found dead on the beach at Restitution Island."

Fell nodded again, waving his glass in a short, impatient arc as if to say, "Get on with it."

Good luck, Roz thought, racking her brains for a plausible story that would take into account not only her presence here but her obvious interest in the plant press she was now prac- tically sitting on, without actually giving away the whole thing. Surely her best course was to stick as close to the facts as possible. "My friend—you met him on the beach, Alan Stewart is his name—you probably noticed he's from the British Isles, or actually Scottish to be precise—" she began, aware that she was babbling, but what the hell? "Anyway, he is really quite a world-famous . . ."—oh, Lord, what was the field that profes- sorship had been in, paleo-something; she couldn't remember! Well, make it up!—"um . . . forensic microbotanist actually"— that certainly sounded high-tech and impressive, and not quite a lie, more an embellishment, considering she was talking about Alan's hobby, at least she was under the impression, or had been until recently, that it was his hobby, but who knows, and anyway, at the moment she wasn't sure about anything—"and as it happens"—here came the lie direct—"when he was search- ing your cousin's boat for some sort of proof of identity, he dropped"—dropped what? a plant press the size of a small suitcase he just happened to be carrying around with him?— "a . . . a . . . rather important piece of paper, so when we heard that you had—"

"I don't think so," said Roger Fell.

"—and we figured it had gotten mixed up . . . been taken off with the rest of . . . ," Roz prattled on desperately.

"I don't think so," Roger Fell repeated. He was stretched out in his chair, looking quite relaxed, a vaguely amused expres- sion on his face. "Let's just cut the crap, okay, hon? You and your boyfriend think I did it, right?"

Roz swallowed hard, then licked her lips and took another sip of her drink, surprised to see it was almost gone. Her head buzzed slightly. "Did what?" she asked innocently.

Fell sat forward, slapped his glass down on the elephant-leg table, and said in an exasperated voice, "C'mon, gimme a break. Killed my cousin Pete, what else? Why else would you sneak on board my boat and start going through all his stuff?"

Obviously Fell was way ahead of her, story or no story. So what was she going to say now? She just sat there, totally at a loss, waiting for Fell to make the next move.

Fell sighed, tossed down the rest of his drink, then got up, refilled both their glasses, and sat down again. "If that's your line, then we might as well call off this charade right now. You obviously think I did it, and have from the very beginning, though why you should pick on me for it I have no idea, let alone how."

"Because you were there?" Roz suggested weakly, painfully aware that virtually anything she said now would be too much. Or not enough.

"Who says?"

"I . . . we saw you. You were coming out from behind Rebel Island . . ."

"That morning, sure. Like I told you and Stiles, I was cruising by on my way to Ellsworth by way of Bucksport—it looks like the long way around but it's really not; you can really cruise a Porsche along Route One there. But I wasn't anywhere near the damned place the evening before, which is when Pete got himself clobbered. Hey, he was dead as a doornail by nine o'clock that night; the medical examiner said so."

"But the officer said—"

"I don't care what the officer said. I wasn't there."

"But . . . but we have only your word for that."

"Yeah, right," Fell replied. "Me and my crew of six."

23

Roz sat there completely thunderstruck, watching the carefully forged chain of reasoning she and Alan had built up link by link indicating Roger Fell's guilt in the murder of Peter Onterdonck disappear precipitately, like an anchor hastily thrown overboard, tackle and all, discovered too late to be completely unattached to anything on deck.

Unless Tom, Pete, Sheila, Steve, *et al.* (never mind the stalwart Captain Sidney) were in it with him, which hardly seemed likely, Roger Fell had an alibi. Not to mention the fact that he appeared to be completely unaware of the existence, let alone the location, of the evidence for his purported motive, the missing endangered-plant specimen. All the more reason not to call his attention to it; anyway, first things first. "But . . . but . . . you were all by yourself in the cockpit, and I thought . . . You mean you weren't alone?"

Fell gave her a withering glance. "You don't really believe I can actually sail this big mother all by myself, do you?" he said, waving a hand vaguely around the room. "Hey, get real. Running a boat this size is a job for professionals. The cockpit's just for the view. Everything's run from the navigation station down below. I just furl the sails and drop the anchors. They can do that from inside, too, but when I'm on board I go up there and horse around to make it look good."

"You mean, your running the boat from the cockpit there, waving at all those buttons and dials—it's all just an act?"

He shrugged, looking at her somewhat sheepishly. "I guess you could call it that. I like the feeling of doing something, you know? Being up there, looking out over the waves . . ." His voice trailed off. "It's just great," he said after a moment, his eyes dreamily vacant for a moment.

"Well, I'll be damned," Roz murmured. The buzz in her head seemed to be getting louder, more persistent; she must have had more to drink than she'd realized.

"Excuse me," Roger Fell said. He got up and went to an intercom inconspicuously placed to one side of the bar. "Yes? Oh, okay. Thanks, I mean, roger, over and out." He hung up and turned to her. "My crew is back. I guess the party's over, at least for the moment."

It took Roz a moment to realize that he was speaking literally; the shore festivities must have reached a temporary lull. And where had Alan been all this while? Probably living it up at the same party, she thought to herself, feeling a little miffed. She wondered if he was even back yet, wondering where *she* had gone off to, as if he couldn't guess. Apparently he had *really* taken her at her word. No more Sir Alan to the rescue; no sirree.

She became fuzzily aware that Roger Fell had picked up their empty drink glasses and now seemed to be in the process of tidying up, swabbing the bar and putting the powder horn away. What a good boy, she thought, smiling approvingly at him. He came out from behind the bar.

"Well, it's been nice talking to you," he said, extending a hand. "I'd ask you to stay longer, but I'm afraid I have another engagement."

Roz stood up, teetering somewhat unsteadily. Was it her imagination or was the boat heeling slightly? "That's fine," she said. "Fine. No problem." Feeling slightly befuddled, she looked around her. Hadn't she forgotten something? Oh, the plant press. She bent down and picked it up, then beamed at Roger Fell. Wasn't it nice how things had worked out?

"Oh, go ahead, take the goddamned thing if you want," Fell said, touching her arm and guiding her toward the passageway into the main saloon. "Maybe you and your botanist boyfriend—but hey, wait a minute, didn't I hear him telling Stiles he was an artist? Oh, never mind, whatever—can figure out what it was Pete was all worked up about. Last time I saw him he'd just been to the islands, and he had some sort of bee in his bonnet. Never got the chance to find out what it was, though. Just like a lot of things . . . Oh, well. Hey, you sure you can make it all right?"

Roz looked down and was surprised to find herself at the edge of the gangplank; she didn't particularly remember coming up the stairs or across the deck, but never mind. Here she was, almost home free, and in full possession of the evidence. Wait till Alan saw this. "Thanks ever so much," she said, still beaming happily at Roger Fell. "Here, would you mind holding this?" she said, pushing the plant press at him while she bent down and took off her shoes. "I'm feeling a tiny bit unsteady on my feet." She handed him her shoes and took back the plant press. Then, carefully putting one foot in front of the other, she crossed the swaying gangplank, turned to smile blithely at Roger Fell, and staggered off down the wharf toward the *Verorum,* holding the plant press out in front of her with both hands like a petrified concertina.

24

Uh-oh, Roz thought as she padded along the floating dock to where the *Verorum* was tied up, I *really* must have had more to drink than I thought. She stopped and squinted, trying to focus, but to no avail—not one but two curly heads of hair were clearly visible in the cockpit of the boat. One of them turned, caught sight of her, and rose upward. The other stayed put.

"Ah, Roz, there you are! Good!" said Alan in a tone so hearty it almost stopped her in her tracks. "I was beginning to wonder where you'd got to. . . ." He hopped onto the floating dock and hurried to meet her. There was the briefest of hesitations as his eyes dropped to the object in her hands, registered surprise, then fixed themselves once again on her face. "Here, let me help you," he went on smoothly, taking the plant press from her and cradling it gently in one arm while he firmly took hold of her elbow with the other. "There's someone here I'd like you to meet. I ran into her while I was scouting out the windjammer *fête,* and we decided to come back here for a drink; didn't think you'd mind. In fact, we'd been rather wondering where you'd gone off to." Eyes still fixed on her face, he continued in a hearty tone, "We've only just now come in; her boat's one of those anchored back over in the cove there. It's that ketch-rig we were talking about before." Roz was about to ask which one, but the firm, almost harsh pressure of his fingers on her arm held another message: Don't say a word.

"Roz darling, this is Biddy Hardcastle," he said as he carefully helped Roz onto the deck of the *Verorum*. "Biddy, this is Roz Howard, my friend and sailing companion, as well as distinguished professor of English literature at Canterbury College." He let go of Roz's arm and in the same instant dodged into the companionway. Aha, thought Roz, so this was why you didn't come looking for me.

"Pleased to meet you," said Biddy Hardcastle, gazing up at Roz with bright blue eyes set in a freckled face reddened by the sun, pleasantly impish, surrounded by an aureole of bright auburn curls. There was something indefinable in the way she spoke, not an accent exactly, but some kind of special intonation that made Roz wonder where she was from. Not anywhere around here, certainly. Canada, perhaps? No doubt Alan had already found this out, along with other pertinent information.

Roz smiled as cordially as she could at the young woman, taking in the sturdy figure, her flowing white shirt open at the throat to reveal creamy freckled skin the color and delicacy of a plover's egg, the shirt tucked casually into baggy denim sailing shorts that did nothing to conceal the very muscular and firm but still feminine shapeliness of her hips and thighs, the dancerlike calves and ankles, the tiny feet in well-broken-in boat shoes. Biddy was leaning back against the coaming, legs crossed, a beer bottle in her hand. That hand, Roz noticed with interest as she sat down across from her, was the only unfeminine thing about the young woman, the skin rough and callused, the fingers square with nails either raggedly broken or cut straight across, clearly the hand of someone accustomed to manual labor.

Alan reappeared in the open hatchway, resting his forearms casually on the sill in his characteristic attitude. Roz wondered where he'd stashed the plant press. "Biddy's first mate on the boat that passed us by rather too closely for comfort out there earlier," he said, smiling amiably. "I tracked her down—the boat, that is—in the crowd over there." Alan nodded in the direction of the cove behind the island where the windjammer fleet was anchored, a bristle of tall masts mixed in with the pointed firs, sails down but all flags and pennants flying. Seen from afar, it looked like the stage set for a medieval jousting tournament.

"Ah, that was terrible," said Biddy, again with that odd, indefinable lilt and a quality to her *r*'s that Roz couldn't quite pin down. "What a rare old scene that was!" She rolled her sapphire eyes to the heavens. "I can't tell you how sorry we are. We did make to come about and see that you were all right, but with a crew of green-as-green passengers all pitching about and hanging over the lee rail and screeching to high heaven . . . Ah! it's quite an undertaking, to be sure, this boat-for-hire business. We're new to it, you know, my old dad and I, this being our first season and all." With a little shrug indicating helplessness in the face of these dire difficulties, Biddy smiled charmingly at Roz.

Right, Roz thought. I'll bet you're about as helpless as a bunny in a rutabaga patch.

"Drink, Roz darling?" Alan inquired, his head and upper body framed in the companionway, his expression as fixed and stiffly smiling as in a Renaissance portrait.

"Just seltzer and a spot of Rose's lime, thank you, Alan dear," Roz replied, giving him a dazzling smile in return. "I had a little something earlier with dear old Roger—that's Roger Fell, who owns that great big sloop just down the wharf there," she explained to Biddy, nodding in the direction of the *Jolly Roger*'s dark shape looming over the wharf. "He's just this minute come back from Boston," she said brightly to Alan, who had emerged from the cabin with a fizzing glass for her and another beer for himself. "We had *such* a nice talk," she added, smiling so hard at him that she could feel her cheeks starting to go numb.

"That's nice, dear," Alan remarked without apparent interest, as he sat down next to Roz, across from Biddy. "Well," he said, lifting his beer. "Bung-ho."

"I'm feeling a little chilly," Roz said. "I think I'll just step down below and put on something a little warmer. Isn't it amazing how things start to cool off once it gets along for dinnertime?" she added pointedly, hoping Biddy would take the hint and go back to her own boat. On her way to the forecastle to change, she noticed that Alan had tucked the plant press under the shelf of the navigation station, next to several books she didn't remember seeing on board earlier. She hurriedly stepped out of her rumpled sundress, resisting the urge to lie down in the foreberth and shut her eyes for just a minute.

When she reemerged in a pair of slacks and a long-sleeved cotton pullover, Biddy was still chatting away, regaling Alan with stories of her childhood spent aboard a Chinese junk with her parents, cruising all over the world, setting up housekeeping in one exotic port after another (though why she would consider New Rochelle exotic in any way was beyond Roz), making pocket money by showing curious onlookers over the funny old boat at a dollar a head. As Roz stepped into the cockpit she was treated to the sight of Biddy leaning back and stretching luxuriantly, her head back, neck arched, breasts obviously just as firm and muscular (and braless) as the rest of her, pushing against the whiteness of her shirt, while Alan watched appreciatively. Roz sat back down next to him, resisting the urge to give him a good pinch.

Meanwhile Biddy had struck a slightly less provocative pose, draped back against the coaming, staring upward at the mast and spreaders outlined against the fading light. "Did you know your jib halyard had gone galley-west?" she remarked.

Alan tilted his head back and peered up the mast. "Why, so it has," he said, slapping his thigh in dismay. "It must have happened when we were striking the sails in such a hurry, trying to make our way around the harbor. We were in quite a taking out there, weren't we, Roz darling?"

Even though he'd said "we," she could tell who was taking

the rap for this little foul-up. And what was with this "Roz, darling" stuff; on the whole, she thought she preferred good old "fair Rosamund."

"We'll just have to jury-rig a boatswain's chair," Alan said with a sigh, then, turning to Biddy, "but that's no concern of yours, Biddy; we can take care of it in the morning. As you were saying . . ."

"No need to do that," said Biddy, bouncing upright in one smoothly energetic motion, kicking off her shoes, and springing onto the cabin top. Before Roz could even blink she had gripped the mast and was shinnying up it, arms stretched up overhead, knees bent, feet crossed in an X, gripping the smooth wooden mast on either side. Roz watched the freckled, sinewy arms pull up, the rippling thighs and calf muscles alternately relax and squeeze, the girl's whole torso contract and stretch in a rhythmic motion like—well, never mind what it's like, Roz thought, watching Alan stare upward, eyes transfixed on Biddy's all-too-visible, impudently round behind gyrating its way up the tall mast. Will it ever end? Roz wondered, as the luscious figure hiked her energetic way upward. Along with whistling loudly through her teeth and climbing hand-over-hand on dangling ropes, shinnying up poles was a skill that had eluded her even in her tomboy years. And here was a young female who was clearly a past master at all these feats . . . and much, much more.

Biddy had reached the top and was standing upright more or less spread-eagled on the spreaders. The boat swayed slightly and Roz suddenly lost her balance, falling into Alan, whose arm encircled her in what was obviously a purely automatic gesture. She stiffened and made to pull away, but Alan's arm tightened, not in the least automatically. "Quite a sight, isn't it?" he said admiringly. "She looks quite like a female version of da Vinci's Vitruvian man, doesn't she?" Oh, right, thought Roz crossly. More like a Playmate-of-the-Month clock.

Meanwhile Biddy had achieved the recovery of the errant halyard and was rapidly descending the mast with it in her teeth, utilizing an entirely different set of moves more or less corresponding to those of a fireman sliding down a pole. She thumped onto the cabin top, clipped the halyard shackle to the mast, and turned to face her audience. Roz almost expected her to execute a sweeping stage curtsy.

"You're all set, nothing to it," Biddy said, leaping down into the cockpit and bending over to slip her feet back into her shoes. That's your version, Roz thought maliciously, glaring at the girl's pert backside. Biddy turned around, glancing at the very professional-looking mariner's watch the size of a wine coaster on her wrist. "Oh, heavens to glory!" she gasped. "I really must be getting along. Me old dad will be wondering where I've gone, and there's supper to get for the passengers and crew, even though they're likely still regaling themselves at the beer tent." She smiled expectantly at Alan.

"Oh, I'll be happy to take you," Roz interjected quickly. "I really could use the exercise. Besides," she said, giving Alan her sweetest "yes, dear" smile, "I'm sure *you* have other things to attend to."

"Ah, yes. It's my turn to cook, isn't it?" said Alan amenably. "So nice to have met you, Biddy," he said, with a gentlemanly bow. "Perhaps we'll meet again."

"Not if I can help it," Roz grumbled to herself as she stepped with some care into the center of the dinghy—even sans the high heels she was still feeling a little uncertain on her feet, thanks to Roger Fell's excessive applications of gin. Biddy, of course, had floated down into the stern seat with the grace and effortlessness of a feather, and sat there now, looking extremely alert and all too competent. "Would you rather I rowed over?" she said innocently as Roz took her seat and began fumbling the oars into the open oarlocks.

"No, thank you, I can handle it," Roz said with elaborate politeness, glancing up at Alan, who was watching them over the stern pulpit. Inexplicably he ducked down and bobbed back up again, grinning over the rail.

"Don't forget this," he said, and gave the coiled-up dinghy painter a toss; it fell into the boat with a plop. Biddy reached down and began to wind it counterclockwise into a neat coil. Alan executed a brief wave, then turned away and disappeared without a word. Roz dug the oars in, praying that she wouldn't catch a crab, and began to stroke as strongly and evenly as she could out into the crowded harbor.

25

When Roz returned, still feeling remarkably woozy in spite of her row across the harbor with the wind in her face, she found Alan down below, sitting at the fully extended drop-leaf table with the plant press still intact in front of him, his hands curled around a steaming mug of tea. "Well," he said, looking up at her. "Back so soon? I thought perhaps you might take it upon yourself to search a few more vessels in the vicinity, so I was just settling myself down to a long wait for your return before I made to dismantle Exhibit A here. I did think you'd want to be here for the main event, the discovery of the incontrovertible evidence."

Ignoring his veiled gibe about her impulsive (and eminently successful, he might also have noted) raid on the *Jolly Roger,* all she said was "Your little Miss Biddy took pity on my lack of rowing expertise and had me let her off at the town dock. Said she'd meet up with the rest of the crew and passengers and go back to the boat with them."

"Ah, yes," said Alan, shaking his head, his eyes still on her face. "Quite a piece of work is our Biddy, is she not?" He lifted the mug and took a swallow.

"Oh, is that what you call her—'a piece of work'?" Roz replied coolly. "Somehow I imagined you might be thinking of another noun in that context."

Alan spluttered in mid-gulp, recovered, and carefully put the mug down on the table. "Ah, to be sure," he said after a moment, lips twitching ever so slightly. " 'In that context,' as you so briskly put it, it was all strictly business, I can assure you."

Oh, Roz thought, I see; strictly business, was it? Hmph. *She* knew very well when somebody was getting the business, all right; it didn't take much evidence of the senses to see that Biddy had the hots for him. She was of the opinion that Alan was being entirely too cavalier about the whole thing. But then, maybe she was making too much of what was no more than an innocent flirtation. After all, she didn't *own* Alan, nor he her. But even so, wasn't he going to say *anything* congratulatory, even nice, about her bearding of the bear in his den, her masterful and audacious retrieval of the indispensable plant press from the bowels—if that was the right word—of the *Jolly Roger?*

"As for that," he was saying, "with my 'little Miss Biddy's' help, I did manage to glean a good bit of information about the various and sundry windjammers hereabouts—all, alas, to very little result. There isn't a single boat in the entire assembled multitude out there that answers to the full description of our mysterious black ship. The closest we came was the *Beauregard* from Portland, but she's a white-hulled vessel with tanbark sails, so unless they've gone and completely refitted her with a paint job and a new suit of sails in less than a week's time, she's hardly a real possibility. Then there's the *Silver Bird,* but she's from Boothbay Harbor, which won't do at all. I had high hopes for the *Admiral Byrd,* from Cousins Island, but she's a Friendship sloop. Ditto *My Backyard* from Portland, but she turns out to be a thirty-five-foot catboat—"

"You can skip the rest of the catalogue," Roz interrupted. Boat inventories aside, Alan's use of "we" had not been lost on her. She had visions of the two of them—Biddy and Alan—

knee to knee, chummily oaring their way out and around every big and little boat in the whole damned harbor, while she was busy being harassed by Roger Fell. "What about your little Miss Biddy Sandcastle's vessel, which, I seem to recall, nearly swamped us out there? You must have had a good look at her—the boat, I mean," she said evenly.

"Of course I did," Alan said with a slightly wounded look. "That's how I came upon her—meaning Biddy—in the first place; she hailed me from afar, and the first thing I knew, she'd swung right down into the dinghy with me—she's frightfully agile, you may have noticed—full of apologies for nearly running us down out there. As for her boat, the hull's dark and the sails white, true enough, but she's a full-rigged ketch, not a schooner. Not only that, the name on her transom in big black letters is *Jas Gardner*. He sighed, twiddling his thumbs around like an old-fashioned reel lawnmower. "So, it appears the boat in question simply pulled up anchor and sailed off to parts unknown. She is gone without a trace, I fear, and whatever insight her voyagers might have provided into our riddle of the sands is lost to us forever." He paused for a moment, still regarding her closely. "But enough of that!" he said suddenly, flinging his arms apart in a wide gesture of dismissal. "*You,* on the other hand, have achieved the real coup! Prima facie evidence of the first water! Or should I say wood?" Here he brought his hands back together with a resounding clap that made Roz jump, then proceeded to rub them together in anticipation. "How ever did you manage it? Come, sit down and tell all." He patted the seat next to him.

Not even a word about her going off without him? No scolding, dirty looks, or further comments on her underdeveloped sense of danger? Well, fine, that's just what she wanted, to be on her own, free and independent, not hovered over, watched, worried about, wasn't it? And that's just what she'd gotten.

Never mind. Back to the matter at hand. Roz sat down next to (but not touching) Alan and began to recount her adventures aboard the *Jolly Roger*. When she had finished, Alan just shook his head in disbelief. "Good heavens, Roz," he said in an awed voice, "what incredible presence of mind!" (At least he hadn't said "luck.") "But really, didn't it ever occur to you that you were taking the most incredible risk, even given your quite logical assumption—based on hearsay, however," he added with a quick acknowledgment in her direction, "—that the crew was on board and Roger Fell was not? One shivers to think. . . ." He fell silent, holding the mug of tea lightly with his long, sensitive fingers. She noticed he didn't seem to be shivering one bit. In fact, he was sounding remarkably casual about the whole thing. It didn't seem to bother him one bit that she had marched straight into danger and had drinks with an alleged murderer.

Now if *she* had come back to find the *Jolly Roger* parked cheek by jowl next door and *him* gone . . . Oh hell, what difference did it make? All was changed, utterly, but as far as she could tell, no terrible beauty had been born. Unless you counted Biddy. She contemplated his profile now as he stared fixedly at the plant press. "Well, you have to admit it all turned out for the best," she said finally. "We've got our evidence, right?"

"So it would appear," Alan said thoughtfully, putting aside the mug and placing both long-fingered hands palms downward on the table in front of the plant press. "And, given our previous line of thought, that in itself is most extremely unexpected, not to say pretty damned odd, wouldn't you agree?"

"You mean, that he would just hand it over like that?"

"Exactly. And not only that, indicate to you in so many words that he had no idea what it was or what was in it . . ."

She stared at him, somewhat taken aback to hear him voicing in so many words her own growing doubts about this whole enterprise. More and more she had the sense there was something not quite right about their dogged, single-minded pursuit of Roger Fell as the murderer. But everything had happened so fast, the run to Belfast, the fruitless search of the *Non-Amo-Te,* the headlong chase down here, her last-minute finesse of the plant press—only to find little Miss Biddy Hardbody ensconced on board . . .

". . . unless, of course," Alan was saying, "what we thought was in it really isn't in it after all, which leaves the possibility that this evidence isn't the evidence we thought it was, and never was . . ."

Roz shook her head, and regretted it immediately. "Stop," she moaned. "You're making me dizzy."

"You were already dizzy. Usual effects of a surfeit of drink, in case you hadn't noticed," he said dryly. "In fact, I'd say you were a good bit more than half-seas-over; in other words, quite swacked. How many did you have, anyway?"

"One? Two? Oh, I don't know. But it was all in a good cause," she enunciated firmly and distinctly, staring him right in the eyes—all four of them. "Look, Alan, this is crazy; this whole thing is beginning to resemble the intellectual equivalent of coitus interruptus. Why don't we just get on with it. The case, I mean. Just open the damned thing up and see what is . . . isn't . . . I mean is . . . oh, never mind, let's just do it! I've had enough of this hanging around, this hermeneutic mind-fucking about who knows what and how! Nothing ever gets settled, not this, not us . . ."

She stopped, dismayed at the sound of her voice—what was she thinking of! She hadn't meant to be so direct; it must be the drink. She made an impatient gesture in the direction of the plant press, then, to her even greater dismay, hiccuped loudly in his face.

She dropped her head into her hands, suddenly overcome by what seemed to be a swarm of gnats revolving busily somewhere behind her eyebrows. And what was this wet trickle traveling down her cheek, around her nose? She licked her lip and tasted salt. Tears? Well, that's a fine kettle of fish. And she'd thought she was doing so well, everything going along swimmingly, no accusations, no shouting, no fighting, no recriminations. . . .

With a little grunt of concern Alan suddenly reached over and pulled her to him. Head revolving, she thought she heard him speak as if from very far away: "Oh God, Roz, darling . . . ," felt a gentle whispering touch across her cheek, her hair. Outside, the sea roared and boomed, drowning out the rest. Or was it inside? She snuggled her swimming head into his shoulder. "You look all in," he murmured in her ear. "Perhaps you'd better lie down."

"No, let's—" she started to say, and hiccuped again, then, to her horror, felt more than a hiccup making its way upward. "Look out," she gulped, struggling out from behind the table and into the head just in time. She was vaguely aware of Alan's presence, holding her, gently guiding her into the forecabin, unbuttoning this, pulling off that, the cool weight of a wet cloth on her face, more soft words in her ear, then warmth and darkness covering all.

She woke up sometime later to find that it was nearly dark. She sat up cautiously; her head was still throbbing gently, but she no longer felt the least bit sick or dizzy, and the only rocking motion she was aware of was clearly related to the gentle swell lapping rhythmically against the *Verorum*'s hull. But where was Alan? The bulkhead door was slightly ajar; a soft wedge of light emanated from the main cabin. She swung her legs over the edge of the vee-berth, discovering in the process that she was completely undressed. Tying her robe around her, she pulled open the door and went through.

The main cabin of the *Verorum* looked like a vacant city lot on a windy day. Alan looked up from where he was sitting at the table. So this was where he'd gone after so efficiently (and chastely) putting her to bed. He hadn't waited for her after all.

The plant press lay there completely disassembled, its contents—newspapers, sheets of waxed paper, blotting paper, plant material—all over the fully extended dinette table, as well as the navigation station and the other settee berth. He looked up. "Ah, you're awake, then. How's your head?"

"Hurts a little bit, but it's nothing a couple of aspirin won't take care of," she answered in what she hoped was a matter-of-fact tone. "I'm all right now. But what about all this?" she asked, nodding at the general disarray. "Did you find what we were looking for?" She moved to the other end of the cabin and perched with her arms folded across her chest on one of the steps of the companionway.

"Hmm, well. I'm afraid this puts a whole new face on the matter," he said, waving a hand around at the various and sundry bits of plant press. "It appears that we have indeed been laboring under a rather large false assumption, or rather a whole series of them."

"What do you mean?"

"Well, to begin with, my somewhat single-minded assurance from the very beginning that Roger Fell was by means of motive and opportunity, as well as by temperament and inclination, the most likely person to have murdered Peter Onterdonck. Certainly, as we have already noted, his behavior toward you on board the *Jolly Roger* is not consistent with this hypothesis, nor is his apparent ignorance of the function and possible significance of the evidence we have before us," he said, gesturing at the remains of the plant press. "Or rather," he concluded grimly, "the lack thereof."

"What?" Roz cried, lurching forward. She stared at the mass of stuff on the table, the bunks, the counters, then back at Alan in total confusion. "How can it lack—I mean, how can the evidence not be the evidence?" She flailed a hand at the dismantled plant press and its accompanying litter. "I mean, there it is!"

"Ah, yes, but what we have here is 'nothing that is not there and the nothing that is,' as one of your more astute and certainly more cryptic poets, Wallace Stevens, put it so beautifully. The plant press is indeed full of plant specimens of many kinds and varieties. All very interesting. Also, unfortunately, for our purposes—quite useless."

Roz smote her brow in sudden realization. "Oh, no," she gasped. "Is it because I didn't get the field notebook? You can't identify or locate any of them without Onterdonck's notations, right? And Fell knew that. That explains why—"

Alan shook his head, smiling. "No, not really. I had everything I needed right here." He picked up a bright red, thickish paperback and waved it at her. "This is the *Red Data Book*, a guide to threatened, endangered, and thought-to-be-extinct plant species, put out at intervals by the International Union for Conservation of Nature and Natural Resources. No self-respecting field botanist ever leaves home without it. All the while, unbeknownst to me, you were having your little adventure—not imagining in my wildest dreams that you would be arriving back here with the thing itself—I was busily thinking to myself that what we might do next in our desperation would be to make a little foray back to the islands on our own and see what we could find by way of *rara avis,* or perhaps I should say *generis.* So I spent some time in that little bookstore-motel across the way—you didn't really think I'd spent the whole time knocking about the harbor totally besotted with the charms of our Miss Biddy, did you? At any rate, I found this"—he held up another book, *Guide to Plants and Wildflowers of New England*—"which I surmised would give me a bit of local background, an idea of what to look for—or, rather, not, since most of these are quite common, in the sense of not the least bit rare. Had any of Onterdonck's specimens been remotely unfamiliar to me, yes, the field notebook would have been a necessity. But in fact, I had no trouble identifying all the plants in the collection."

Roz dropped her arms to her sides, staring at him in dismay.

"What this all tells me, then," Alan went on, gesturing at the various flattened plants laid out in their waxen envelopes like so many hands in a game of gin rummy, "is that though these are all perfectly nice, rather interesting specimens of flora indigenous to this habitat, not one of them in the entire collection could be considered even remotely endangered."

"So that's why Roger Fell was willing to let the plant press go without a fuss! He knew there was nothing there either to incriminate him or to interfere with his plans for the islands!"

"Ah," said Alan, holding up a cautionary finger, "but the plant press had not been opened. He couldn't have known what was actually in there, for the simplest reason that he never looked. No, I'm afraid the simplest explanation is the real one, that it never occurred to him that there would be anything incriminating in the thing. He was telling the truth when he handed it over to you. He not only had no idea on earth what the plant press was for, he couldn't have cared less what might be in it."

He gazed at her in silence, letting the full import of his words sink in. She stared at him in dazed comprehension; he nodded. "It does rather knock into a cocked hat our idea about Fell's motive for getting rid of Onterdonck, doesn't it? Then there's the 'crew-of-six' alibi he produced for your benefit—and presumably the authorities before you—which appears to put paid to our notions about opportunity as well, never mind the means. Which in turn puts our chief suspect, old jolly Roger Fell, right out of the picture, wouldn't you say?"

"But what about the specimen from the plastic bag?"

"Ah, that. Whatever it was, if it was what we're after, it never made it into the plant press; nor, I suspect, was it noted in the field book; my guess is Onterdonck had only just found it and hadn't recorded it yet."

"So what do you think happened to it?" she asked.

Alan shrugged. "Who knows? If it wasn't a rarity, Onterdonck might simply have tossed it away himself; which makes sense, actually. Being the stern environmentalist he was, of course he wouldn't leave the plastic bag behind to litter up the landscape." Alan sighed heavily. "At any rate, I'm afraid it's lost to us forever. Too bad. I can't abide loose ends."

Roz slumped in the companionway, completely deflated. No chance now of bringing Onterdonck's murderer to justice, let alone of saving the endangered islands from Fell's depredations. "So our most likely suspect has become the least likely," she said finally. "End of the line for sure this time. Case closed."

"So it would appear," Alan said ruefully. "Of course," he went on after a moment, "you know what the experts say."

"What experts?"

"Whodunit experts. Detective story theorists—Knox, Sayers, Symons, the whole boiling. The law of the least likely person."

He wasn't serious. Roz looked at him closely. Yes, he was. "What law?" she asked.

"The one that says the least likely person is always the one who did it," Alan replied. "Sayers formulated it most clearly in her introduction to *The Omnibus of Crime*. She thought it was rivaled in importance only by the rule of the unexpected means. In other words, 'why' taking a backseat to 'who' and 'how' in the ingenuity sweepstakes."

Roz thought this latest ramification of the logic of detection over for a moment. "So let me get this straight. Without any motive and with an alibi, Roger Fell is the least likely person to have killed Peter Onterdonck. So what you're saying is that according to Sayers's formula, that automatically makes him the most likely. Is that it?"

Alan nodded. "Right-o, you got it in one. In other words, I'm not prepared to give up on our illustrious and ingenious Mr. Fell just yet. I smell a double bluff, or is it a triple?"

"Who's counting?" said Roz. And she'd thought she was dizzy before.

"This whole plant business may have been a massive red herring," Alan said. "But that doesn't mean there can't be other motives; think of the sunken ship, the treasure pit—and that's only for starters. And failing that, fair Ros—whoops, forgive me, I forgot: plain Roz—there is always Lord Peter's formulation, you know—you must, you quoted it off to me verbatim when I got it wrong before: 'If a thing could have been done only one way, and if only one person could have done it that way, then you've got your criminal, motive or no motive.' "

Roz groaned inwardly. So it was back to that. "But, Alan," she said wearily, "we still don't have the faintest idea about the one way."

"All the more reason to hightail it back to the islands first thing in the morning. No ifs, ands, or buts. We've gone along as far as we can on speculation, hearsay, and analogy; it's time to go back to the evidence of our own senses. I have a feeling that the unexpected means is going to come back into it somehow, and that our 'one way,' motive or no motive, will provide the key. That's the most important thing now." He paused. "Or perhaps the second most important thing."

He was looking straight at her, an oddly intent look in his eyes. Roz adjusted her robe, which had come open slightly, more closely around her.

"I quite feel," he said slowly, "we have been rather badly neglecting the most important matter at hand." He leaned back and stretched his arms along the back of the settee berth; his blue workshirt had come untucked from his pants to reveal a flat, tanned, muscular expanse of abdomen, the paler demarcation of skin defining the smooth line of his hips just above the loose beltline of his rumpled jeans.

Roz's mouth went dry. "Which is?" she managed to croak, leaning back against the companionway.

Eyes still on her face, Alan plunked his hands with finality down on the tabletop. "Dinner. Unfortunately, since what with one thing and another we've neglected to do a shop, and there's hardly a morsel on board, not even cheese and pickles."

Cheese and pickles? Cheese and pickles! That's all he had to say on the subject (and she didn't mean dinner)? She pushed herself up from the companionway and took a step toward him. "Alan . . ."

He didn't answer. With one fluid motion he slid out from under the drop leaf, unfolded his long body, and moved over to stand in front of her. Taking hold of her hands, he gently pulled her the rest of the way to him. She was suddenly aware of his body pressing along the length of hers, emanating warmth. She wrapped her arms around his back. He bent and buried his face in her neck, sliding his arms around her inside her robe and pulling her to him.

"Oh, God, Roz, when I got back and you were nowhere to be found I was so worried about you," he said in a muffled voice. "I'm sorry. I just can't help it."

"Never mind," she said, tilting her head back to look at him. "It's all right . . ."

Slowly he removed his hands, then gently picked up one of hers, lacing her small cold fingers between his large warm ones. Eyes still fixed on her face, he began to back up slowly in the direction of the forward cabin, dragging his shirt out the rest of the way and unbuttoning it with the fingers of one hand, the other one still holding hers, pulling her with him.

Watching him remove one article of clothing after another as they went, Roz found herself thinking quite irrationally that he did a much better striptease than Roger Fell. But then, he clearly had more to work with.

Eat your heart out, Biddy Rockcrystal, she thought as she followed him into the forecastle.

26

Roz awoke to the aroma of burning coffee and the realization that not only was Alan no longer in the foreberth with her, but the space he had occupied wasn't even warm. Just as she was taking in the fact that, the lack of dinner notwithstanding, she had slept long and hard and the morning was already quite well along if not over, she was startled by a series of loud thumps, which appeared to come from somewhere outside the *Verorum*. Hurriedly pulling on her robe, she went through into the main cabin.

Alan had clearly been up for hours, hard at work. Coffee steamed on a wire ring on the stove, and a covered frying pan held warm muffins. Half a grapefruit sat on what passed for a kitchen counter, and there was a fresh block of ice perspiring gently in the icebox, along with a carton of orange juice. Two bags of groceries sat on the navigation station waiting to be stowed. So he had done the necessary shop. Not only that, he had picked up all the assorted plant specimens and reassembled them back inside the plant press, which now sat innocently on the bookshelf behind the settee berth, looking like no more than an old-fashioned souvenir scrapbook run to fat.

On the table were several sketches torn from one of his pads; boats of various sizes and configurations, from the tops of their masts to the bottoms of their keels, with what Roz took to be various contours of the ocean bottom drawn in as well, the waterline barely suggested, as though the boats were floating in water as clear as air, drawn from the perspective of someone more or less submerged. Scribbled figures and faint lines running here and there apparently at random decorated the sketches, suggesting that these were merely preliminary studies to be used later in a more finished work. But work on what? Did this have something to do with their urgent trip back to the islands?

Leaving the sketches as she had found them, Roz quickly disposed of the grapefruit, then fixed herself a cup of coffee, cradled the remaining muffins in a paper napkin, and went up on deck. She wanted badly to see Alan.

She peered over the side, expecting to see him busy at some mysterious task involving the dinghy and the *Verorum*'s hull; how else to account for the bumping and thumping emanating from back here somewhere?

The dinghy was there, but Alan wasn't in it. He was in fact nowhere to be seen. What was to be seen was a large metal air tank in the bottom of the dinghy, weighting it down so that as the smaller boat rose and fell with the slight swell, it thudded solidly against the hull instead of glancing off with a light tap as it would normally. Still no sign of Alan.

Munching absently on her second muffin, Roz shaded her eyes and looked around the harbor. The thicket of masts in the back cove had thinned considerably, and several more wind-jammers were engaged in the process of getting under way.

A splash followed by loud spraying noises from the other side of the boat made her lurch and drop the remains of her muffin in the water, where an enterprising sea gull wasted no time gliding in to scoop it up. Ah, that's it, she thought happily, Alan engaged in his morning ritual, all's right with the world, back to business as usual.

Well, almost. There was still the mystery of the body on the beach to contend with—they couldn't call it a case anymore, could they? Because there wasn't one, the elaborately built-up series of assumptions about Roger Fell's guilt having gone completely by the board in the light of the zero evidence of the plant press.

She heard another splash right behind her and turned, expecting to see Alan churning around to the ladder—and was greeted by the sight of a strange alien life form bobbing next to the dinghy, sleek seallike head smooth and black and shiny, no stubborn tufts of hair springing up, eyes obscured by large blue goggles, mouth bulged out around a mouthpiece connected to some sort of flexible tube that ran around its back. The creature swam to the dinghy, grabbed hold, spat out the mouthpiece, then with a complicated series of maneuvers shrugged out of the air tank and lifted the whole apparatus into the dinghy. Pushing back the goggles, Alan grinned up at her. "Ah, I see you're finally back among the living. Find the muffins all right?"

While she was wondering what sort of perverse variation of the morning constitutional this might be, Alan swung up the ladder and plopped on deck, water streaming from the wet suit that covered him from crotch to crown, leaving his legs bare, except for the large flippers he now proceeded to pull off and lay to one side, followed by the goggles and a clip-on belt apparently filled with weights that clanked heavily as he put it down. The wet suit covered his torso so closely it could have been a coat of oil. As he reached up with one hand to pull off the hood, the other dangling casually at his side, he resembled nothing so much as one of those classical statues of warriors encased in molded breastplate armor designed to be not so much protective as anatomically correct. Roz decided it was a toss-up which was more fetching, Alan in the form-fitting wet suit, or Alan just plain wet.

"Well, then, now you're up and going, we can be on our way," he said, plucking off the hood. With one motion he zipped down the front of the wet suit and shrugged his arms and shoulders out of it, eyes on her face, still smiling. Roz watched it peel down past the pale demarcation below his waist.

"Uh, Alan . . . haven't you forgotten something?"

Alan glanced downward. "Oops! In my enthusiasm I seem to have put this rig on over what a Scotsman purportedly wears under his kilt, or so the story goes," he said wryly, clutching the suit together and heading for the companionway, giving her a quick kiss on the way by. "Back in a jif." She could hear him rummaging down below, the sound of bags being emptied, food being stowed. He popped his head out momentarily. "You might get dressed as well, you know. We've got a good two hours' sail before us, and I want to get to the islands with plenty of time to spare."

She looked at him curiously. Time to spare for what? Another session on the sands with magnifying glass and metric rule? Tweezers and sticky tape? What *was* it he thought he could accomplish by going back? And what was he planning to do with the scuba gear?

Alan, now more decorously dressed in a pair of pull-on painters' pants, hustled back up on deck and wasted no time stowing the selfsame scuba gear in the rear compartment.

"May I ask where all that stuff came from and what it's for?" she asked.

"I rented it in at the wharf there," he said to her curious look as he hopped back up into the cockpit and started revving up the engine. "I'll explain later." Roz stood still for a moment, while several relevant lines from "The Charge of the Light Brigade" ran through her head—hers not to reason why, hers but to do or die? Let's hope not. She went below to get dressed.

When she came back on deck, Alan had already untied all the docking lines and was tossing them onto the *Verorum*. He joined her in the cockpit. "I'd suggest that we imitate Longfellow's Arabs and silently steal away, but with this old banger that's hardly a real possibility. I've already settled our account with Jack the dock boy, so let's just get out of here as expeditiously as possible."

And so they did, Roz at the tiller steering the boat out of Camden Harbor under power, while Alan uncovered the main and hanked on the genoa. All around them boats were starting up and moving out, so that as they threaded their way through the already considerably less crowded inner harbor, it was in a bevy of other vessels, large and small, schooners, ketches, sloops, and lobster boats. Roz scanned the company briefly, wondering if Biddy's boat—or, faint hope though it was, even the long-lost mystery schooner, for that matter—was among them, but dark hulls seemed to be everywhere as the line of windjammers streamed out one after another, some under their own power, some pushed along by tenders, sails of various hues just beginning to flutter up the multitude of masts. It was impossible to tell one from another; they looked like a flock of multicolored wild swans setting out on some sort of mass migration. Quite a day for sailboats on Penobscot Bay, she thought as she turned her attention to the passage of the *Verorum* past the complicated series of channel markers, nuns, and cans that marked the circuitous route out into the bay.

Alan did not hoist the sails until they were well past Curtis Island and coming up hard on the red bell buoy that marked the outer limits of Camden Harbor. The wind was brisk; frills of white danced along the waves farther out in the bay. "Could you hold her for a bit?" he inquired as he threaded his way back along the deck toward the cockpit. "I want to have a look at the charts to see what's the fastest route."

"Fine," Roz said. Resting her hands lightly on the tiller, she adjusted the main and set the *Verorum* sailing across the wind on a comfortable broad reach, the wind at her back as she sat to one side of the cockpit facing the mainsail. She glanced back at the picturesque toy village of Camden fading into the hills beyond, the trail of boats like cut-out paper triangles dotting the channel and the waters beyond.

And there, just barely visible, moving out from behind the furthest headland, a tall, steeplelike sail: the *Jolly Roger* on the move again. She wondered where he—she, it?—was headed this time. Surely he (this was Roger Fell, not the boat) couldn't be following them; at this distance even with the most powerful spyglass he couldn't possibly distinguish them from the dozens of other boats of roughly the same dimensions flitting about the ocean this fine day. Or could he? Given all his other accoutrements, he would surely have an observatory-sized telescope on board as well.

Alan came up from below, chart in hand, and sat down close to her, thigh to thigh. "I think our best bet is to set a course straight for the gong marking this sinister little set of ledges ever-so-picturesquely called the Graves—and well named, I'm sure, poking up as they are virtually in open water, not a hint of land anywhere about—and then hang a left, as my nephew Derek would say, and shoot through the passage between Mark and Saddle Islands." He rattled the chart to flatten it, pointing somewhere in the middle. "Then straight on till morning . . . just joking," he added in response to her startled look. "It shouldn't take more than a couple of hours in this wind. Wake me when we come abreast of Mark Island." With that he stretched himself out along the other seat, wadded up the towel and stuck it behind his neck, propped his head up against the cabin, and shut his eyes.

That's it? Roz thought, staring at his supine figure in disbelief. That's all he has to say about what we're doing? "Hey, wait a minute, Alan," she said. "What's going on? Why all the diving gear? You said you'd explain later."

"Thought it might come in handy for the sunken wreck, not to mention the supposed treasure pit–*cum*–mine shaft," he said, not even opening his eyes. "If it's anything like the ones I've read about—Oak Island and of that ilk—it's probably full of water. I decided to try to kill two birds with one stone, test out the rig and get my morning constitutional in as well. Had a good look at *Jolly Roger*'s keel while I was mucking about— ruddy great flanges on either side, looks like an underwater version of the Starship *Enterprise*." He adjusted his position slightly, folding his arms neatly over his chest. "I've had a further idea or two about our most vexing question of means, not worth talking about yet. It's what I hope to find back on the island that really matters. Evidence of the senses, and all that. We must leave no store—of evidence, that is—interred. Or perhaps I should say, 'no trove unstirred.' " With that he pulled a flap of the towel down over his forehead to block the sun, and closed his eyes again. End of discussion.

Roz sighed. Clearly that was all she was going to get out of him (puns aside), at least for the time being. She didn't know whether to be relieved or not that they weren't engaging in further exhaustive "ratiocination." Then at least she'd know what was on his mind.

Could it be that he was still smarting about the mammoth false assumption he'd—they'd both—made? But so what if they had? They'd done the best they could with the information at hand. And besides, they *were* in this together, weren't they? Now more than ever, since they had quite effectively made things up between the two of them last night. She hadn't been doing it (nor had he) as a mere pretext to stay on together in spite of the apparent collapse of their relationship; she had her own moral, intellectual, and humanitarian investment, too— she wanted to see justice done just as much as he did, and the islands protected from Roger Fell's—or anyone else's—depredations, if that was humanly possible. She knew enough about criminal law (and who didn't, except, apparently, the criminals) to know that if they could somehow still prove that Roger Fell was guilty of Onterdonck's murder and the subsequent cover-up, then he couldn't go through with his plans for developing Rebel Island, for the simple reason that he'd be in jail. That Alan had been doing his frogman foray around the hull of the *Jolly Roger* seemed to indicate he hadn't entirely given up on that score. But was that all he had in mind? What was the point of all the sketches, the diagrams? Did he really believe they could get to the bottom of this by finding out how the body got on the beach, as in "When you know how, then you know who": the law of "only the one way"?

Oh, well, there would be time to thrash this all out later; they had at least another hour's sail in front of them, and given all his strenuous activity this morning (not to mention last night), he could probably use some sleep. Keeping her eye on the barely visible speck on the southern horizon she took to be the navigational aid that marked the hazard ever-so-appropriately named the Graves, she steered gently into a broader reach, eased the sails, and settled back to think a few matters over by herself.

27

Alan was a peaceful sleeper, so her first inkling that he was awake came when she glanced over at him after about an hour's sail, just as they were coming up on the first of the islands that formed a bumpy spinelike barrier down the middle of the bay. He smiled at her, stretched his arms, neck, shoulders, then got up and moved back across to sit beside her. "Want me to take a turn?" he said, settling his hip in close to hers and snaking an arm around her back.

"I can manage," she said, smiling at him.

"Right," he said, shading his eyes and looking over his shoulder toward the bumpy blue line of islands some distance to the east. "That's where you want to head next, just there, Saddle Island to port, keeping Mark Island well on your right," he instructed, pointing toward a clear stretch of water between two of the smaller and closer-appearing land masses. It was hard to distinguish exactly what was part of what, the way they all seemed to blend into one another, though one, she now saw, clearly did resemble a saddle, two humps and a dip. The other, rounder one to the south must be Mark Island. She was just about to adjust her course and tighten sail when he said, "You'll have to harden up a bit more."

"I know," she said agreeably. Even though she'd known that perfectly well, she no longer felt the need to defend herself from his sometimes peremptory behavior. During last night's reconciliation, he had confessed to her that he hadn't even realized how directive, at times even overbearing he was being before their blowup that night in the cove—as soon as they had set foot on board the *Verorum,* for that matter—his seemingly constant hovering, telling her how to do this, barking orders about the right way to do that, as though she'd never been on a boat before. And for this he was, he had told her at some length, with appropriate demonstrations, heartily, abjectly sorry.

It was all part and parcel, or rather a further extension, he now realized, of what they had in earlier days together, during the Montfort Abbey episode in particular, jokingly referred to as his White Knight routine—his rescuer complex. During their quarrel, he had come to understand suddenly and in no uncertain terms how very wearing it was for her to be always on the receiving end of his constant solicitude. In thinking it all over in the intervening days, he had come to the conclusion that this need of his always to be on the watch and ready to dash to her rescue at the drop of a hat was in fact a flaw in his character. In addition to (or perhaps as a result of) his sense of universal expertise, he was, as she well knew, an inveterate fixer, a tinkerer, someone who took real joy in the random putting of things to rights. But he now saw that, in personal terms, left to run unchecked, this impulse could be felt as interfering, condescending, even patronizing, in that it invariably called into question and impaired the competence of its beneficiary.

Certainly this impulse, which he in many ways had always regarded as second nature, had been greatly exacerbated when he had met her. Having fallen so deeply in love with her, it was more than he could stand to watch her trip off into danger not just once but repeatedly ("There is, you must admit, that underdeveloped sense of danger of yours, my love"). He had come to feel that the price of loving her and keeping her safe from harm required no less than his eternal vigilance.

She was glad that he had thought everything over and finally brought himself to admit all this; his willingness to see her side gave her a whole new perspective on the problem—and on him. To his credit—even more now that she understood the difficulty this entailed—he had clearly been trying to temper his overwhelming need for vigilance, his compulsion to run to her rescue at the drop of a hat, or (to his mind), better yet, always to be there on the spot, watching and hovering to prevent anything bad from happening in the first place. For her part, now that she understood the reasons for his overprotectiveness—that it came from an excess of loving her—she was better able to accept a certain amount of it with better grace. They would work it out somehow. And what was it he had been going to tell her before everything went to pieces? When all this was over, he had said, almost pleading with her; when the case is settled and off our minds, and we have time to talk. It was a consummation devoutly to be wished.

When this is over, she thought, when things are settled. But when would that be? When the mystery was resolved, he had said, but was there really any hope of that? They'd been at it for nearly a week, and where were they now? Heading right back where they started, without a word to her of why or wherefore. But why? What could it be and what was so important—or strange and difficult—about what he had planned or arranged that he couldn't just tell her right now? Was it really still just his involvement in the case, or was this unforthcomingness symptomatic of some deeper rift between them that last night's happy reunion had merely temporarily glossed over?

What *had* he arranged or planned about their future together without consulting her, and why couldn't he bring himself to tell her now? Could it be that it was something *really* inappropriate or, worse yet, irrevocable, especially in the light of last night's discussion? She racked her brains for the worst thing she could think of. Not the professorship in paleobotany, or the cottage at Pittenweem; she had already had her say on these. She thought a moment longer.

Wait a minute! Could it be he had decided to solve the problem of their long-distance relationship on his own by pulling up stakes and moving in with her, in her tiny apartment—hardly bigger than this boat!—and into her life at the college? He couldn't fight her, so he was going to join her? Oh no! For all their new understanding, their happy rapport together, for the reasons she had so baldly stated both to him that night and to herself the morning after, she didn't think she was ready for that much close proximity. But what else could it be?

She couldn't stand it any longer. She felt her sense of their new rapprochement, her hope for their future together, slipping away; in sudden panic she turned to him. He was staring over the bow, face turned away from her, his strong profile limned by the sun, his figure unmoving, almost statuelike in its detachment. The image suggested by this stillness almost stopped her heart. "Alan, why do we keep doing this?" she said to him. "We just aren't getting anywhere. Are we? What's the point?"

Slowly he moved his head around and, frowning slightly, studied her face, reaching up to run a finger down the line of her cheek and jaw. "It seems that way, doesn't it?" he said after a moment. "I'm sorry. But be patient with me, Roz. I'm trying, I really am." Then, with an apologetic shrug, he added, "We both know we can't just let matters go on like this. We shall simply have to work it out as best we can."

Matters like this. Work it out. He meant the case, of course; the mystery still came first. However things had changed between them since last night, she ought to have known this much at least: he would never let a crime or a criminal go unpunished, not as long as he thought he could do anything about it. Given a choice, he would prefer to keep bad things from happening in the first place, rather than have to face the consequences afterward.

"You're right," she said, trying her best to smile at him. "We couldn't possibly let it go. We'll just have to do the best we can." She felt his arm tighten around her shoulders.

"Don't worry; it will all come right, I promise," he said quietly, gazing off into the distance. In that instant, she didn't know—or care—whether he meant the case.

They sat in silence for a while longer, while the two small islands bracketing their passage eastward bobbed closer.

"Did you see Biddy when you went ashore?" Roz asked after a few minutes.

"No," Alan replied, "nor the *Jas Gardner*. They must have been up and off early with their latest boatload of holiday trippers—sorry, make that passengers." He grinned. "What with all these 'skinboats' flitting about the waters and only a limited number of fascinating ports of call to choose from, I'm sure it's a case of the race being to the swiftest, first come first served, full speed ahead and the devil take the hindmost-o. Tell you whom I did run into, though. Our old friend Thaxter Waite, roaring about in that stripped-down sharpshooter lobster boat of his. Said he was here to pick up a part. Asked where I was off to with that 'mess a' scuba gear there.' "

"Did you tell him?"

"Not on your life. I said we were headed down the bay for a bit of gunkholing, then back to meet up with your Auntie Jess at Bayside. He just nodded, said 'uh-huh' several times, and that was that. End of conversation, and off he zoomed." Alan paused briefly. "Now there's something very important I need to ask of you that may help to solve the mystery."

"I'd say it's about time, my dear Holmes."

"Seriously now, Roz," he said, with a slight frown. "I want you to describe to me once again everything you saw on board the *Non-Amo-Te* after we found the body. Steady on, step by step, and in minutest detail." He glanced down at his watch. "At a guess, if you start now, you've just about time before we get to our jumping-off place—Rebel Island, that is."

Rebel? she wondered curiously. Why Rebel? The body had been on the beach at Restitution. Oh, but of course; he was back at square one, which meant investigating the wreck and the treasure pit, both on Rebel, not Restitution. But why everything she had seen on the boat, in the order in which she had seen it? She didn't see how this directly related to the means by which Onterdonck's body had gotten on the beach or the motive for his murder either, but oh well. Another case of "hers not to reason why," at least not for the moment.

"Here, you take the tiller, then. I don't think that I can achieve total recall and sail the boat at the same time," she said. She got up and scooted past as Alan put a hand on the tiller, his attention momentarily diverted by the necessity of making minor adjustments to the course and sails. Roz stretched out in the place he had vacated, closed her eyes as though she were on an analyst's couch, and tried to concentrate on recalling all that she had seen that first day on board the *Non-Amo-Te.*

"Bang-on," Alan said when she finished her catechism a little over an hour later. "Good show. Good timing as well, for here we are."

She looked up to see the fuzzy, wedge-shaped silhouette of Rebel Island, hard by the smaller, prickly-hedgehog outline of Restitution. From this angle, they looked like parts of the same island, in turn superimposed on the massive headland of Cape Rosier looming what appeared to be directly behind, but as the *Verorum* drew nearer, the various land masses drew apart, and the channel in between came into view. Roz realized with a start that, much as she had had the islands on her mind this past week, particularly the beach, the actual sight of them was oddly unfamiliar to her. But that was only to be expected. When they had come here before, they had approached them in the dark, shrouded in fog, invisible, and when they had left after the discovery of the body, she had not looked back. Then she had another thought. "Alan, what if there's someone there? Schooners, windjammers, whatever, more casts of thousands, running all over the place?"

"Not to worry," he said imperturbably, running the boat up the channel toward the nearest mooring log. "It's off limits to the windjammer trade, remember? And the odd sloop or two won't matter, as long as it's not our Roger, and we should see him coming from miles away, shouldn't we? Ah, my dear, we're just a pair of day trippers on holiday, looking for a nice place to have a picnic, a spot of frolic in the sun, all strictly on the up-and-up," he said, favoring her with a look of wide-eyed innocence followed by a wink so shockingly lascivious she had to laugh out loud. "So if you will just man the binoculars— sorry, unfortunate choice of phrase there, make that 'take charge of'—I will suit up for the first order of business." Here he paused with an eyebrow raised. "Unless you'd care to be the one to dive down and investigate the wreck?"

She considered his offer for a moment, uncertain whether to accept it as a sincere effort to treat her as an equal partner in this enterprise, or as what it sounded like, an afterthought. She decided to give him the benefit of the doubt. "Thanks anyway, but I've never used one of those things," she said, gesturing at the tank. "I'm strictly mask and snorkel. It's all yours."

Alan ducked below to put on his gear. He reemerged some minutes later encased in black latex from head to toe, having added long johns, she (ever mindful of the paralyzingly chilly water) was relieved to see. He had a chart tucked under his arm, and also, inexplicably, a pot and a metal spoon, which he handed to her without a word as he bent to peruse the map.

"Hmmm. No secret there," he said after a brief consultation of the perimeters of the islands, which clearly showed the lo- cation of the purported treasure ship as a bland notation "*wreck*" in the same small italic script used to warn of boulders, kelp, piles, and various other more arcane points of interest cryptically labeled "*obstr.*" or "*rep.*" "And," he added wryly, pointing out the spot to her, "if one were to fail to catch the drift, so to speak, there's always the name of the ledge on which it obviously came a cropper in the first place, aptly named— can you guess?—Shipwreck Rock. The whole lot has no doubt been pillaged clean long since. This begins to feel like an ex- ercise in futility, I daresay, but we must leave no store interred, wet or dry; at this point it's more a matter of elimination than anything else, isn't it?" He gave her a quick smile, and shrugged. "Or so I keep telling myself. Hence, to the boats," he intoned, motioning her toward the dinghy. "You wouldn't mind rowing, would you? I must see to the regulator."

While Alan busied himself with various dials and valves of the diving apparatus, Roz rowed into the closest landing point on Rebel Island, a narrow, uninviting rim of pebbled beach directly across the cove from the sandier expanse on Restitution where they had found the body of Peter Onterdonck. Roz stared at it as she was rowing, relieved to see that it had returned at least temporarily to its pristine, undisturbed state. If only things could stay that way; if only they could assure that. But it was too late; whatever Peter Onterdonck had found out about the islands that might have stopped any development had died with him. The dinghy crunched on shore.

Alan hopped out and hauled it well above the waterline, then turned to Roz. "I don't suppose you'd care to do a bit of exploring on your own while I'm down under, to see if you can locate the next item on our list, the purported treasure pit?" he inquired tentatively. "You might try the far side; there's a bit of a bog near what appears to be a large freshwater pond, at least according to the chart."

Roz nodded. "Sure, why not?" she replied. Why not indeed? She'd marched right on board the *Jolly Roger* without a qualm, hadn't she? What was the big deal about a deserted island? And to his credit, Alan hadn't said a word about her "underdeveloped sense of danger" or told her to stay put till his return. "I could start by climbing up that knoll over there," she answered. "I can probably see the whole island from that vantage point, not to mention most of the bay for several dozen miles, and any boats that might be coming our way. So I can kill two birds with one stone. If you don't need me here, that is," she added. "Are you sure you'll be all right?"

"Not to worry; I shouldn't be too long sorting out the wreck—only to see if it's been messed about recently," Alan replied without looking up. "If you see anyone suspicious, say our jolly Roger—I mean the chap, not the boat—for instance, just wade out a bit and beat smartly on this pan under the water. I'll hear you and come right up."

Roz watched him dubiously as he bent to slip on the webbed flippers, then strapped on the unwieldy metal tank as effortlessly as if he were fastening a pair of suspenders. Come right up? she thought with a twinge of real anxiety. Was that really advisable? Years of watching *Sea Hunt* as a child came back to her. Wasn't there something about the bends if a diver swam up too quickly? She was about to say something when she realized he probably couldn't hear her anyway with the hood and mask on. She would just have to assume he knew what he was doing.

She watched him move backward down the beach, flippers shuffling a blurred trail in the loose gravely surface, looking like the Creature from the Black Lagoon in reverse as, still facing her, he began slowly to submerge himself in the murky green water. When all she could see was a trail of bubbles, she turned and walked along the beach toward a break in the trees that appeared to mark the beginning of what looked to be a path leading to the interior of the island and up toward higher ground.

She wound her way along the path with very little difficulty, noting that it seemed surprisingly well trodden for an uninhabited island. The grass was thoroughly tramped down, in some places even worn away completely to the bare ground, crisscrossed with exposed roots that showed splintered scars still white from recent scuffing. How recent? The back of Roz's neck prickled, and she stopped to listen for any sounds not attributable to nature undisturbed by any human presence other than her own. Standing stock-still amid the scraggly second growth of scrub pine, thin-leaved beech and ash trees, all she heard was the rustle of the wind rising and falling in the trees, the hum of wings and random twitter of bird song, the steady buzz of insects, punctuated by a faint staccato chorus of frog croaks. No cracking of stepped-on sticks, no sound of tentative stopping and starting, no bated breath of someone listening, no grunting and snorting of any animal larger than a squirrel, human or otherwise. But that was only to be expected on an island. Unless bears could swim.

And even if she were to meet another human, would this necessarily mean danger? With its proximity to the mainland, its position near the entrance to Eggemoggin Reach, this must be a favorite stopping place, windjammers aside, for boaters in need of a respite from the close quarters, a welcome interlude from pitching and rolling, even though fires and overnight camping were strictly forbidden (and any self-respecting sailor would honor these caveats), a chance to put one's feet on solid ground.

So it should have come as no surprise, as she mounted the high knoll, for her to see on the far side of the island, past the freshwater pond that filled a deep declivity spanning a considerable portion of the interior (considering that the whole island was barely two miles long and no more than half that wide), surrounded by a swamp whence the frog song clearly emanated, beyond the squared-off, timber-rimmed pit showing signs of recent excavation, the long dark hull of a large single-masted sailboat moored not more than twenty feet offshore.

FOUR

THE
FELL SLOOP

28

At first glance she thought it was the long-lost black ship come back to haunt the island, but as she fumbled for the binoculars she realized it couldn't be. It was narrow enough for a sloop but easily twice as long as the *Verorum*; seen from this high angle, the bow looked snub-nosed, almost bargelike. She still might not be the world's foremost expert on sail rigs, but she could count, and thanks to all the coaching she'd gotten from Alan and Thaxter Waite, she knew that, length and shape not-withstanding, a boat with only one mast had to be a sloop. So the question was, what was this particular sloop doing here?

She scanned the deck looking for signs of habitation. No crew was visible at the moment, but there were a couple of good-sized crates lined up next to an open hatchway. There was also what appeared to be a thick roll of canvas wound around some-thing resembling a big log, wrapped up in ropes and coarse netting and lashed amidships several feet in back of the mast—some sort of fishing apparatus? Even with the binoculars it was hard to make out detail from this distance, but there also seemed to be some sort of double line running from the mast to a tree on shore. Roz wondered what it was for; had they been doing their laundry? No, that was silly, it was probably some sort of insurance against dragging anchor in such shallow water; she vaguely remembered something about depth and scope and having to have two anchors if the ratio wasn't right. But how, come to think of it, could a boat that size be anchored in so close to shore in the first place? Not to mention why. Hadn't the book said it was off limits to commercial vessels?

Roz lowered the binoculars and ducked down behind a thicket of high-bush blueberry as a figure came out on deck. She watched as the person, sex indeterminate but short and sturdy of build, in baggy seaman's clothes, began to maneuver one of the crates, which seemed to be attached by some sort of pulley arrangement, almost like a come-along, to the line overhead, toward the open hatch. Seemingly without effort, the figure hauled the crate up, angled it into the opening, unclipped the rope, and gave it a push. The crate slid precipitously out of sight. Down the hatch, Roz thought wryly, another metaphor come home to roost. The figure bent to maneuver the second crate.

Ducking even lower, Roz wondered if she could risk raising the binoculars again to see if she could make out the name of the boat. She didn't want a chance flash or reflection to give her away, at least until she had a better idea of what the people on board the sloop were up to, what they were doing on the island, and whether or not they'd mind being seen doing it. She tended to think they might, particularly if the activity had something to do with excavating the pit, which, she seemed to recall, was on the list of activities forbidden by Roger Fell's father some time ago.

Unless of course the crates had been full of clams and lobsters and they were cleaning up after a clandestine clambake, which on the whole she didn't think was very likely. The pit showed no signs of having had a fire in it, and anyway that, too, was on the list of forbidden activities. So who was on board and what were they doing here? She squinted to see where the sun was—almost over her head, naturally, since it was getting on for noon—shifted her position slightly so that her back was as much to it as possible, then carefully lifted the binoculars and peered through them. Unlike the darker hull, the wide-up-turned stern of the boat was painted white, which should have made it easier to read the name.

But no luck; from whatever angle she tried, as though aware of her intentions, the boat seemed to swing its stern around out of range as perversely as a white-tailed deer in a pen. She heard someone shouting and ducked down farther into the bushes, hoping she hadn't been sighted. But it was just one of the crew members calling out some sort of order to someone else down below; the rope running into shore sagged, then seemed to whip backward toward the boat. With rapid arm-over-arm motions the squat seaman hauled it in and expertly wound it into a coil on deck. Frustrated, Roz let the binoculars drop and scooted backward on her hands and knees until she was hidden from view by the contour of the hill, and then ran down the path toward the other side of the island as fast as she could.

Alan was standing on the beach dismantling his gear when she came tearing out of the woods. "Hullo, Roz!" he said, looking up curiously. "What's news? Company coming?"

"Company's here," she said breathlessly, and told him what she'd seen.

"Hmm. An old wooden sloop seventy feet or more in length, and that close to shore, you say?" Alan said when she was finished. "That's passing odd. We'd best have another look. Lead me to her." They turned and jogged down the beach together toward the opening in the trees.

"By the way, I came up dry, so to speak, regarding the wreck. Nothing left but ribs and knees," Alan informed her as, bare-foot, still in his wet suit, he squelched behind her up the trail. Leaving her to ponder at her leisure this latest insight into the curious anatomy of boats, he added, "She was probably a small coaster from the look of her keel, obviously picked clean long ago, no doubt by a professional salvage outfit. So much for treasure ships. Now where's this mystery sloop of yours?"

"Shhh," Roz ordered. Head down, she bent herself almost double into a crouch and slunk movie-Indian style along the crest of the knoll to the point where she had seen the boat. Motioning to Alan, she cautiously lifted her head and peered over the blueberry thicket . . . and groaned in disappointment. In the time it had taken them to get over here, the crew had finished whatever they were doing, pulled up anchor, and left. She could see the boat already some distance off, moving slowly, with only a single large sail flying.

"Aha, to be sure. And a most fell-looking sloop—as in dark and sinister, not our Roger—she is. That makes not one but two fell sloops." Alan continued to gaze at the departing boat. "Hmmm. A bit of an odd duck if you ask me, for a sloop, that is," he muttered, as though talking to himself. "Mast is so far forward, she could almost be a catboat. Except that they don't come in that big. Mainsail looks a bit short as well. Wait, here come some more headsails—one, two, three; jib, flying jib, and jumbo. Some sort of cutter rig, then? No, hang on a bit!" he said, suddenly standing upright next to her and squinting into the distance. "Here, Roz, give me the glasses, quick!" He snatched them from her.

She watched as he trained the binoculars on the boat, wondering what it was he thought he could see from this distance; surely not the name, and what else mattered? Standing up herself, she saw the mainsail flutter up the mast and swing out, filling with wind.

"Well I'll be blowed! She *is* a schooner, minus her mainmast, and dark-hulled into the bargain. I say, Roz! She could well be our mysterious black ship."

Roz looked at him in amazement. What, did he think she couldn't count? "What makes you say it's a schooner?" she demanded. "It's only got one mast!"

"The look of the mast partners," Alan answered, still training the binoculars on the now more rapidly moving boat.

"The what?" She'd never even heard the term, let alone knew what it meant. She knew a hawse from a handrail, but there was obviously more to these big boats than she'd ever suspected.

"The mast partners," Alan said imperturbably. "Those framelike braces there that support the mast weight going through the deck. She has two pairs fore and amidships, hence two masts. You can just barely make out the other mast lashed down along the deck there. I wonder why it's down? It must have been damaged somehow.'' He made as if to hand her the binoculars but she pushed them aside.

"How do you know it's not a ketch?"

"Just a guess, really, based on the placement of the mast fittings," Alan replied as if this were perfectly self-evident. "That and the relative length of the mast on deck. It looks to be roughly the same as the other, if you include the topmast." He was peering intently through the glasses again. "Hmm. They must be in an awful thrash to get somewhere to have just struck the whole mainmast and stowed it rather than have it repaired. Unless that's where they're headed now." He turned to her. "But all this is beside the point. The real question is, what were they doing larking about on Rebel Island in the first place?"

"How should I know!" Roz almost shouted in exasperation. "But why are we standing here discussing it? Why don't we just go find out?" With that she marched off through the bushes down the hill toward the now-deserted beach.

By the time Roz had reached the beach, she wished that she, too, had been wearing a head-to-toe wet suit; it would have saved her numerous whips and scorns from the thick underbrush. Alan, on the other hand, was scratch-free, but sweating profusely in his rubber garments. They stood next to each other, looking down into the empty pit. "An old wellhead or mine shaft of some sort," Alan panted, wiping the sweat out of his eyes. "Recently reinforced—see the new timbers?"

"Also recently excavated by the looks of it, and something heavy lifted out," Roz said, running her hand along the edge where the squared-off timber showed signs of fresh scarring and splintering, deep V-shaped gouges in the wood, the timbers dented, even crushed in several places. "Do you suppose this could be the alleged treasure pit *manqué*?"

"Hmmm, quite *manqué*; as whatever it once contained is clearly gone without a trace." Alan paused, gazed fixedly at the ground around the pit, then back along the beach. "But then how would they get something heavy enough to gouge these timbers down to the beach and across into the boat without leaving any marks? I don't see any signs of dragging, and you can't just run an evergreen branch across a shingle beach and sweep up all the guilty traces."

"Maybe it had something to do with the rope-and-pulley arrangement I saw," Roz remarked.

Alan whirled around to face her. "Rope? What rope?"

Roz quickly described the line she had seen running to the shore, as Alan stared down at her with a growing expression of mixed disbelief and enlightenment. "That's it!" he yelled, grabbing her hand. "Come on, then, there's not a moment to lose!" And before she had a chance to ask him what he meant by "it," he had leaped back up the hill and was crashing through the underbrush as fast as he could go, pulling her behind him.

29

Within a few breathless seconds, it seemed, they were back on the *Verorum,* hauling up the anchor, starting up under power, Roz taking the tiller while Alan ran up the sails. They came out of the small cove just in time to catch sight of the alleged schooner, now a mere rag of white in the distance, rounding the first small spit of land that marked the island-dotted entrance to Eggemoggin Reach. Roz looked back briefly at the swiftly receding islands. Uh-oh. Was that a tall, peaked triangle of sail looming behind the high knoll on Rebel? She squinted, tried to make it out. Who could it be besides the *Jolly Roger*? Roger Fell was following them! But when she pointed this out to Alan, he simply shrugged as if to say: Let him come on, then, I can't do anything about that now. He was clearly fixated on the fell sloop–*cum*–one-masted schooner.

"Bloody hell," he muttered, looking down at his watch and back again at the diminishing triangle of white. "They've got a good half-hour start on us, and those fore-and-aft-rigged schooners go like the blazes except when they have to beat to windward. Of course they'll be up against it with that jury-rigged single-mast setup, but still. We'll just have to hope the wind stays in their face, so they'll have to tack a good deal, or we haven't a prayer of catching them up. Try to keep your eye on her, if you can," he finished, thrusting the binoculars at her. "I'll trim the sails."

And so he did for a fair-thee-well, winching in the jib and then yanking the mainsheet down so tight his forearms bulged and his knuckles whitened, until the *Verorum* was screaming along, heeled over nearly sideways, the whole rail buried under the waves, and Roz had to hold on to the tiller with both hands, so that she was quite grateful when Alan came to spell her at the helm.

Feeling as though she were bowling along in a giant pinball machine, Roz hung on for dear life as they careered past islands and around marks that flashed and dinged and whistled, until to her relief they entered the long, straight, relatively unobstructed stretch of water known as the Reach. By now the errant schooner was completely out of sight. Cursing gently under his breath, Alan abruptly handed her the tiller and dived belowdecks. Roz heard him shuffling charts and thumping down books. Finally he popped back up with a small, businesslike-looking book entitled simply *Down East Directory*.

"What are you doing?" Roz asked as he sat down and began thumbing through the pages.

"I'm looking up boatyards, to see if there are any along the Reach that could repair such a large mast on short notice. They'd need a spar crane of some sort, or deep water off a high dock and a heavy block and tackle at the very least. If there's one such around here, I'll give you odds that's where we'll find our mystery schooner has headed. Either that or they're making a run for it, mast or no mast, in which case they'll still have to put in somewhere for supplies." He closed the book with a snap and put it to one side. Hauling out a chart, he pointed to several small indentations in the sandy-colored land mass that bordered the pale blue-rimmed swath representing the waters of the Reach on the chart. "We'll just have to assume they're making for one of these three harbors. It's all by guess and by gosh, but at this point it's our only hope, I'm afraid. Head for there," he said, pointing out a small promontory, and abruptly disappeared back down below.

When he reemerged some while later and plopped down next to her, she noticed that he had changed back into his regular clothes and toweled his hair dry, and now seemed set for a long afternoon's sail. She looked up toward the sun; it was barely past the meridian. She wondered how far it was to the farthest harbor—which looked to be roughly three fourths of the way down the ten-mile length of the Reach—and how long it would take them to stitch their way there, tacking back and forth down these narrow rock- and fir-fringed waters. Long enough for Alan to explain what he'd meant by "that's it"?

But when she asked him, all he would say, as he looked up briefly from the chart, was that he didn't have time now, hadn't quite worked out all the details yet, and he'd explain later. For now, they had to concentrate on catching up to the one-masted schooner. Then, after inquiring if she was quite comfortable at the helm, he went down below, made sandwiches and coffee, and brought them back up into the cockpit.

After they had finished their repast, without a word he went back to studying the charts and the waters, his head bobbing up and down as he squinted from one to the other, his finger denting first one place and then another on the map. Roz decided not to press him; someone had to figure out where they were going and how to get there the fastest way possible, and he was clearly intent on this, so she held the tiller and looked to windward, considering not so much Phlebas the drowned Phoenician sailor as Peter Onterdonck, who had once been as handsome and tall (or so the poem went) as he. Meanwhile, she continued to aim the boat at whatever Alan bid her, trying not to look as though she were holding on for dear life. But when eventually he came and sat down next to her, and offered to take over the helm, she gladly let him.

The first marina was clearly visible from the mouth of the harbor, and they could see that at the moment it was empty of anything larger than a dinghy, so they just blew in and out. As it turned out, rounding the Triangles off Eggemoggin Head into the Reach itself, blown along by a fresh, steady wind from the southwest, they very shortly settled into a steady beam reach (hence the name, no doubt, as she ought to have expected), and before she knew it, they were threading their way between the towers of the Deer Isle bridge, that spindly-looking span of green metal that arched high above the Reach between Sargentville and Little Deer Isle (she was now in charge of the chart, her finger tracing each landmark as they sailed past), the deep cleft in the hills that marked the Benjamin River inlet at Sedgwick. "Too hard to get in and out of, and beastly shoal," Alan said, peering closely at the narrow entrance dotted with buoys and day beacons. "Besides, that yard doesn't have the equipment to raise a mast."

Past the red nun marking off the rocky hazard in mid-channel at Bridges Point, there they were, coming into the next harbor a few miles farther down, nearly at the end (or was it the beginning?) of the Reach, a shallower horseshoe-shaped inlet partly masked by a small island, channels on either side passable with some care at mean high tide. "No crane here, but the wharf is far enough out of the water at low tide to restep a good-sized mast if the boat has a shoal draft, which the evidence indicates she does."

Sure enough, as soon as they put in at the dock belonging to the Yacht Club and looked around to get their bearings, Roz saw a long dark shape with a single mast alongside another wharf some distance farther in, running off at right angles to the one they were tying up to.

"Look!" she shouted to Alan. "There it is!"

Alan turned in the direction she was pointing. He was silent for a moment. "Surely not, Roz," he said flatly. "It can't be."

"Alan, I tell you, that's it!" She looked from the boat to Alan and back again. Didn't he understand what she was saying? "I mean, that's her! She! The boat I saw at Rebel Island!"

"But it can't be, Roz," he repeated slowly. "I can't quite see the name on the transom from here, but I could swear that's Biddy's boat."

Roz stared at him openmouthed, then at the sinister-looking fell sloop (alias the Black Ship) again. "What do you mean, Biddy's boat? It can't be Biddy's boat. Biddy's boat is a ketch-rig, and that's not the same as a schooner, right?"

"You're right," said Alan, staring at the dark-hulled boat with a deeply perplexed expression on his face. "But even so, I'm all but certain that's the *Jas Gardner*. Narrow and somewhat small as windjammers go, barely seventy feet on the waterline. Accommodations for twelve plus crew. But even so, Roz," Alan went on with a trace of impatience, "as I told you before, Biddy's boat can't have been our black ship in any case. Rigs aside, her name and port of call aren't even close."

"Well," said Roz, with more than a hint of impatience herself, "unless you can prove otherwise, black ship or no black ship, that's the boat I saw hitched up to the beach at Rebel Island. Look, only one mast, the other lashed on deck, not to mention your precious mast partners. Come on, Alan! What are the chances of there being two such boats around here with a downed mainmast? Biddy or no Biddy, name or no name, *that's* the boat I saw on Rebel Island. So, given the island is off limits to the windjammer trade, and Biddy's boat is most certainly a windjammer whether it's a sloop, a ketch, a schooner, or an oceangoing banana peel, what do you suppose friend Biddy and company were doing there, may I ask?"

Alan was busy making the *Verorum* fast to the yacht club dock; she couldn't see his face. "I'm sure I don't know," he said coolly, standing upright on the dock and dusting off his hands. "But, to take a page from your book, the easiest thing to do is go and ask, isn't it?" He paused, peering across the way at the boat in question. "Come to that, she's riding awfully low; her Plimsoll lines are underwater. Perhaps there's something else amiss besides the broken mast—I wonder if she's gone and got herself holed somehow. Maybe that's why they put in at Rebel."

Roz restrained herself with some difficulty from commenting that perhaps nimble little Miss Biddy had gotten *herself* holed cavorting around on the beach at Rebel Island. Alan finished coiling a bit of line according to his prescribed pattern, then hopped over the lifelines onto the dock and started to walk away in the direction of Biddy's boat.

"Hey, wait a minute!" Roz called after him. "You're not really going to just march right over there and ask, are you?"

Alan turned and came back, clasped his hands behind him, leaned over the lifelines, and looked at her with a bemused expression on his face. "And why not, may I ask?"

"Because it might be dangerous, that's why not! Now who's running around with an underdeveloped sense of danger? They could be in this up to their necks! If they think you know something . . . Here, I'll go with you."

Alan straightened. "Come now, Roz," he said dismissively. "Don't you think I can take care of myself with our dear little Biddy, who, may I remind you, is roughly half my size?"

"She's in awfully good shape," Roz retorted. "And besides, what about the crew? The passengers, not to mention dear old Captain Dad? Maybe they're all in on it, too, whatever 'it' is!"

"I see. Well, I appreciate your concern," he said formally, "but I think I can handle Miss Biddy and her friends perfectly well all by myself. Besides, someone has to stay here with the boat. See the sign?" He jerked a thumb toward a large sign that read: LOADING AND UNLOADING ONLY, DO NOT LEAVE BOAT UNATTENDED. Then, with a conciliatory smile, he added, "I really don't think there's much danger, Roz, particularly since we're in such a public place. I'm sure there's a perfectly good explanation for why they were at Rebel Island—so this has the appearance of a purely social call. And even if they are up to something, there is the fact of all those passengers on board, isn't there? Safety in numbers and all that, eh, what?" Still smiling, he leaned closer so they were almost nose to nose. "If worst comes to worst, I'll just give a shout and you can come running. So don't worry, love. I'll be back shortly." He gave her a quick, firm kiss on the mouth, then walked off down the dock and along the wharf toward Biddy's boat.

She watched him as he strode along casually, hands in his

pockets, looking dapper and debonair, until he came abreast of the damaged windjammer. She had to admit his reasoning made sense—and sounded familiar. He stopped and called out, "Ahoy there"—or so Roz assumed, since she could only see his lips moving. But if he was out of earshot, how was she going to hear a call for help?

Too late now. A red curly head appeared in one of the hatches, shortly followed by the rest of compact, enthusiastic Biddy, who, after a brief moment of surprise, leaped toward him and flung her arms around him, hauling him on board, chattering happily in his ear. After a moment Roz stopped watching the empty deck of the *Jas Gardner*, or whatever its name was really, and went down below to change her clothes and tend to the scratches she'd acquired beating through the bushes at Rebel Island.

She should have asked him to define "shortly," Roz realized some twenty minutes later when Alan still had not returned. She had settled herself in the cockpit with a hat pulled down over her eyes, pretending to read, but actually keeping a fairly constant eye on Biddy's boat. It was now getting on for three in the afternoon, and there was no sign of Alan, or anyone else on board the *Jas Gardner*, for that matter. Whatever they were doing on board, they were apparently doing it down below. Not only that, for a windjammer purportedly on a cruise, there seemed to be damned few passengers around. Maybe they had all been sent ashore to shop while the crew attended to other matters. They certainly seemed to be conspicuous mostly by their absence.

But wait a minute, what day was it? She calculated quickly: Saturday afternoon! She racked her brains, trying to recall the article she had read on windjammers. A windjammer week went from first turn of the tide on Monday to Saturday morning, at which point all the passengers disembarked and went home! She slammed her book shut in agitation. That meant there *were* no passengers, just Biddy and Dad and whatever crew they had on board! Maybe not the passengers, but the crew could certainly be in on it—it being whatever they had been up to that required the murder of Peter Onterdonck, and the subsequent cover-up thereof.

And that in turn made her think with renewed urgency of Alan—or rather the absence of Alan. Without the safety of numbers, he was at their mercy, and had been for the better part of a half hour. He could even be dead himself by now!

She looked around her in panic; there wasn't another soul in sight. And even if there were, who would believe her? She could just imagine the looks as she ran breathless down the dock to stoppeth one of three. Excuse me, but my Scottish lover has been taken prisoner on board that up-to-no-good single-masted schooner—I mean ketch—oh never mind! By the time she explained everything . . . No use. She was going to have to go after him by herself.

All right, Roz, think. No sense getting both of us shang-haied . . . or worse. She had to think of a way to get on board, or even close enough to find out what was going on. Then what? She was no match for the athletic Biddy, let alone Captain Dad and crew; she'd have to sneak on board and stay out of sight somehow until she found where they were keeping Alan. Then the two of them . . . if there *were* still two of them.

She stared down unseeing at her book as though she were still engrossed in reading it and hadn't noticed anything unto-ward going on, in case anyone *was* watching. Well, why not? That was as good a ploy as any—to act totally oblivious. Just wander over there looking interested but slightly out of it (there was ample precedent for that; she'd certainly been three sheets to the wind the only other time Biddy had seen her). Didn't Mainers have a word for it: "gormless"—without a clue? Once she'd gotten that far, she could figure out how to get on board without being seen, and on from there.

Briefly considering the backless sundress (only slightly mussed from her encounter with Roger Fell, but it had worked before), she settled instead for her white baggies and a denim shirt, knotted a navy Shaker knit cotton crewneck sweater around her neck, slipped on her boat shoes, adopted the spacey demeanor of a quintessential preppy airhead on a stroll. Fluffing up her hair as best she could—after this was over she was going to have a good, long bath—she stepped off the *Verorum* and strolled down the dock, in no particular hurry should anyone be watching, in the direction of the *Jas Gardner*. As she rounded the corner and started down the other wharf toward the windjammer, she happened to glance at the wide transom looming just in front of her. Sure enough, there was the name *Jas Gardner*—and something else that chilled her blood and froze her in her tracks.

JAS GARDNER, it read.

And in smaller letters underneath—

Belfast, ME.

30

Recovering herself as best she could, Roz turned on her heel and walked quickly back up the dock to where a number of lobster traps stood stacked in a pile. She ducked behind, her breath coming in short, uneven gasps, and peered cautiously around at the schooner, still unable to believe her eyes. But there it was, in so many words, black against the white expanse of the transom:

JAS GARDNER

Belfast, ME

And as clearly and distinctly as though he were standing right next to her, she heard Thaxter Waite saying in no uncertain terms that there were no schooners, ketches, ships, windjammers, or any other vessels of that size or description in Belfast, nor was it likely there would be.

Obviously the name had been altered, in haste and somewhat sloppily, to disguise the boat's identity. And why would anyone do that, except for one reason—whoever it was had been up to no good, and had been seen, or near enough, doing it. What the original name and port of call might be she had no idea at this point, but she was willing to bet they ended in the letters -RD and -*land*. She was also willing to bet that not only were there no passengers on board right now, but *there never had been*. Just Biddy, her old dad, and whatever skeleton crew they needed to run the boat for their nefarious purposes.

And Alan, having ruled the *Jas Gardner* out because it was a ketch and not a schooner (and how any boat could be one and then the other—or both—was quite beyond her) had never mentioned in so many words the so-called *Jas Gardner*'s purported port of call. For her part, communication being as it had been between them, she had never thought to tell him the one crucial fact that Thaxter Waite had let drop (granted, she had not thought it particularly important herself), that no schooners, ketches, brigs, or ships—in fact no windjammers of any kind, sort, or description—called the port of Belfast home. And as a result of their lack of communication on this point (as well as numerous others) Alan had unwittingly waltzed right on board the one and only—if heretofore unrecognized—Black Ship, to inquire blithely what Biddy and company had been doing at Rebel Island.

And had not returned.

And speaking of Thaxter Waite, she thought in dismay as she huddled behind the pile of traps, wasn't that his souped-up mahogany-colored lobster boat tethered to the dock at the far end there? What was *he* doing here? But of course! He must be involved as well, in it up to his sailor's hornpipe—that phony accent, his evasiveness, the misleading and confusing information about which boats were which. And what was it that nice man Clyde had said—some sort of rivalry, no love lost between him and Peter Onterdonck? Suppose "Dad" wasn't really Biddy's dad at all, or "from away"? Suppose this whole operation required an accomplice, somebody local? Could Thaxter Waite and Dad be one and the same?

But before Roz could consider any further the full implications of Thaxter Waite's presence here, she heard voices coming from the rear of the schooner. Quickly drawing in her head and flattening herself against the rough slats of the lobster trap barricade, she turned and pressed her face against the lattice-work, the coarse netting digging into her nose and cheek as she squinted through the slats, trying to see without being seen.

What she saw was two figures dressed in baggy seamen's clothes emerging one after another onto the afterdeck of the black vessel. She watched as they crossed over the gangplank onto the wharf, then turned and walked quickly up toward shore, pulling some sort of an empty pallet on wheels, almost like an airline baggage cart, behind them. What were they doing? Surely not picking up any passengers and their luggage; the whole windjammer act had been simply that, a ploy to disguise their true purpose. And both she and Alan had fallen for it. Talk about your false assumptions! Hearsay evidence—or was it by analogy?—in spades!

And what was their purpose? Roz mentally ticked off the possibilities—smuggling, drug-running, treasure-hunting—or all of the above. Whatever it was, Peter Onterdonck had caught them redhanded and been knocked dead for his pains. And whatever it was they were doing—and whoever they were really—clearly they had been interrupted that morning Roz had seen them leaving the islands. The intervening time had been spent laying an elaborate smokescreen until they could some-how get back and finish the job. Which they apparently had. So what now?

She poked her head out and saw them rattling up the hill toward a small grocery store, two short, sturdy figures, one head of auburn curly hair, the other gray—could Thaxter have had his own brown hair dyed? a wig?—with some sort of cap-tain's hat perched on top. Groceries. Stores. They were laying in supplies, from the looks of the trolley, for an extended voy-age. Oh, no! Roz thought in horror. The bogus *Jas Gardner* and crew were about to make a getaway to parts unknown with whatever they had taken off the island!

Not to mention Alan.

She had to get him off the boat, which meant getting herself on it. But what about the crew? Speaking of crew, it suddenly dawned on Roz that she had never seen anyone other than Biddy and her cohort on board the windjammer at any time. So where *was* the rest of the crew? Surely Biddy and her old dad or whoever he was couldn't be the only ones sailing this boat?

Or were they? A skeleton crew indeed! She remembered Biddy rather pointedly mentioning that she had to catch up to the crew and passengers when Roz had rowed her to the dock at Camden. But had anyone ever laid eyes on this purported crew? Of course not! Phantom passengers, why not a phantom crew? As unlikely as it seemed, it looked as though there were just the two of them running this boat, pretending to have passengers, pretending to have crew, all part of the disguise! The only assumption left was that the *Jas Gardner*—a.k.a. the Black Ship—was clearly up to no good.

All right. This made things easier. Biddy and Captain Dad had gone ashore, and in all likelihood there was no one else on board except for Alan; anyway, she'd just have to take the risk. Their shopping should occupy them for at least a while, even if the local store wasn't exactly a major supermarket. There wasn't a moment to lose. Roz glanced quickly from side to side; the coast seemed clear. Breaking from behind the lobster traps, she darted over to the schooner, hopped over the rail, and scuttled down the nearest hatch.

31

Negotiating her way somewhat precipitately down what turned out to be little more than half a stepladder fixed underneath the hatch, Roz found herself in a remarkably Spartan galley. A big black cookstove on gimbels stood to one side next to a well-chopped butcher block with a small cupboard underneath, a similarly gimbeled picnic-style table with two wooden benches opposite. The rough, gently sloping walls—bare weathered boards set edge to edge with lines of heavy caulking in between, clearly the inside of the hull—were lined with narrow shelves obviously meant for stores. Not much room to hide a person here. Not much in the way of stores, either, she saw as she perused the empty shelves; no wonder they needed to go shopping. From the looks of it, they wouldn't be back for a while, either, especially if they were provisioning themselves for the duration (but of course a skeleton crew wouldn't eat much, ha ha). Oh, well, hysteria aside, she was here now, she might as well take a quick look around to see what she could find by way of evidence.

Like, for instance, these traces of fine white powder on the butcher block. She wet a finger the way she had seen it done in movies, tapped one of the lines, and tasted the residue. Not bitter. Not sweet, either. In fact, it had almost no taste at all. Coke perhaps? (though she had a vague sense that coke should taste bitter). She opened the cupboard underneath; several paper bags containing more white powder were stacked inside. Hmm, so that was it. Drugs. Banal as it seemed, Biddy and Dad were running a drug drop on the islands, and Peter Onterdonck had stumbled on one of their operations. Case solved, right?

Wrong. She dipped a finger in one of the bags inside the cupboard, tasted it. Sweet. Another bag; salty, with a bite to it. Suspicious now, she took a good pinch from the pile on the butcher block and rolled it between two wet fingers—and felt it turn to dough. Flour. Powdered sugar, baking powder, and flour. If Biddy and Dad were running anything down here, it was a bakery.

Disgusted, she turned and gave the galley one last look. Obviously there was nothing here—no evidence; even worse, no Alan—and she was wasting valuable time. As she climbed up the stepladder that passed for stairs, her eye was caught by a set of louvered bifold doors she had missed. She reached over and opened one and folded it back—and was confronted with an ultra-modern, ultra-sleek instrument panel full of dials and levers and gauges and digital readouts that rivaled the one she had seen on board the *Jolly Roger*! A state-of-the-art navigation station if there ever was one—so that's how they did it, just the two of them! She'd guessed right; there was no crew on board and never had been. With all this electronic gadgetry, who needed one?

Not that that made her task any simpler. She still had to find Alan. Cautiously she climbed up the rest of the way and stuck her head out as far as eye level, peered up and down the dock and all around. As far as she could tell, the coast was still clear. She scrambled onto the deck and scurried forward along behind the downed mast until she came to a second hatch opening. This must be the main cabin and sleeping quarters. She swung her legs over and started down.

She wasn't sure exactly what she had expected, even with her recent tours of various vessels (and a good thing, too, considering: she'd had plenty of practice finding her way around the inside of a boat), but it wasn't this dark, enclosed space at the bottom of a companionway ladder that was scarcely more than a set of two-by-fours nailed to the wall. She felt as though she were at the bottom of one of those tiger traps she remembered from old Tarzan movies. The only light there was filtered in from the open hatch and as her eyes gradually grew accustomed to the dimness, she saw that she was in an area no more than six feet square, surrounded by several paneled doors of a dark wood, somewhat the worse for wear but shabbily elegant. They were also closed. She could almost reach her hand out and touch each one of them, the space was so small. The space was bisected at one end by a narrow wooden trunklike casing that she could have sworn was for a centerboard. It was the first she knew that boats this big could have centerboards, but why not? That would explain how they'd gotten so close to the beach. Anyway, it didn't open, so that was that.

So what kind of arrangement *was* this? For some reason she had pictured a windjammer as having one long passageway off which the cabins opened, doors to this side and that, a galley or mess at one end or the other where people gathered to sing songs and tell stories, not this frustrating system of vertical cul-de-sacs. How was one supposed to get from one part of the boat to another?

But this was no time to be dithering about floor plans. She had to find Alan. She reached forward and pulled open the door opposite her.

It was a cabin, or what had been a cabin, obviously, with bunks built into the curved side of the hull. The whole space, bunks and all, was now filled with wooden boxes the size of orange crates stacked on top of one another, sealed shut with heavy staples. So that was it. Smuggling. Boxes and boxes of contraband. Roz gave the nearest one a good push, and was greeted with the clink and rattle of metal on metal. She stared at the boxes for a moment, trying to imagine what kind of cargo would clink like that. Not just your average contraband, stereos, cameras, dope, and the like. So what was it, pieces of eight?

Of course, that was it! Not drug-running, and not smuggling, either! Biddy and Captain Dad were treasure hunters, and they had found the secret of the treasure pit on Rebel Island! Roz had seen them transferring the last of the treasure on board ship in those wooden crates, and now they were getting ready to make away with their illegal booty.

She backed out and quickly pulled open the rest of the doors one after another, four more cabins filled almost to the ceiling with similar wooden crates, all sealed. It must have been quite a haul. She wished she could get into one so she could verify what was inside, but without a crowbar it was hopeless. And silly, too: what else could it be? Biddy and Dad were rival naturalists and beachcombers, and the boxes were full of sea-shells and sand dollars? Those didn't clink. Besides, there wasn't time. She still had to find Alan and get him off the boat. She could always report this little operation after he was safe; even if they took off with the goods, the authorities would certainly catch them before they got beyond the three-mile limit.

She opened the last door. Damn, a dear little miniature por-celain toilet gleamed up at her, and nothing more. In other words, no Alan.

So where could he be? She counted on her fingers, five double cabins, accommodations for ten, plus head—everything except the head filled to the brim with boxes. Alan had said—no, Biddy had *told* him, ye olde hearsay again—the boat accommodated twelve plus crew. So there must be more cabins somewhere, even if only for Biddy and Dad. Unless, of course, they were bunking in with the loot. She racked her brains. *Captains Cou-rageous. Mutiny on the Bounty. Two Years Before the Mast.* Ha! That was it! Crew quarters in the forecastle; that meant more cabins up front. She had to get to the forecastle somehow. But there was clearly no access from here. Okay. That meant she had to go back up on deck again.

Cautiously she climbed up the ladder—and quickly ducked

down as she heard the sound of voices shouting, the rattle of wheels. It must be Biddy and Dad coming down the path toward the dock with a trolley full of stores. But they would head straight for the galley to unload the bags, wouldn't they? If not, and she was discovered, she could always scramble off the boat and run for help, even though it meant leaving Alan behind temporarily. If they did make for the galley, which in all probability they would, there might still be time for her to search the rest of the boat. Either way, the first thing she had to do was get back up on deck and into position to run for it.

Feeling like some sort of nautical jack-in-the-box, Roz popped out of the main hatch and scuttled around the side of the deckhouse, keeping it between her and the dock. The voices, loud and chipper, calling out thanks and goodbye in that lilting, unidentifiable accent, came nearer. At her back she heard a heavy tramp, tramp, tramp. Rattle, rattle, thud, thud, all moving well aft. She heaved a sigh of relief. The galley it was, then. She heard the murmur of voices, the sound of grocery bags rustling. Roz hoped they had a lot of stores to stow. She couldn't see them from here, which meant, she fervently hoped, that they couldn't see her.

What she could see right in front of her was another, slightly lower, deckhouse with a companionway leading down, and what looked like an open skylight at the far end, almost to the bow. Silently she hitched herself forward, and popped down yet another hatch—this time, she hoped, into the forecabin, where, by process of elimination, Alan had to be. Unless, she shuddered to think, she was too late, and he was already—

Somewhere else.

32

Here we go again, she thought, opening her eyes wide in the gloom. Five doors, all closed, two pairs opposite each other, the fifth door, the one with louvers, facing the companionway ladder. So which is it to be, she thought as she reached for the nearest door, the Lady—make that the Gentleman—or the Tiger? Holding her breath, she yanked it open . . .

And found herself staring at a stack of crates identical to the ones she had seen being taken off Rebel Island. They were oblong and much larger than the ones in the other cabins, and not only were the tops of these crates nailed down tight, but heavy metal strapping encircled each one in two places. But that was not their most interesting feature. These crates were marked with numbers and letters stamped in red. M-16: quan. 30. AK-47: quan. 20. Anyone, even a pacifist, non-violent-protesting professor of English literature specializing in medieval studies in the wilds of darkest Maine, would know what those numbers meant, from watching the evening news, if nothing else. Not dope, not contraband, not stolen treasure. Weapons. Assault rifles. Guns.

The *Jas Gardner* was running guns.

And all those smaller jingly boxes in the main cabin were filled not with gold and jewels and pieces of eight, but with bullets. Crates and crates of guns and ammunition. The whole boat was filled with them; they must weigh tons. No wonder it was riding low in the water.

But guns for whom? Who *were* these people? Biddy and Dad, International Terrorists? So who else would be running guns, never mind to where? But from Maine? In July? In a wind-jammer with one working mast?

She shook her head; hers not to reason why. She had accomplished part of their mission—hers and Alan's—to discover the motive behind Peter Onterdonck's murder, to find out what no good the Black Ship and its crew of two had been up to. All very well and good, but she still had to find Alan and get him—and herself—off the boat somehow.

Obviously he had stumbled on what she had—unless he had worked it out beforehand. Was that what he had meant by "that's it"? But then why had he taken such a chance by going on board? Just to verify it by the evidence of his senses? Only to be captured for his pains, the stupid nit! And he thought she was reckless! Underdeveloped sense of danger, my foot!

And while we're on that subject, Roz old girl, she thought in sudden chilling realization, there's something you may have overlooked yourself. Biddy and Dad would obviously be counting on me to get worried sooner or later, come looking for Alan, and fall into the same trap, thus disposing of both of us in one fell sloop—I mean swoop! Now who's the stupid nit!

Roz smote her brow. They probably even knew she was already on board, and were just biding their time before they grabbed her and deep-sixed her as well. And all because Alan hadn't seen fit to take her into his confidence and tell her what he suspected. And if by some miracle they both managed to survive, would he ever admit he'd been a jerk? Of course not!

All right, enough of that. And enough of this nonsense with one door at a time. Reaching out with both hands, she simultaneously yanked open two doors in front of her.

And there was Alan, lying in one of the coffin-narrow bunks, surrounded by more wooden crates, cocooned in ropes, a gag around his mouth, eyes closed. He looked asleep, or drugged, or both. She bent down, undid the gag, gently shook him. He didn't move. Her heart sank. How was she going to get him off the boat? First things first; she couldn't carry him trussed up like a chicken, asleep *or* awake. The ropes first. Frantically she set to work undoing the ropes around his legs, no mean trick as they were tied up with what was obviously some sort of seaman's mystery knot that looked about as untie-able as a wad of chewing gum. Not only that, one of the ropes was looped around the bunk rail. Damn it, where was his famous jackknife of all trades? Rummaging through his pockets, she snatched out the L. L. Bean megaknife and began to hack away at the knots, to no avail. The rope must be coated wire! Desperately she pulled out the toothed wire chain saw and began to saw away at the bunk rail.

Just then Alan stirred, groaned faintly. She looked at his face just as his eyes fluttered open, fixed themselves on her with a perplexed expression. "Hi, Roz," he said with a beatific grin, and took a breath as though he were about to say more. She leaned closer to listen. "Asgard," he croaked in a tone of breathless urgency, then something that sounded like "aerie." She watched his eyes roll back in his head. His eyelids fluttered as he strained to stay awake; his mouth struggled to form words. "What an idiot," he said quite distinctly. "I should have known . . ." Roz started to ask, "Known what?" but Alan went right on, dazed, oblivious, ". . . Tabernacles, not mast partners. They let them down." His eyes closed and he began to snore.

She stared at him in disbelief. Tabernacles? What the hell did that mean? In imminent danger of his life, had he gone religious on her? Let who down? And what was this nonsense about 'asgard'? And 'aerie'? That meant 'eagle's nest'; but what was *that* supposed to mean? Did he think they were rustling eagles? Talk about unanswered questions!

But she couldn't stop to sort it all out now; whatever he was trying to tell her would have to wait until later. Anyway, he was out cold again. She turned her attention back to the rail.

Ah, there it went, sawed through! Thank God for modern technology! Dropping the knife on the floor, she pulled him free and was just unraveling the ropes around his arms when she heard the tramping of feet, and another voice, harsh, not Biddy's melodious fluting but with a similar accent, shouting orders directly overhead. Roz froze.

"Bridget, love, look sharp! One of us should be going down to have one more look at our passenger, see if we need to pop him another dose to keep him quiet until we get clear. There'll be time enough to put him over the side when we get beyond the three-mile limit."

Oh, no! Footsteps coming nearer, what little light there was momentarily blotted out as a shape appeared at the top of the ladder. A dark figure climbed down backward. But not before Roz had ducked out of the cabin containing Alan's unconscious form and shut herself into the one next to it, which she found, cursing silently as she barked her shins on the cold porcelain, to be another head.

She flattened herself against the wall and held her breath, praying that whichever of them was coming down to check on Alan didn't decide to answer a call of nature for convenience' sake. A small brass hook and eye meant to foster the illusion of uninterrupted privacy dangled in front of her; flimsy as it was, she reached up and fastened it, taking care not to let it clink. She heard a door creak open and shut, then another. There was a pause, then her heart nearly stopped as she heard the sound of footsteps moving around closer to her. They stopped; another door creaked open. How many more doors? She counted on her fingers but to no avail; she'd lost track.

Groping around the small space, she picked up the first thing that came to hand as a weapon, what felt like a sawed-off broomstick handle propped in the corner, and tensed herself, heart pounding now, ready to leap out flailing as soon as the door opened. She would whale whoever was out there about the head and shoulders and scream bloody murder. People would be bound to hear and come running . . . wouldn't they?

Or would they just assume it was a spot of slap and tickle on the skin boat?

Silence. What was the someone doing, standing outside the door listening?

The ropes! Of course. What an idiot, Roz! Whoever it was would have noticed the missing gag, the sawed rail, the partially untied ropes. Of course they knew she was in here somewhere! It was just a matter of time . . . and doors.

Roz tensed herself. Aware of a prickly sensation against her leg, she raised the weapon in her hand and looked at it. It was a toilet brush (at least she assumed it was a toilet brush; in fact it looked more like a belaying pin with bristles, and capable of giving someone quite a good knock). She could see it quite plainly; in fact she could see everything inside here quite plainly. It was much lighter in here than in the rest of the cabins.

She looked up. There was the skylight, and on the wall underneath, a series of metal hand grips, leading upward. What a novel idea. An escape hatch through the head.

Just then the handle of the door rattled as whoever was outside pulled on it, then began to yank, straining the little hook and eye. Still clutching the special schooner-sized international terrorist–strength toilet brush, Roz leaped onto the toilet bowl rim, grabbed for the handholds, and swung herself up, flinging the brush down hard behind her at the person's head just as the door flew open. Then she was over the top and out the skylight, running for dear life, hurdling the downed mast and leaping over the rail and onto the dock, looking wildly all around for help as she ran.

But the only face Roz saw was Biddy's, her mouth a circle of surprise, in the act of casting off the docking lines, as the bubble and spurt of an engine coughing to life disturbed the waters under the *Jas Gardner*'s stern. So it was Captain Dad doing the dirty work down below. Roz looked up and down the dock. There wasn't another soul in sight. Where *was* everybody? Where were all the damned tourists when you needed them, not to mention the natives, dockhands, yard apes, whoever? It was pointless to stand in the middle of the dock and scream, but how far was she going to have to run for help?

She looked back over at the *Jas Gardner* and saw to her horror a gap widening between it and the dock. They were leaving! Right now! Making a run for it! With Alan virtually comatose and helpless on board!

She swiveled her head wildly from side to side. There must be someone around here who could do something!

Too late. The *Jas Gardner* was already steaming through the harbor, rocking boats in its wake, the wash rippling along the dock in a taunting ruffle of foam. She couldn't let them get away just like that, help or no help.

With one last desperate look around, she sprinted down the dock toward the *Verorum,* cast off the lines, jumped aboard, cranked up the reluctant old crock of an engine, and set off after them at full speed.

33

What a fool she was. Biddy's Captain Dad had known she was there the whole time, had probably seen her through the louvers in the door, silhouetted in the light from overhead. She should have just burst out and bopped him with the toilet brush instead of running away. After all, there were only the two of them on board, Biddy and Dad, and even though she couldn't match Biddy in pole-climbing ability, she could still give a pretty good account of herself in hand-to-hand combat, thanks to the lessons her friend and colleague Iris had given her in the gentle art of self-defense. But it was too late now.

Masts and pilings hove into view, whipped by, and faded into the landscape at an alarming clip, like landmarks seen from a speeding train. There was the day beacon marking the ledge at the entrance to the harbor, and the black can at the edge of the channel; the engine thumped furiously as waves washed against the hull in a continuous sluice. What would happen once they were out of the harbor? What indeed? They wouldn't be expecting her to follow—Biddy had obviously thought she was virtually helpless in a dinghy, let alone a full-sized sailboat, and Alan's behavior certainly hadn't contradicted this impression any. And who would she get to believe her story, anyway? Once they were beyond the three-mile territorial limit, there probably would be a rendezvous with other international-terrorist gunrunners, Biddy and her old dad would throw Alan overboard and off-load their illegal cargo to go back for more. Or, knowing their cover was blown, just keep on going to parts unknown.

Roz pondered this for a moment. From what she had seen, as well as what Alan had said about the whatever lines—why did she think it had something to do with rubbers, the kind you wear on your feet?—the boat was heavily, even dangerously overloaded. But if this whole thing was part of a systematic gunrunning operation, why hurriedly (and rather sloppily) disguise the name, then proceed to load the creaky old windjammer from stem to stern with heavy crates, stuffing every nook and cranny, cabin and bilge, with guns and ammo all the while proceeding in a highly suspicious manner that had all the earmarks of a getaway?

No, everything about their movements up to this point fairly screamed damage control, an *ad hoc* salvage operation. From the moment Roz and Alan had first seen them leaving Restitution Island, they had been engaged in making a desperate and hurried run for it, taking any and all evidence with them. The guns had been hidden in the old mine shaft on Rebel Island, and while Biddy and friend were in the process of transferring them, Peter Onterdonck had unluckily stumbled across them in his search for some form of rare plant on Rebel that would stop Roger Fell's proposed development. Biddy and Dad had killed him on the spot, and then to gain time and divert suspicion from Rebel, had waited until dark, then transferred the body to the other island, making it look like an accident by using that rope arrangement that Alan had been so interested in.

But how was Roger Fell involved? He must be, mustn't he? Or was that another false assumption? It was his island, and he had certainly been in all the right (or wrong) places at the right time. She racked her brains, trying to remember something he had said that first time they saw him, the feud between the families, his remark about the fathers not liking each other's politics, old Fell and those "radical republicans." Something about that didn't quite square.

And then it dawned on her. Of course. Not the G.O.P., that elephantine, old-line conservative American Republican Party of which Onterdonck, according to his death notice, had been a card-carrying member, even a higher-up; no one would describe those Republicans as radical (though, come to think of it, they were not above engaging in a spot of alleged gunrunning now and then). No; Fell's description of his father's affiliation and sympathies, she now realized, must have been in reference to another group that also used the term "Republican"—the IRA, or, more accurately, the outlawed Provisional wing of it that had long engaged in terrorist activities, gunrunning primary among them since the days of Roger Casement. That's what Alan had been trying to say: "IRA," not "aerie." But Fell hadn't included himself in the description—it had been "my old man's politics." Was it possible that Fell's father, honoring the age-old connections to the Auld Sod, had been one of those surreptitious fanatical American supporters of the illegal organization, isolated pockets of whom still purportedly existed in certain areas of the United States, particularly New England, offering Rebel Island as a way station, a safe storage base for arms, a fairly clear shot to the open ocean . . . it all fit! So *that* was why all the excavations and explorations had been halted some years ago, why it was off limits to boat traffic! So the gun smugglers could go about their business undisturbed!

But then a year or so ago old Fell had died unexpectedly, leaving Roger Fell as his sole heir, entrepreneur *extraordinaire,* with no ties to the old country, no clue about his father's secret activities, and big plans of his own for the island. And the terrorists had been faced with the necessity of having to get their cache of weapons off the island in jig time, before the bulldozers moved in, or all would be lost. Then Peter Onterdonck had gotten it into his head to save the islands for posterity . . .

Roz's speculations were interrupted as she suddenly realized the thumping of the *Jas Gardner*'s engine had stopped. The windjammer glided through the water just ahead of her. As the *Verorum* and the *Jas Gardner* came out of the mouth of the harbor almost neck and neck, the windjammer plowed a course straight into the wind; she could see one lone figure on deck busy with the halyards, apparently getting ready to raise sail. Oh, no! Now what was she going to do? As long as they were under engine she knew she had a chance of keeping up, but as soon as the *Jas Gardner* got under sail it would be all over; the windjammer would outdistance her in no time. But wait a minute. Was it really possible for only one person to raise the sails of such a large boat, even with electronic aids?

Apparently so, for as Roz watched, taut little Biddy leaned into it, and with a rattle of metal against wood, a great triangle of sail began to flutter upward. The rustling turned to faint booming, followed by the sharp *floomp!* of the sail filling with wind. Roz's heart sank.

Hold on, though, only one mast and one sail; maybe she still had a chance as long as . . . But what was that whining, whirring noise?

As she watched, eyes glued on the windjammer, to her utter astonishment the downed mast began to rise like a shrouded corpse in a macabre magic show, until it stood upright once more, its huge sail now fluttering free, then filling slowly with wind. She stared at the apparition before her—two masts nearly identical in height, the second one with an extension that made it slightly taller. She stared at the boat as it gathered speed. The *Jas Gardner* was a schooner after all, and unmistakably the one she had seen leaving Restitution Island that day.

What next? What else but a great crosspiece swinging up and out from the topmast to form a yard, shaking out a square topsail as though it were a tablecloth. All this, and a topsail schooner, too! And wait a minute, wasn't there something awfully familiar about that other figure who now appeared at the wheel, short, gray-haired, and sturdy? Not Thaxter Waite—no wispy brown hair or fringe of beard, but even more important, no wishbone legs. And if not Thaxter, with his unmistakable rolling gait, who of those she had met around these parts could it be? Gray-haired, round-faced, rosy-cheeked, long eyelashes . . .

Clyde! Clyde Merithew pronounced "Matthew"! Clyde, who had been in the boatyard that day, who seemed to know everything, and had sent her and Alan off on a wild-goose chase after Roger Fell! Of course—it had to be Clyde! As Roz stared in consternation, Biddy and her gray-haired companion—Captain Clyde?—moved down the deck to the forward hatch, slammed it shut, and padlocked it! So much for any chance Alan had to get himself out of there, ropes or no ropes, dope or no dope. It was up to her to rescue him, come hell or high water. She was his only chance.

So what was she doing sitting here speculating on where and why, let alone who, twiddling her thumbs and carefully working out the puzzle on both hands while a couple of terrorists made off into the open ocean with God knows how many tons of high-powered munitions, never mind the powerless Alan?

Think a minute. The windjammer was heading straight down the southeast-running Reach that provided the only passage to that selfsame open ocean. And if she was not mistaken—she held a wet finger up—at this very moment, the wind was blowing up like stink from the southeast, straight in their faces. Anyone who wanted to get down the Reach in the foreseeable future would have to beat. Hadn't Alan said that schooners, fast as they were, one mast or two, topsails or no, did not beat well to windward? Maybe there was still a chance.

But the only way to catch up with them was to beat to windward after them herself.

Mouth dry, breathless, heart thumping, Roz tied off the tiller and started forward to raise the *Verorum*'s sails. She had sailed on this boat in her youth with Aunt Jess and Uncle Lou, and now on this cruise with Alan, but from the first he had laid claim to the running of it as if this were a matter of course, even his right. But never mind that now. Suppose she did manage to keep them in sight, even catch up? And then what? Ram them? Grab hold, hang on like grim death, and scream for help?

Scream for help. Of course, the radio. Why hadn't she thought of it before? Wrapping the mainsheet around the tiller the way she'd seen Alan do to hold it steady, she reached into the companionway, picked up the transceiver, pressed the button, just as she had before that day on the *Non-Amo-Te.* No time for explanations as through the crackle of reception she quickly gave the boat name and position, and the signal "Mayday." Not even waiting for a reply, she simply left the distress channel open. With any luck, Stiles and the Marine Patrol at Castine would respond. So, she hoped, would everyone else within a five-mile radius. Anyway, it was the best she could do.

She raced forward and with less difficulty than she expected hoisted the main, then the genoa, cleated off the sheets, ran back to the cockpit, and freed the tiller. Still standing, she headed the boat off the wind just enough to fill the sails. The *Verorum* picked up speed, began to heel. Sleek and narrow, it was, she knew, a very fast boat to windward. Almost as an afterthought she switched off the engine and was startled by the sudden quiet, the deceptive sense of peace.

All right. Now where was the *Jas Gardner,* anyway? She scanned the horizon to her left—make that to port—and gasped in surprise. For there, swooping down the Reach toward her, looming across the sky like some giant leaning tower, was the unmistakable, impossibly tall, peaked outline of the *Jolly Roger*!

Roz stared in horrified fascination as the huge sloop sluiced through the water in what seemed like an instant replay of the first time she had laid eyes on it over a week ago, charging full tilt toward the beach at Restitution Island. And there in the Phantom of the Opera seat, hands hovering, making motions while the hidden crew of six sailed the boat, was the unmistakably piratical figure of Roger Fell. She could just make out his face now as he raised a pair of binoculars to his eyes and began scanning the area. What was he looking for, or, more to the point, what was he doing here?

Dummy, what else? He had been following the *Verorum* the whole time, ever since she'd spotted him coming out of Camden Harbor! That *had* been the *Jolly Roger* she'd caught a glimpse of at Rebel Island. And why would he do that—unless he was in cahoots with the crew, such as it was, of the *Jas Gardner*? And here she'd been thinking he was innocent after all! Fat chance!

He was probably getting ready to head her off or, worse yet, run her down. And that would be the end of it. She might be able to outmaneuver a lumbering schooner, but she'd never have a prayer against that high-tech behemoth, the *Jolly Roger*.

Meanwhile, if that was what he had in mind, why was Roger Fell still waving madly in her direction as though trying to attract her attention? Did he honestly think she could miss seeing him out here? Or was he waving at the schooner? But where *was* the schooner? Fell's waving motions stopped abruptly; he shouted something down below and pointed beyond her. Aware of a hissing, creaking noise, Roz turned and looked in that direction, but saw nothing until she ducked and looked under her own main. There, not more than ten yards ahead and just off her starboard bow, where it had been almost totally hidden from her view by the *Verorum*'s sails, was the *Jas Gardner*—in the process of bearing down on the *Verorum*! They were going to run her down, too! A pincer movement! She and the *Verorum* would be crushed to splinters between the two great hulks!

Too frightened even to think of taking evasive action, Roz stared transfixed as the great hull loomed over her, its shadow blocking out the sun, the towering sails like great swans fluttering, flying, twin masts like huge trees leaning farther and farther over in her direction . . .

And watched in horrified fascination as the schooner kept right on going over, its treelike masts moving in tandem through one long, stately arc, plummeting now like felled timber toward the surface of the water, the sails fluttering and flapping like great wounded birds. With one last billow, the sails ballooned upward, then settled into the water like collapsed parachutes as both masts hit the surface of the water simultaneously with a surprisingly gentle splash, then seemed to rebound upward slightly as the schooner lay there on its side like some great wounded black leviathan, the hull heaving up and down as though with labored breathing, the sails washing around it like old rags.

34

Sorry, Aunt Jessie, Roz muttered to herself as she flung the tiller to one side and leaped up onto the *Verorum*'s deck; it's goodbye, old boat.

Then she was overboard and in the water swimming as hard as she could toward the nearly perpendicular deck of the *Jas Gardner*. There wasn't much time; a boat loaded with tons of guns would surely sink in a matter of seconds. Alan didn't have a chance; even if he was conscious by now, he was still tied up. But if she could only get to him, get herself on board as the boat was going down, there might be air pockets. . . .

In a few strokes she had reached the skylight leading to the head, still above water—barely. Whirring, hissing noises, yells and screams, cracking and groaning, and above it all, the rush of water pouring in.

She wriggled through into the cabin and stopped dead for a moment, mildly disoriented by the sight of the boat on its side, everything—cabin doors, companionway, floors, and walls— now at a ninety-degree angle from what they had been before, the main hatchway no longer overhead but to her right, water now pouring through it as though over a great waterfall.

"Alan!" she shouted. Doors lay everywhere, ripped off their hinges, and the crates of guns lay higgledy-piggledy where they had crashed through. The water was rising rapidly up into the lower half of the hull.

She stepped out over the collapsed head door and picked her way over the crates tumbled every which way against the cabin walls like flung-aside children's blocks. Only one door was still closed. She turned the knob . . . and Alan's rope-cocooned form dropped through into her arms, knocking her back against the crates. The water was up to her neck and freezing, bone-shattering cold. She struggled to get Alan's head above water, but it was rising rapidly around both of them.

Alan's eyes popped open. "Hullo, Roz!" he said in an impossibly chipper voice, then shivered mightily, his eyelids fluttering, then dropping to half-mast. "Damn, that's cold."

Well, at least he was awake. But how was she going to get him out? Obviously there was no time to fiddle with ingenious sailor's knots. What about his precious knife, on the floor somewhere! But never mind that now; if they got out of this, she'd get him another one, this time with an outboard motor.

She grabbed him by the nearest rope, crossed like suspenders over his shoulders, and climbed up as high as she could on the jumbled pile of crates, while the water swirled and foamed higher. It wouldn't be long now. As the water surged up around them, she looked around at the crazily tilted space around her, trying to figure a way to get out, and fast.

Calm, keep calm, there's still time. And how deep could it be here, anyway? She tried to remember the numbers on the *Verorum*'s depth sounder; thirty, maybe forty feet? Even if they sank to the bottom . . .

Stop that! She was going to get them out somehow! She tried to remember all the safety tips she had read about getting out of submerged cars, movies she had seen, rescues she had witnessed on the news. Silly as it seemed, she'd never thought that much about getting out of a submerged boat. But perhaps the principle was the same: stay calm, stay in the air pocket, and plan your escape until the water stops pouring in through whatever exits are available, then take a deep breath, open the door or roll down the window, and swim for it.

Okay, but through what? It wasn't as though she could roll down the windows. The hatch was underwater, but it was also shut tight and locked from above. The skylight, too, must be nearly submerged, from the rate at which the ocean was rising in the cabin.

"I say, all these crates are filled with guns and ammo, you know," Alan said in a conversational tone. "That's why the bloody boat went over; overloaded to the gills. I'd say we haven't got a chance in hell. But I'm still awfully glad to see you." He shrugged his arms and shoulders mightily against the ropes, to no avail. Leaning forward, he gave her a cold, hard, saltwater wet kiss on the mouth. "Leave me, Roz. Swim for it. Get yourself out before it's too late."

Roz shook her head, just as the boat gave a great lurch. Water rolled and gushed in their faces, then subsided once again. Pulling Alan's head back above the surface, she stopped struggling for a moment and studied the water level. Was it just her imagination, or had the boat paused in its rapid progress downward?

Too much to hope that it had gone over on a ledge or a shoal, no, that was impossible; it was just a momentary shift before the final plunge. But she knew what she had to do. She looked over toward the little skylight running from the head; it was now completely submerged, an underwater tunnel leading— where? She peered through the dark, roiling water, could just barely make out a paler square of blue-green light that marked the opening, if not into safety, then at least out of this death trap.

"Alan, listen to me! Take a deep breath and hold it!" she ordered. Filling her own lungs with air, she grabbed Alan by the hair in her best senior lifesaving carry, ducked under the water and into the narrow space, pulling herself forward awkwardly by means of one handhold after another, dragging Alan behind her toward the faint square halo of light. She squirmed through and kicked her way free of the schooner's hull as it ever so slowly, even imperceptibly—and that was odd; you'd think a boat loaded to the gills with several tons of guns and ammunition would sink like a rock—continued its inevitable way to Davy Jones. Damn, there goes the real evidence, she thought in passing as she churned her way toward the surface, still hauling Alan by the hair.

As her head broke through, gasping for air, supporting a sputtering Alan with one hand and treading water as hard as she could, Roz looked around—to find they were surrounded by a veritable flotilla of boats. There was the faded khaki-colored hull of the Marine Patrol, with Stiles and Rancourt hanging over the side, gesticulating madly at two bobbing and drenched wet heads clinging to the tip of the schooner's mainmast. There was Biddy—but who was the other one?

Not Clyde Merithew. Not Thaxter Waite. Not anyone she had ever seen before, that was certain. Not only that, she was, as far as Roz could tell, a woman. Not Biddy and Captain Dad, but Biddy and Captain Mom?

And here came Thaxter Waite now, in his snazzy hot-rod lobster boat, spewing exhaust, churning slowly up the Reach toward them with the *Verorum* in tow. And there was the *Jolly Roger,* looming clifflike over all of them, with its two huge plow anchors poking through the hull of the *Jas Gardner* like giant fishhooks, the schooner on her beam ends but still afloat and steady in the water, masts, sails, crates of guns, and all.

And coming alongside them in the *Jolly Roger*'s longboat was none other than Roger Fell himself. "Hi, there," he said amiably, shipping the oars as Roz reached up and feebly gripped the side of the boat with one hand, the other arm still clasped tightly around a bedraggled Alan. "I'm glad I finally caught up with you," Fell said, reaching behind him.

As Roz stared at him in astonishment, he held up a pair of familiar-looking objects. "You forgot your shoes."

35

They were all standing on the beach at Restitution Island—Roz and Alan, Stiles and Rancourt, the District Attorney for Waldo County, the State Medical Examiner, Roger Fell, Thaxter Waite, and several state policemen, waiting for high tide. Conspicuously absent were Biddy and Mom—actually no relation, as far as anyone could ascertain, since neither woman was giving away any information other than name, rank, and serial number—now confined without bail to the Waldo County Jail, awaiting indictment for, among other crimes and misdemeanors, murder, kidnapping, assault, and conspiracy, not to mention piracy on the high seas.

Anchored in the little cove and in the channel beyond were the former *Jolly Roger,* now renamed *Ellie W.* (after adjudicating various suggestions, mostly obscene, in the boat-renaming contest, Roger Fell had given up and decided to call the boat after his mother, a choice apparently exempt from the bad-luck clause, and very pleasing to the crew of six, who were in fact her brother the captain and his five children of the same last name, beginning with W), the *Verorum* with Aunt Jessie True at the helm, assisted by her old friend Clyde Merithew, and several other official-looking vessels. And hard by the beach, comfortably floating at anchor, was the sailing vessel now revealed to be, once the various hastily painted-over and taped-on alterations to the original insignia had been removed, the canalboat schooner *Asgard*, of Belfast, N. Ireland, alias the topsail schooner *Sea's Garden* of Newfoundland, as well as the ersatz ketch-rig windjammer *Jas Gardner* of Belfast, Maine. The peculiar qualities of these now-rare schooners—which were used in the last century to carry freight from coastal seaports through the various canals into the Great Lakes—included not only retractable centerboards, but twin masts set in tabernacles that allowed them to be raised and lowered at will to pass under the many bridges en route. Or—as in the case of the *Asgard*—enabled the crew of two, with the aid of hydraulic motors and pulleys set up on deck, to dismantle the topmast and yards, even shorten the rig to alter its configuration if need be, to throw pursuers off their trail. As Alan said, it might better have been named the good ship Moriarty, for it was, in truth, a boat of many disguises.

Alan had just finished running a line from the foremast around a good-sized pulley that he had found attached to a large pine tree at the edge of the beach (obscured by several branches from ordinary view unless specifically looked for), and back again to the boat. "What we have here, as most of you will no doubt recognize," he was saying, "is a very serviceable makeshift breeches buoy. Our Miss Bridget, with her well-demonstrated shinnying ability," he explained with a quick wink at Roz, "brought the rope along by way of the rocks over there, then up the tree and through the block she'd already affixed to the tree, tying it into what is called an endless whip, rather like those clotheslines one used to see strung out upstairs windows for hanging out the week's washing. Then, hanging on to said knot, she hauled herself, with the aid of her partner still on board, I surmise, back onto the schooner." Alan looked down at his watch. "About now, I think," he said, motioning to Roz and Roger Fell. "The tide's just coming on full. Hurry, we've got to be done and gone before the water starts to drop away too fast.''

The three of them ran down the beach to the *Non-Amo-Te*'s dinghy. Roz and Roger took their seats, while Alan lay face-down, one arm outstretched in the bottom of the dinghy. Thus arranged, they rowed out to the schooner, which now was floating high enough for its reinstated mainmast to be nearly on a level with the trees. Leaving Alan and Roz in the dinghy, Roger Fell scrambled aboard the schooner.

As the various witnesses watched with interest as well as skepticism on their faces, Roger Fell clipped what appeared to be an oversized child's safety swing seat but was in fact a state-of-the-art boatswain's chair to another pulley running along the line to shore, then jumped back down into the dinghy, holding a smaller line attached to the sling. Then he rowed the three of them into shore, pulling the sling along with them almost as though it were a puppy on a leash.

As soon as the dinghy grounded on the beach, Roz and Roger went to work. Roz pulled off Alan's shoes and placed them on the sand just above the dinghy while Roger Fell hoisted Alan—who resisted bending with an eerie cadaveric stiffness that made Roz shiver—upright. Together they maneuvered him into the sling, the upraised arm causing some difficulty at first, until they simply wrapped one of the ropes supporting the sling around it, which also served to keep him from falling over sideways.

Roz now carefully stepped out of the boat and stood next to it in the ankle-deep water, while Roger Fell guided the body so that the legs came down around her neck, the mostly supported weight of the body resting ever so slightly on her shoulders. Roger Fell stepped out of the dinghy, also into the water, and, still holding the line, handed Roz the dinghy's long painter, which she tied tightly around her waist. Then she stepped forward into Alan's shoes.

Grasping the body's legs around the calves, Roz trudged straight up the beach well above the high-water mark to where the rope overhead sagged downward slightly. Taking a deep

breath, she reached up and unfastened the sling, ducked out
from under the legs, and carefully let Alan's body, still supported by the sling, slide out and down her own, until his feet
were touching the sand. She hesitated for a moment, then
stepped back and let go, resisting the impulse to shut her eyes
as Alan fell solidly forward on his face, landing in the sand with
a soft thud, his stiff profile turned slightly to one side, one arm
upraised.

Overcome by a horrifying sense of *déjà vu,* she stared at him,
his prostrate figure coalescing with Peter Onterdonck's, so that
for a moment she was back on the beach, looking down at the
body of a dead man. . . . *No chance now to make amends. Oh,
Alan, don't worry; whatever it is you have to tell me. . . .*

Alan's fingers scrabbled restlessly in the sand, reminding her
that she had more to do. Without turning around, she untied
the dinghy painter from around her waist, and with some difficulty pulled the dinghy up the beach until Roger Fell called
out, "There!" The empty dinghy now rested several feet above
the high-water mark, where it could not float away at high tide.

Roz dropped the painter in the sand. Taking a deep breath,
she kicked off the shoes, gritted her teeth and stepped onto
Alan's back, then swung herself up into the boatswain's chair,
which Roger Fell pulled gently back by means of the steadying
line to where he was standing at the water's edge. As it reached
him, he swung upward, clinging to Roz in the boatswain's seat.
The schooner was now riding lower by almost two feet due to
the rapidly falling tide, and with one or two jerks on the steadying line, the two of them slid easily down the inclined rope onto
the deck.

Back on the boat, they dismantled the breeches buoy and
untied the knot in the endless whip, after which a hefty yank
on the part of Roger Fell made the line fly right out of the
pulley in the tree, landing some distance from the body. Carefully they pulled it across the sand and back into the boat,
leaving only a barely noticeable drag mark. The tide washing
back down the beach had already obliterated all signs of where

the dinghy had landed, leaving it and the body high and dry.

There was silence on the beach as the witnesses stood transfixed, contemplating the final effect. Finally Thaxter Waite, breaking into the hush, was heard to murmur in an awestruck down-east drawl: "Uh-*huh*! Well, that's the ballgame—homicide during the commission of a felony; in my book that's murder one for sure!" From her seat on the *Verorum*, Aunt Jessie clapped loudly, ending with an earsplitting whistle. Roz climbed down into the dinghy and began to row back in.

"All right!" shouted the district attorney. "Get busy, everyone!"

Stiles, Rancourt, and the other officers present jumped to attention, bringing out cameras, notebooks, and measuring devices, and swarmed in a phalanx over the beach, scribbling diagrams, taking photographs, and sticking things in the sand. The M.E. stood to one side with his arms folded, nodding his head.

Almost unnoticed, Alan got up and brushed himself off, then walked thoughtfully up the beach toward the trees. Roz landed the dinghy and came up the beach to stand beside him. "Congratulations," she said quietly. "You did it."

"*We* did it," he corrected. "Mostly you, for that matter. If it hadn't been for your—" He stopped in mid-sentence. "All right, then," he said in response to her don't-be-condescending look, "we did it together."

"Nonsense," Roz replied. "You knew everything right along. You had it all figured out practically from the word go. What I want to know is what you knew when, and how you knew it."

Alan gave her a bemused look. "To be sure," he said, then turned and began to pace back and forth, talking as he went. "We know now that Onterdonck was killed on Rebel Island, put into cold storage in the schooner's bilge until dark, then brought over here by Biddy and the erstwhile Dad, who turns out not only to be no relation, but undeniably female as well, though, like Bridget, an exceptionally sturdy as well as ruthless member of her sex." Here he paused in his tramping. "And by the by, I don't believe for an instant that Bridget's last name is O'Shaughnessy, any more than her friend's name is Irene Adler, do you?"

Roz, who hadn't given it a second's thought, shook her head, waiting for the upshot.

"No," Alan continued, "it was after we came a cropper with Roger Fell and the plant press that I realized we—or rather I—had been reasoning from one mammoth false assumption, namely that Roger Fell was the only one who had motive and opportunity, not to say means. I had some vague ideas about how the body could have got there, including being swung from a crane—not far off your skyhook gibe, for that matter—but they all involved getting a large boat in very close to shore. Upon reflection, particularly after my subaqueous explorations in Camden Harbor, I realized that Roger Fell and his *Jolly Roger* couldn't possibly have been involved in the planting of the body by any stretch of the imagination, motive and proximity notwithstanding. But that still left me with no real clue about the means by which the footprint dodge *could* have been accomplished, let alone by whom. In other words, I hadn't quite got as far as 'only the one way, and only one person who could have done it that way.' And that was because I'd completely discounted the Black Ship as a possibility, simply because I took it for a windjammer full of passengers. That was the original false assumption that led me down the garden path."

"You weren't the only one," Roz said. "We were both reasoning from analogy. It looked like every other windjammer, so we just assumed it was one. All windjammers carry passengers; therefore this one must have, too. Not that Biddy didn't do everything she could to foster that assumption; it was their cover."

"Mere hearsay. I should have known she was having us on," Alan murmured.

"Not necessarily," said Roz. "There was all that fiddling with the rig to throw everyone off the scent, removing the topsail yard that Roger Fell had seen, taking off the main topmast so it looked like a ketch, finally even lowering the mainmast, while all the time they were keeping a very careful eye on our whereabouts and the progress of our investigation. Who could ever have guessed there was such a thing as a schooner with folding masts?"

"True enough; canalboat schooners are not a regular feature at the Greenwich Maritime Museum," Alan admitted. "But it wasn't until after you told me about the rope you'd seen being used to haul the crates that I realized how easily it could be used for a makeshift breeches buoy to transport the body. But only a good-sized schooner would have been heavy enough to support the breeches buoy and body, and only a shallow-draft schooner with a retractable centerboard could get in close enough to shore to rig it. Furthermore, it had to be done right at high tide so the rope would be near level, or the breeches buoy wouldn't work, and any much past high tide, they couldn't count on the ocean to clean up after them. But I already knew that Onterdonck had not been killed anytime that morning, but a good while earlier, and in all probability somewhere else."

"How did you know that?"

"Onterdonck's foul-weather gear," he answered. "Remember on the way back to the islands, when I asked you to go through everything you'd seen on his boat?" Roz nodded. "The foul-weather gear was quite dry, which indicated he hadn't been wearing it that night, which he naturally would have been, had he been wandering about the beach at Restitution on his own in the dark of night, in the rain, thus leaving more than just those footprints we found. What had to have happened—the only way all the evidence can be accounted for—was that Onterdonck surprised Biddy and her compatriot at the pit on Rebel much earlier in the day, was knocked senseless with some sort of cylindrical blunt instrument, probably an oar or a whisker pole, causing an epidural hematoma from which he was shortly to expire. Meanwhile the pair—with reckless disregard for human life, since it is possible that, given proper medical treatment, he might have survived—put his body face down into the cold bilge until they could figure out a way to get him onto Restitution Island with no one the wiser, and divert suspicion from Rebel until they could get everything away. Which they did. Almost."

"When you know how, then you know who," Roz said. "When a thing can only be done one way, and only one person could have done it . . ."

"Well, not exactly," said Alan. "I'd managed to work out how and where by the time we were tearing down the Reach, but I still hadn't the foggiest who or why. Not until I woke up with a fierce headache, bound up like a Christmas joint, and saw the gun crates. Onterdonck must have suspected something immediately he saw the boat's real name when they were getting ready to sail for a rendezvous offshore. He even had Erskine Childers's book *The Riddle of the Sands* on board. Childers, as you no doubt already know," he added with a quick, apologetic glance at Roz, "was an Irish propagandist and revolutionary, executed by the British for treason, whose alleged crimes included running guns along with Roger Casement for the rebel cause in his yacht, *Asgard.* I should have dropped to it earlier, I suppose, but I just missed it. Too wrapped up in working out the details of 'how.' Careless of me, not to say self-indulgent, and it almost cost us our lives. That will teach me to jump on my horse and ride off in all directions. I didn't even drop to Biddy's accent; she sounded perfectly ordinary to me, more or less what I was used to hearing at home, unlike the rest of you Yankees. Another oversight on my part. Sorry, love."

With one last, oddly troubled look at Roz, Alan bent down and made faint scratching marks that feathered outward, vaguely scalloping, across the sand. "So that's the story," he said, then added ruefully, "But not quite all of it. There's still one thing that hasn't been accounted for, a little matter of unfinished business. . . ."

Oh, no, Roz thought with a surge of disappointment. The case was solved, wasn't it? What else was there? Aside from Roger Fell's plan for destroying Rebel Island, which now, unfortunately, would go forward unimpeded. But that was none of their affair. It couldn't be helped. They had done their best, and now it was time to get on with their own unfinished business.

But Alan was pointing to the faint marks on the sand next to the imprint of his body. "See those? Those marks I made scrabbling with my fingers are nothing like the ones we saw here when we found the body, and, in any case, we now know Onterdonck couldn't have made them in the first place."

"That's pretty obvious," Roz said, "since he'd been dead for some time when they put him down, with rigor well established. . . ."

Alan stood up, dusting off his hands. "Right-o. We know all that. What we don't know is what made the marks. Another puzzle." He whirled around and faced Roz with a look of pained distress. "Oh, bugger all! When will it ever end? I simply can't abide loose ends."

Roz stood there, stunned, taken aback by his sudden echoing of her own sentiments. "Then there's the Rebel Island Theme Park and cargo port," she added to cover her confusion. "There's a loose end for you, even though it's not exactly a puzzle."

Just then there was a faint rustling in the underbrush. Roz looked down just in time to see a turtle poking its nose out a few feet away. It was about the size of a small soapdish, with a coarsely plated shell, bronze-colored, rimmed with red around the bottom. Cautiously swinging its bleary prehistoric gaze from side to side for a moment, it lurched forward turtle-fashion and began to plow its way doggedly across the sand toward the water. Roz nudged Alan. "Look," she said. The turtle immediately retracted itself into its shell, so it now resembled a beach rock.

"My God," Alan whispered, staring down at the scalloped track the turtle had scratched in the sand. "That's *it!*"

36

"Guns and turtles," Alan said from the huge bed he was lounging on. "As unlikely a final conclusion to a mystery as one's ever likely to meet."

"The last loose end bites the dust," Roz murmured from the deep old-fashioned footed tub she was soaking in.

After they had delivered up the turtle—tentatively identified by Thaxter Waite ("Hey, hold her, Newt! I seen that little fella on the latest set of National Wildlife Federation stamps!") as a rare and endangered species called the Redbelly, long thought to be extinct in all but one small area of Massachusetts, the field identification shortly confirmed by a phone conference with the New England Aquarium—Aunt Jessie, in a charming exchange with Alan (during the course of which Roz realized that her elderly aunt was not only quite taken by his physical presence, she was actually *flirting* with him), suggested that they take a few more days on board the *Verorum* to "catch up with each other," a quaint euphemism if Roz ever heard one. "No more boats," Roz had said firmly, at which point Aunt Jessie, twinkling and winking, countered with an offer to stand them several nights at the poshest bed-and-breakfast place in Camden, an architecturally unique shingle-and-stone mansion overlooking the bay and strongly reminiscent of a Black Forest cuckoo clock made for giants.

So here they were, Alan lolling on the huge bed, and Roz in the huge tub. If she craned her neck a little, she could just barely see him around the corner of the bathroom door. Not a comfortable position. She subsided back into the pleasantly hot water, remembering those final moments on the beach.

"You're asking me?" Alan had said with a puzzled look, when Roz picked up the turtle and held it in his face, expecting an instant identification and explanation of the significance of this pocket-sized reptile. "I don't know the first thing about turtles."

"Then what did you mean by hollering 'That's it!' as if it were some sort of ultimate revelation?" she had demanded. "And not for the first time, either, I might add!"

"Only that it was obviously what had made those strange marks in the sand," he'd said in a bewildered tone. "No more than that."

Roz had just stared. It was the first time she could remember hearing him admit in so many words he didn't know a blessed thing about a subject . . . any subject . . . and wasn't prepared to give a disquisition on it. But in her heart she knew she was being unjust.

In fact, it had been Thaxter Waite who had recognized the turtle's significance; Thaxter Waite, who, with his honors degree in biology from Williams College, had been a friendly rival to Peter Onterdonck in the realm of amateur field taxonomy as well as in Little Ivy football, the bad blood between them amounting to no more than whose field notebook and whose college team was ahead of whose at any given time. Dead even on plants (and football), the two of them had begun to branch out, and Thaxter Waite had been busily getting up rare and endangered reptiles and amphibians, in order to "bust Pete's chops, God rest his soul." Aunt Jessie claimed that this explained the come-and-go down-east accent as well, Thaxter taking pains to suppress his academic background and be just one more good old boy around the yard for business' sake.

It had also been Thaxter Waite who, looking for a part for his restored sharpshooter pride and joy at Seafarer's Marine, had heard the strange story of the odd-looking ketch-rigged windjammer "from up your way" putting in at the crack of dawn for diesel fuel, "in an awful thrash to get a move on." Knowing there was no such windjammer, ketch-rig or otherwise, registered in Belfast, Thaxter had smelled a rat, and had followed after, tracking the one-masted schooner on his fishermen's network of CB's.

"And Rebel Island was originally Redbelly Island. So much for the Tory connection," Alan said from the other room. "That's what Peter Onterdonck had in his pocket all the time. He'd picked it up by the pond there on Rebel, where there's a whole colony of them, the northernmost remnant of the nearly extinct species. That's why there were traces of mud in his pocket; he could hardly stuff a live animal in a plastic bag; that did in fact contain a plant specimen, which the turtle, being omnivorous, was perfectly happy to make a meal of. The turtle must have gone into mild hibernation while they were in the cooler . . . er, bilge . . . and revived after being in the sun all morning. Then our last little bit of evidence simply crawled out and walked away." Alan chuckled. "But alas! wrong island. Poor bugger's probably been trying to figure a way back ever since."

"Well, anyway, he's—or is it a she, do turtles have sex?— safe now." Roz made little splashes with her fingers in the tub, rippling the water over her bare skin.

"Though I wouldn't have expected Roger Fell to give up so easily," Alan said, "just shrugging his shoulders like that and saying, 'Well, so much for that project. Guess I'll give the Nature Conservancy a call and tell them they can complete the set.' Though as far as that goes, I suppose anyone who would name a boat after his mother can't be all bad. Robber baron or no, his heart seems to be in the right place."

"And he only took the boxes off the *Non-Amo-Te* as a favor to the Maine Chapter, because they called him up and asked him to. So that's that," Roz said with finality. "How, what, where, when, who, and why. Case closed; cargo port scuttled. No more loose ends."

Silence from the other room. The bed creaked softly, Alan changing position. She couldn't see him anymore, even craning her neck.

"Well, not exactly," came his disembodied voice. Silence. "If you'll recall, there is one more thing."

Roz suddenly began to shiver, which was odd, since she was up to her shoulders in the almost-too-warm bathwater. Perhaps that was also why her heart was thumping so hard she could see her chest moving. But she knew that wasn't the reason. This was it, the moment of reckoning. He was going to tell her the one last thing he'd been keeping back from her all this time, since the night of their quarrel. She wished she could see him. But if he'd wanted to address her directly, all he had to do was get up and walk across the room. Maybe what he had to tell her was something he couldn't quite bring himself to say right to her face. But what could it be? She had an awful thought; what if he was going to tell her it was all over between them? "And what's that?" she said finally, trying to keep her voice steady.

"Um, well. Remember before this whole bloody mess started, you asked me about our . . . er . . . well, ah . . . about what was going to become of our relationship, how we were going to carry on, that is, the current transatlantic arrangement not having proved to be very satisfactory, and I said something on the order of 'As for that, I've something to tell you, but it must wait for the right moment' and so on and so forth? Silly of me to put it off, because then the body turned up and we were in a flat spin for the nonce."

A noncommittal "Mmmnn" was the best she could muster. She sank lower in the water, waiting.

"Well, the fact is, I'd rather taken the matter into my own hands and done something on my own hook, and I thought it would be a nice surprise. I meant to tell you right off, but then I began to have second thoughts that you'd be upset I hadn't consulted you first . . ."

Roz sat up, sloshing bathwater from side to side. Consulted me first? About what? This certainly didn't have the ring of a marriage proposal; on the other hand, it didn't sound as though he were planning to break things off, either. But what else could it be?

"And then things started to fall apart between us, having to do, I suspect, with being so much together on your aunt's boat (which had seemed like such a jolly idea at the time, but just the wrong thing for us, worse luck), and then we quarreled for what seemed to be the very same reason that I'd put it off in the first place, too much taking things into my own hands, and going off half-cocked. Then there was the murder—though that actually seemed to help things a bit, gave us something less personal to think and talk about—and all the while I was trying to work it out on both hands, wondering what I'd done to aggravate the situation, and knowing all the time I'd gone and done something really rash and committed myself to something we might both regret, and I was so afraid the whole thing would come undone. In short, I funked it. . . ."

Roz couldn't stand it any longer. "What? What!" she all but shouted at him. Then more calmly: "Never mind all that now. Just tell me."

"I'm trying to, Roz, but it's fairly complex, even for water over the dam. At any rate, I'd of course been thinking about things between us, and had the distinct feeling that at this stage in your career, just getting back on track at the college, so to speak, you wouldn't want to just up stumps and throw in with me in my rather rattling-around life. Nor had you exactly invited me to join you there, but that's all right, I shouldn't have cared much for that idea either; Maine is quite nice but rather off the beaten track, especially for such a traveling jack-of-all-trades as I am. So I was casting about for a solution to what seemed an insurmountable problem—you here, me there and about, and never the twain shall meet—and then one day this policeman friend of mine mentioned an exchange program between the British Police Staff College at Bramshill and your most prestigious John Jay College of Criminal Justice in New York City, to which, it seems, someone, not even necessarily police, with a modestly useful expertise relevant to, say, their program in forensics might come and hang his hat for a time—"

"You're kidding," said Roz.

"Not a bit of it. So, to make a long story only slightly less so, I called up the Dean of Studies and arranged to be taken on for a term starting next fall as a—"

"Don't tell me," Roz choked out. "Forensic microbotanist."

Silence. "No, not really," Alan said after a moment. "Wherever did you hear that term?"

"I made it up." She slumped back in the tub, not knowing whether to laugh or cry. Alan. In New York. Little more than an hour by plane, and no oceans between them. Not too near, but not too far, either. They could be together, but within the boundaries of their own lives. For now. Together, but not too close. Not yet.

"Oh, I see," Alan was saying now. "Hmmm. I don't think there is such a field, actually; what I shall be offering has to do with the toxicology of substances from poisonous plants, alkaloids and the like—not a huge concern for your modern-day police force—still, one never knows. In any case, they were willing, not to say enthusiastic, and frankly, Roz, at the time, at least, it did seem to be *meant*—"

"It's perfect." Roz stood up, letting the water run over her in rivulets, and stepped out of the tub. She picked up a towel and walked over to the doorway.

Alan looked up from where he was reclining in the middle of the bed. "Wait," he said somewhat anxiously. "There's something else I think I should tell you."

"Never mind. I'm sure we can work things out," Roz replied, flinging the towel aside and starting toward him.

"No, really!" he said with some urgency, holding a hand up as she leaped toward him, landing squarely on top of him, only to be overcome with a familiar sensation that the world was once again awash.

It was a waterbed.